SAVAGES

CHRONICLES OF WARSHARD BOOK TWO

KATHERINE BOGLE

Patchwork Press

Copyright © 2017-2018 by Katherine Bogle

http://katherinebogle.com

Cover Design by Katzilla Designs

Third Edition — 2018

No part of this publication may be reproduced in any form, or by any means, electronic or mechanical, including photocopying, recording, or any information browsing, storage, or retrieval system, without permission in writing from Katherine Bogle.

❀ Created with Vellum

SAVAGES

CHRONICLES OF WARSHARD
BOOK TWO

KATHERINE BOGLE

MAP OF
WARSHARD

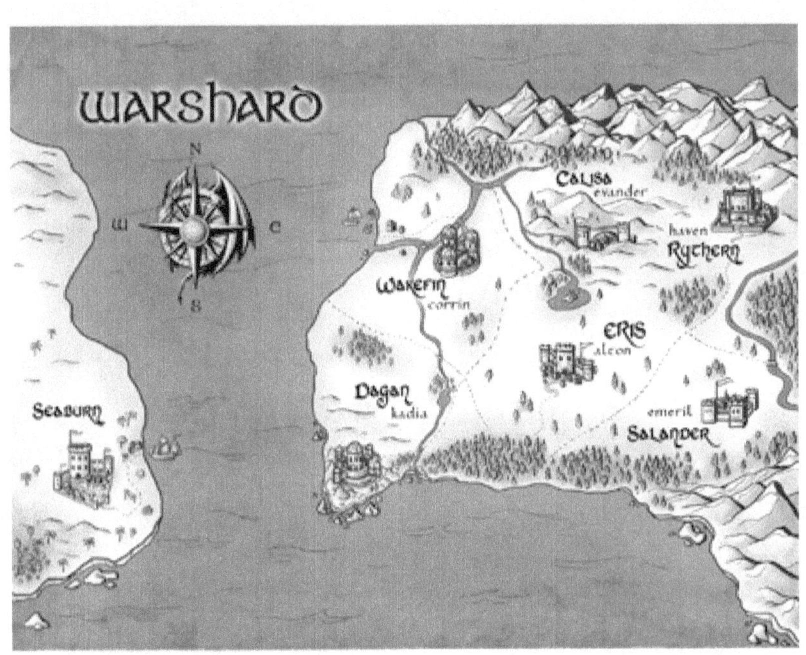

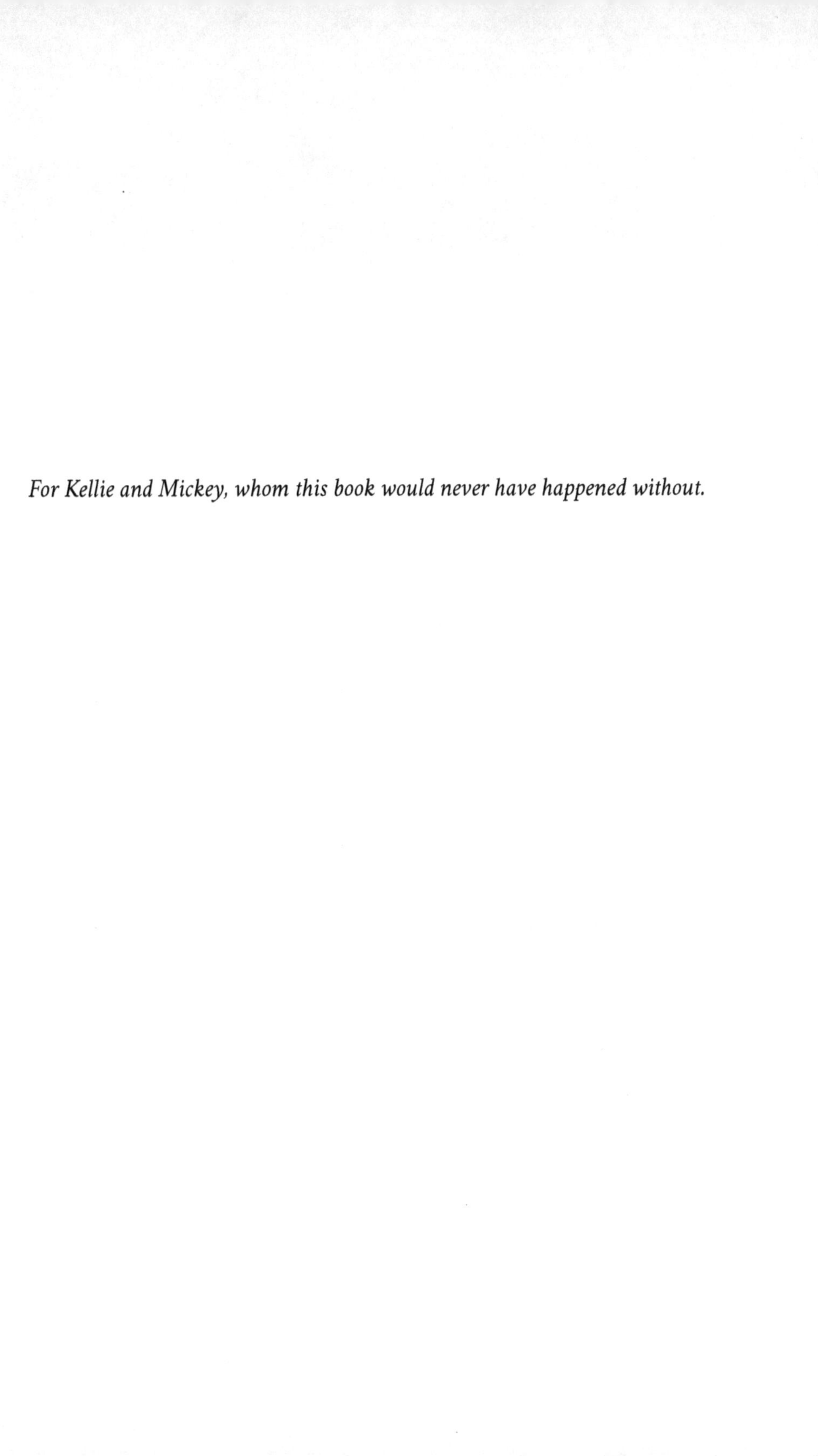

For Kellie and Mickey, whom this book would never have happened without.

PART
ONE

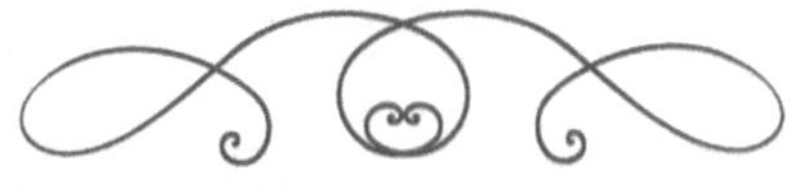

SURVIVE

ONE

The sun beat against her face, lending fire to her veins. A smirk pulled at the corners of her full lips and sweat beaded on her forehead. Hot sand pushed between her toes, unable to burn her calloused feet. Breen stared down her opponent on the opposite end of the ring while the surrounding Delica tribe howled for the fight to begin. Their savage song strengthened her bones and told of her victory.

Breen never lost.

"Are you ready to lose, my betrothed?" Lukerin grinned, stretching the tawny skin of his cheeks. He danced from foot to foot, his weight sinking into the sand.

Breen's brow furrowed. Lukerin knew very well that their betrothal wasn't solidified. Though her father, Chief Ruin, urged the young man to stay and win her hand, her heart belonged to no one but her tribe.

"I never lose." Her fingers itched at her sides. Her heart raced. As long as she was patient, Lukerin would lunge first. He always did.

Lukerin shook his head. His gaze wandered between her feet and her hands, most likely watching for the tightening of her muscles. He tried to guess her movements time and time again, but he had yet to learn she never leapt the same way twice—not with him. The only man to ever best her in a wrestling match; she would keep her guard up at all times and wait for his hasty steps.

"I've taken you down before, Breen." "Hardly."

Sand brushed over his feet as he inched closer. She kept her eyes on his, and his movements in her peripheral. *Don't move,* she urged herself. Like a wild jungle cat, as long as she kept still, Lukerin would grow tired of waiting.

"I suppose I'll have to show you again."

Breen smiled, her lips quirking to one side. She said nothing.

Lukerin's grin slowly twisted into a frown, and his brows cinched. There. His impatience betrayed him.

Her opponent lunged across the sand, sending thin grains into the air. Breen leapt from his path, her thick black braids tapping her shoulders and breasts. Lukerin spun, reaching for her wrist. She pulled away, dancing easily from his reach.

"You've got to be faster than that," she taunted.

He leapt again, his movements quick, but uncontrolled.

Breen stepped away once again, but this time, Lukerin spun and slipped his foot behind her calf. Her breath rushed from her lungs as her feet flew from under her. She caught herself on his leather vest, using all of her strength to flip him over her head. Sand assaulted her limbs as she rolled over Lukerin, bringing him onto his back beneath her. Her hands held him down.

"Good try." She flashed her teeth.

Lukerin growled and flipped her over. His rough hands tossed her like a sack of rice. Hot sand burned her bare arms. She leapt to her feet.

Her not-quite-betrothed waited opposite her. The howling tribe called for more. Their cries lent strength to her limbs, and a grin to her face. Her brothers and sisters, the fellow tribesmen, though not related by blood, encircled the sand ring. A line of dark brown rocks marked the borders.

"Is that all you have?" Lukerin raised his brow.

Breen shrugged. "Why don't you come and see?"

He took the bait. Leaping through the sand, he grabbed her forearm and twisted; giving her the momentum she needed to fling herself around his torso. Her worn leather tunic pressed against his back as she held her forearm to his throat, gripping her wrist with her opposite hand to keep him immobile. She pressed hard, bringing him to his knees.

"You should have learned by now, Lukerin," she breathed next to his ear, her voice husky and sharp.

His fingers clawed at her forearm, but she held too tightly. He'd never get the grip he needed to pull her off. Breen took a few deep breaths to still her heart. Any moment, she'd win. Lukerin would tap out, and the fight would be hers.

With a loud grunt Lukerin dove forward, swinging her over his head. Her eyes widened and a yelp pulled from her throat before she could stop it. She flew over his arched back, losing her grip. Her back hit the sand. Air exploded from her lungs.

Lukerin sat back, gasping in air.

Blue sky and a blazing sun shone overhead, stealing the color from her sight. She blinked white dots from her vision and leapt to her feet, dusting sand from her shoulders.

The weight of a wild horse collided with her chest, flinging her feet from beneath her. Breen instinctively latched on to Lukerin's arm and swung up and over so that her legs wrapped around his neck and she pulled him to ground.

Sand burned her bare skin, but she held on tight, squeezing his neck between her thighs while she pulled his arm back, stretching it at an awkward angle. Lukerin cried out. Though his muscles bulged with the effort to rip her legs away, again, she held too tightly.

"Give up," she hissed. Her arms strained with the effort to hold his heaving arm in her grasp. If she couldn't tame his arm, she'd lose her hold.

"Never," he choked.

"Breen!"

They both froze. The savage cries of her tribesmen died as her mother, Kianne, stepped between two of her larger brothers.

Delicate dark brown braids weaved in patterns secured the hair from her face, while thick waves drowned her shoulders and bosom. She smiled, her hooded gaze warm as she motioned to Breen. Thin golden bands upon her fingers glinted in the afternoon sun.

"Enough with the wrestling," her mother chided. "It's time for the young ones' lessons."

Breen heaved a sigh and slowly released Lukerin. He gasped for breath and rolled onto his stomach, coughing into the sand. She stood, hands on her wide hips as she met her mother's dark gaze.

"Mother, I'd nearly received Lukerin's surrender." She stepped across the ring to join her beautiful mother, clad in a dark blue gown, woven with gold stitching and leather belts.

"Nearly." Kianne smiled.

Breen frowned. "Lead the way."

Her mother dipped her narrow chin, the opposite of Breen's square one, and entered the maze of tents.

The tribesmen clapped her on the back, and sung her praises as she passed them by. Though she hadn't *officially* won, it was clear who the winner would be. She grinned, and thanked them, weaving through the few dozen men and women until she crossed the sand between the white tents.

Children younger than five ran between the homes, chasing chickens and swiping wooden swords at one another. Their laughter rose on the hot breeze. They grinned and ducked around Breen and her mother, waving as the small troupe disappeared behind a gnarled bush.

"You really are your father's daughter." Kianne glanced over her shoulder, mischief in her eyes. "He always prefers to fight than teach."

Breen smiled. "I'm sorry I didn't inherit your gift of lessons, Mother."

Kianne shook her head. "I'm not. But you could go easy on your betrothed."

Her joy seeped from her chest. Not this again. "*Mother.*"

She laughed and waved her ringed fingers. "I know, I know. *He's not your betrothed, simply an observer.*" Kianne recited the message Breen had given her parents time and time again.

Though she liked Lukerin and enjoyed his company and their wrestling matches, she couldn't see a life with him. She couldn't imagine being a wife to anyone, let alone mothering children yet. She'd gladly strengthen the numbers of the Southern Delica Tribe one day, but at sixteen, she wasn't ready for either of the things expected of her.

"Exactly." Breen nodded. "I can't imagine Father would be all right with me marrying someone I could best in battle."

Kianne laughed, her voice high like a bird's. "He wouldn't."

The large white tent of her mother's *Lesson Hut*, as she called it, rose above the sand, glaring in the sun. Breen narrowed her eyes against the white.

"What shall I teach today?" she asked.

"Your Father insists on more swordsmanship." Kianne's shoulders slouched, as if disappointed. She much preferred educating the children on the ways of the tribes, from the plants of the desert, to the wild horses that roamed the distant hills. None of these things kept the interest of babes, but she insisted on teaching them nonetheless.

"Perfect." Breen grinned.

Her mother narrowed her eyes, most likely sensing a conspiracy. Chief Ruin knew Breen's passion to train the young ones in battle, and often spoke on her behalf. The folds of the tent entrance parted and a thin girl of maybe six slipped outside. She glanced back and forth before spotting Breen and Kianne. The girl froze, her eyes flying wide. Aura. She hadn't been doing well in their battle training, preferring to focus on taming wild horses and identifying the desert fauna she could use to survive. Her large innocent eyes met Breen's, and her throat bobbed as she swallowed.

She was trying to flee before Breen's arrival.

"Aura." Breen inclined a brow. "Where are you off to?"

"Um..." Her eyes darted around the camp, searching for an answer.

"Get back inside." Breen motioned her in. Aura sighed before she spun back for the shadows of the interior.

"She's been doing well in all my classes." Kianne paused by the tent flap.

"Of course she is. Her thumbs are as green as yours." Breen grinned and her mother laughed.

"She'll get better with a sword, I'm sure."

Breen said her goodbyes and slipped inside.

Her whole body cooled in the shadows as she stepped from the hot sand and blazing sun into the tent. Though she preferred the freedom of the outdoors, she had to admit getting away from the sun during the day was a welcome relief.

"Good afternoon." Breen waved at the dozen children inside. Ranging from six to twelve, the young ones sat in a half-circle at the center of the tent, legs crossed, and dark eyes eager. All but Aura's.

Breen stepped from the entry and into the main area, rough cloth beneath her bare feet. Furs and tanned pelts lined the walls. Leather flasks hung from a dark brown lattice fashioned from jungle trees.

The Lesson Hut wasn't the most lavish of tents, but it served its purpose.

"Afternoon, Breen," they echoed back.

Opposite her small class, Breen placed her hands on her hips and smiled at the group. "We've gotten through the basics of holding a weapon and blocking. Most of you have done well and will move on to spar in pairs. This will help get you used to anticipating your opponent's moves."

While most of the children grinned beneath their heads of dark hair, Aura's lips turned into a frown, and her brows furrowed. Breen met her gaze briefly and nodded. She'd teach Aura separately to help her understand the importance of sword skills.

In the past, most children didn't start learning how to fight until at least eight years old. Their young years were for play, curiosity and exploration. But with Seaburn's glutinous Emperor ravaging the Savage Lands for soldiers, they hadn't a choice but to train children younger and younger.

Their tribe needed protection against the Empire raids. Seaburn soldiers took the young warriors, such as herself, and her brethren. If they were one day taken, the younger generations would need to step into their place.

"Grab your swords. Be mindful and pretend you wield iron or steel." Breen raised her brows and met the children's gazes. She wanted them to take this seriously. Though right now it was all a game to them, one day it wouldn't be. "Watch your footing, guard your face, chest, and abdomen. Remember, those are the killing blows. A cut to your arm or leg will only slow you down."

Each of them leapt to their feet, racing the short distance from the main floor to the edge of the tent where a wooden rack held small carved swords in varying sizes. Though the wood wouldn't cut them like a real sword, it could still hurt enough to make them think twice about each block and hit.

Once her students paired up, Breen took Aura aside. She plucked a long, curved wooden sword of her own from a nearby rack, and handed a shorter blade to Aura, who twisted her lip nervously between her teeth.

"It'll be all right." Breen smiled. She hadn't always been good with a blade either. Although daughter of the chief, Breen had struggled for many months to learn the most basic of steps. She'd started around the same time as Aura, and could see herself in the young girl's round eyes.

Aura nodded.

They stepped near the entrance of the tent, while the other pairs took up the center. Clashing wood, and tiny grunts filled the space, while Breen focused on the small girl before her.

"Hold your hilt tightly, but not with such force your knuckles go white." Breen demonstrated, her blade a mere extension of herself. "Your sword is part of you, an extension of your arm. Treat it as such, and you'll move effortlessly."

She dipped her narrow chin, avoiding Breen's gaze. Her brows furrowed as Aura adjusted her grip and parted her feet on the sand, holding her wooden blade straight from her body.

"Relax your elbow, like this." Breen shook her arm, relaxing her elbow. Her blade crossed a foot from her chest.

"All right." Her tiny fingers twisted around the hilt and she relaxed her arm.

"Good!" Breen smiled. She could get this. Breen was sure of it. "Now that your sword blocks your chest, you can easily move to block an attack aimed for your abdomen." Breen slowly thrust her sword forward as if she were going to stab Aura's chest.

Most likely sensing her intention, Aura shifted the wooden blade to slap Breen's off course.

Breen grinned. "Excellent! See, I knew you could do it."

Aura's cheeks flushed, and she lowered her blade. "It's still a bit heavy."

"I know. Usually you wouldn't start training for another year or two. But you know how deep the Seaburn soldiers have come. They've been sighted near the Northern Tribe across the river. I only want you to be ready in case a day comes where I'm not around to teach you. Someone needs to protect the horses you're so fond of."

Aura's brows furrowed and her eyes grew wide. She knew as well as the rest of them, and somehow seemed to understand better than the other children. Once her surprise faded, determination set her gaze. "What next?" she asked.

Breen held her sword aloft, and so did Aura.

"Protect your head." Breen swiped her sword for Aura's braids. The small wooden sword shot up to block her attack. "Now your stomach." She twisted and thrust her blade out. Aura jumped back from reach. "As good a tactic as any."

"Thank you."

"Would you like to try swinging at me?" Breen stepped back into her ready stance.

Aura's brows shot up, and she glanced from the other children swinging wildly at one another, back at Breen, who waited patiently.

"I'm not sure I can do it."

"You can. Pretend I'm one of the Seaburn maggots." They both smiled. "Pretend you're not only fighting me for the honor of your clan, but for survival. Protect your kin from me. Protect your mother."

Aura's lips pressed into a thin line. Her father had been taken two years ago by Seaburn's army. He'd ventured too far into the jungle blocking the Savage Lands from Seaburn's great Empire. When he emerged north of the forest, he'd been captured. Aura's mother had barely escaped alive.

Breen held up her sword as Aura's fingers tightened around the hilt. The fire of the gods flashed through her dark gaze. It was that fire that gave Breen hope. Aura would one day be great, do great things, fight great battles; her determination and strong will would aid her in this. This mock battle was only the beginning. Someday Aura would mirror her warrior father's skill in battle.

Aura swung. Though her footing was awkward and she simply hit Breen's sword, there was determination in her gaze. "Again," Breen said.

The small wooden sword sliced through the air. Breen blocked the blow for her chest. Aura lunged, thrusting her sword at Breen's gut. Breen parried, sending the small blade flying from her hands.

Aura's gaze flew wide, and she breathed hard.

"Very good." Breen grinned. "Again."

The small braids at Aura's cheeks shook as she nodded. She plucked her sword from the ground, and stepped opposite to Breen, raising her blade in the ready stance she'd been taught.

The beating of horse hooves over sand made her freeze. Breen's brows furrowed as she looked at the edge of the tent, in the direction of the river running to the east. No hunting party had come or gone from the tribe today. No sentries stormed the land, or watched the southern hills.

Then who could it be?

Breen lowered her sword, as did Aura. Her small prodigy followed her gaze.

"What is it?" Aura asked.

Her jaw set and her fingers tightened around the hilt of her blade. "Trouble."

Breen sprung into motion, placing her wooden sword back on its mount before flying to the door. She peeled the flap of the tent back.

The ground rumbled, and war cries split the hot desert. Her breath caught in her throat. "All of you stay here." Breen glared over her shoulder, silencing the protests of the older students. "Do not leave this tent, no matter what you hear."

Wide eyes followed her as she fled the Lesson Hut.

Breen ran across the hot sand as cries of panic rose all around her. Her brethren ran through the tents toward the commotion, curved swords drawn, and scowls gracing their faces. She dove between tents until she reached the largest of the bunch—that of the Chief. She pushed the flaps aside and embraced the cool shadows. Sunlight poured through the opening as she raced between lavish fur rugs, and ornate tapestries her mother had woven.

She found her quarters beyond the main room, the space broken by wooden dividers and jungle cat furs. Breen grabbed her boots from the floor and yanked on the dark leather. She laced them to her calves before tearing her long burgundy sheath from her bedside. Glass jars of candle wax toppled to the floor in her haste.

Her heart raced. Whoever was here—be they raiders, foreign tribesmen, or worse—she had to protect her people. The faces of her students flashed before her eyes. What if one of them wandered from the tent to see what was going on?

They weren't ready. They wouldn't be for some time.

Breen fled the chief's tent, fear and anticipation quickening her movements. She joined her brothers and sisters, sword in hand, boots crushing sand.

Several mothers ushered their children by, pushing them inside their tents, and ripping daggers from the leather sheathes at their hips.

The tribe was united in this. United against anything that dare threaten their home, their family, or their way of life. Gritting her teeth, Breen leapt over the sand to the edge of the Delica tribe's camp. Steel glinting in the harsh sunlight, she froze atop the slope.

The river stretched to her left, heading east to the sea. On their side of the canal, unheard of before this day, dozens of horses stormed across the open sand. Soldiers clad in metal armor with the gold seal of the Emperor at their hearts, rode the beasts. With swords in their fists, and the flag of Seaburn whipping in the wind, the enemy had finally arrived.

Seaburn had come for them.

TWO

S words clashed at the top of the hill. Horses reared and whinnied. Shouts tore across the desert, and panic ensued.

Breen dove between her brethren, nearly twenty men and women on the sand, half as many as the Seaburn warriors. The once wild horses of the hills tore past the tribesmen on all sides, slipping through to the camp, while others engaged in battle.

Her gaze flew from the small matches before her, and the tents at her back. Seaburn soldiers weaved between their homes, searching for something. More soldiers for their army?

Would they dare take the children now?

A snarl ripped from her throat, through her teeth. Fire burned through her chest and licked at her heart. She leapt for the nearest soldier, thrown free of his horse.

The man leapt to his feet, heavy armor slowing his movements. Breen spun and sliced at his chest. His sword rose to block hers. Metal clanged loudly in the chaos. She spun again, faster this time. While men had strength on their side, she had speed. Her blade clanged against his armor this time, denting the metal.

His boot slammed against her stomach, sending her flying. Her breath whooshed from her lungs. Hot sand burned her bare arms, though she hardly noticed it against the anger consuming her chest. Gasping in a breath, she leapt to her feet in time to block the man's swing. Her lips pulled back and she growled, inches from his face.

He pushed hard against her blade.

She jumped back.

All of his weight toppled forward. She jammed her sword through the break in the armor at his waist. Blood poured from his gut onto the sand. He gasped, wide brown eyes meeting hers. The familiar hooded eyes of a fellow tribesmen met her gaze.

Her breath caught in her throat.

So it was true.

Seaburn was using their own kind against them.

Breen pushed him back, and he slid from her blade. He hit the ground hard, and didn't get up.

Cries rose from the tents. Breen spun towards them, her eyes wide. No. Not them. Not the children. Panic bubbled in her chest. She fled the battle for the white tents dotting the sand in a wide misshapen circle.

I'm coming, she thought desperately.

She had to save them. Had to protect them. They were her family.

They were children.

Her boots pounded the sand as she ran. Soldiers clad in armor pulled two of her students from the Lesson Hut. Their screams rose above the fighting.

"Stop!" she cried.

One soldier looked up in time for her blade to slice clean through his arm. Her student flew back inside the tent, tears streaking his cheeks. The man's arm hit the sand, blood sticking the fine grains together.

The soldier shouted in a foreign tongue, his eyes wide as he dropped his sword to hold the stump where his arm once was.

The second soldier spun on her, dropping Aura back to the ground.

"Aura," she whispered. Rage stabbed her chest like knives. She lunged across the severed arm, blocking the man's path to Aura. "Stay away from her!"

Aura skittered back, whimpering quietly.

The soldier grinned, his dark hair sweeping across his forehead in the breeze. He spoke in the same foreign tongue. His words were clipped, arrogant and angry. Though she didn't understand the words, she got their meaning. Breen lashed her sword at his chest. He leaned back, the tip of her blade scratching the metal plate protecting his breast.

"Get back inside," Breen snapped at Aura. She didn't dare turn her gaze from her opponent.

The soldier narrowed his eyes and lunged. She leapt to the side, his blade sailing over her shoulder. With all her strength, she tackled him into the sand. Aura crawled back inside the tent while Breen leapt to her feet.

Slowed by his armor, the man rolled to his back. Breen dove, her sword held to his throat. He froze. Her hand trembled around the hilt.

Never had she been so angry. Never had she wanted to kill so badly.

Blood pumped through her veins and angry tears stung the back of her eyes. "You will not hurt my family," she hissed between her teeth. She pressed her blade closer to his flesh.

Garbled words and a smirk were his only response.

Breen thrust her sword through his neck.

He choked, blood gurgling from the back of his throat and between his lips. His eyes rolled back and he lay still.

The roaring of hooves across the sand stole her victory. She spun toward the noise, her bloodied sword ready. A black-skinned man in golden armor flew toward her. She leapt from his path. The horse flew passed, but the back of his sword slapped her back. She fell face first. Harsh grains rasped her tongue.

She spat the sand from her mouth, rising to her knees.

The ground trembled as the huge man leapt from his horse and hit the ground. Breen glanced over her shoulder as he bore down on her.

Scrambling to her feet, Breen stood in time for him to slice a curved steel blade at her chest. She leaned from reach, giving him time to step into his swing and kick her feet out from under her.

Air exploded from her lungs, and she gasped for breath.

Cold metal pressed against her exposed throat. She froze. Anger seeped from her trembling limbs. No. She *never* lost.

The man narrowed his dark eyes, his lips twisted in a frown. "You killed my men." He slurred the words of her language, but she understood.

"Your men would kill *mine*," she spat.

Steel pressed closer, nipping and stinging her skin. Something hot dripped down her throat. Blood. She hissed, her teeth snapping together.

His eyes roamed her from head to toe. "You will do."

"Do what?" The tip of his blade rose from her throat to her chin. She tilted her head until it touched sand, and she had nowhere else to go.

"Silence."

She glared. Her fingers twitched against the hilt of her sword. If only she could get the momentum, she could swing his sword from his hands and jump to her feet. Her chin stung as the sharp tip of his sword cut through, as if he sensed her intention.

"Drop it." His voice was monotone, deep, and merciless.

She released her hold on her hilt. He kicked it out of reach.

"You'll pay for this." She held his gaze.

His dark eyes gave away nothing. "Stand." He stepped back, the sting leaving her skin. Once given a foot of space, Breen slowly stood, her eyes never leaving the soldier. "Turn around." She did. "Move." He poked her spine with his blade.

Her fists clenched. But she listened.

Marching ahead, silence stilled the desert sand. The sounds of battle had died, and the scent of copper wafted through the air. Her heart leapt into her throat. How many had they killed? How many of her tribesmen were dead? Were her parents alive?

Breen stepped through the maze of tents, and into the open where the battle had been. Several soldiers lay dead. Several of her tribesmen joined them. Their blood soaked the sand. Their eyes turned to the blue skies, unseeing.

Her eyes widened and burned with tears.

Between her brethren and the Seaburn soldiers, at least a dozen were gone.

Why?

Why must they do this? Why did they wish to steal the lives of her family, and ravage their lands? So many lives had been needlessly lost. And for what?

Breen gritted her teeth against the coming tears. She would not cry. She would not show such weakness in front of these men. Steeling herself, Breen followed where the soldier directed her, to a line of her brothers and sisters kneeling in the sand. The man pushed her to her knees.

Lukerin met her gaze. Blood poured down his face, matting his short dark hair and bathing his harsh cheekbones and angular jaw. His eyes mirrored her sorrow, her fear, and her anger.

Another soldier stepped up behind her, his boots crushing sand. A cold blade pressed against the base of her skull.

The soldier clad in gold stepped to the front of the line of eight. He slipped his sword back into its sheath and crossed his hands behind his back. He walked the line slowly, inspecting them like livestock.

Her lips pulled back in a snarl and her fists shook at her sides.

They were outnumbered. Hardly any of their best warriors remained.

Cries of protest broke the quiet. Several soldiers led the rest of their tribe to the far end of the slope, closer to the tents. Dozens of children, elders, her parents, and some of the older warriors were forced to kneel.

The dark gaze of her father found hers across the sand. The leather band that typically wrapped his forehead was gone. His thick brows furrowed, and his beard trembled as he mouthed words to her.

Be strong.

She nodded. Breen would be the strength their tribe needed. She'd kneel because she had to. She'd kneel because she'd rather die than let these men hurt her tribe. And they would. The spears facing the large group by the tents told her as much.

"These eight will do," the black man said. He nodded to the guards at their backs.

"We should fight," Lukerin whispered, barely audible over the breeze.

Breen shot him a glare. "No." She wouldn't have his desire for revenge outweigh the lives of those left.

Rough twine encircled her wrists and burned her skin. Gloved hands pulled her to her feet and thrust her down the hill to a smaller pack of soldiers waiting beside two horse-drawn trolleys. Bars of wood created a box atop the back of the carts. Cages. She gulped the lump in her throat.

This is what they wanted. The fighters. The young warriors. Those who would grow and become one with their armies.

Breen shook her head. She had no choice. She had to follow.

The man at her back thrust her forward. She stumbled ahead, but kept her footing. Glaring over her shoulder, Breen cursed them for this. A curse for hurting her family, endangering the children, and for causing fear to stir in her chest. She didn't know how Seaburn could create such loyal soldiers out of those they called *savages*. Yet, the men she had fought proved they could.

Clenching her fists, she paced across the sand, the rest of the clan's warriors following. She'd follow as long as she had to, but then she'd escape.

* * *

THE JOURNEY from the Savage Lands to Seaburn was long and arduous. Desert sand and hills spread out on all sides. They crossed the river at the single wooden bridge to the east, before turning west to escape the jungle. The trolley bumped along the rough terrain, keeping sleep at bay.

They didn't stop for food, water or rest. The soldiers were determined. After a full day's ride, the horses came to a stop somewhere north of the jungle—far from any tribe village. They were on their own. Breen needed to escape.

"We could head for the jungle." Breen nudged Lukerin's arm with her elbow. They sat side by side at the back of the cage. Three others accompanied them, while the remainder of the warriors taken occupied the smaller cart behind two dark mares.

"We have no weapons." He glanced at her, his lips pressed in a thin line. For hours she'd spouted possible plans of escape, but he had yet to agree with any.

"We'll take them from the soldiers."

"With our hands tied behind our backs?" He scoffed.

Shouts rose from the soldiers at the front of the party. Breen glanced nervously at them before returning her gaze to Lukerin.

"I can get mine in front of me." She'd done it before as a test long ago in her lessons with Kianne. Her mother's foresight had to be excellent, for Breen never imagined she'd need to use this knowledge.

"Without anyone noticing?"

At least thirty soldiers led the party, all on horseback or atop benches at the front of the carts. While maybe a dozen led the way back to Seaburn several feet ahead of their wide wooden cart, fewer stayed behind to watch their captives. She took pleasure in knowing their numbers had diminished since their attack. At least they'd made a dent in Seaburn's army.

"I may need a distraction," she admitted.

Lukerin nodded. "What do you have in mind?"

"Make a scene. Shout. Holler. Pretend you're injured—" She glanced at the blood dried to his face. "—More injured than you are."

"And what will you do?"

"Get my hands in front of me. When the soldiers check on you, I'll grab whatever weapon I can and stage our escape." The dark eyes of the other warriors flickered in their direction. Soldiers at the front of the party dismounted their horses and approached the rear.

So they were taking a break. This was the perfect time to spring an escape plan. They were weary from the journey, sleep deprived and hungry.

Her own stomach rumbled. She narrowed her eyes at the leather covering her gut. Hungry or not, she'd use every last bit of her strength to get away.

Several yards to the south, the dark jungle rose out of the sand, as if by magic. Thick green moss covered visible stones and vines hung from the tall trees, brushing the desert's edge. How could such dense forest survive in this heat?

"I don't know, Breen." Lukerin sighed.

He didn't meet her gaze. Instead, he stared at the wooden floor of their prison. She'd never seen this side of him before—the side that would give up. She was glad she'd never accepted his proposal.

"Then what do you suggest?" she hissed between her teeth.

"Someone's coming," one of the others snapped.

Her teeth clacked together, cutting off their conversation. She leaned back against the bars of the cage. Rough wood dug into her spine.

Foreign mumbling approached. Two men dismounted their horses at the rear of the pack. Another two joined them from the front.

Cursed traitors.

Breen barely held back her snarl. The faces of tribesmen, not her own, but of others to the north. They'd given in to Seaburn. She could never forgive such an act. Her fists clenched at her back. She waited. Maybe they'd move them. Outside this prison would be easier to flee.

"We're camping for the night," one of them said. His soulless black eyes looked right through her. "Try anything and you'll be beaten. Try again and you'll lose a hand. Try a third time—" He smiled. "—and we'll bury you in the sand and leave you out here to die."

She couldn't help the widening of her eyes. How cruel.

Breen set her jaw. She'd have to choose her moment carefully.

The man slipped a key into the thick metal lock barring their exit. He turned it and the lock clicked. The gate creaked open.

"Out." He motioned to the sand. "One at a time."

Three soldiers waited at the man's back. She sighed. She had no other choice. Slipping from the cart and onto the hot sand, Breen stepped from the trolley, only to be grabbed by one of the men. His rough fingers wrapped her bare bicep. He thrust her forward.

She stumbled, and turned a glare on her captor. He stared back with hard eyes.

What had Seaburn done to these men? They were vacant. Barren of feeling. Did they not see their own brothers and sisters here? How could they go along with whatever this was? How could they obey the Emperor?

The man pushed her forward again.

She didn't bother glaring.

The others dismounted, led by one soldier each. A small camp formed around them. The sand darkened with the setting sun, casting long scorched shadows over the surrounding dunes.

The soldiers brought tents up on either side of their party, building fires outside each. One remained tall and lavish, most likely for whatever General led them. The other was small, worn beige fabric and brittle polls to hold it aloft.

The soldier leading her grabbed her shoulder. His fingers dug into her skin as he forced her to the ground. "Sit," he commanded.

Breen's fingers itched against her restraints. She pulled on the ties, but did as he said, sitting cross-legged on the hot earth. The others joined her until eight of them sat about a foot from each other.

Five soldiers stayed to guard them, surrounding the tribesmen in a small circle.

By the time the camp had risen from the dust, the sun had disappeared behind the horizon. It would take some time for the sand to cool. At least her pants were thick enough to keep her from burning.

Two more soldiers approached their party. "Eatin' time," one of them growled. He tossed two burlap sacks and a leather water canister to his comrades.

Another slurred back in the foreign tongue she assumed belonged to Seaburn. The soldiers joined in laughter, while she glanced at her brethren. What was so funny? A soldier kneeled at her back and grabbed the twine at her wrists. It dug into her skin, rubbing her already raw flesh.

She gritted her teeth until a dagger snipped the thin rope and her hands were freed. He stepped away from her and another soldier placed the water canister in her lap.

"Share," he slurred, motioning at the circle around her.

Irritation flashed through her chest. She nodded.

She wasn't an imbecile.

Breen uncorked the bottle and took a quick sniff of the contents; just to be sure they hadn't been poisoned. Nothing but the scent of her own sweat met her nostrils. Fresh water. Finally. Her dry lips parted and she took a deep gulp. Warm water washed down her throat. She sighed blissfully.

Reluctant to give up the water, though knowing she needed to, Breen took one more quick sip before passing it to Lukerin. His brows rose and his hard features relaxed. Relief. Breen sat back

With one of her present concerns cleared, she could think clearly.

Though seven soldiers stood nearby, there were eight of her tribesmen. Even with armed opponents, her tribe should be able to fight their way through them. But they'd need to do it together. Glancing around the circle, Breen assessed the warriors.

Two sisters and five brothers.

Three half-asleep from the looks of their drooping eyes and hunched shoulders. Two on alert and two injured, including Lukerin. With only three ready to fight, including herself, it would be a blood bath.

They'd never be able to pull this off.

Her stomach soured. She still wanted to try. Death might very well be better than finishing the journey to Seaburn. Whatever waited for her to the east, she didn't want to know.

Lukerin met her gaze. His brows furrowed. He knew she was up to something. She flicked her fingers against the sand, motioning in a circle to the guards surrounding them. He narrowed his eyes. No. He was telling her no. But he wasn't the Chief's daughter. She was.

Breen sought out the other two on alert. One sister, Osana, a year older than she, and one brother, Gryn, a year younger. She made sure they were paying attention to her before glancing at the surrounding guards.

Her short-haired sister nodded, determination setting her hard gaze. Osana wanted blood. She wanted escape. She wanted freedom. Just like Breen.

Gryn hesitated, his lips parted as he glanced between the guards and their warriors. He had the same concerns as Breen. They'd be well outnumbered in this fight. But it would be a test of her strength and resolve. All she needed was a sword, and she'd have them.

The soldier behind her stood at attention, though his gaze wandered to the setting sun. He wasn't paying attention. With his sword held carelessly at his side, she could knock it from his hand and sweep it from the sand before he could attack.

Lukerin shook his head in her peripheral. He knew her plan. Would he try to stop her? Or join in the fight?

It was time to find out.

Breen leapt to her feet and slammed her knee into the guard's groin. Breath fled his lungs in a gasp as he buckled forward, releasing his sword. She grinned and swept it from the ground, turning back to the enemy.

Lukerin and three of the other tribesmen joined her, sending fists, knees and feet at their opponents.

Yes! They could do this.

Two guards lunged at her, swords brandished. Breen parried the attack of the first, slipping through his defenses and slicing open his gut. Before he hit the ground, she spun to block the swing of the second. A snarl passed her opponent's lips. He gritted his teeth and thrust her back.

She leapt away, in case he moved to counter. He didn't. Not right away.

Blood soaked the ground at her feet.

The second soldier swung wide. She stepped from his path and kicked his unarmored knee. The man's eyes flew wide before he toppled to the sand.

Breen lunged after him, swiping for his hand.

The man cried out as her blade sliced his flesh. He released the sword, giving her a second to work with. Plucking it from the sand, she held both swords to the back of his neck. He froze, mid-crouch.

"Release him, *savage*." The black-skinned, gold armored man who'd taken her, held his long curved blade to the throat of the kneeling Lukerin.

Her breath caught. Her heart sped.

"Release *him*," she countered.

Osana and Gryn had been taken down, pinned to the earth. Osana met her eyes, an apology on her lips.

Breen shook her head. Damn.

"Release my soldier *now*," he commanded. Blood trickled down Lukerin's exposed throat. He winced.

Breen gritted her teeth, looking left and right. Soldiers stepped up on either side of her. It was no good. She was trapped.

And she couldn't risk the lives of her tribesmen.

She dropped the swords and stepped away from the soldier. They didn't hesitate on grabbing her arms and throwing her into the sand. Grains irritated her eyes, nostrils and throat. She coughed them from her lungs and looked up at the gold-clad man.

His boot pushed her head back down.

She gasped, struggling to push herself up.

Two soldiers held her arms behind her back.

She sputtered, sand filling her mouth and throat, stealing her saliva and the sweet relief of the water she'd been given.

"You are no longer a warrior," the man droned. "You are a *slave*. You will obey me, and my soldiers. We are your betters. We are your masters. If you want to live, you will *listen*."

Breen struggled against their grasp. Her cheeks and eyes burned. She thrashed her shoulders.

"Stop!" Lukerin shouted.

Something heavy hit the ground nearby.

"Silence," a soldier said.

"You will learn to obey, *slave*," the man continued.

Her lungs burned. She couldn't get air. She was suffocating. Panic lent strength to her limbs, while oxygen deprivation stole her senses. They held her to the ground until pain filled her chest and her movements slowed.

The boot lifted from her skull.

They pulled her up before throwing her back down. Coughs exploded from her chest. She gasped in air, her sides heaving with the effort. She'd nearly died. He'd nearly suffocated her on the sand.

"Let that be a warning." The man spun on his heels and trudged away from the group of tribesmen.

Weakness seeped into her muscles. Her cheek lay against the earth as she blinked sand from her lashes.

So this was Seaburn. This was their army. Cruel. Merciless thugs.

Her fists clenched around the cooling sand beside her face. She took another deep breath. If this was Seaburn, she needed freedom. Whether she found freedom in life or death—she would soon find out.

THREE

reen awoke to sun burning her skin and the rock of the cart below. Three days. Three. Damn. Days. They travelled over sand and hills for miles, through heat and high-winds with little rest.

Her head ached as she opened her eyes. The soft cotton beneath her cheek caused her brows to furrow. She didn't remember falling asleep in the cart. She didn't remember curling up next to anyone.

She glanced up.

Lukerin watched the coming road, his lips pressed in a thin line and his jaw hardened. She was lying on his lap. On the man who wanted to marry her, yet whom she had no desire for. If her cheeks weren't already burning from the sun, they'd have burned with embarrassment.

She sat up quickly. Her entire world spun. The aching of her skull grew worse. She closed her eyes and rubbed her temples as she groaned.

"Good morning." Lukerin's lips quirked to one side as if he might smile. He didn't. She hadn't seen him grin in days.

"Morning." She sat back against the wooden bars of their prison. "Where are we?"

Lukerin glanced out the front of the cage. A dirt road stretched beneath them. The jungle was no longer to the south, and sandstone homes rose in the distance, clay rooftops peeking over the hill.

"I think we're close." He frowned.

Close to Seaburn.

Cold fear stole her heat. She rubbed her arms. The rest of her brethren rested, lying where they could, leaning against one another in the small space. No wonder she'd fallen asleep where she did. There was nowhere to move where she didn't touch the limbs of her comrades.

"Is that it behind the sun?" she asked, pointing to the homes.

He shook his head. "I don't think so. Probably an outer village."

She nodded. That made sense. She'd never seen a foreign village, or Seaburn itself, but she'd heard stories. Lukerin's father had been a traveller and was well versed in the ways of Seaburn. He'd taught his son many things, and Lukerin passed on some of that knowledge to her.

"How long was I asleep?"

"A few hours."

"You should have woken me." She hadn't given up on escaping before they reached their destination.

Lukerin shrugged. "You need your rest. We don't know what's coming, Breen. We need to be ready." He met her gaze. He meant she shouldn't make another escape attempt. They were all weary from travel, and trying to break free on the road wouldn't do any good, especially if they were close to civilization.

But would it be any easier to escape once they'd arrived? She doubted it.

"All right." She'd keep her eyes peeled, but she couldn't flee without her tribesmen. She wouldn't go. Not yet.

The dirt road widened as the trolley scaled the hill. Sandstone homes peaked on the rise. Gnarled trees and bushes marred the land. The squat homes passed on either side of the cart. The path became smooth. Less bumpy. Black-skinned men, women and children walked by the road, some with swords and rucksacks, others with pails of water or arms full of straw.

The children paused to watch them go, dark eyes following the carts.

Her fingers wrapped around the bars of the cage. Did these people know what the soldiers would do to them? Did they know how Seaburn made its warriors?

Hours passed with the same landscape of homes and periods of wasteland. Some small farms spread across the land, with horses ploughing the fields and soldiers marching by in pairs. They didn't stop to watch. They didn't check to see if those in the cages were their friends or family.

How did they get like this? How was it possible to forget all about your brothers and sisters? She couldn't imagine life without her tribal family, and refused to think about it here. They would escape. They would return home, whatever the cost.

"Look." Lukerin nudged her arm.

Breen turned toward the front of the caravan.

Salt air brushed her nose. A tall hill rose from the edge of the sea, several miles of sandstone, smooth stone and regular wooden homes spread from the sandy shore, up the slope to the great walls of the Emperor's Palace. That had to be it. Beyond the thick walls, trees rose, followed by three tall, rounded buildings, all attached by smooth sandstone. Golden domes covered each section, steeples pointing from the tips.

Her eyes widened.

This was Seaburn.

And it was beautiful, in a strange way she wasn't accustomed to. Though natural beauty was everywhere in the land surrounding the Southern Delica Tribe, Seaburn was different; architectural beauty, unique to this land. She'd never seen anything like it. Even her mother, Keeper of Knowledge for the tribe, hadn't ever described such a place to her.

The cart lurched down the slope towards the surrounding city, following a cobblestone road. If she didn't know her fate as a slave lay somewhere inside this city, she might have wanted to explore. She might have spent more time inspecting the waterfront and the tall windows of the palace.

But Seaburn was the enemy. Seaburn could be her end.

Breen clenched her fists in her lap. Her nails dug into her palms.

It was too late to escape. She didn't know these streets and could be lost too easily in a land these soldiers must know. But what could she do? Wherever their journey ended, would be dangerous. More dangerous than here.

She met Lukerin's dark gaze. "What do we do?"

"I don't know."

Neither did she. And that was the problem.

THE CARTS PULLED to a halt outside the palace walls. A three-story stone structure with pillars holding up the lip of the long slanted roof rose forbiddingly to block out the sky. Soldiers clad in tan leather costumes and some in armor, marched across the open courtyard, their boots stomping in rhythm with one another.

She gulped.

They were gone. Whoever she had been, whoever the tribesmen had been, it was over. There was no escape now. The lock on their cage clicked open and two guards with rough hands yanked her out. Her knees scraped the stone courtyard before they hauled her to her feet. Her hands were still bound, this time at her front. She waited in a circle of soldiers for the rest of her brethren to be yanked from the cart.

When they did, the soldiers gathered the prisoners in an orderly line, pushing them none-too-gently into place. She narrowed her eyes at them, but said nothing. Instead, she hoped she'd never see these men again. If they often left the city to hunt for tribesmen, she may not.

The gold-clad man joined them then. Whereas half a dozen soldiers had left their group upon entry to the city, the black man still accompanied them. He stepped in front of her at the head of the line. His dark eyes continued past her to look at the others. His lips curved in a frown.

"You have arrived at the Academy. Here you will become soldiers of the Emperor." He glanced between each of them before continuing. "I am General Mace. You will be under my direct supervision should you continue to training."

If, they continued. So, what happened first?

Her gut soured. Her heart sped.

This couldn't be good.

"Obey. Follow orders. Do what you're told. Become one of Seaburn's soldiers and you will be given good food, drink, and quarters. Should you try and escape, you will be punished. Should you not pass the Cleanse, you will die."

He tilted his chin towards the sky, looking down his flat nose at the eight of them. He'd given this speech many times, that much was clear. Though she was tempted to demonstrate her irritation, she couldn't stop the dread boiling in her gut.

The Cleanse.

It didn't sound good. She had no idea what it could mean.

"Follow me."

The group behind her mumbled as they were jostled forward. Lukerin pushed her forward gently. Her feet grew heavy like lead, stuck to the earth. With each step forward, it was as if she somehow sealed her fate. Each breath could be her last. The passing moments might be her last free ones.

She took a deep breath.

No, this wasn't it. She'd get out. She'd escape without incurring the wrath of General Mace. Her fingers shook as she followed Mace past the marching soldiers and through the front gate.

Two guards standing on either side of huge wooden doors stepped forward to push them open. The thick wood creaked against the iron hinges before slamming off the inner wall. Mace, and two of his subordinates led them inside.

Twin sandstone staircases rose on either side of the main hall, leading to the second floor above. High vaulted ceilings opened the room. Shadows danced in the rafters. After a glance or two at her surroundings, her fellow prisoners were forced forward. Even as she paused to look, Lukerin ushered her forward.

The heels of Mace's boots clacked against the floor until they reached the space beneath the second floor balcony. The soldiers ushered them through a door to the left.

Down and down they went, following the stone staircase deep into the earth. The lavish halls stopped quickly, turning to ragged stone blocks and musty air.

She wrinkled her nose. They were far beneath the earth. Only the torches lining the walls lit their way. What seemed like hours later, they reached the ground and entered a long hall.

Prison cells lined the right wall. Dark wood slated doors with a barred window in the top half too high for her height stopped her from seeing who, or what, lie inside. Moans drifted from further down the dark hallway. Cool, damp air brushed the base of her neck.

She shivered. Goose bumps rose on her flesh.

She shouldn't be here. None of them should be. What did they *do* to them down here? Her eyes widened, and her fear stole the courage she'd been desperately clinging to for the last few days. Her pace slowed. Her feet itched to run. Her muscles braced for flight.

A soldier grabbed her arm and thrust her forward, muttering something in the foreign Seaburn tongue.

"Welcome to your new home." Mace's thick lips twitched in a smirk. He paused, as the narrow corridor became a wide room. The cells continued up the right hand wall, mere inches from her shoulder.

Several brown-skinned guards stood from their seats by the far wall. Torchlight cast shadows across their faces. Dark, black eyes. Menacing stares. So these were their keepers. Their jailers. And what else? Their cleansers?

She shook her head.

The leather-clad soldiers stepped forward. Each of them resembled the other Seaburn natives. Were there no tribesmen in the dungeons?

A rough hand clasped her bicep and thrust her forward. He whipped open a cell door. Only the torches in the outer room lit the shadowed cell. Straw covered the rough stone floor. Dark, wooden walls stood on either side, while sandstone rose on the back wall. A metal bucket lay in one corner.

He pushed her inside.

The door slammed behind her. The lock slid shut.

She spun for the door. The foul odor of feces and vomit slid up her nostrils. Her stomach flipped. Breen wrapped her fingers around the bars at the top of the door. They were just low enough for her to peer through on her tiptoes.

"Why are you doing this?" she hissed. "What do you want from us?"

General Mace hardly glanced at her cell before motioning the rest of the men to continue. They nudged Lukerin, Osana, Gryn and the rest of her tribesmen into their cells. Heavy doors slammed on either side of her, rattling her own door. She kicked the door hard, gritting her teeth.

"We don't belong here. Why do you people do this?" She rattled the bars of her window.

No one looked at her. No one payed any attention to her pleas. No one met her eyes. No one even glanced at her.

"Seaburn rats!" Osana spit out the window of the cell next to her.

Lukerin slammed against the door to his cell. "Let us go!"

Questions which had been circling her brain for the last few days forced their way back into her mind. Her indignation wouldn't be shoved aside. Who were these people? How could they be so hardened? So heartless?

General Mace turned from their cages and trudged back down the hall, leaving them to their protests.

So this was it; this was the great Seaburn.

She wasn't impressed.

THE DOOR to her cell slammed against the wall, waking her from an uneasy sleep. Breen's eyes flashed open, and she sat up from the hard stone floor. Her body ached all over.

A soldier with a dark leather mask stepped inside and grabbed her braids in his hand. She yelped, and clawed at his hand. He pulled her across the floor, dragging her by her hair.

"Stop!" Breen screamed. Her eyes stung from the pain. She sank her nails into his hands. Leather. Damn.

To stop the wrenching pain in her scalp, she grabbed the base of her braids, holding on tight to keep him from pulling all her hair from her skin.

The large room outside the cells, seemingly etched right from stone, with twin pillars keeping the ceiling aloft, passed her by with little more than a glance.

Two soldiers marched past, holding Lukerin by his elbows. He was soaked to the bone. His head lolled forward, water dripping from his dark hair.

She gasped.

What had they done to him? She thrashed with her legs and body, but her eyes blurred with tears. She could see no escape. What had they done to Lukerin? Had they been doing this all night and she had yet to hear?

The pressure left her skull and she fell from the soldier's grip. Her back hit the cold ground. Her breath whooshed from her lungs. Breen struggled to her feet while simultaneously wiping tears from her eyes and regaining her breath.

"What is going on?" she wheezed.

The haze of tears disappeared, revealing another room, this time carved from gray stone. Darkness crept from every corner. Only two torches lit the wide space. At the center, a lone wooden chair sat dripping with water.

"What is this?" Her voice was small. Her eyes flew wide.

The man who had dragged her inside slammed the door shut closing them in together. It rattled on its hinges. The quiet *plop* of water drops filled the silence—the only sound aside from her ragged breath.

Her fingers trembled and cold slithered down her neck. This deep in the earth, there was no heat, no light, no warmth, but it didn't matter. The cold came from more than the dankness of the room. She was scared. Breen gulped.

He jailer pushed her forward. Her heels dug in.

He grabbed her hair in one hand, and twisted her arm behind her back with the other. She gasped; her head wrenched back so far she met his eyes through slits in the leather. Dark menace stared back. He urged her forward and forced her into the chair, never releasing her hair. The men emerged from the shadows occupying each corner of the space. They strapped her arms and legs to the wooden seat. Goose bumps rose on her tawny skin.

The man gripping her hair held her head back while another placed a thin sheet of cloth over her face. Her breaths came in quick gasps. Her heart raced. No. She didn't like this. She wanted to see. She didn't want the darkness, couldn't handle the darkness.

"Ready?" someone whispered. His hot breath brushed her ear.

She shivered.

No.

"As a recruit to the Seaburn armies, you will learn our mantra," the rough voice of a man said. "Listen closely, and repeat."

The grip on her hair tightened, sending knives through her scalp. She winced.

"I accept my place." He paused. She didn't repeat the words. "I accept my place," he repeated more forcefully. Again, she did not respond.

Breen accepted *none* of this.

"I'll begin again."

Ice-cold water bathed her in painful daggers. She gasped for air, but water filled her mouth. She coughed, trying to suck in air, but only receiving more wetness pressing against her face.

"I accept my place."

She spit as much as she could from her mouth with the sheet

sticking to her skin. It clung to every inch of her head, muffling his words and freezing her skin while trying to suffocate her.

"I accept my place. I will perform my duties."

Another bucket of water filled her mouth and lungs. She spluttered, drowning against the wet fabric. How could they do this to her? This was inhumane. Cruel. But what had she expected from the same men who would threaten children and lock potential soldiers in putrid cells?

"I will obey."

She refused to speak; couldn't really, even if she'd wanted to. Her lungs burned and her eyelids fluttered. She gasped in more water. It tore down her throat and up her nostrils.

"I will follow.

Ice struck her cheeks again. She couldn't breathe. She couldn't think. Why wouldn't it stop?

"I will surrender."

Her fists clenched against her restraints. She bucked hard, trying to pull from the chair, trying to strike someone—anyone.

"I will live by Seaburn laws."

She screamed through the next gallon. Her voice cut off to more fits of coughing. All the while, rough hands kept her head back, and her throat displayed.

"I will adhere to my Seaburn masters."

Her lungs filled. She couldn't do it anymore. She couldn't breathe. Panic bubbled in her chest and rose into her throat as she thrashed against her bindings, trying to get free, to shed the wet second skin the sheet had become.

"I will heed all above me."

She gasped. No air came. Blackness pulled at the little light she could see beyond the sheet. Her limbs grew weak. This was it. She couldn't do this. She couldn't escape. She'd never be free.

"I will obey."

The fight fled her limbs, and darkness took her.

COLD BURST THROUGH THE BLACK.

Breen sat up, coughing as water hurled from her lungs. Her entire upper body tensed with pain. Her limbs trembled and her shoulders quaked.

Soaking wet, she rid her body of the ice, until she gasped in air.

Sweet, sweet air.

It rasped against her sore throat, but she swallowed it with pleasure. Every lungful gave her life.

Slowly her trembling died, and she blinked drops of water from her lashes. Her lips quivered as she looked up at the masked man standing before her, a bucket in his hand.

She glared. Him. He'd done this to her. She'd nearly died—drowned—because of this stupid ritual. *The Cleanse*. It was torture. Their mantra was a joke. She'd never say it. She'd never follow them, no matter how much they tortured her.

"Repeat the mantra." The man bore down on her, his dark eyes nearly black behind his mask.

Breen spit water from her mouth and sat back in her chair, glad to be free of the hands clutching her hair.

Though shivers wracked every inch of her, she would not give in. She would not obey. She would not follow these people, and she certainly wouldn't surrender to whatever rituals these men concocted.

"Never." Her throat was raw and stung as she spoke.

The man stepped back and nodded to the man at her back. This wasn't over. Not yet. Fear bubbled in her chest despite her resolve. Her weak limbs drew what little strength they had back into them. She leapt to her feet, yanking her wrists and ankles from the restraints. The floor was slick beneath her boots and they slid as she lunged forward.

The masked men grabbed for her. She dodged their outstretched hands. She would not let this be the end. She would not let them take her down.

"Stop!" one of them hissed behind his mask. With no holes for their mouths, she hadn't a clue which spoke.

Breen danced between them until she reached the thick wooden door. Her fingers closed on the cold metal handle.

Rough hands grabbed her shoulders and threw her to the ground.

"No!" Her heart raced as she spun to her stomach and pushed herself up.

A boot crashed down on her spine, pinning her to the floor.

"You *will* obey." The man who'd brought her here pulled her to her feet and nearly tossed her back into the wet chair.

Her breaths came in quick gasps. Her adrenaline was fading. She didn't have the strength for this. She didn't have the energy to defend herself.

They snapped her restraints back on her wrists and ankles. Leather dug into her exposed skin. She gritted her teeth and waited. From a water trough hidden in shadows by the wall, they filled another bucket. Her heart leapt. No. Not again.

Please no.

She pulled at her restraints. They would not give way a second time. The man at her back gripped her hair and forced her head back.

The wet sheet chilled her face and clung to her features as they draped it over her a second time. She gasped in great lungfuls of air, trying to savor it.

"I accept my place."

Ice crashed down upon her.

FOUR

$\mathcal{P}$ain ate at her abdomen as her stomach growled for the hundredth time. Her eyelids fluttered open. Clutching her gut, she pulled herself from the cold stone floor. Straw clung to her bare arms. She sat against the wall, leaning her head back.

For days they tortured them all. They hardly fed them a thing, or gave them water aside from drowning them in it. Only a couple of hours passed in which she was given rest before they took her back again. Time and time again they blasted her with ice water and drowned her until she passed out.

But she would not repeat their mantra. She would not give in to them.

"Breen?" Lukerin croaked through the wall.

She glanced at the door, praying it wouldn't open; that whoever lived to torture her wouldn't hear the desperate whisper of the man next door. Or her own as she answered him. She didn't want any more time in that room. She didn't want to drown anymore, but she needed to speak with someone—anyone. She needed to remember what life was like before this so she could one day get back to it.

Despite the fear welling in her chest, she whispered, "Lukerin."

Breen pressed her ear against the wall, her dry, cracked lips nudging the boards separating her from her friend.

"We should have tried harder to escape when you wanted to." His voice cracked. She could hardly hear him, though she could almost feel his presence on the other side of the worn wood. "We should have gone."

Her fingers brushed the wood. "It's all right, Lukerin. We would have been beaten, or worse, for trying again."

He took a loud rasping breath. "I know. But death would have been better than this."

She agreed.

"There is no honor in this death. There is no fight," he continued. "There is only suffering. There is only pain." The wall shook.

"I know." Pain stabbed her heart like a knife. Her eyes stung as she gazed at the dark ceiling above. He was right. There was no honor here. There was no fight. There was only suffering.

"We have to stay strong."

"We will," she assured. Her fingers clenched.

"We can't go down like this."

"We won't."

The creak of a door broke their conversation. They were coming for one of them. Coming to take her tribesmen into that hellhole. She closed her eyes and prayed they didn't come for her.

A gasp sounded through the wall.

"No, please no," Lukerin pled.

Her eyes flew wide, and she turned to her side, kneeling on the stone. No, not Lukerin. Not now. Though she could still feel the strength of her ancestors in her bones, Lukerin's was fading. It wasn't fair to keep torturing him this way.

The door to the neighboring cell cracked off the wall, echoing in the dungeon. She stood and rushed for her own door. Her fingers wrapped around the metal bars.

Two soldiers pulled Lukerin by his elbows outside the cage. Her fellow tribesman tried to fight. His arms shook and he dug his heels in. But, like her, his strength was failing. Without food, water or rest, they couldn't fight anymore. That had probably been their plan all along.

"There is no honor in this," Lukerin hissed. He pulled his arm from their grasp and swung to his feet.

One of the masked men drove his fist into Lukerin's gut. He collapsed onto the floor, gasping for breath.

"What do savages know of *honor*?" The guard's boot slammed into Lukerin's chest, spinning him onto his back.

"Stop!" she cried.

They ignored her.

Lukerin groaned and held his injuries, while the two guards hoisted him back up. They dragged him across the floor. Lukerin's moans bounced off the walls.

Her fingers clenched around the metal. Her heart sank. This wasn't right. None of it was. How could they do this to them?

* * *

HER BODY QUAKED as two soldiers tossed her back in her cell. Her eyelids fluttered beneath heavy drops of water. Her lips quivered. For what felt like hours, they dowsed her in water and forced her to drown. Their manic laughter echoed in her ears as she pulled herself to the back of her cage.

The door slammed shut.

Breen curled into a ball. Every inch of her ached. Her stomach no longer growled with hunger. She lost all track of time. Was it day? Night? She couldn't be sure. With no sunlight, no windows, and only darkness, she hadn't a clue what her body should be feeling. Should she be asleep? Should she be awake?

Waves of exhaustion attempted to pull her under.

She let her lids shut and her body fall limp. She didn't care what time of day it was. She didn't care about anything.

The door creaked slightly, the worn wood of the bottom scraping against the rough stone floor. She opened her eyes.

A small plate slid inside with a puffy roll and strip of dried meat atop it. Her eyes widened. A small canteen slid in next before the door closed with a soft click.

"Wait," she choked out. Her fingers dug into the floor, and with the little bit of her strength left, she pulled herself across the floor and kneeled in front of the plate. Her fingers hesitated over the meat.

Could she trust it?

What if it was poisoned? It'd be a much swifter death, she was certain.

"It's not tainted," a rough voice said beyond the door.

A brown-skinned soldier, with short black hair and dark eyes, gazed through the bars in her door. His brows pulled up and his lips pulled down in a frown.

"How do I know you're not lying?" Her voice rasped against her raw throat.

He paused. His round eyes regarded her with pity.

Her lips pulled back in a snarl. How *dare* he pity her? He, and the rest of the soldiers were to blame for this.

"You don't," he said at last.

Breen sat back, her legs bent beneath her, and her shoulder leaning against the wall. Whether he was lying or not, she wanted the food. She would die without it.

She snatched the roll from the plate and devoured it in a few bites. It stung her throat, and weighed heavy in her stomach. But it was *food*. Plucking the dried meat from her plate, she tore off a long slice. Salty, savory meat. Possibly of a cow or a sheep. She couldn't be sure. But she didn't care.

Boots echoed off the walls, approaching fast.

"It's her turn," the rough voice of one of the masked men. Her heart leapt and she slid to the back wall of her cage. Not already. Please no. It was so soon.

"Not now," the generous food-giver said.

"It's *her turn*."

The man's jaw hardened and he narrowed his eyes. "She's had enough for one day."

The masked man hesitated, narrowing his eyes behind the eye slits. He turned on his heels and left.

Breen stared in astonished silence. What had just happened?

The man at the door shifted to step away.

She swallowed the bite of meat quickly. "Wait."

He stopped, and glanced back at her through the bars.

"Why are you doing this?"

His gaze roamed to the food in her hands, then back to her eyes. "Because this isn't right."

Her brows furrowed. What? Her heart pounded against her ribs. Could it really be? Were there Seaburn-born soldiers who disliked the treatment of prisoners as much as the prisoners themselves? Or did he disagree with stealing savages entirely?

"Enjoy your dinner. I'll be back later." He stepped from sight, heavy boots colliding with the stone corridor.

Breen leaned back against the wall and finished her meat and savoured her water. Once she was done, she slid the plate back to the door and hid the canister behind a pile of straw.

The weakness in her limbs faded slightly. Relief flooded her chest.

Maybe she could survive this place after all.

* * *

CRIES ECHOED through the stone halls outside her prison. Breen opened her eyes slowly, fog sticking to her brain. How long had she been asleep for? It seemed like ages since she'd been awoken for more torture.

Rubbing the sleep from her eyes, Breen sat up.

Whimpers filled the hall.

Her brows pulled together. What was going on? Were they taking another of her tribesmen? Breen stood. Her legs didn't shake as they had been for days. The little bit of food the man had given her, helped much more than she'd thought it would.

Her feet chilled against the stone, even through her boots. She stepped up to her cell door and peered through the bars.

The typical darkness, lit only by a couple of torches, greeted her. The masked men were nowhere to be seen. Then what was going on? Wrapping her fingers around the cold bars, she stuck her cheek to the metal, trying to peer further down the hall.

Several cages down, a door remained ajar. The wails came from inside. Her heart plummeted to her stomach. What were they doing to that woman?

Her fingers trembled. Should she shout? Should she raise a fuss, try and get their attention? But what if they came for her next? What if they dragged her back inside the torture chamber and dowsed her in buckets and buckets of ice?

What if they did something worse?

She shivered and stepped away from the wall.

A scream rang out, shrill and filled with fear. She lowered herself to the back corner of her cell and wrapped her arms around her body. Cold wracked her bare skin.

Why didn't they just kill them already? What was the point of keeping them alive, only to fill their lives with despair? Was this how they broke their soldiers? Is this why the soldiers taken from the Savage Lands had vacant eyes, and refused to glance in their direction? Had they been through the same?

Her lips quivered and she buried her head in her arms. How much longer would this last? How much longer would she be subjected to this madness?

Nearly an hour passed before the wailing stopped and the door to a cell slammed shut. A man cleared his throat and locked the cage. His heavy boots retreated down the hall. This wasn't fair.

This wasn't right.

But there was nothing she could do to stop it.

Head buried in her arms, and thoughts running rampant, she didn't hear the approaching footsteps until her door creaked open. Her heart skipped, and fear sent a knife into her chest. Was it her turn?

She looked up, her eyes wide.

A plate slid through the crack in the door, followed by another canteen.

Her racing heart slowed. Her parted lips closed. The man who'd given her food had returned.

"This is all I could bring today," he whispered through the bars. His face was level with the window. He had to be tall to reach it.

Breen glanced at the plate. A ball of rice and a few slivers of dried fish. She lowered her shaking limbs. Why was he doing this? Why was he the only kind soul in the Academy? Was it all a trick?

She hesitated.

She couldn't help it. The man waited, watching her as she slowly rose to her feet. She didn't approach the plate. Instead, she went to the door.

"Who are you?" she asked.

He shrugged wide shoulders. "Drakkone."

She held his gaze. "Drakkone. Can you get me out of here?" Her voice shook.

His brows pulled together and he shook his head. "No. I'm sorry."

"Why bother being kind when it only prolongs my fate?" Her lips pressed into a thin line. Irritation soured her stomach.

Drakkone started back, his eyes flying wide. He said nothing. There was nothing to say. He knew she was right. Every morsel he gave her. Every pint of water. It only kept her body running longer, so that she took longer to starve to death.

Even if it prolonged her fate, Breen couldn't resist. She reached down and plucked the meat from the plate, tearing a piece off with her teeth. Her stomach rumbled. She had to satiate her hunger. It was too painful.

"I'm sorry." His fingers wrapped around one of the bars.

She glanced at him. His brows furrowed over round eyes.

If he was sorry, he'd find a way to stop this. If he was sorry he'd help her escape. No, Drakkone wasn't sorry. If he was, he wouldn't be a soldier.

Breen turned her back on Drakkone and ate.

She waited until his footfalls disappeared and quiet fell in the dungeon. Her chest ached. Though the manners passed down from her mother begged her to thank him, she couldn't bring herself to. She was sure he fed her with the best of intentions. But whatever drove him to kindness, she couldn't let it harm her.

She would die here before she recited their mantra.

* * *

BREEN LEANED against the door to her cell, her shoulders brushing worn wood. Drakkone visited her on an almost nightly basis. He kept the torturers at bay, and slipped her whatever food and water he could. But her days continued to drain her.

In the cramped cell she could hardly exercise. Her muscles were beginning to weaken, as was her mind. How much longer would she endure this?

Drakkone leaned on the other side of the wooden slats. His warmth radiated through the door, and Breen kept close to it. She hadn't felt any semblance of warmth in days. Weeks. How long had she been here? When had she last seen one of her brethren? When had one of them spoken last?

She had no idea.

"Have you finished?"

His deep voice made her jump. The slur of his words and thick accent had begun to fade as he used her language. She took a deep breath, and nodded before realizing he couldn't see her. "Yes." She slid the plate to the entrance. She wiped breadcrumbs from her lip and tilted her head back against the door.

Drakkone made no move to retrieve the plate.

"Why do you do this?" she asked.

He hesitated. "It's the right thing to do."

Breen scoffed. "The right thing to do would be never to have let this happen at all."

He sighed. "I know."

Tears burned the back of her eyes. "Then *why* let them?"

"Seaburn… the Emperor… things weren't always like this, Breen.

There used to be volunteers in the cities. Men and women from all over would come to join the armies, until Emperor Ragus took the throne. *Untapped potential,* is what he calls all of you." He paused. "I don't know why he turned to your lands."

Breen stared at the grungy back wall, the rough stones etched with mold. "Why did you volunteer then?"

"I wanted to serve my country. My home."

"Then why work in these dungeons? You aren't serving anyone but a greedy old man." The growl in her voice bit off her words.

"They don't allow tribesmen to work here. They fear they'll sympathize too much, or help you all escape. Or worse, know someone."

Breen gritted her teeth. Damn the Emperor. Damn the Academy. And damn the men who kept her here. If her people, the Tribes of the South, were to work in this section, they *would* help them. They would. She was sure of it.

Her anger turned to despair. She turned her back from the door and leaned her forehead against it. She closed her eyes against the darkness.

"If you hate it all so much, why can't you help us escape?" Her voice hardly travelled in the confined space.

His breath caught in his throat, creating a small choking sound. "I can't."

"*Why?*"

"They'd kill me too."

Breen shook her head. Let him risk his life. Why was his life worth more than hers? More than those of her brethren? Why were the lives of any of Seaburn's citizens worth more than theirs? Her fists clenched.

"I don't want to end up like your soldiers. I don't want to be like the other women down here." Her gut twisted with fear. For days, wails and screams had broken the quiet of the dungeon. It had taken her awhile to figure out what was going on, but now that she had, she refused to let it happen to her. She'd fight with every bit of energy she had left.

She'd kill them if she had to.

"I'm sorry." His voice hardly travelled through the slats. "I'll do whatever I can. But I can't help you escape."

She squeezed her eyes shut. "Then kill me."

Anything was better than this. Anything was better than the uncertainty of tomorrow.

He shifted against the door and slowly rose to his feet. She sensed him staring through the barred window. She didn't bother looking up. She didn't want him to see the tears streaming down her cheeks although she was sure he heard them in her voice.

"You aren't serious," he said.

"Death would be better than this. Death would be kinder." Her voice quivered. She hated how weak she sounded. She hated how this place stole her energy, her drive, and her strength.

"Breen."

"*Kill me!*" Breen glanced up. His face was in shadows.

Drakkone stepped away from the door. "I can't."

A humorless smile pulled at her mouth, and a laugh bubbled from between her lips. "Of course. You can't do anything." She shook her head and turned from the door, pulling her legs to her chest and resting her forehead against the wall instead of the door.

He hovered for several moments.

She couldn't imagine what he wanted to say, what he thought. But this was the reality of it. If he couldn't help her escape, if he couldn't relieve the pain by killing her, then she needed nothing from this man.

Drakkone's footsteps echoed down the hall, leaving her in silence.

FIVE

She hadn't seen Drakkone in days.

Her stomach ached and her lungs were on fire. They'd hardly allowed an hour of rest between sessions. The voices of her brethren slowly dwindled in the dungeon. Had they given up? Recited the mantra? Or were they dead?

Ice poured over her face. She coughed and spluttered, struggling against her restraints. Her face numbed and her struggle grew slow.

She couldn't do this anymore. She couldn't.

Her gasps for air grew ragged. The fog on her brain became heavy. Breen drifted from blackness to sudden cold. She couldn't focus, could hardly move.

And she didn't want to.

She didn't want to do this anymore. She should just let them kill her. She should let this be the end.

Another bucket of water. Her lungs burned. Her limbs grew still. She wanted to die, like she'd never imagined before.

Darkness blessed her with its embrace.

Cold spewed from her lungs. They held her hair, tipping her

forward out of the chair. The cloth was gone, leaving her chilled and gasping. She took in deep gasping breaths. Her entire body shook.

So cold. Everything was just so cold.

Before she'd fully regained her breath, the man grabbed her braids and forced her back. Her scalp stung, but she hardly felt it. Her eyelids were heavy. She wanted to sleep. She needed rest. She hadn't eaten, hadn't drank any water that wasn't from being drowned, in days.

Where was Drakkone? The one light in her day. The one thing that helped her endure her trials.

Cold wood dug into her back. They replaced the cloth.

Her heart raced.

Not again. *Please* not again.

"I will accept my place."

No. She wouldn't.

"I will perform my duties."

Ice water collapsed like a waterfall upon her face. Her cheeks and nose grew sore from the pressure. She held her lips shut as long as she could. Her lungs burned from holding her breath.

"I will obey."

Never.

Finally, she couldn't take it anymore.

She gasped for air.

Another bucket dumped over her mouth. Water flew inside, numbing her tongue and throat.

She gagged, trying to force water from her lungs.

"I will follow."

Her limbs were too weak. She couldn't fight back anymore. She could only lay there helpless.

"I will surrender."

She'd never given up before. Never given in. She'd *always* won.

Until the day they stole her from her tribe.

"I will live by Seaburn laws, adhere to my Seaburn masters and heed all above me." Hot breath on her ear. Burning in her chest.

She couldn't listen to this. So let her die. Why wouldn't they just let her *die?*

"I will obey."

Blackness stole her.

DARKNESS ROLLED THROUGH HER MIND.

She groaned, blinking slowly. Her brain shifted and rolled through waves of black. In and out she came. The stone ceiling of her cell came into view. Dirty, and smudged with mold.

She blinked again.

Straw, that on the floor of her cell.

Again.

Dirt at her fingertips, digging into the cracks in the stone.

Again.

Pressure on her skin. Cold licking her back. She shivered as she faded into darkness again.

Blackness held her mind for several sweet moments. No pain, no nothing. She was numb. The world retreated. Was this death? Was this void the end? She'd always believed in the gods of her tribe—the tamers of wild horses and keepers of the harvest. The gods kept them fed, gave them their lands, and watched from on high. They were the eagle in the sky, the grass they walked upon. They were everywhere and everything.

No, she wasn't dead. Couldn't be. She blinked slowly. The numbness gradually left her skin. Warmth. Somewhere. But where? Her fingernails dug into the dirt, scraping at stone.

No. This wasn't right. Something was wrong.

She tried to push up onto her hands and knees.

Pain exploded through her chest as she was forced down again. Cold stone pressed against her bare chest, finding skin above the top of her worn leather shirt.

Darkness called her back, enticing her. It slithered at the edges of her vision, calling her to its murky depths. She groaned again. She didn't want this. She didn't want to die yet—not if this black was all that remained.

Pain exploded through her cheek. Something sharp dug into her skin. She trembled. The warmth fled, replaced by cold. She cried out, clawing at the ground. Why couldn't she think? Why could she hardly move?

Weakness overtook her.

Her cries echoed off the wooden walls until shouts overtook the dungeons. The pressure, the pain, left. She sighed with relief, rolling to her side and pressing her back against the wall of her prison. She blinked slowly, unable to think, unable to get past the numbness.

Voices outside. Thumps. Something solid hit the ground.

"Breen!" someone gasped.

She couldn't keep her eyes open. Let her rest. Let her be for just a few minutes.

Her lips trembled and she whimpered. She lifted her arms, heavy like lead, and buried her face against them. Maybe the darkness was better than life. Maybe in the void everything would be painless. Maybe she could be free there. Maybe she could survive.

"Breen, I'm here."

Warmth embraced her arms, chest and back. She hadn't been held in so long. She hadn't been touched except to be hurt. She leaned into the warmth. It soothed her cold cheeks and stopped the clacking of her teeth.

"I'm so sorry," the voice rasped. It held her close, soothed the pain she hadn't realized was there. Her whole body ached.

No. She wanted the numb back.

"I'll get you to the infirmary. It'll be all right."

Strong arms wrapped beneath her legs and back, hoisting her from the ground. Her breath caught in her throat, and her heart sped. She fought a moan and lost as it ripped from her throat without her consent. Her mind started up again. Who was holding her? Where was he taking her? What was going on?

"Just hold on a few minutes."

She recognized that voice.

Drakkone.

He'd come back? She thought he'd abandoned her to the dungeon, to the masked men and torture. What was he doing here?

"What's happening?" Her words tumbled slowly from her tongue, garbled by her raw throat. She wrinkled her nose. How would she get her answers if she couldn't even speak properly?

"It'll be all right," he repeated. She wasn't sure who he was trying to reassure.

Heavy boots beat the floor, then her body bounded as they ascended. Her head throbbed with every step he took. His strong hands held her tighter, keeping her close to his chest. She didn't try to speak. The darkness at the edges of her vision started to whisk in like clouds, blossoming around the corners of her sight.

Dark was good. It meant sleep.

"We're nearly there."

Breen blinked. She hadn't realized her eyes closed. How long had they been that way?

Sandstone walls passed on either side of them. Smooth. Not like the dungeon. Her brows furrowed. Gold arms held torches aloft against the walls. No, this couldn't be anything like the dungeons. It was too pretty. Too nice. Nothing like what Seaburn thought its prisoners deserved.

Drakkone's boot slammed into a wooden door at the end of the hall. Bright lantern light spilled from the doorway. He lurched inside. High walls. Tapestries in brilliant colors. Several white cots and pale wooden furnishing.

A man spun from an occupied cot by a tall window at the back of the room. Stars shone from the sky above. She hadn't seen the sky in so long.

"What is happening?" the short black-skinned man bellowed. Clad in beige robes stitched with gold, he let his patient be and stepped across the wide room. His shaven head glowed beneath the lanterns hanging from the ceiling.

"They've gone too far," Drakkone growled.

Breen wasn't sure what he meant. Then again, she had hardly any clue what was happening.

"I see that," the man said. "Put her there."

She couldn't see where he motioned to, but Drakkone stepped

further inside what she assumed was the infirmary. His thick muscles bunched against her limbs as he lowered her to a bed. *A bed*. How long had it been since she slept on something but a hard stone floor? Her body relaxed against the smooth cotton. It brushed her skin like silk.

"Get the water basin, there." The doctor motioned toward a long table against the wall by the door.

Her eyelids lowered. What a lovely bed. So soft. So warm. Maybe she could sleep now. Maybe they'd let her.

The two men shuffled around the room, knocking against furniture, shifting water and banging metal. Why were they so loud? Couldn't they see she was trying to sleep?

"She's falling unconscious," Drakkone said. His voice was high, concerned.

"That's all right. She needs her rest," the doctor replied. "We'll wake her later."

Thank the gods. This blessed man was going to give her a reprieve, allow her rest. Breen smiled and let her mind go. Drifting down and down, she found sleep.

* * *

"Breen." A pause. "Breen."

She shifted on soft cotton. Sheets wrapped her arms and tangled between her legs. Darkness was good. She savoured it. She didn't want to wake up. Sleep was warm, safe, and untroubled.

The world was chaotic and scary. The world *hurt*.

"Breen."

Drakkone's voice pulled her from unconsciousness. She awoke with a groan. Bright light behind her lids turned her world red. She blinked slowly. Everything hurt. Everything ached. Though for the first time in days—weeks?—she wasn't cold. She drew her legs to her chest.

"What is it?" The haze of sleep faded like morning mist in a valley.

"The doctor needs to speak with you."

Breen glanced up. Sunlight filtered in through the tall window.

Blue skies and fluffy white clouds. It had been so long since she felt the sun's rays on her skin. Her heart ached. She was desperate for it. The freedom of the open desert. She missed home.

Drakkone sat at her bedside, hulking in a tiny wooden chair. The bridge of his nose was flat, and his nostrils wide. His smooth brown skin wrapped his carved cheekbones and sturdy jaw. Short dark hair stuck from his head in all directions. Though she'd thought it had simply been the shadows in her cell, his eyes *were* black, like a starless night.

The doctor cleared his throat. She started, her eyes peeling from Drakkone's handsome face, to that of her caretaker. The short man nodded now that he had her attention.

"Breen, is it?" His accent wasn't nearly as heavy as Drakkone's. He must have spent quite some time with her fellow tribesmen.

"Yes." "I have some good news." A small smile broke across his thick lips, but it never reached his eyes. "But it isn't all good."

Her brows pulled together.

What was he talking about? Last night. What *had* happened? After her torture, everything was a blur of darkness broken only by pain, numbness and snippets of her outside world.

"What happened?" She glanced between the pair.

They exchanged a pitying look with one another. She bristled. She didn't want their pity, no matter what had gone on.

"You were... assaulted, I'm afraid." The doctor spoke slowly, raising his brows as if she were supposed to understand some hidden meaning within the words.

"Of course I was. They torture us every day." Her stomach soured. He had to mean more than that. But, what?

The doctor sighed, and avoided her gaze. Drakkone reached for her hand. His fingers were warm against hers. She should pull away. She wanted to pull away. She didn't know this man. But the warmth was soothing.

"You were raped, Breen."

Her heart stopped. Her eyes went wide.

What? How was that possible? It wasn't. She'd have been woken by such a foul act. Yet the ache in her limbs, and lower abdomen spoke otherwise. No. This couldn't be. She didn't want to have the children of a Seaburn *rapist*. She didn't want to bear babes in such a place.

Tears burned the back of her eyes. How was any of this good news?

"I'm sorry. It isn't a practice condoned by the Academy." The doctor cleared his throat and continued, as if her world wasn't falling apart at the seams. "The good news, I'm afraid, is that I've discovered you are barren. You will never conceive a child. Under normal circumstances *this* would be the worst of the news, but I'm afraid it might be a blessing in this case."

Her heart restarted, ramming painfully in her chest.

How was any of *this* good news? Though she was thankful she'd never have to bear the children of a terrible man like this, she still *wanted* children. She wanted to raise little ones, see them grow and become warriors. It was her *duty* as a woman of the Tribes. She needed to continue on her line. She needed to have an heir to become the next Chief after her father. How could she do that if she was barren?

Drakkone squeezed her fingers.

She yanked her hand away.

"This can't be right." Her lips quivered.

"I'm sorry." The doctor's brows cinched. His eyes spoke for him too. He *was* sorry. Truly.

"I can't be." She stared at the cotton guarding her lower half. Her own womanhood had betrayed her. Her own body.

But was it really so awful?

Though she'd never bear children for her tribe, she wouldn't bear a rapist's babe either. She shook her head. It was that awful though. She couldn't believe this. It wasn't fair. After all these people had put her through, and still, something else to add to the pile.

"You may experience pain or soreness for a few days." The doctor turned from her bedside and picked up a small stone bowl from his worktable. He handed it to her. Bright purple liquid swirled inside.

"This will help to numb any discomfort. If you need more, Drakkone can come to me."

Breen stared into the murky liquid.

A tonic would cure nothing. A potion couldn't fill the emptiness growing in her chest, or the dread turning her stomach. This wouldn't help her. Nothing could.

Pulling her legs up to her chest, she buried her face in her lap and wrapped her arms around her legs. He was wrong. He had to be. She wanted a child. She wanted a daughter or a son. She wanted someone to pass her legacy to.

But what legacy did she have? What legacy *would* she have now that she remained trapped by the Academy?

She blinked back tears and took deep breaths. She wouldn't cry in front of these men. She wouldn't cry in front of anyone.

After several long moments of silence, the doctor excused himself from the room. She was the only patient left inside the infirmary.

Drakkone stayed, a silent sentinel at her bedside. She could feel his desire to comfort her. His warmth radiated through his leather armor. She hoped he wouldn't. She hoped he'd go away. She couldn't stand the confusion he brought. Or the uncertainty he left her with.

Seaburn was bad.

But Drakkone wasn't. As the product of such a vile nation, how could he be born good? She sighed.

"Breen?" he asked at last.

She froze.

"I don't know how common barrenness is within the tribes. But here in Seaburn, many are affected by it."

She glanced up.

"Including myself."

She wouldn't cry. She would not commiserate with this man, but her eyes wouldn't cooperate.

Hot tears burned her cheeks against her will.

"I can't say that it'll be all right, but I'm here for you." His fingers tightened in his lap.

She nodded.

"You can't let this go on."

Breen scoffed and rubbed the tears from her eyes before turning a glare on him. "*I* can't let this go on? You're the one not trying to help me. You're the one keeping me here. You're just as bad as *them*."

He winced. She didn't care. Finally, she'd spoken her mind.

"I know." His eyes lowered to his knees. He leaned forward to rest his elbows on his lap. His wild hair remained inches from her bicep. "I can't help you escape the Academy, or Seaburn." Anger flared inside her chest. "But—" He glanced up, meeting her gaze. "I can help you escape the dungeons."

Her heart leapt. "How?"

"You have to give in. Say the mantra. Go along with what they want you to do. If it means your safety and your life, you *must*." He took her hands, his skin rough against hers. He squeezed her fingers.

"I can't."

"You have to. There's no other way. You'll die down there." Again, he squeezed her hand.

"Why do you care if I live or die?" She worked her jaw, uncertain.

He smiled. It was the first time she'd seen it. The tiny grin lit the entire room. "I care about every living thing. You're a person. A living being created by the gods. You don't deserve this more than an animal would."

Her brows furrowed. What gods did he believe in? Certainly they weren't of Seaburn. If any gods occupied this world, she couldn't see how the people of Seaburn did such things and still remained faithful.

"You'll have to make it believable," he continued. "You'll have to pretend they broke you. But *do not let them*. You're strong, but now you need to be cunning."

Breen nodded. This wasn't giving up; it was finding a way out of her pain, a way out of her torture.

But to do it, she'd have to give up her pride. She bit her lip.

"Be meek. Do what they say. Recite their mantra back to them and they'll free you. You'll rise out of the dungeons and join the Emperor's legions."

She snapped back. "I will *not* fight for him."

"You might not have to." He held her gaze, brilliant amber flashing through his dark eyes. "Get yourself to safety now, and worry about the rest later. Outside of here you'll be able to train, eat, drink, and sleep. You'll grow strong again. Better than ever."

Her brows shot up. Stronger than ever? If what he said was true, she could escape the dungeons and join the army. In doing so they'd arm her with new fighting skills, and equip her with the strength she needed to make her escape.

"I'll do it." The words left her lips before she'd finished her thought.

A sigh of relief warmed the air between them. Drakkone grinned, flashing white teeth. He released her fingers and sat back in his chair. "Thank the gods above."

For the first time in weeks, Breen smiled, for her future wasn't over. She could get out of this awful place and this terrible mess. She could get out of here, and when she did she'd bring their world to its knees.

SIX

"I accept my place. I will perform my duties." Breen kneeled on the floor of the dungeon cavern. She kept her eyes on the ground as Drakkone had instructed. She had to appear weak, like she'd given up. But with every word, fire licked her raw throat. "I will obey. I will follow."

Two masked men stood before her, feet spread apart, arms crossed. Even if she looked up, she couldn't read their faces through the masks. She could hardly see their eyes.

"I will surrender. I will live by Seaburn laws, adhere to my Seaburn masters and heed all above me."

Don't look up, she urged herself. It was almost over.

"I will obey."

She kept her head hung, and her arms limp. She hunched as if the weight of the world sat on her shoulders.

Believe me, she thought desperately. She needed them to listen. She needed them to think her capable of this. If they didn't, she'd be back inside that prison, waiting for the next foul thing to happen to her.

"Rise," the man at her left said. She didn't glance up, no matter how much she wanted to. She stood.

Breen wasn't the last of her kin inside these walls, but she wasn't the first to go. She hoped they'd see the ruse behind her eyes. She hoped they'd do the same, and join her in the Academy.

Join her for her escape.

The second man stepped forward, the tallest of the duo, the one who constantly grabbed her messy braids. He inspected her with eyes black like the darkest ravine, where no light could ever reach.

Rough hands ripped her hair back.

Instead of snapping back, or slamming her fist into his gut, she remained limp. Her lip quivered in a whimper. *Meek*, Drakkone had said. That's what she had to be. Meek. As much as it killed her to do so.

His dark eyes roamed her face, down her throat and over her body. She took a quaking breath. It was almost over. It had to be.

After a few moments he released her. The sting of her scalp faded and she quickly lowered her gaze. He'd pay for all of this. Every bit.

The first masked man nodded. "She's ready."

The other motioned her to turn. She did. He stepped in front of her. "Follow."

She took a deep breath. It was over. Finally, she'd see the sun again.

The men led her past her cell.

Lukerin glared from the bars of his window. He spat at her feet with what little saliva he had left.

"You've dishonored your tribe." His eyes hardened. "I can't believe you've given up, Breen."

Her heart clenched. No, Lukerin, she hadn't. She wanted to say so. She tried to convey as much in the widening of her gaze. One of the soldiers pushed her forward, tearing her sight from her tribesman.

* * *

WARM WATER EMBRACED HER SKIN. Breen stepped naked into the hot spring. Aqua green water steamed the surface, surrounded by large dark brown rocks. A wooden fence enclosed the large area, separating the women from the men, and all of them from the outside world.

They said she was in training. But before she joined her class, there was one thing she needed to do. After her mental Cleanse, came the physical. Once she was bathed, she'd be fed, and shown to her quarters. Tomorrow she'd begin.

Two other women sat at the other side of the spring. Their hard gazes flickered between each other and Breen. So now she was a pariah. It was probably for the best. She didn't want to grow attached to any of the soldiers here. That'd only delay her escape.

Heat wrapped her ankles, her calves, and her thighs. She stepped further. Her hips, and her waist were enveloped in sweet heat. The cold of her skin prickled. It had been *so* long since she'd had a bath. Though the constant pouring of ice water over her upper body kept her mostly clean of dirt, beneath her clothes, her skin had grown sticky and uncomfortable.

Her leathers. They'd taken those too. They were from her old life —something Seaburn wanted desperately to destroy.

Breen's feet hit bottom. The water rose to her shoulders. Ten feet sat between her and the two other women. She didn't know or trust them, so she had to be careful. She had to be careful of everyone. One wrong step could get her thrown back into the dungeon.

She gulped.

She couldn't go back there. Not now. Not ever. She'd throw herself from the cliff behind the palace before she let them take her back.

Breen submerged her head. Heat soothed her face, and stung her scalp. She ignored it. She wanted to enjoy every minute of this. When her lungs began to ache, she resurfaced. She gasped in a breath, pushing away the memories of being drowned. She wouldn't let them ruin her bath.

Thick wet braids clung to her back and shoulders. Loose hair drifted atop the water like black snakes. She ran her fingers through it. Before she'd come here, they'd been tied and woven with thread, feathers, and gold string her mother had procured. They told the story of her life. She'd hardly ever cut her hair.

Twisting the ends of her braids undone, she unwove them from the bottom up, until her hair encircled her in the water.

With lavender-scented soap given to her by the soldiers, she cleaned her hair and her flesh. Her bruises ached, even in the warm water. They marred her skin, her arms, her legs and her abdomen. Some purple, some yellow, others fading to brown. She wrinkled her nose. How ugly.

Breen took her time scrubbing every bit of dirt away, ridding it from under her nails, behind her ears, and especially her hair.

Ignoring the glares of the other soldiers, Breen splashed suds from her shoulders and hair.

Garbled words interrupted her.

She froze and met the gazes of the two soldier-women. The first, with a narrow chin, small almond-shaped eyes and shoulder-length dark brown hair, approached. The second hung back, biting her nails, her brows furrowed. Though the second was most certainly another tribeswoman, her eyes weren't dark like most. Instead they were startlingly blue.

The first stepped closer, her bosom nearly exposed at the top of the water. She was at least several inches taller than Breen.

Her brows furrowed. Though she spoke, she hadn't a clue what these words meant. After a moment, the woman quirked a brow, seeming to realize this.

"You need to learn their language." She scoffed.

Breen tilted her head, and searched her peripheral for a weapon in case this woman stepped too close. "Why?"

"They'll force you to, either way." She shrugged and paused halfway between her fellow soldier, and Breen. "Where do you come from?"

"The south."

The woman rolled her eyes. "Obviously."

"You're a soldier?" Breen felt silly asking, but she wanted to make sure. The woman's ample curves were obvious below the water. She didn't have the muscles of a soldier; instead she had the body of a harlot.

"Yes," she said. "I am Moigrin of the Arkon Tribe."

That explained her slender features and elongated nose, so different from those of her people. North of the Delica River, the Wastelands occupied miles upon miles of land. While several tribes occupied the desert, further north still, the Arkon Mountains bordered much of their land.

"Breen of the Southern Delica Tribe."

Moigrin's eyes widened, and she stepped back. "*What?*"

Her lips pressed together in a thin line.

"If they've gone that far south, there is no stopping the Emperor's madness." Fear crept into her voice.

"There has to be a way." The words tumbled from Breen's lips before she could stop them. She covered her mouth, eyes wide, hoping her careless words wouldn't throw her back into the dungeon.

Moigrin looked up, her eyes wide and sparkling with hope. "So you're a warrior then? You didn't..." She paused, her fists clenching beneath the water's surface. "Give in."

Breen shook her head. "Never."

Moigrin's lips twisted into a rueful smile. She glanced briefly over her shoulder. The younger woman at the back of the spring remained frozen to the spot. Whereas Moigrin had clearly not been broken, the blue-eyed girl definitely had.

"This is Elka." Moigrin nodded at the small girl. "My little sister."

Breen nodded in greeting, but Elka's eyes lowered quickly to the water. Was there any going back from this type of brokenness? For Elka's sake, she hoped so. Breen couldn't imagine living the rest of her life devoid of hope. She had to return home. She had to save herself and her brethren.

"Let me give you some advice, Breen." Moigrin's gaze hardened. "Protect yourself, and those you love. Trust no one. Do what they say, but do *not* believe in their lies. I'm going to find a way to get Elka out of this place eventually."

Hope bubbled in her chest. Her first ally in Seaburn. "When you come up with a plan, I'll be there to help."

Moigrin's shoulders lowered, as if relieved. "Thank you."

She shook her head. "Don't thank me. Just find a way out of here."

"I will."

"It is time for your dressing," one of the guards called from inside the dressing hut at her back. The one-storey wooden building sat with the door open, light streaming out.

Breen nodded her goodbye to Elka, and met Moigrin's gaze for several long moments. Strength remained in their dark depths. But could she trust this girl?

She'd have to find out.

* * *

Sun beat against her flesh, warming her skin and lending fire to her determination. Outside the Academy walls, next to the cliff giving way to the rest of Seaburn, Breen waited in line with her fellow trainees.

After her bath, they'd given her clothes, baggy cream pants that tucked into new leather boots, and a cloth shirt of the same color. The fabric breathed well, keeping her cool against the rising heat of morning. Since giving up her pride to escape her torture, she'd been bathed, clothed, fed, and given a proper cot to sleep on, even if it was in a dorm of her fellow tribeswomen.

"For those of you who don't know me, you will address me as General Vargas." The black-skinned man paced back and forth on the sand, following the line of a dozen new soldiers on either side of her. His black eyes roamed each of them, his brows furrowed. His gaze wasn't emotionless like that of the other General she'd encountered, nor twisted like the masked men in the dungeons. Instead, he assessed them from head to toe—like the warriors they were born as.

"Yes, sir," the other tribesmen said. Their loud timber nearly made her jump. No Seaburn recruits joined them on the training field. She froze against the sand, glancing at those on either side of her.

They must have already been training for some time. If she wanted to appear broken, she'd need to follow. Breen mimicked their stances, her feet parted and her hands behind her back.

Obey. Follow.

The mantra was ingrained in her memory.

"We have new recruits today. Do your best to welcome them, and show them what they've already missed." Vargas glanced at Breen, and the other few men and women who appeared lost. At least he spoke in their language, though his accent remained thick. "We'll start off with one on one duels. Hand-to-hand. No weapons."

Why? Her brows furrowed. It could be to assess their strength.

"But before we begin, let me briefly instruct you on how the Academy works. You are in the First Rank. There are four. You will advance through each at my sole discretion. I work with all my soldiers, all the recruits that enter the Academy, and *I* will decide if, and when, you are ready for more responsibility. Once you've completed all four ranks, you will join the rest of the military in their usual duties." He nodded to the pack of twenty men and women jogging at the far side of the sand-covered field.

Instead of cream, they wore tanned leather armor, elaborately fashioned, with patterns carved into their shoulders. They all stared directly ahead, and marched in unison, kicking up dust as they ran.

"Now then, let's begin." Vargas smiled and motioned to the First Rank men and women who clearly already knew what they were doing.

Six stepped forward and turned to face the new recruits. Their hard eyes met the new recruits'. They didn't glance between them, simply stared at their faces and raised their hands, shifting their feet into a ready stance.

"Begin."

A tall man approached, towering several inches above Breen. His dark eyes met hers, vacant, his expression hard like stone. He threw a fist at her head.

Breen ducked, rolling from his shadow. Her heel slammed into the back of his calf. He collapsed to his knees, where she leapt on his back.

A growl rumbled in his chest, vibrating against hers as she clung to his neck, wrapping her forearm around his throat. She locked her wrist with her free hand and held on as tightly as she could.

He choked for breath and clawed at the skin of her arms.

She hadn't wrestled, let alone fought since she'd been taken. It seemed like eons ago that she'd faced Lukerin in the ring, and now here she was slipping into her old role like it was her second skin.

Breen held on until his body started to go limp and he tapped her arm quickly.

"He's given up, recruit. Let him go," Vargas barked over the grunts and shuffling of the surrounding fights.

She released him without question. She had to keep up her ruse. Breen stepped back, giving the man room to recover. He buckled over, coughing into the sand.

"Good." Vargas materialized at her shoulder. She froze to keep from jumping. "Very good, recruit. What is your name?"

She kept her gaze on the sand at her feet. Meek. Be meek, she instructed herself. "Breen."

"Sir."

"*Sir*," she quickly added.

"I haven't seen a recruit best another that quickly in a long time." He stepped around her shoulder, circling her. Breen remained still, waiting to see what he'd do. The rustling of his armor stopped directly before her. "Do you think you can do it again?"

She quirked a brow. She couldn't help it. "Sir?"

"Do you think you can do it again?" he repeated.

Breen bit the inside of her cheek. Should she confirm, that yes, she was a great fighter, one of the best in her clan, or should she keep a low profile? Then again, if she wanted to leave this place, training to her best ability would only allow her to grow stronger, independent, *more* capable of the last thing they wanted from her.

"Yes, sir." She risked a glance up.

He smiled. "Good."

Vargas called for another. A woman this time. She stood opposite to Breen, her fingers dancing at her sides. Breen glanced behind her, at her previous opponent. The man lay unconscious several feet away.

Breen held her hands at her sides, refusing the urge to twist her newly woven braids around her fingers.

"Let's begin."

SEVEN

Breen passed the smooth sandstone walls of the Academy, heading to the back fields an hour later than the previous day. It was time to meet with the Second Rank. After taking down every opponent Vargas paired her with, he agreed it was best to advance her to a group more suited to her skill level.

Her fingers clenched and unclenched at her sides. She wasn't sure if she should be proud of this. Every bit of strength she possessed got her a step closer to freedom. But in doing so, she'd be leaving her brethren behind. Should she wait for them to get to the First Rank? Form a plan of escape together? She shook her head. It'd be sometime before Lukerin gave up. She shook her head. Though she'd always thought herself stronger than him, maybe he'd been the strongest all along.

"Breen." Warm fingers brushed her elbow.

She jumped, her eyes widening as she spun on Drakkone. He blinked in surprise at her sudden reaction. "Drakkone." She caught her breath. "What are you doing here?" Her heart slowed. It'd be some time before she got over the dread of the dungeons. Each moment she was above ground was another they could use to send her back.

He smiled. "I do work here."

She sighed. Yes. He did, didn't he. "I'd almost forgotten."

"Do you have time for a walk?" he asked. His fingers danced by his thigh and his brows pulled up. Was he… nervous?

"I don't know." Breen glanced to the end of the long carpeted hall. Used to no sleep at all recently, having any left her well rested. She'd already devoured her breakfast, and she thought she'd go for a run to warm up for the day. Her strength hadn't fully returned, and she was determined to get it back.

"I could accompany you to training then." He didn't leave room for argument.

"Fine." Breen continued on, leaving Drakkone to catch up with her.

"How did your first day go?"

"Well."

"Aren't you a little tardy for First Rank?" His brows pulled together. She couldn't imagine why he constantly appeared concerned for her, but he had yet to let up.

"General Vargas moved me to Second." She shrugged.

"Already?"

Breen levelled him an irritated look. "I'm not as *meek* as you'd like me to be."

Drakkone's eyes flew wide. "I don't want you to be meek. But the dungeon guardsmen did. It was the only way to get you out."

She raised her brows at him, disbelieving. "Are you certain?"

"Yes. You're from the Savage Lands, I couldn't imagine any of you are weak."

"We're not as primitive as you might think." She rolled her eyes. They passed through the main hall and out into the glaring sun. Warmth bathed her skin. She sighed, relishing the feeling, and refusing to ever take the sun for granted again.

"I didn't say that."

"You didn't need to."

Across the large sand fields, nothingness stretched to the cliff side. The First Rank must have already finished for the morning and were taking a reprieve from the sun—or whatever else they did after training. Just outside the Academy, a large overhang blocked the sun, or at least it would if it weren't so early in the morning. Along the sandstone walls, rows upon rows of curved swords, metal shields and long spears leaned and glinted in the early morning sun.

Her eyes widened slightly. These hadn't been there yesterday.

Breen glanced from each end of the sand. No one. Not a soldier, not a General—no one to see her take a weapon. She could hide it, beneath her cot or in the bathhouse. Anywhere she could return to easily and grab it for her escape.

She stepped toward the weapons rack. Drakkone's rough fingers wrapped her bicep and spun her to face him. She startled as she looked at him. She'd forgotten he stood behind her.

"What are you doing?" His dark eyes grew hard, and his fingers squeezed. "Do you want to be sent back to the dungeons?"

Her heart leapt. "Of course not."

"Stealing a weapon will get you there. You're supposed to be broken, remember?"

How could she forget? "I remember."

"Then please, for your own sake, behave for now."

"I don't take orders from *you*." She yanked her arm from his grip.

Drakkone sighed, gazing to the sky as if the gods held the answers to make her listen. She'd never been good at following others, certainly not men she wasn't related to.

"I'm not trying to give you orders, only suggestions to keep you alive." He met her gaze, brows raised, dark eyes desperate to make her understand.

She sighed. "Fine. I won't steal a sword." She paused. "For now."

Drakkone shook his head and smiled. "Good enough."

Heavy footfalls marked the entrance of the other Second Rank trainees. Drakkone stepped back, keeping a good few feet between them. "I have to return to my station, but I'll be back."

Breen raised a brow. She didn't need his promise to return. They barely knew each other. Yet, he saved her life in the dungeons and was oddly semi-supportive of her desire to escape. Her gut clenched in anticipation or anxiety, she wasn't sure. "Goodbye." She turned back towards the cliff, dismissing him.

Drakkone hesitated a few moments before his boots crunched through the sand towards the Academy. She glanced over her shoulder as he disappeared inside.

He confused her. He was the enemy, yet he protected her, rescued her from a hell she'd wish on no one, tried to steer her away from trouble; perhaps he was a good man. Yet she couldn't shake the caution warning her to remember he was one of *them* and he could be playing some twisted game.

Breen sighed and shook her head. She had no idea how she was supposed to know who to trust, and who to stay away from. She said a silent prayer to whatever Gods were listening to send her a sign.

"Breen!" Someone nudged her shoulder and she rounded to greet the voice.

Moigrin.

"Didn't think I'd see you so soon." She smirked, dark eyes dancing with mischief.

"Here I am." Breen shrugged.

Vargas stepped onto the sand. "Line up," he barked. Hands held behind his back, he marched across the sunlit earth.

Moigrin's amused expression fell. She stepped back to join at least a dozen others. Breen fell in line, mimicking their poses; feet parted, back straight, hands held behind her back, eyes straight in front of her.

The general passed back and forth in front of them, much like he had with the First Rank. "As you can see, we have new equipment today." He motioned to the weapons lining the Academy wall next to the entrance. "It's all fairly dull, but useable. All of you should have some experience with these sorts of weapons, I imagine." So someone in Seaburn was finally taking into account the fact they plucked *warriors* from their tribes.

Her shoulders stiffened as Vargas paused in front of her. His gaze roamed from the end of the line, back to her.

"We'll start in pairs."

Without question, the other recruits broke off into pairings, leaving Breen with Moigrin. The tribeswoman nodded and stepped opposite her, waiting further instruction. The trainees moved like children commanded by a stern adult. They'd been taught to obey Vargas without question. She wrinkled her nose.

"Before I give you all weapons, show me your offensive stance, as if you held a sword and shield." He continued to pace their ranks, observing the trainees as they took their stances.

Breen dropped one foot back and slid into her ready stance, feet parted, one hand at the ready, fist tightened as if she held a blade. Her other arm remained rigid, forearm bent for a shield. She'd never been particularly fond of shields, but she knew how to use one.

"Good." Vargas paused by each pair, adjusting each of their stances.

It took several long moments until he paused at Moigrin and Breen. He nodded to the dark haired woman, and then stepped over to Breen. He nudged her elbow up, where her shield would be before moving on. So her stance was acceptable then. Good.

"Now then, we'll begin."

Each of them fetched iron scimitars and heavy metal shields from the wall. She hoisted the straps around her forearm and held it aloft. It pulled at her muscles. She'd lost more muscle during her imprisonment than she thought; she'd be sore tomorrow.

Once all the trainees were back in line, their opponent standing opposite them, Vargas stopped at the end of the line. His sword *shinged* from its sheath as he withdrew it. He stepped back into a fighting stance, no shield, but arm still ready. He swung forward in an impressive display of strength. Though the man had to be reaching his fifties, there was no doubt he was still a great warrior.

"We'll take turns practicing this move. While the soldier on my left attacks, the one on my right should block."

So Moigrin would attack and Breen would block. Fine then. They moved into fighting stances, and waited for Vargas's signal. After several moments, he nodded. "Begin."

Moigrin leapt forward, swinging in a wide arc. Though the general chose a drill meant to use her shield, her instincts kicked in. She parried the attack, knocking Moigrin's sword from her hand. It thumped against the sand.

"Trainee!" Vargas paced up the line.

Breen froze. What had she done this time?

"Impressive display. Not many choose to block with their sword." Vargas nodded his approval.

A sigh of relief passed her lips. "Thank you, sir."

Moigrin plucked her sword from the ground, her jaw working back and forth as she stood opposite Breen again. Her eyes hardened. She clearly did not like to be beaten.

"Now switch." Vargas continued down the line.

While Moigrin shifted her shield in front of her, Breen brought hers back and her sword forward. She waited for the signal.

"Begin."

Her muscles bunched, and Breen leapt forward. Her sword flew through the air, an extension of herself. She hadn't realized until now how much she missed it. Moigrin raised her shield to protect her head. Breen's sword slammed against it, the clang of metal reverberating in the open space.

"And switch."

Breen stepped back. Moigrin shifted forward.

"Begin."

Moigrin lunged. Breen used her shield this time, but instead of blocking, she thrust forward, knocking her back. Moigrin's eyes went wide as she fell back against the sand.

"Another impressive display." Vargas paused behind Breen. "Trainee Breen." She turned to meet his eyes. "Keep this up and you'll move to the front lines quickly. Train hard, and you'll go far." He raised his eyebrows in recognition.

This was supposed to be an honor—this praise. Then why did her stomach boil and her fists clench?

"Thank you, sir. It is an honor." She nodded, her jaw hard like stone.

This is what she wanted. She needed to rise in the ranks, be strong, and earn trust. Once she earned all of the generals' trust, she would go on missions and she would escape.

That was it. That was her plan.

Breen steeled herself and turned back to Moigrin, who glowered over her shield. Her heart clenched. She didn't want this woman's loathing, hate, or whatever else her glare could mean. If she were to advance far, having Moigrin as an ally could be a good thing.

"Let's continue." Vargas walked the line, barking orders and sending them each into useless formations. Their tactics were dated, their moves simple. She'd been teaching the children these sorts of tactics by age ten, and here they were demonstrating these to adults like this was new information.

Breen resisted the urge to roll her eyes. Let them try to teach her. With this heavy sword and shield, she'd regain her strength in no time. And when she did, she'd be ready.

* * *

DAYS UPON DAYS OF SIMPLE, childlike training passed. Sparring was common with the dull blades, but unchallenging. She longed for a real battle, but the dulled blades ensured injuries were minimized; this was simply training after all.

Again, Breen faced off against Moigrin. While the rest of their class waited in a wide circle, Moigrin paused opposite her, sword and shield at the ready. Her eyes narrowed, determined. Breen waited patiently for their sign to begin. She'd been put against Moigrin many times, and knew her tactics well. She went for strength above speed, attack above defense, and used her shield as often as her sword.

Moigrin was an excellent fighter. Though fights with the other trainees had grown boring, her fights with Moigrin only improved her skill. Breen focused on her own speed, the movements passed down from her father. If she remained quick with a blade and ignored the use of the shield, she might just win.

At least her muscles no longer ached beneath their weight.

"Begin," Vargas said from the edge of the ring.

Breen slid back into a defensive stance. Moigrin always attacked first.

As she'd anticipated, Moigrin slid forward as if to attack. Only she didn't. She paused, watching Breen above her shield. Her stance was half offensive, half defensive. What was she doing? This wasn't like Moigrin.

"What are you doing?" Breen whispered.

Moigrin circled. Breen was forced to follow, rounding the circle like a cat stalking its prey. She didn't respond, only smirked at Breen over her shield.

Breen's brow quirked up. She didn't have time for these games. She needed to advance to Third Rank, and if that meant leaving Moigrin in the sand to do so, she would.

Breen shot forward, swinging her sword out. It clanged off Moigrin's shield. The woman pushed back, knocking Breen's blade away from her chest. While she was exposed, Moigrin went for a stab at her abdomen.

Her eyes widened. There was only one thing she could do.

Breen dropped her shield in the way of Moigrin's blade.

Though the blade was dull, it dented the smooth metal, and forced Breen back, nearly toppling her into the sand.

"You're not the only one with tricks, southerner." Moigrin smiled maliciously and leapt again.

This time Breen was ready.

While Moigrin's sword came down, Breen twisted out of her reach and slapped her sword against Moigrin's exposed shoulder blades. The woman's eyes widened as her feet flew from beneath her. She fell face first in the sand.

Breen stepped back.

Moigrin coughed grains from her lungs and rose to her knees.

"You cheat!" she snapped.

"All is fair in battle, Moigrin." Vargas crossed his thick arms over his chest.

Breen smiled and raised her brows at Moigrin. Her heart beat wildly in her chest. It had been a while since she had a true challenge. "You should have guarded your back."

Moigrin's lips pulled back in a snarl. She barred her teeth and lunged.

Dodging out of reach, Breen slapped Moigrin's blade away with her own. Again, Moigrin rounded, leaping forward. Breen's sword met hers with a *shing*. Moigrin leaned all of her strength forward, pushing Breen's own blade back towards her face.

Her muscles ached with the effort of keeping Moigrin's blade back. She struggled for a moment to get the upper hand, but her strength was too great.

Fine. She'd use her speed then. Breen gave one last push before she spun to the left of Moigrin. Her blade *shing*ed free. She twisted around to Moigrin's back, slipping her sword in for Moigrin's throat.

The length of her blade pressed to the tawny skin of Moigrin's exposed neck. The woman growled, but froze, unable to move with Breen in such a good position.

"Excellent work!" Vargas clapped his hands together twice.

Breen lowered her blade and stepped back. Moigrin rounded, a growl on her lips, but said nothing. She stalked to the opposite end of the ring, throwing down her sword and shield.

"That'll be all for today," Vargas said. "We'll continue tomorrow morning."

Breen nodded, but paused while the others filed away. Vargas returned inside the Academy and the other trainees slowly followed.

Only Moigrin remained standing on the opposite side of the field near her fallen sword and shield, hands on her hips.

"That was a good fight," Breen said.

Moigrin rolled her eyes. "You beat me, again."

"But you were much closer this time."

She sighed. "I suppose." Moigrin's animosity faded for an irritated quirk of her brow and stern set of her lips. "Do you think he suspects anything?"

Breen smiled. "That we're truly getting along just fine?"

"Yes."

"No, I don't think anyone suspects." They exchanged a conspiratorial smile before separating.

Every day or two, they met in the baths, where they shared dreams of escape, advancement, and other tactics. But elsewhere, under the watchful eyes of Seaburn soldiers, Vargas, and the other trainees, they acted like enemies. It was the only way they could plan their escape together.

"See you later." Moigrin left for the weapons racks. Her angry scowl returned.

Breen resisted a laugh and followed after a few moments. No. No one would suspect a thing. And while they grew closer, the outside world would only see their distance. It was Moigrin's plan—a smart one at that. She only hoped it'd keep working until they were free.

After waiting for Moigrin to slip inside, Breen mounted her own sword on the wooden rack by the door. The others were long gone, leaving her alone in the shadows. She replaced her shield on the hanger and wiped the sweat and sand from her palms on a rag hanging on the wall by the shields.

"The riots are getting worse," the voice of a patrolling soldier drifted from the doorway. Breen glanced in his direction.

What riots?

"I heard," said another. "They're spread to the towns on the Outer Rim."

"Really?" the first gasped.

"I heard Vargas mention it to Mace this morning."

Her skin crawled at the name. General Mace had been the man to steal her from her home and bring her here. She'd never forgive such an act.

"How?"

"They had me stationed outside Vargas's quarters."

"They're brothers aren't they?"

"I think so."

Her brows pulled together. She didn't see the resemblance. Though they shared similar tones of black skin, Vargas had bright eyes, a slimmer build and wasn't the worst of human beings. Mace on the other hand was cruel, vile, much wider, and had eyes dark like night.

"They're worried they'll riot closer to the palace."

"Probably. I've heard several teams were dispatched in the last few days to take care of them."

Silence. Footsteps moved away slowly.

Whatever these riots were, they gave her an idea. A spark of hope lit in her chest. She could use the turmoil of these riots to escape. If only they drew closer to the Academy.

She shook her head and went inside.

EIGHT

arm swaths of heat followed her from the hot springs to the dressing rooms. It soothed her throat and filled her lungs with the aroma of lavender, shortening her breaths. She padded across the wet wooden slats into the women's side of the rooms. She plucked clean clothes from where she'd left them—a simple set of cream pants and shirt. With a thin piece of cloth, she dried what she could from her skin, leaving her braids to dangle down her back.

She pulled on her clothes, and they clung to her damp skin. It took several moments to shimmy them around her wide hips and down over her naval, but once she finally had them back in place, she yanked on her leather boots and proceeded to the wooden door barring the entrance.

Moigrin hadn't shown up to their typical meeting. Worry had her heart fluttering inside her chest, sending pricks like needles over her warm flesh. What if something had happened? What if she'd been found out?

Breen bit her lip.

No, Moigrin was too smart. Too savvy. She'd never let them catch her.

The oak door creaked as she pulled it inward. Cool night air pushed in, brushing loose strands of hair from her forehead.

"You do take long baths, don't you?"

Drakkone leaned against the tall trunk of a tropical palm tree. The ridges dimpled the skin of his bicep. He raised a brow expectantly, an amused half-smile on his face.

"Women have much more hair to clean." She walked passed him, hoping he didn't see how dry the top of her head was. She hadn't cleaned it, simply washed her body and left her hair as is. It would only dirty quicker if she cleaned it all the time.

"That they do." He caught up to her in several easy bounds. She cursed his irritatingly long legs.

"So you're following me again?" Breen glanced at him. He watched her from the corner of his eye.

"I want to make sure you stay out of trouble."

"I can handle myself."

"I know you can." He smirked. "I've seen you practice."

Her heels dug into the packed-dirt walkway. "What?"

He shrugged. "I've kept an eye out on the training yard when I'm not on duty. You seem to be doing well in Second Rank."

Breen narrowed her eyes.

"You don't have to take the compliment." He chuckled.

She sighed. What an irritating man. Not only did he insist on stalking her training, but now he waited for her outside the bathhouses. The behavior was disconcerting.

Yet, the quirk of his lips and girth of his muscles made her pause. She'd never minded the interest of her fellow clansmen when it came to courting her. It had always been fun to see how far they'd go to win her hand. But this man was different. He didn't best her or win her over. He simply lent her aid without asking for anything in return.

Breen twisted her jaw, uncertain what to think. Could she trust him, or this newfound attraction? She'd never been interested in one of her fellow tribesmen. They were her brothers. Practically her kin, at least in her mind. But Drakkone was not. He was new. Different. Something she'd never had in her tribe's village.

"No need to go silent on my account."

Her gaze snapped up and she flushed, unable to stop herself. Could she trust him? Should she? While her head told her no, something in her gut told her yes. He had helped her out of the dungeons after all

"I have a plan." She paused. "And I may need your help."

Drakkone raised a brow. He slowed by the gardens to the right side of the Academy. Hardly any light spilled on the dark recesses of the yard. They'd be nearly invisible among the shadows. He motioned for her to walk ahead of him into the garden. At least he would listen to her plan. Pushing away the anxiety that he may still betray her, she took the first step.

Breen led the way, picking through the brush, tall ferns, and exotic orange flowers until she reached a mostly open area. A break in the clouds shone starlight down upon the garden. Here they'd be far enough from the path, and hidden by ferns. She took a seat on the packed dirt—forgetting she'd just been to the bathhouse.

The tall greenery rustled as Drakkone joined her. He brushed through the flowers and sat opposite to her, his head nearly the height of what had to be four-foot tall ferns.

She quirked a brow. "This will have to do."

"What is your plan for?"

"Escape, of course."

Drakkone sighed dramatically. She imagined him rolling his eyes in the dark, though with clouds drifting back over the stars; they stole the light from his face.

"Can you really blame me?" She'd had enough of his protectiveness and desire to keep her safe. She wasn't afraid of the risks. If she managed to escape, she'd be happy, but if she died trying to gain her freedom, at least she'd go down fighting. She couldn't go on pretending to be meek. If she stayed, her spirit would eventually be crushed, and she would cease to exist. She must escape; freedom or death were the only acceptable options. Whether she fled Seaburn by foot, horse, or in death didn't matter. She had to get away.

"No. I suppose not."

"Then will you listen?" He nodded; the back of his head illuminated by lanterns more than ten yards away. "Good. I plan to escape during the riots. The chaos will cover me. I can take to the streets or scale down the cliff side if I have to."

"You'd die if you tried that."

"The streets then. If I can get free of the city, I can lose any pursuit I might acquire in the jungle south of here. They might not even notice I've left in the first place. I'll watch the nightshift guards, and find a way through. Once I'm out, if the riots are close enough to the palace, I can slip away."

"You think you've thought of everything, don't you?"

A growl broke through her teeth unbidden. "Then *help* me. What am I not thinking of? What don't I know?"

He hesitated for a long moment. If she'd been on the other side of the small clearing she might be able to see his face in the lantern light. But instead she left hers illuminated, and his emotions unknown.

"I can't help you escape."

Her breath fled her lungs in an irritated gasp. "Are you serious?"

"I'll only be contributing to your re-incarceration in the dungeon." While her voice rose, his fell.

Breen leapt to her feet. "I've had enough of this."

She passed him into the ferns. They rustled around her hips and flicked against her back as Drakkone jumped up. He grabbed her elbow and spun her to face him. "I don't want to see you hurt. Why can't you see that?"

Dim light lit his raised brows and wide eyes. He was concerned for her. But he didn't even know her. Her brows pulled together and she shook her head, but didn't pull away. Not yet.

"I don't want to go back to the dungeons," she surprised herself by saying. Cold goose bumps broke across her flesh, stealing the remaining heat from the baths. "But remaining here, fighting for the enemy that kidnapped me, tortured me, and raped me is its own special death."

Drakkone yanked her forward. Her eyes flew wide as she fell into his arms. He embraced her for a quick moment, his muscles pressing against her chest, her arms, her back.

She flushed.

"I won't let anything else happen to you," he said. "I'll find another way to gain your freedom."

Breen blinked in surprise, glad her warming cheeks were pressed against his chest. At least here he couldn't see the embarrassment and confusion flooding her face. At least here she was safe—even for a moment.

He stepped back, letting his arms fall to his sides. Breen avoided his gaze as she turned to the path.

Her heart clenched. She'd always wanted to feel this way with someone, like her mother said she felt for her father. Her parents had wanted that man to be Lukerin, her semi-betrothed, a man she thought of as a brother, not a lover. Her heart didn't flutter for him though. Her cheeks didn't warm in Lukerin's presence. She'd never felt her words catch or her mind swirl until now, with one of the enemy who had turned out to be a friend.

She had no idea what to do with it.

"It's getting late." Breen pushed through the remaining garden and returned to the path. Drakkone didn't follow.

"Good night," he said.

She returned to the Academy before he could fluster her further.

* * *

Night fell heavily on the Academy grounds. She'd avoided Drakkone at all costs for two days. She'd gone so far as to duck into the men's bathhouse to avoid him walking by. Once she even hid in the stairwell leading to the dungeons. Her skin prickled at the thought. She couldn't face him knowing what she was about to do.

Breen hid amongst the shadows crowding the walls of pillars. She slipped through the darkness, searching the high walls surrounding the compound. Three guards circled at different intervals, pausing every so often to peer inside, or out.

While one turned his back, she leapt across the yard, more than fifty feet of open expanse. Before the man turned against the light of the moon, she dove behind a crop of gnarled bushes. The thick leaves scratched her arms and cheeks as she pressed into their folds.

She glanced back at the walls.

The armored men continued, their shadows moving slowly.

She breathed a sigh of relief. Thank the gods. She only had to wait a few minutes, then she'd be able to escape.

For several days she had watched the guards, and inspected the walls. A side gate to the inside of the palace would be her best bet. She'd be able to flee through the main gates at the very least.

Once the shadows disappeared from sight, Breen leapt from the shadow of the tall gnarled tree and ran for the door. Her boots beat the sand, her steps muffled. Her breaths came quickly, not from exertion, but from fear of being caught.

She would not return to the dungeons. She would not be put through torture again. No man would touch her unless *she* willed it.

Breen slid to a stop before the slab of wood. She glanced at the walls. No shadows moved in her direction. Perfect. She reached for the metal handle. It clicked open.

A relieved sigh brushed loose strands of hair from her face. This was it. Her freedom. She swung the door open.

Across the yard, a soldier spun in her direction.

No. Her eyes flew wide, and she froze in the doorway.

"Hey! What are you doing here?" he barked. His voice travelled over the yard. Too loud. *Too loud.* She could deal with one soldier, dispatch him and get away. But not all of the night shift. She wanted the cover of darkness to slip away under—not an army at her back.

"I-I'm—" she stammered. She needed an excuse. A good one.

The man stopped inches from her chest. His lips twisted in a scowl and he narrowed his dark eyes at her.

"I asked you a question *recruit*," he snapped.

"The General," she began. Could this work? This lie was her only chance. "General Vargas's men. They sent me for wine in the palace kitchens. They told me to hurry as fast as I could or I'd be punished." She feigned innocence, flashing wide eyes and a quivering lip.

Believe me.

His eyes narrowed further. Suspicious. Damn. He wasn't going to leave this alone. She glanced at the shadows roaming the walls. They all continued their trek. None had heard the loud soldier. Maybe she could still knock him unconscious and flee.

"Which of the General's men?"

Damn.

She racked her brain for names. None came to her. Every moment she hesitated, the man's suspicion only seemed to grow. He grabbed her bicep. "You're coming with me."

He spun her toward the Academy, holding her wrist behind her back. She had to do this now. She had to act fast.

Her fists clenched and her muscles bunched. *Now!*

"Soldier!" Drakkone's deep voice cut through the night.

His tall frame emerged from the shadows of the pillars. He stepped beneath the starlit sky, staggering and grinning like a fool. What on earth was he doing?

"Sergeant." The soldier snapped to attention.

Sergeant?

"I see you found my errand girl." He'd overheard them. How long had he been following her without her taking notice?

"So you did send her for wine?" The soldier glanced between the two of them with furrowed brows.

"Yes, yes." Drakkone waved the man off. "I sent her ahead before realizing how strange it'd look. Someone should have accompanied the girl."

The soldier nodded slowly. Sweet gods. He believed Drakkone.

"I thought she was trying to escape, sir." The soldier released her arm.

She immediately stepped from his reach, joining the supposedly drunken Drakkone.

"Escape?" He tipped his head back in laughter. "Not this one."

The guard nodded slowly, a smile curving his lips. "I should return to my post. Try the wine in the cellar. It's hidden behind the rice crates."

"It is?" Drakkone gasped comically. "I betchu old Argen hid it on me! Dirty rat."

They both laughed, while Breen remained confused. She glanced between the two. *End this Drakkone.* She wanted to return to her escape and get on with this night. Just as she thought it, he heaved a heavy arm over her shoulder and drew her back toward the Academy.

"'Ave a good evening." Drakkone slurred and did a sloppy salute while the soldier returned a perfectly poised one. The man turned back to his duty and disappeared into the palace yard.

Once he disappeared, Drakkone stiffened, and dragged her into the shadows of the pillars. Once safely in the darkness, he pushed her up against the cold stone and pinned her, his forearm to her collarbone.

"What were you thinking?" he growled.

Pressure against her chest restricted her breathing. He eased up when she gasped for breath. "That I want to go *home.*"

"Why won't you listen to me? Why do I keep having to come after you?"

"Why didn't *you* tell me you're a Sergeant?" She pushed him back.

He staggered away, hitting the smooth stone of the Academy.

"It doesn't matter."

She scoffed. "Maybe you should have told me before letting me mindlessly agree to your plan to escape the dungeons. You led me to believe you wanted to help me!"

"I do want to help you."

"But you're one of *them!*" Though they only whispered, her tone grew louder, untamed. Her fists clenched.

He sighed and shook his head. "If you believe that, you really haven't been listening to a word I've said."

"I have listened. But you only speak of keeping me here."

"Because you're safest here for now. One day you might be safest elsewhere. But today is not that day." His eyes grew hard, like stone. He meant it. He did want to keep her here, but only for her safety.

"What kind of life is this?"

He started back as if slapped.

"I have to live in constant fear that if I don't do what they say, they might kill me *or worse*. I can't live like this, Drakkone. I won't." She met his eyes, fury lighting her veins. Why did he not realize how much he was asking of her; how much being here cost her? "I'm leaving. I need to escape, or die. There is no other way."

Breen spun for the edge of the shadows, ready to escape this Academy, this city, and this life. She needed to return to her family, or die trying.

Drakkone grabbed her arm.

His fingers dug in hard. He yanked to spin her, but she dug in her heels. She was tired of him forcing her to stay, keeping her grounded and stuck in this horrible situation.

She glared over her shoulder. "I'm going, whether you like it or not."

"I can't let you." He pulled her back. Using her own momentum, she twisted from his grip and jabbed him in the ribs with her elbow.

Air exploded from his lungs.

"Do *not* try and stop me." She yanked her arm from his grip.

Drakkone winced. He gritted his teeth and narrowed his eyes. His jaw set. He was determined to keep her here. But she couldn't let him.

Hot anger burned through her chest. Who was he to keep her? Her heart raced. He couldn't keep her any more than the men in her village could best her in a fight. She could take him. She had to. Her escape depended on it.

Drakkone lunged for her in one graceful motion. How he did so as such an enormous man, she couldn't be sure.

Breen jumped back from his reach and spun to slam her heel against his jaw. He ducked back before she could hit. His fingers wrapped around her ankle and pulled her from her feet.

Damn.

He towed her ankle high. Wrong move. Breen wrapped her thighs around his neck and spun, forcing him to the ground. His back cracked against the stone floor, and knocked the air from her lungs.

She grabbed his wrist and pulled it behind him. He pulled back, unbelievably strong.

Damn.

Drakkone peeled her legs away and spun to pin her with his weight. She rolled out from under him just in time, her heart racing as she leapt back to her feet. The door to her escape mocked her across the yard, nearly lined up with the pillars.

She gritted her teeth. She was *so* close.

In the moment her gaze flickered towards that door, Drakkone leapt. His arms wrapped around her waist and towed her to the ground.

Damn.

She gasped as they collided. She only had a single second to reclaim her advantage. Using his size and momentum against him, she drove her boots into his abdomen and flipped him over her head.

He didn't sail far. He caught himself on the ground. She slammed her fist into his cheek. He grabbed her arm. She spun away, tripping him with her heel. Before she could run, he grabbed both of her forearms, pulling her after him.

She landed on top of him, hard muscle pressing against her abdomen. She tried to pull back, but his grip had gone rigid.

Her breath fled her throat in an irritated hiss.

His warm chest pressed against hers. The contours of her thighs, cradling his waist, were hot. Flush rose to her cheeks before she could stop it.

Mere inches separated their faces. Her braids dangled over her shoulders, brushing his shoulders and ears. His breaths warmed her cheeks, and stole her sense.

She froze.

Dark eyes met hers, equally stubborn, equally confused and flustered. His grip on her arms softened, but she didn't get up. Her hands lay on his chest, which rose and fell slowly as his breathing evened out.

Her mind flew in all directions. She should knock him out now while she had the chance. She should flee back to the door, even if only the palace lay beyond. She'd find a way out. She had to.

But Drakkone's earnest gaze held her captive. His thick lips parted to speak. Before he found his voice though, he seemed to change his mind.

Flames of uncertainty welled in her chest.

He reached up, his thumb warm as it brushed her cheek.

Why wasn't she trying to escape? Her body remained glued to Drakkone's.

"You're covered in dirt." An amused smile quirked his lips at the corners.

She sucked in a breath and sat back, rising quickly to her feet. "It's your fault."

His smile only grew as he stood. "It'll look suspicious if you go to the bathhouse now. You can clean up in my private barracks."

Breen fought the flush from her cheeks. She hoped the shadows hid her embarrassment more than her filth. "Fine."

Drakkone nodded, unsuccessfully taming his amused glances. "Follow me."

NINE

Their boots tapped the smooth stone floor quietly as they crept through the Academy. Torches lit the hall, casting amber light across her skin. She followed Drakkone, against every instinct that told her this was a bad idea. Her skin crawled with what she could only describe as anticipation, but she wasn't sure what for. Her heart raced, even though they'd hardly scaled any stairs.

She should turn back. She should return to her own dorm where she belonged. But she couldn't. Not with dirty clothes and skin. If any soldiers saw her, they'd assume she attempted to escape—especially in the middle of the night.

Breathe, she urged herself.

Breen inhaled deeply, trying to calm her racing heart. She was simply going to clean herself up, and head back to the dorms.

Drakkone paused by a tall wooden door and slipped a thick bronze key into the lock. The door clicked open. This was her last chance to back out. Her last chance to flee him and perhaps the palace too.

She followed him inside.

Dim lantern light illuminated smooth sandstone, a thick fur carpet, and a colorful tapestry woven in vibrant blue-green hues, forming the sea and a ship atop its surface.

The door closed behind her, clicking shut.

The room wasn't lavish, but small and simple. A wide bed occupied most of the narrow space. Furs of unique colors; orange with black and white stripes, and yellow with black speckles, occupied the surface. A rack held up weapons, a spear, two curved scimitars and a thick steel shield with the Seaburn crest upon it. Leather armor and other clothes dangled from hooks along the wall beside the single third-storey window overlooking the gardens.

"You're much more ragged than I thought." Drakkone raised a brow, his gaze scanning her from head to toe.

Finally in suitable lighting, she could make out scuffs of dirt on his cream shirt and dark trousers. She hadn't realized how much dirt they'd rolled around in.

"So are you," she said.

Drakkone shrugged and motioned towards another door that stood ajar. He stepped inside, bringing with him a small lantern.

"You can use the tub first of course." He set the lantern on a small wooden table. At the center of the small room, a large basin held still water. "I had it filled this morning, but never used it."

Folded cloth was piled beside the lantern, ready for her to dry off. Moonlight filtered through the single window, arched and etched from the very stone. No glass interrupted the light.

"Thank you." She waited for Drakkone to leave before stepping inside.

Once he left, she shut the door.

It occurred to her that she was in the bathing room of a man she hardly knew. Though he'd saved her numerous times now, she owed him a debt, though not one that allowed him to see her naked.

She sighed and undressed. Cool air filtered through the window and brushed her skin. After the heat of the day, the cold was soothing.

Breen plucked a bar of soap from the same counter the lantern occupied, and stood before the water basin.

Clear water occupied the wide tub carved from some sort of smooth stone. She tested the water with a fingertip. It still retained some semblance of warmth—though just barely. She stepped inside the tub and slowly slid in.

The water rose a few inches short of the top. How Drakkone ever expected to fit inside, she couldn't be sure.

Scrubbing the soap over her limbs, she worked the dirt from her arms, chest, legs and face. Once they were clean, she felt her hair. Dirt, pebbles and sand clung to her braids. She wrinkled her nose.

Damn. She'd have to wash it.

Breen pulled out her braids one by one, her fingers working through the thick strands until she reached her scalp. Once her hair was free, she sunk into the water, letting it wash over her head.

She held her breath. Bubbles rose from her nose. The stillness below the water enveloped her like an embrace, keeping her safe below the surface.

When her lungs began to ache, she sat up, her head breaking the surface. She inhaled deeply. Cold lapped her wet shoulders and head.

She wiped water from her face and blinked away the thick drops clinging to her lashes. How nice it must be to have a single tub. Though she'd been enjoying the hot springs, she missed having a private bath like she did back in her tribe. Since her father was the Chief, they had a specially crafted tub in their tent, one she readily used instead of the river water. On occasion, she'd even boil her water before slipping in. She smiled at the memory. Would she ever return home?

Her lips curved downward and she sighed.

Now that she was clean, she should go. But the soothing water continued to tempt her. It had been kind of Drakkone to allow her the use of his personal bath. He was right. If she'd gone to the bathhouse so late at night, suspicions would rise. If she'd returned to the dorms dirty, things might be even worse.

Why did he continue to be so kind to her? Why risk himself at her expense?

She shook her head. She may never understand that man.

Breen took one last calm moment submerged to her shoulders before she stood. The stone was smooth against her feet, but not so much she'd slip. She rang water from her long dark hair and stepped free of the tub. Large drops dripped from her skin, leaving a wide puddle beneath her.

She plucked a cloth towel from the wooden shelf and went about drying her hair and body as best she could. Outside the tub, her temperature lowered. Cool air nipped her bare skin. She wrapped the cloth around her chest, folding it so it concealed from her chest to her thighs.

She glanced at her pile of dirty clothes. Damn. She'd nearly forgotten.

Before she could leave the bathing room, Breen reclaimed the bar of soap and set to washing the dirt stains from her outfit.

After several long minutes, she rung them out and folded them over the windowsill to dry. But until they did, she was stuck here.

She sighed. She should have thought of this.

Refusing to remain in the bathing room for the rest of the night, Breen opened the door back to Drakkone's quarters.

Amber light bathed his bare umber skin. His shirt lay in a pile on the floor. His back was turned; revealing the hard muscles of his shoulders and back. Her imagination played with the rest. She froze in the doorway, lips parted.

As if sensing her stare, he turned.

Though she'd seen many shirtless men in her life, they had been her brothers, and Drakkone was certainly not one of them.

"Breen?" He stepped toward her.

Her lips snapped shut. "Apologies, I didn't mean to burst in on you... dressing." Her voice was high—much higher than usual. She spun back for the bathroom, only to have Drakkone's warm fingers brush her elbow.

"Are you all right?"

Damn.

She was making an utter fool of herself. Normally she had every bit of control over herself. She was practiced, ready to fight, and always the master of her emotions. But every moment she spent alone with Drakkone tore down those walls, and sent her into a confused frenzy.

"Yes." She squeaked her answer, nearly gulping her tongue at the sound of her own voice.

He gently turned her to face him. She avoided his eyes. He laid the back of his hand on her forehead. She only flushed further.

"You're warm." His brows pulled together.

"I'm fine." Her voice was low, hardly audible.

His fingers lowered to her chin. She raised her eyes to meet his.

Breen bit the inside of her cheek. She didn't understand the kindness and concern in his eyes. She didn't understand why he did any of this. And she had to know.

"Why are you so kind to me?" Her lips pressed into a thin line.

He didn't even so much as quirk a brow at her question, only left his fingers gently against her raised chin.

"I don't believe in what the Academy does." His eyes hardened. "Or how Seaburn soldiers are made." He lowered his hand, but didn't step away. Mere inches remained between them. "I've been... keeping my eye on you, trying to protect you because..." He sighed, lowering his gaze. "Because it's the right thing to do."

Her lips parted in shock. Though she'd suspected something along those lines all along, she always imagined he had an ulterior motive, almost hoped he did. But that was the most honorable thing she'd ever heard a man say. Never before had someone spoken to her so deeply, so honestly.

She closed the space between them.

Breen wrapped her arms around his neck and pulled him down to meet her lips. She kissed him, letting the heat rising inside her take over. She'd never let her passion guide her. She'd let instinct and logic guide her hand, but never this raw fire that leapt inside her breast.

Gentle hands rested on her hips and smoothed the lines of her back. They soothed her tightened muscles before pausing just beneath her shoulder blades.

She held on tightly, and pressed harder. Her curves molded with his bare, sculpted abdomen, and he gasped against her lips.

She couldn't help her teasing smile as she gently nipped his thick lower lip. He wrapped his arms around her waist, and in one quick motion, hoisted her from the ground.

It was her turn to have the breath flee her throat. She wrapped her legs around his hips instinctively, to keep her aloft, though she didn't need to with his thick muscles holding her up. His lips sought hers this time, embracing them with unexpected passion.

The heat that rose in her chest stole all thought from her mind. She simply yearned, for more of something she'd never quite experienced.

Drakkone turned and crouched, gently laying her among the furs of his bed. They brushed her bare arms and tickled her neck. He refused to let go for even a moment, his chest pressed to hers as he lay with her.

Breen lost herself to that heat as their kisses burned between them.

* * *

BREEN AWOKE to the caw of circling vultures and sun bathing her bare skin through the open window. Heat pressed against her back, toned arms holding her close beneath the furs wrapping her legs.

She took a deep breath. The cool air of morning filled her lungs before she expelled it.

Her eyes flashed open. White dots spread across her vision as the sun blinded her. She shielded her eyes with her hands. Morning. *Late* morning. She had training to get to. Her heart leapt. She glanced back at Drakkone, who continued to sleep soundly. With his eyes gently closed and his lips parted against her hair, he hardly seemed a threat at all. She'd never seen anyone look so innocent.

A smile pricked her lips.

Another caw. She started. Yes. Right. She had to get to training.

Breen slowly eased from Drakkone's embrace. Cold air assaulted her on all sides. Her lips quivered and goose bumps ran across her flesh. She crept quietly back into the bathing room, where she plucked her dried clothing from the windowsill. She slipped on her clothes and boots, then quickly braided long chunks of her hair. The thick braids bounced against her back as she returned to his chambers.

He continued to sleep.

She crept to the door. Pausing, Breen listened. No sound in the hall. She inched the door open. It was clear.

Breen slipped from the room and made her way quickly back to the first floor. She sprinted past patrolling guards, other soldiers-in-training, and fled the Academy onto the practice fields.

Vargas was nowhere in sight.

She breathed a sigh of relief. She had no idea how she would have explained her tardiness.

Moigrin stood on the sand several feet from the building, wielding a sword and shield. She'd clearly been practicing, her feet already parted and ready to lunge. She glanced at Breen, her eyebrow raised in a question.

She hadn't been back to the dorms last night, and Moigrin had noticed.

Taking deep breaths, Breen attempted to control the flush rising to her cheeks. Last night. It had been, different, wonderful. Something she'd never experienced before, but had been told of by her mother many times in preparation for her would-be marriage.

She shook her head. No, now was not the time to think about such things.

"Attention, trainees." Vargas stepped from the back doors of the Academy, hands grasped behind his back, and chin tilted high.

They all leapt into line. Breen joined the others, feet parted, and hands clasped behind her back.

"Trainee Breen."

Her heart leapt. She stepped forward. "Yes, sir."

"You're being moved to the Third Rank. Go occupy yourself elsewhere for the next hour." He motioned over his shoulder.

Her eyes went wide. What? Already? She glanced at Moigrin, who's wide eyes mirrored her own. She was being moved up before any of the Second Rank trainees who'd been there long before her. A few of them shot her dirty glares, while Moigrin's lips twitched to smile as she tried to hide behind her own glare.

Breen nodded at the General, and did as commanded, fleeing back inside the Academy.

She couldn't believe this. She was being moved up. That meant only one thing—she was getting strong, stronger than she thought possible in such a short time. Maybe even strong enough to escape.

BREEN RETURNED to the training fields an hour later. Across the sand, a dozen men and women fought furiously, swords flying, metal clanging and angry glares in every direction. These warriors were *fierce*.

Their muscles bunched and curved as they sprang. One leapt like a viper, another a wild cat, a snarl at his lips.

She paused near the rack of swords and shields. Adding Breen to the mix, they'd have an odd number. She had no one left to pair with. Her fingers itched at her sides, dancing up and down on her thighs. Anticipation ate at her. She wanted this challenge—this fight. She hadn't been truly challenged since her bout with General Mace weeks ago in her village. She was stronger now.

If she were sent back to her tribe, and the same thing occurred, she'd be able to stop him. She'd drive her sword through his chest and snuff out what little light remained in his black eyes.

"Trainees!" Vargas barked.

Breen started from her reverie and launched across the sand to join the others in line. She joined the end, getting a few curious glances as she assumed the typical pose.

"Two laps of the outer rim. Now."

Her brows pulled together. Though they'd run laps of the fields a few times, never had they done the outer wall. She was the only one to hesitate. The rest took off, loping across the field.

Breen leapt after them. Clearly this was a typical exercise. Or were they just that obedient? She hoped to find another Moigrin, perhaps someone more powerful, more skilled, but equally intelligent and loyal to their tribe.

Her legs worked hard to catch up with the others, her thighs burning. She took even breaths, her heart rate increasing.

The heat of the sun beat down on her limbs, warming her skin and drawing sweat from within. She swiped it from her forehead as she joined the tail of the troop. They ran in two rows, side by side, evenly paced. She brought up the rear, pumping her arms like they did. So this is when they became a unit—Third Rank. She'd wondered about the synchronicity of the soldiers, and when they began to teach it. It seemed now was that time.

The group banked around the Academy's outer wall, jogging in the shadow. Breen couldn't help her relieved gasp as cool shade descended upon her shoulders.

They circled the wall closest to the palace. It took nearly five minutes to jog from the back field to the door she'd tried to escape from the previous night.

Her cheeks warmed at the thought.

Drakkone had saved her, protected her, again.

The sandstone wall curved up ahead, breaking off from that of the palace. If she were up high, maybe on the third floor, she'd be able to see past the wall and down into the city. The sea would spread beyond it in infinite possibilities.

Her foot slipped in the sand.

Her eyes widened and she quickly righted herself, her breaths heaving in an attempt to slow her startled heart. She glanced at the group in front of her. No one had noticed her blunder. Good.

Distant shouts carried on the breeze.

Her brows furrowed. She glanced at the wall, but couldn't see if any guards stood atop it while this close. They continued. The shouts grew louder.

Could there be riots this close to the palace already?

Breen took slow breaths, trying to hear their words over her own huffing. Garbled words met her ears in the native tongue of the

Seaburn people. She understood a few, though she couldn't be sure of the translation.

Unfair. Poor. Glutton. Emperor.

So the citizens of Seaburn were unhappy with their Emperor. They weren't the only ones.

The curve of the wall brought them back away from whatever riots lay outside the Academy. She glanced back, but could see nothing but blue sky over the fifteen-foot stone wall.

She looked ahead. She didn't want to trip again.

After about another five minutes, they arrived at the training fields, sweat gleaming on their foreheads. Breen was glad to see she wasn't the only one unable to bear this immense heat without sweating.

By the open doors to the Academy, Vargas spoke with a soldier in hushed tones. She cocked her head to hear their words, but only mumbles drifted on the breeze.

After a few long moments of rest, Vargas nodded to the soldier and joined his class. He assembled them in a half-ring before tilting his chin.

"Today marks your first expedition exercise. I'll be accompanying you into the city to help the city guards with civilian unrest." His tone rasped from his throat—irritated. He'd had something else planned for the day. "Follow me to the armory."

TEN

The stomp of their boots echoed off the city streets. Beautiful sandstone homes with intricate patterns carved into their pillars rose on either side of them. Cobblestone lay at their feet.

Breen couldn't help glancing from one side of the road to the other. Men, women and children skittered by, fleeing the noise at the far end. While the riots lay to the south of the Academy, they'd come through the Palace grounds to get the advantage and approach from the west.

Clad in tanned leather armor, Breen rubbed her thumb over the belts at her hips. In a sheath at her waist, the hilt of her sword stuck, rubbing against her inner forearm. How she'd missed carrying a blade, wearing real clothes, and being away from the sadness the Academy pulled from her.

Here, her heart soared with possibilities. Here, she was in the open. Only the metal wristlets wrapping her wrists separated her from Seaburn warriors. This way her fellow trainees couldn't be mistaken for true soldiers and slip off unnoticed. Only a key back at the Academy could remove them.

That very thing crossed her mind with every bend in the road. She could flee. She could run. She had no more walls to cross, only the city, which sloped down from the Palace atop the hill, revealing blue sea for endless miles beyond the shore.

A cool breeze ruffled the loose strands of her hair. She brushed her braids over her shoulders. Marching with the Third Rank was simple. Follow their steps, and listen for the orders given by the General.

Vargas led them. Now in lines of three, they occupied the center of the road, allowing enough space for pedestrians to flee the riot behind them.

The rioters had to know they'd be coming. The thump of their boots might as well be the rumbling of thunder.

Around a bend in the road, they emerged onto the crowded street. The Academy walls rose to their left behind the one and two-storey homes. Further down the street, the rioters screamed at the front entrance to the school. They waved sticks, and torches, but none held swords. A few wielded long-bladed daggers, or cooking knives, but these weren't warriors. They would stand no chance against the Third Rank.

Before they'd left the compound, Vargas briefed them on the situation. They'd been called to duty after several soldiers had been taken hostage by the rioters. There was no sign of them, but the forty or so men and women could be hiding them in one of the neighboring homes.

Vargas didn't pause. He marched straight through the bazar toward the group wielding makeshift weapons. Long cords hung from home to home between the alleys, holding up clothes, and drying meat.

The vendors had long since vacated, leaving wooden carts and empty shops on either side, shades drawn.

"Citizens of Seaburn, cease your acts against the Emperor at *once!*" Vargas bellowed.

He held up a hand. Breen and her fellow trainees came to a halt twenty yards from the gate.

The rioters grew silent, confusion twisting their brows as they turned to face Vargas, now clad in golden armor just like his brother General Mace had been when Breen had first met him. In the golden armor, the resemblance was unmistakable.

Breen resisted reaching for her sword. She had to remain controlled, pretend to obey. If she could keep this up, she might very well find a moment to escape within all the chaos.

"We're within our rights to protest!" one of the men shouted, inciting cheers of agreement from the crowd. Breen quirked a brow, surprised they spoke the language of the tribesmen, and not that of Seaburn.

Upon closer inspection, the man who spoke had the same tan tawny skin as she and the rest of the tribes. But his bright green eyes and wild blond hair were foreign, not even those of Seaburn, let alone her tribesmen.

"You will return my soldiers at once, and disperse," Vargas continued. "This is a disruption of the peace, and will not be condoned."

Rising shouts of protests spread through the crowd. Some called in Seaburn's language, others in hers. Her brows pulled together. What was the purpose of these rioters? Were they revolutionaries and rebels, or simply those seeking change to better their own lives? Her heart leapt faster.

This was a change she could get behind.

Breen glanced at her fellow trainees. None batted an eye, or shared her unhampered excitement. So they were as broken as she'd expected.

"Return my soldiers *now*, or appropriate force will be exercised to assure their safe return." A growl seeped into the General's voice. He did care about his men. It was too bad not many of his fellow Seaburn-born soldiers shared the feeling. Such a fact was clear by her treatment in the dungeons.

"Never!" the blond man shouted.

The crowd lunged across the cobblestone, trampling several among them in order to be the first to swipe at the General.

Her eyes widened.

Vargas drew his sword with a *shing*. As did the others around her.

Breen followed close behind, her curved blade heavy in hand. She smiled. Sunlight glinted off the well-polished metal. Now this was a blade.

"Find them," Vargas instructed two by his side. They nodded and fled to the back of their ranks, while the first wave of three leapt forward.

Soon, each row of the twelve dove in.

Two men took down one of her fellow trainees. They crashed to the stone street in a pile. Two women with large sticks mobbed another. The rest of the trainees pushed forward, using their strength as they had to, while avoiding the use of their swords.

Watching her fellow soldiers while dodging blows from the citizens filled Breen with hope. They'd been instructed to use as much force as needed, but avoid unnecessary bloodshed, yet they took care in avoiding hurting the citizens. They were almost gentle, despite being mobbed, and this care for the common citizen made her heart lift just a little.

A man with a torch swung the burning log toward her.

She leaned back, the heat of the fire scorching her cheeks. She had to be careful and stop thinking outside the immediate danger she was in. Breen leapt back the second the fire was clear, and slammed her heel into the man's gut. He flew back, gasping for air.

A woman with wild black curls leapt on her back, her nails biting into the leather at her shoulders. She was even more thankful for the wardrobe change.

Breen whipped forward, throwing the woman off. She toppled to the ground, rolling down the incline.

The torch man returned, swinging at her with fire lighting his eyes.

"Damn soldier scum!" he cried.

Fire burned through the air; smoke wisping to the sky above.

Breen leaned out of the way, bumping into her fellow trainee who grappled with a dagger wielding man.

She bit the inside of her cheek and thrust away, leaping from the torch's reach. She swiped the torch with her sword, cutting it in two.

The end wielding fire rolled down the hill, flames flickering as it skittered off the cobblestone and into the mud.

"Give up." She swung for the torch again. Another clean slice of wood fell to the floor.

His eyes widened and he stepped back, fear registering in his eyes. Her heart clenched. She didn't want his fear. She wanted him to quit attacking her, and create a larger upset. With something large, she could flee. With only a small angry crowd, she was certain the trainees would be able to overcome the riot. She needed something they *couldn't* handle, something to help her escape.

The man turned and ran.

She sighed. Good.

A crash sounded behind her. Breen spun, sword up and ready.

Moigrin froze in the middle of the street, her eyes wide and a long cloak wrapping her shoulders. Beneath her arm, the blue-eyed Elka cowered.

Her heart leapt. They were going to get caught. She'd seen them, and it wouldn't take much for one of her fellow trainees to catch them too.

Breen glanced between the fighting crowd at her back, and Moigrin. She tilted her head in the direction of the alley across the street.

"Hey, you there!" she shouted, waiving her sword about to distract anyone who might look her way.

Moigrin nodded in understanding beneath her burgundy cloak and rushed Elka into the alley, out of sight from the prying eyes of Breen's fellow trainees.

With shadows soothing the heat from her shoulders, Breen joined them, hurrying the pair back as fast as she could.

Clotheslines hung overhead, fabric of every color hanging from the cords. The scent of salted fish filled the alley, stirring her hunger. Her stomach rumbled.

"Moigrin, what are you doing?" she hissed. Moigrin had missed the last few meetings in the bathhouse. She'd feared the woman had been sent to the dungeons.

Moigrin turned, lowering her hood and glancing over Breen's shoulder to the end of the alley. "Helping Elka escape."

"This isn't a good time. Someone might have recognized you." Sweat trickled down her forehead. Breen glanced over her shoulder, straining her ears in case any footsteps approached.

"I had to get her out, Breen." Her brows turned up, and her eyes widened with desperation. "She can't do this. She's not a warrior like us. She'll never pass First Rank."

"What do they do if you don't pass?" Breen's voice was small, distant. Fear for Elka knotted her chest. Moigrin glanced down at the metal cuffs wrapping her wrists. There was no way for Breen to accompany them.

"I don't know… but I've heard rumours." She paused. "Let's just say, death would be kind."

Breen's jaw clenched. She knew all too well. "Then go. Get your sister free. Before it's too late." She stepped back toward the end of the alley.

Moigrin grabbed her wrist. "Wait. Breen, I'm not going anywhere. I'm only getting Elka to the edge of the city, and once I've secured passage for her, I will return. I should be back by nightfall."

Breen's brows pulled together. "Why?" There were no cuffs keeping her here. "You should go with your sister while you can."

When they'd first met, Moigrin would have done anything to escape. But here she was telling her she was about to escape, only to *come back*. It was unthinkable. Why would she do such a thing?

"Because *someone* needs to bring the Academy down from the inside." Her eyes hardened.

Breen couldn't help the gasp that escaped her. "You're serious?" Is this why Moigrin had avoided their meetings?

"I am."

She nodded brusquely. "Then go. Quickly, before you're caught."

Moigrin nodded.

"And be safe."

She smiled. "Of course."

Moigrin took Elka back under her arm and led her to the end of the alley, where they slipped from sight behind a sandstone home. Once they were gone, Breen rushed to the other end of the alley where the shouts of rioting continued.

The battle had yet to die, though the numbers of both sides had diminished. Her fellow trainees slashed through the citizens with vigor. Her hope died with them. Where was the gentleness she'd seen in the beginning?

Her heart should clench, or leap, or feel something about the loss of her fellow trainees. But it didn't. She felt nothing for them. Because they'd given up. And there was no worse fate than giving in to the darkness.

A man with two daggers lunged at another trainee. His sword flashed up to block the blow, but the man slipped one free and stabbed the soon-to-be soldier in the gut.

Blood gushed from the wound, and the trainee's eyes flashed wide. Damn.

Breen rushed to join the fight, her leather boots slamming against the cobblestone. As the trainee lowered his sword, staring in horror at the blood drenching his soldier outfit, the man lunged for his throat.

She crashed into the man, throwing him across the body of a fallen rioter. She leapt after him, holding her sword to his throat. "Surrender!" She pressed the tip of her sword to his flesh. Red welled in the thin cut. He stared at her with wide eyes.

Shouts emanated from the far end of the street. She glanced up. Four soldiers ran from the tall building at the end of the street. Two tore ropes from their wrists, while the other two, the ones who'd been sent for the captured soldiers, led the way.

So their first mission had been a success.

"*Never*," the man spat.

Breen looked down in time for the man to sit up, pressing her sword to his flesh. It sliced clean through his throat, until blood gurgled between his lips and drowned his exposed neck in red.

She gasped and pulled back quickly, stepping away from the insane man. He'd killed himself on her blade. But why? Did his cause mean that much to him? Or were Seaburn's prisons similar to the one she'd been kept in?

Suppressing a shiver, she glanced back at her fellow trainee, who she'd narrowly saved from suffering a similar fate. He met her gaze and gave her a stiff nod. His breaths came heavy and his fingers shook against the wound. He held it tightly, but blood still seeped between his fingers.

He needed to get to the infirmary at once.

"Retreat!" Vargas called as the four soldiers reached him.

Breen lowered her blade, and joined the bleeding trainee. She swung his free arm over her shoulder.

"What are you doing?" he hissed through pained breaths.

"Helping you." She rolled her eyes and stepped forward, dragging him with her.

His jaw hardened, but he said nothing.

The remaining trainees, eight out of the twelve they'd arrived with, not including herself, and the bleeding man she aided up the hill, joined them. Two had died by the hands of the rioters. Two had lost their life, and for what?

She shook her head and joined the others on their trek back to the Academy.

ELEVEN

The streets of Seaburn quickly became familiar. Vargas sent them out with regular city patrols to get a feel for what their duties might be. After the riots, more soldiers on the street had been needed.

Three weeks had passed on duty, and the soldiers continued to watch the trainees like vultures circling prey. Her fingers itched, and her eyes darted toward every bit of movement. She wanted to escape. She *had* to. But after her first botched attempt, she had to be careful.

Drakkone might not be able to save her again.

Their boots beat in unison against the wide stone bricks. They patrolled the upper rings of Seaburn, working their way down the winding streets. Heat beat against her skin from the afternoon sun. It burned her bare shoulders, and scorched her cheeks.

Her breaths grew heavy, and she squinted in the light. Day after day, they went halfway down to the shore before turning back up. Her legs ached as they mounted the hill. It'd be at least another hour before they returned to any semblance of shade.

Heat waves rose from the stone street. Children didn't play

outside, and scarcely any pedestrians occupied the bazars they passed. After the riot had been disbanded, most civilians stayed indoors as much as they could. It was a stark contrast to the first time she'd entered Seaburn, riding in a cage on the back of a wooden cart while countless civilians went about their business.

Children had kicked balls across the street, running between the legs of adults, screeching with laughter. People had smiled. People had roamed leisurely. Now only Breen's and her fellow soldiers' footsteps broke the whispers of the ocean's wind.

Her stomach soured and rolled with nausea. Too much sun. Too much heat. She needed water. Breen unclipped her leather canteen from her belt and unscrewed the top. Only a few drops of water graced her tongue. She shook the bottle. Empty.

Damn.

She returned the canteen to her hip, and shielded her eyes from the glare.

When she did try to escape, she wished it could be after nightfall, when darkness embraced her and cold air swept her skin. But would she be so lucky? She doubted it. Though Drakkone hadn't been able to stalk her near as often, she had a feeling he kept an eye out from his window whenever possible.

Her days were occupied by drills, patrols, training and very little rest. Never before had she felt so sick, and so overworked.

Sweat dripped down her forehead, and her back. She bit the inside of her cheek to keep from groaning. Maybe she could convince Drakkone to allow her the use of his bath once again. She wouldn't mind lying in cold water for a few hours.

She licked her lips to moisten the dry cracks. But then again, maybe he didn't want to see her. His presence had been scarce enough, despite most of her days being occupied. By dinner, she was so exhausted that she simply ate and slept; occasionally she bathed. Maybe, hopefully, Drakkone didn't have time to approach her in the short moments of freedom she had.

Breen drew in a deep breath. Her stomach rolled. Nausea rose into her throat, but she bit it back. She would not be sick on this road. She would not be sick in front of her fellow trainees, or these soldiers. She took another shuddering breath.

"You don't look so good." The trainee marching at her left furrowed his brows. He was the one she'd saved during the riots. It had taken a couple weeks for his wounds to heal. This was the first patrol they'd been put on together.

"I don't feel so good," she murmured.

His brows furrowed.

The world swirled beneath her. Her legs weakened. Nausea rolled through her again, hot and uncomfortable.

She snapped her lips together and held her stomach.

Only a few more streets. She could make it.

Every step was arduous. Every street seemed to take hours instead of a few minutes. She squinted against the glaring sun, and wiped sweat from her forehead. The Academy walls came into sight above the homes.

She sighed in relief, and clenched her gut. She could do this. Nearly there.

Her legs became lead, aching, painful lead. She gritted her teeth. Only thirty feet. Twenty. Ten.

The great wooden doors creaked inward, allowing them entry. Their small party passed through onto the packed dirt and sand. Now that she'd returned, she was only forty feet from shade. Only.

Forty feet seemed like forty miles.

Her world swirled, and she swayed with it. Her brows furrowed. No. Not yet. Black speckled her vision. Every bit of her skin burned like fire.

"Breen?" someone asked her.

Her feet fell from beneath her. Darkness took her.

* * *

BREEN BLINKED AWAKE, her heart racing.

Soft cotton embraced her shoulders and back. Heat didn't burn her skin, and her limbs didn't ache. She rolled her dry tongue in her mouth. When was the last time she'd had anything to drink?

"You're awake." The doctor who'd assisted her last time smiled from his desk. He rose and shuffled across to her cot. "Nice to see you again."

Breen nodded faintly. Though she didn't feel sick anymore, her world continued to tilt. "What happened?"

"You passed out." He handed her a cup of water from a small table at her bedside. "Here. You're probably just dehydrated."

Breen took it. Cold soothed her warm fingers. She brought it to her lips quickly, and gulped the entire glass. Cool liquid numbed her tongue and throat. Moisture spread across her lips and a drop or two slipped down her chin.

"Careful now. You don't want to bring it all back up!" The doctor chuckled and took the empty cup. He refilled it before handing it back to her.

"Thank you," she mumbled against the dull iron. She drank more slowly this time.

The door burst open, cracking off the stone wall behind it.

The doctor spun, and she looked up with wide eyes. Drakkone stood in the doorway, his brows furrowed, and his breaths quick.

His dark eyes met hers, sparking with concern. "Breen." He came to her bedside. "What happened?"

Breen glanced between Drakkone and the doctor. The man raised his brows, a smile pulling at his lips. "I'll be right back." He slipped from the room. The door clicked quietly behind him.

Drakkone pulled up a chair and sat. His fingers wrapped around hers and squeezed. Her heart fluttered, and she bit back a smile, unsure she enjoyed how easily he pulled warmth into her chest.

"I fainted, that's all." She shrugged.

"You're pale." He felt her forehead with his other hand. "And warm."

It seemed like so long since she'd seen him. It was just as she'd hoped—he hadn't been avoiding her. She'd simply disappeared too early every night. Something like relief settled her racing heart.

"I'm fine," she assured him. "Dehydrated is all."

She couldn't fathom another reason. She simply hadn't had enough to drink, and had been in the heat too long. That explained her dizziness, nausea, and even her fainting spell.

"I'm glad you're all right." He sighed and sat back in his chair. He didn't release her fingers.

"You're afraid I wouldn't be?" she teased. The corners of her lips quirked.

Drakkone raised a brow, a smile pulling at his lips. "Of course."

"It's good to see you as well."

He squeezed her fingers. "So you've been well then?"

She nodded. "Tired and sore from drills, training *and* patrol, but fine otherwise. And you?"

"Busy in the dungeons." His lips snapped shut before he could catch himself.

Her shoulders went rigid. She had nearly forgotten he continued to work in the bowels of the Academy, assisting her captors with gods knew what. She slid her fingers from his grip.

"I'm sorry." He sighed. "You know I don't condone it, but that is where I've been stationed. They won't shift me elsewhere until we have more Seaburn volunteers."

Her jaw hardened. "Why do your people insist on relying on mine for protection?"

Drakkone sat back, his hands empty in his lap. "They haven't always. It used to be a great honor to be involved in the military. But when the Emperor came into power, he changed things. Nobles seemed overly pleased by it, but I know there are some who refuse to allow such poor treatment of your people."

Like the rioters.

Her stomach rolled. She bit the inside of her cheek. "Would they do something about it? Those who feel like you?"

Drakkone glanced off into the distance. Sunlight drifted through the glass window at the other end of the room, warming his dark eyes.

"Maybe."

Her breath caught. Drakkone leapt to cover himself.

"It depends, Breen. Some like my family would. The few rioters in the city would. But the nobles, most certainly would not. The middle class are mostly happy with how things are. Their children aren't being stolen from their beds anymore. No one is forced to enlist. They see stealing *your* children as best for the Empire."

"But what about *us*? It isn't best for any of us." Her fists clenched in her lap.

"I know."

"It isn't fair, Drakkone."

"I know, Bree."

Her brows pulled together. "Bree?"

He smiled shyly and glanced away. "I usually refer to you as Bree in my head."

So he'd given her a nickname. Were they familiar enough for that? Her mind drifted back to the time they'd spent in his chambers. Her cheeks flushed. Yes, they were familiar enough.

"It's fine," she decided. Why not let him call her what he like?

Drakkone smiled.

The door creaked open and the doctor reappeared in the doorway. He stepped inside, the same amused smile glued to his face.

"All right, Breen. I have a few questions to ask you before I can release you." He paused by her bedside, and stared pointedly at Drakkone.

Drakkone cleared his throat and stood. "I'll see you later then."

Breen nodded. "See you later."

He disappeared from the infirmary, giving her a small smile over his shoulder before he departed.

The doctor sat by her side and took her wrist. He held his fingers there a few moments, checked her forehead, and her throat. "You seem to be improving already."

"That's good, I assume." She quirked a brow.

"Very much so. It indicates you were most likely just dehydrated and in need of rest." He smiled. "I just have a few questions to ask you to be certain." She nodded. Ready. "How much water do you generally consume in the day?"

"A few cups in the morning, some in the afternoon if we're given a break." She paused, staring thoughtfully at the ceiling. "Then in the evening of course. A canteen on patrols."

He nodded. "Good, good. And how are you sleeping?"

"Well." As well as could be trapped inside the Academy against her will.

"Do you generally feel tired and overworked?"

Yes. "No."

"Good. And when was your last monthly bleeding?"

She froze. She hadn't had one since her arrival. "I don't know."

His brows furrowed. "It could be from the stress." He didn't meet her eyes. It must be common for women to cease their monthly cycle in this place. There was plenty of stress around every bend.

"Since you're barren, it can't very well be pregnancy." He stood. "I believe if you be sure to consume extra water whenever you're able, continue to eat appropriate proportions, and stay well rested, you'll be fine."

Breen nodded. "Thank you, doctor."

The man waved her off and stepped back over to his table. He poured her another glass of water, and handed it to her. "Hydration is important when you're out under the sun all day."

She knew this very well. After all, she'd lived in the desert her entire life. In all that time she'd never fainted from the heat, and never become dehydrated. Could stress have caused her bout of dizziness? Or was it truly lack of refreshment?

Her stomach soured.

Or was it something else altogether?

"You should be good to go today," he continued. "I'll recommend to the General that you be free of your duties until morning. Get some rest."

Breen nodded and flung her legs over the side of her cot. She downed the cup of water handed to her, and stood. Her world didn't tilt, and her legs remained steady beneath her.

"Thank you."

"It's nothing." He took her cup and gave a small wave goodbye.

Fleeing the infirmary, Breen paced the length of the sandstone hall back to the main corridor. Though she was no longer dizzy, some rest truly sounded wonderful.

Maybe a good sleep would rid the unease clinging to her gut. She hoped he was right, and simple dehydration caused the problem. Though it seemed impossible, her symptoms lined up with one other possibility she refused to admit.

If she was truly barren, she could bear no children. Pregnancy would be impossible, and thus it couldn't be it. Her stomach rolled once more.

She hoped it wasn't a sign of the unthinkable.

TWELVE

ngry embers kindled inside her chest the next day. Heat burned through her boots and bathed her skin. Beneath the hot sun, sweat trickled down her forehead and glistened on her skin. Sand billowed in the breeze, and clung to her limbs.

She shook it off, swiping angrily at the grains.

Breen stood opposite another trainee, the man she'd saved on patrol. She couldn't quite recall his name. Raven? Ren? Rook? She shook her head. It didn't matter. None of them mattered. The Third Rank was full of men and women who'd abandoned the ways of their clan. They'd given up. They were nothing. Useless.

She gritted her teeth.

In training, they were to spar today, practicing for future battles with mixed weapons. Her opponent stood with a long sword, while she held two curved scimitars. Her fingers tightened around the hilts, the cloth wrapping the ends itching her sweaty palms.

"Begin!" Vargas barked from the edge of the training field.

The man lunged, swiping in a long arc toward her abdomen. He wasn't used to the blade—none of them would be. The metal was heavy, and awkwardly long. His footing didn't compensate for it, allowing her plenty of time to step out of the way. His swing was too slow. He'd have to be faster than that to catch her.

Breen stepped in and swiped her twin blades.

He leapt back, eyes flying wide as her swords cut the leather of his soldier outfit. His chest heaved as he glanced down at the damage.

Another half-inch and she'd have sliced open his stomach.

He met her gaze, brows furrowed.

She didn't give him a moment of reprieve. Lunging in, she danced out of the way of his blade, and sliced at the back of his knee, his spine, and his shoulders.

He ducked and dodged, unable to swing his sword in time to block. He was much faster without it. If he were smart, he'd give up on it and try to snatch one of hers. Not that she'd ever allow that.

Breen ducked low beneath his blade and swiped for his hands.

A long cut sliced his knuckles as he pulled back. He hissed. Blood speckled the sand.

"What was that?" he snapped. They weren't supposed to draw blood during their fights. Breen tensed and stepped back.

"You should have been faster." Her jaw hardened.

"Are you serious?"

"Switch partners!" Vargas called from the sidelines. If he'd seen the cut, he didn't make note of it.

The man, whatever his name was, narrowed his eyes as he switched to the right while she went left to her next partner. A woman with bright hazel eyes and short dark waves. She held a typical shield, but wielded a spear as well.

Her flat nose and almond eyes reminded Breen instantly of Moigrin.

Her heart clenched. She hadn't seen Moigrin in weeks. She hoped she hadn't been caught.

"Begin!"

The woman held up her shield, eyeing Breen from the other side of it. Instead of jumping in, the woman waited. Smart. The tip of her spear remained inches from the sand. She'd have much more range with it. Breen would have to be careful.

Heat continued to compress her chest. Her heart raced as she lunged. The woman snapped her spear forward. Her heart leapt as the pointed blade at the end sliced inches from her skin.

Her eyes widened. She dodged to the side.

The woman leapt back, spinning her spear in hand, crouching with her shield up. She was quick. Maybe even faster than Breen.

A growl rumbled from her throat. Her fingers clenched around the hilts of her twin blades. She would not be out done. Not today.

Breen leapt again. She sliced for her shield. The woman thrust out to knock her blade away, while simultaneously shooting her spear toward her. Breen expected this, and used her second blade to whack the spear away.

She spun inside the safe zone between her shield and her body, thrusting her blade at her chest.

The woman stepped aside. Her blade sailed passed.

What? How was she so *fast*?

Breen fell forward. She had far too much momentum behind her. The woman slammed her boot into Breen abdomen, sending her flying across the sand.

She rolled through thin grains, sand clinging to her sweat coated face and limbs. She finally stopped several feet from her opponent. Her gut soured with nausea. Breen rubbed her stomach with her free hand.

She froze. She'd lost one of her blades.

Between the two of them, her blade waited. Damn. How could she be so careless?

Breen leapt to her feet. Her body ached as she did.

The woman smiled, taunting her with a quirk of her brow. She knew if Breen went for her second blade, she'd be within reach of her spear. Either she could go for her second blade, and return her advantage, risking a hit in between, or she could forget it and attack with a single blade.

She bit her lip. A horrible choice.

Her chest burned. Her fingers tightened around her blade. Her mind swirled with possibility. She was taking too long to decide. The woman's taunts only grew more obvious.

Breen narrowed her eyes. This woman was nothing to her. She'd beat her, and then see how smug she'd be. Breen lunged across the space between them, her boots kicking up sand. The woman smirked and thrust her spear out.

She ducked, skidding across the sand. She grabbed her sword and leapt. The woman's eyes widened as she tackled her shield, pushing her back to the ground.

Before Breen could pin her, the woman used the one trick Breen had used countless times. Using Breen's own momentum against her, the woman threw her over her head. Warm air embraced her entire body for a long moment.

Her back hit the hot sand. Air exploded from her lungs.

Cold metal pressed against her throat.

"Nice try," the woman gloated. She smirked down at Breen.

Breen gritted her teeth and pushed the woman's blade away. She leapt to her feet. "I want a rematch."

She raised a brow. "A rematch? Why? I just bested you."

Fire licked her throat. "What? You think you can't beat me a second time?"

"I know I can." She scoffed. "Why waste my time?"

"Practice is over!" Vargas bellowed. He waved his hands to get their attention. "We'll meet tomorrow at noon."

Her fists clenched around her blades. Damn. Why now?

The woman departed with the rest of the trainees, leaving her alone on the sand. She worked her jaw, unable to rid herself of the anger lending adrenaline to her veins. Her breaths continued to come quickly.

What was wrong with her? She'd never picked a fight like this before.

Shaking her head, she returned her weapons to their rack and stepped inside. Shadows soothed her shoulders and cooled her scalp.

She sighed.

"Bree!" Drakkone stepped from the wall. He'd clearly been waiting. "I see you're done with practice."

Instead of the usual flutter she received at the sight of him, her heart clenched painfully. She could be pregnant. And if she was, he was a liar. He'd told her he was barren, like her. They'd commiserated over their inability to have children. She'd cried in front of him. And he'd *lied*.

Fire pushed through her veins and closed her fists. She narrowed her eyes at him.

Drakkone's brows furrowed with confusion. "Are you all right? I just wanted to see if you'd like to dine together."

If she was pregnant, the doctor was wrong, Drakkone had lied, or both. Which was it? Her eyes stung with frustrated tears.

"I don't want to see you anymore." Venom laced her words.

His eyes flew wide. "What?"

"I will not see you again. Stay away from me." She turned for the hall.

His fingers wrapped her elbow, spinning her to face him.

Fury gave breath to the burning embers in her chest. She slapped him, and he released her.

Breen stepped away. "*Stay away from me.*"

Confusion and hurt registered in his eyes. His lips parted to speak. She spun for the hall, marching quickly away.

Drakkone didn't reach for her again, and he didn't follow.

* * *

BREEN STOOD at attention in the open sand, her back straight, but aching. Her feet parted and her hands held behind her back. Vargas paced the line. After two months of training, he'd finally moved her to the next level. The Fourth Rank. Just in time for a bump to grow from her belly.

She was really and truly pregnant. And though it should be a time of joy and celebration, fear swallowed her. How was she supposed to bring up a child in this world? How was she supposed to explain to her superiors that she'd had relations with Drakkone? Would she be punished for such an offense? Would she be placed back in the dungeons?

Or worse, would they take the child from her?

Cold fear chilled the sweat coating her skin. She needed to flee. She needed to escape. There was no other way.

"Good job today, trainees." He paced back and forth along the line of ten men and women, including herself. "We'll meet tomorrow afternoon after your patrols."

"Yes, sir," Breen said, in unison with the others.

"Dismissed."

The other trainees lowered their hands, and returned to the Academy. Instead of fleeing in the same direction, Vargas waited until she passed him. He grabbed her elbow gently.

"I'd like a word with you, trainee." He didn't meet her gaze.

No. He knew. He had to. What could she say? How could she explain?

"Follow me." He spun on his heels and led the way back to the Academy.

She paused for only a moment before following. Her feet grew heavy. Every step was a burden. The arch of the doors passed overhead, and shade descended upon them. She took a deep breath, trying to calm her racing heart. It didn't work.

"Breen. You've shown incredible skill and improvement over the last few months," he began. She bit her tongue, waiting for the *but*. "I want to groom you for a new role. A leadership role."

Her heart skipped. What?

Though she'd been sure he'd somehow discovered her pregnancy, instead he offered her a new rank. Could it be a trick? It had to be. It didn't make sense. She was one of the few unbroken by Seaburn. They'd be fools to give her any sort of role.

"I think you could play a crucial role in our society. You've been deft at leading your fellow trainees, excelling in combat. Soldiers respect power. They respect strength. I believe you could command them." Finally, he glanced at her.

She tried to smooth the shock from her face. He smiled.

"I know this may come as a surprise." Vargas gazed ahead. "But with less and less soldiers coming from Seaburn itself, we need leaders to come from your ranks."

He didn't say it. But she felt the words he didn't say. *Her* ranks. *Savage* ranks. Her fists clenched at her sides.

Nausea rolled to the surface. She'd spent weeks with it. Not simply in the morning, but at all hours. It remained distracting, feeding off her. The bigger her bump grew, the more her discomfort became. Though she'd hidden the bump beneath baggy clothes, it would be too big to hide soon. Too big not to notice.

Vargas wouldn't be offering her this if he knew.

"You can take as much time as you'd like to think about it." He stopped in the front lobby of the Academy. A gold statue of the Emperor stood at its center. "But the sooner the better. There's much to do to prepare you. You'll be my apprentice, and learn the ways of leadership. I can teach you much, I promise you that."

Breen met his gaze. "I'll think about it, sir."

He nodded. "Good." He turned. "Enjoy your evening, trainee."

"Thank you, sir."

Vargas departed through the front doors of the Academy, leaving her to stand alone in silence. She'd think about it all right, though it wouldn't be the same train of thought he'd come to expect. If she were to stay, she'd undoubtedly face more pain, more despair, than she ever had before.

It was time to go. There was no putting it off.

* * *

FEAR SENT HER HEART RACING.

Breen clung to the shadows outside the Academy. Clothed in her soldier uniform, she left her metal cuffs back in the dorm. There was no one to lock them to her wrists anyway. This way she'd appear a full soldier. It should be simple to get away beneath this new identity.

Or so she hoped.

Darkness shielded her from the watchful eyes on the wall. Slipping between tall pillars, she searched for the door to lead her beyond the wall. Hopefully whoever occupied the night shift wasn't familiar with her. If they were, they'd know she was a trainee, and she'd be caught. But she saw no other way.

Breen gulped the lump in her throat. She crouched at the edge of a long shadow cast by a thick sandstone pillar. The moon lit the sky, hovering above the sea, casting silver upon its surface.

Two guards stood at the front entrance. Three circled the wall. Another two would stand on the other side of the closed gates. What were the chances *none* of them would recognize her?

Not good.

She would have to risk it.

Biting back a sigh, Breen stood tall and stepped from the safety of darkness.

I belong here, she thought. She had to emulate the other soldiers, had to pretend to fit in. Keeping her chin low and her steps even, she marched down the packed dirt path to the main gates.

Twin wooden doors with iron hinges and intricate carvings held her and her brethren within these walls.

Her fists clenched. She took a deep breath. Her heart continued to race. She had to remain calm. Had to pretend she was one of them. She could do this. It wasn't just about her anymore. The life of her child depended on her success.

As she made her approach, the two guards, both men with spears and shields, turned her way. She didn't recognize them. But there were so many soldiers in the Academy, she wasn't sure if they would recognize her.

"Speak your business." His garbled words were the language of Seaburn. Over her several months incarcerated, she'd come to learn it, not fluently, but enough to know the gift of what other soldiers and Seaburn natives spoke of.

"Late patrol." She spoke in the language of the tribes, hoping that wouldn't give her away.

The other man inclined a brow, but didn't speak. Her lack of knowledge of Seaburn's language must be unusual for fully trained soldiers.

"No one spoke of this," the first continued. He stepped forward.

"It was only decided a short time ago." She swallowed her anxiety. Sweat trickled down her temples. "With the riots, General Vargas wants more patrols around the clock."

"Typical," the other snapped. "No one informs us of anything."

The first narrowed his dark eyes. Shadows clouded his face beneath a gold helmet. Maybe this hadn't been the right approach. Maybe the front gates of the Palace would have been simpler.

"I'll check with the General." The first stepped around her.

Her heart leapt. No. No. No.

"There isn't a need." She spun, reaching for his arm.

He froze and glanced over his shoulder. Damn. That was the wrong thing to say. "Seize her," he snapped.

The second stepped forward and grabbed her biceps.

Instinct took over. Breen drove her elbow into his gut. He buckled. She leapt from his grip, ripping her sword from its sheath. The first spun, pointing the tip of his spear in her direction.

She hadn't faced off against someone wielding a spear in ages. What had she learned? They had range. But would be slow with a shield and armor. She could use speed to her advantage once again.

He thrust the spear at her stomach. Hot fear flashed through her chest, and widened her eyes. She turned from its path and grabbed the shaft of the spear.

She yanked forward.

He fell, his momentum too great. Foolish. Her fist collided with his face. Blood exploded from his nose. She spun and slammed her elbow into the back of his skull. He fell to the sand unconscious.

The second let out a battle cry as he lunged. *Damn.* Too loud. The guards on the wall would hear. They'd come to check on them. No. This wasn't how it was supposed to go.

Breen jumped back from the spear's long reach. The man narrowed his eyes at her and growled.

"There is no escaping!" He thrust his spear toward her.

She leapt from its path. He was wrong. She would prove it to him.

Breen flipped her blade to her other hand and swiped at the shaft of his spear as it flew passed her.

He drew it back too quickly, as if sensing her intent.

Shouts sounded on the walls, breaking the quiet of the Academy grounds.

No.

Heavy footsteps raced along the top of the sandstone walls, back to the stairs carved from it several yards away.

She had to go *now*.

Breen drove her sword at the man. He blocked with his shield, sending her sword astray. Her heart leapt. She couldn't lose. Not this time. She swung again. He stabbed her sword with his spear.

The force behind the blow sent her sword flying. She was defenseless. It was all over. "Give up," he growled.

She slowly shook her head.

Footsteps pounded the stairs nearby. She backed up for the Academy. There was nowhere to run. Nowhere to hide. Nowhere to go.

Her heart sunk. She spun to run, somewhere. Anywhere.

Four soldiers surrounded her on all sides. Four spears pointed at the baby forming in her belly. She froze. She couldn't let them harm her. She couldn't help them harm her child.

Her limbs went limp. She dropped her fighting stance.

It was over.

THIRTEEN

The door to the cell crashed open. Two soldiers dumped her inside, none too gently. Her breath flew from her lungs, and she rolled onto her back. The wooden slats slammed in her face.

She stared in wide-eyed horror at the prison. No. Not again. It had been so long since she'd seen this place. Though she still had nightmares about it, it had been *over*. It had been done. And now she was back.

Hay and dirt clung to her skin. Fear wormed inside her belly, souring her insides. How could she have let this happen? Why hadn't she fought harder? Longer? She could have died trying. But that would have meant the death of the beautiful child growing inside her.

Tears burned the back of her eyes. She squeezed them shut. She would not cry. She would *not*. This wasn't over. It couldn't be.

Breen opened her eyes to the dark walls of the hell she'd spent weeks inside. Its rank stench was all too familiar. And now she didn't even have Drakkone to save her. He probably hated her now. *She* hated herself. For allowing this to happen, for not being better, for not throwing herself from Seaburn's cliffs sooner.

She slammed her foot into the door. It rattled as the burn of anger filled her chest and smothered her breath. She kicked again. Not to escape. Not to break the door, but because her frustration was too great. She wanted to hurt someone. Anyone. She wanted them all to pay—every Seaburn citizen that let this happen. Every noble who preferred the enslavement of her race over volunteering to fight for their own country. She wanted to kill them all.

Her fists shook, and hot tears poured down her cheeks.

No matter how much she willed it, nothing would change. Not from in here. How had she been so stupid? Why did she try and flee at such a moment? How foolish. She should have waited. Once she was a Sergeant, or Lieutenant, or whatever trivial role Vargas gave her, she could have used it to escape.

She was sure of it.

Her breath hissed from her throat in a sigh. She leaned against the cool wood. It soothed the warmth seeping from her skin.

But nothing could calm the rage boiling and rolling in waves through her stomach.

Breen buried her face in her hands, running her fingers back into her braids. She squeezed. She would die here. Her child would die here. How was any of this fair? How could any of them live with themselves?

The tears continued to burn, slipping down her throat.

Silence descended on the dungeon.

Were any of her brethren left? Were any of them still alive? Though she'd seen several wandering the halls and cafeteria, their expressions had all been slack. Their eyes vacant. They were broken. Gone. Never to return.

Her heart sank.

Would she be next? Would she join their ranks?

Fear clawed at her heart and pulled the breath from her lungs. She was stuck here. They'd drown her again and again. They'd starve her. Leave her weak and beaten and alone until she could no longer take it.

They'd force her to recite their mantra. Though the words were forever burned in her memory, she couldn't say them. Not again. But was the lie worth it? Maybe she could say it. Let them think she'd been broken for her baby's sake.

Or could anyone fall for that a second time?

Goose bumps rolled across her skin.

The crash of the dungeon's torture chamber door, echoed off the carved stone walls. Her heart raced. As much as she wanted to stand, peer through the bars and see whom they brought out, she couldn't. It could be Lukerin. But she wouldn't let them pick her next. She couldn't. Not yet.

The cell next to her opened and closed with a slam.

Her breaths came in quick gasps. Her fingers trembled. Footsteps slowly stepped across the stone. Closer. Closer.

They stopped.

A masked man stared through the bars at her, his eyes black like coal. Her heart sank. She could never forget those eyes. The ones that racked her flesh and stole her innocence.

The lock clicked and her door opened.

"Welcome back." His deep voice rumbled like storm clouds. He stepped inside. She scurried across the floor to the back of her cage.

"You can't do this to me," she spat. "Not again."

He chuckled. "And why is that?"

Her teeth clacked together. Because it wasn't right. It wasn't just. It wasn't human. "You can't do this to me." Her voice hardly broke the quiet.

The corners of his eyes wrinkled beneath the mask. If she could see his mouth, she was sure he'd be smiling.

He was *happy* she'd returned. He was *happy* she'd come back to suffer.

He grabbed her braids. Her scalp stung, and she gasped.

Breen slapped his hands, digging her heels in as he attempted to pull her from the cage. She was strong now. She was nourished, and filled with energy.

She had to fight.

He pulled her from the cage. She didn't pull against him this time.

Instead she leapt, grabbing his masked face and pushing her fingers into his eyes.

His scream ripped through the dungeon, echoing on and on in an endless loop.

He grabbed her shoulders.

She pushed harder, something hot and wet squishing beneath her thumbs. "You won't do this to me again!" she roared, fuelled by the protective fire working through her veins since her pregnancy began.

He pulled her from his face and threw her to the ground.

Air burst from her lungs. Cool stone burned her bare arms. She rolled to her feet. Two soldiers, both masked men, rushed from the torture chamber.

The masked man's howls didn't cease. He pressed his palms to his eyes, blood dripping over the leather hiding his identity.

She smiled.

Finally, she'd done it. He may not be dead, but she'd *won*.

And he deserved the pain. He deserved much worse.

But at least she'd finally got him.

More soldiers came racing down the corridor. They threw her back inside her prison and locked the door.

Breen rose to her feet and wrapped her fingers around the cold bars. She watched every minute of the man's agony, every second of his cries. She watched until they dragged him down the hall and out of sight. When he was gone, she smiled and listened until his whimpers disappeared.

She's done it. She'd won.

* * *

THEY CAME for her the next day in pairs. The door flew open, waking her from deep slumber. Her eyes flashed open, and she slipped to the back of her cage before they had even stepped inside.

They reached for her, she kicked out. One fell back, while the other lunged, using all of his weight to secure her to the floor.

"Get in here!" he barked.

Two more guards came inside. They carried her by her wrists and ankles while she thrashed and shook, fire lending her strength.

But it wasn't enough.

The darkness of the torture chamber embraced her. Dim torch-light cast eerie shadows on the walls. Her heart rammed in her chest. She thrashed harder.

No. Not again.

Something heavy collided with her skull.

Black dots danced across her vision. She tried to blink them back, but they pushed forward to douse the only light she could see.

ICE WATER RETURNED her to life. She gasped for air, sitting upward. She must have passed out. She was already secured to the chair. Thick leather straps held her wrists and ankles to the worn wood. A new leather strap held her neck to the back of the chair. So much for pulling-hair-man.

"I will obey."

A man narrowed his eyes behind a worn leather mask. He held the bucket that had woken her. A second soldier passed him another. A third threw a cloth over her face.

This again.

Her jaw hardened. She steeled herself. She could do this. She had to. Breen could make them believe she'd been broken. She just had to endure this a little longer.

She took a deep breath.

Cold burned her face through the cloth. It poured and poured over her cheeks, and down her neck as her lungs ached. She needed to breathe, but breathing meant drowning.

She kept her teeth clamped shut, her eyes squeezing tightly. She could do this. Her lungs burned and her chest tightened. Damn.

She gasped.

Water slid down her throat. She choked, yanking on her restraints and thrashing for freedom. She remained immobile.

How had she let this happen again?

Breen inhaled, her lungs burning as she sought air.

Ice water continued to assault her face and lungs until her lungs were full and black danced at the corners of her vision. Her fingers dug into the arms of her chair like claws. Her entire body tensed.

She was going to die down here.

She was going to die never having had her child, never having seen it grow and learn. Her heart clenched.

The water stopped. The soggy cloth peeled from her face and the strap at her neck loosened. She buckled forward, vomiting water from her lungs.

Her whole body heaved and quivered. Her teeth chattered and her eyelids fluttered with thick drops of water holding them shut.

Darkness continued to push in around her. Nausea rolled through her stomach. This wasn't good for her baby. This wasn't good for *her*. Her sanity had been tested once, and she wasn't sure she could hold onto it again. Not with the drowning. Not with the cloth smothering her face and men dragging her from sleep every few hours.

Her lips quivered.

The men untied her straps, hoisting her by her armpits to her feet. Her legs shook beneath her, but she could still support herself. Surprisingly.

She half walked, half dragged her feet back to her prison. They dumped her inside. She crawled to the back wall, curling up in the hay and grime. How had things gone so wrong?

Breen took a deep breath and slid onto her side. Cold stone made her shiver harder. She embraced herself, stealing what little warmth she could.

* * *

"Breen?" someone whispered.

Darkness smothered her vision. Thick braids lay across her eyes. She groaned and curled her legs in closer to her torso. She shivered against the cool dungeon air.

"Breen?" the voice continued.

So it hadn't just been in her dreams.

Breen brushed the thick hair from her face and blinked up at the barred window to the outside world. Someone stood silhouetted against it, though in the dark it was hard to tell who.

She slowly eased up onto her side, bracing herself with her hands as she took long, deep breaths.

"Are you all right?"

Drakkone.

Her heart clenched, and her eyes stung. She bit the inside of her cheek.

"No." Her voice was hardly a whisper.

He sighed, leaning his head against the bars. "You tried to escape again, didn't you?"

She glanced up, trying with every ounce of her being to hold back the tears pushing to the surface. She'd never been this weak. She'd never cried in front of any man but her father. Yet she wished the door between them would disappear so she could throw herself into his arms.

"Yes." Shivers shook her shoulders.

"You shouldn't have."

Her teeth clicked shut. "I know." But she didn't need him to tell her that.

"Why did you do it?" He paused, his fingers tightening on the bars. "I heard you're in Fourth Rank. There's a rumor Vargas wants a new apprentice, and he asked you."

Her lips twisted in a humorless smile. "He did."

"Then *why*, Breen?" His breath passed his lips in an irritated hiss.

Breen couldn't look at him, couldn't meet his gaze. How could she tell him he was going to be a father? How could she tell him she'd done it for her child, not for herself? Would he understand why she'd done it? She hugged herself, pressing her fingers into her biceps.

"I'm pregnant."

He gasped.

It was the only sound in the quiet dungeon. A long moment of silence stretched. She shouldn't have said it. Shouldn't have told him. It was the wrong thing to do. The wrong thing to say.

"How is that possible?"

"The doctor was wrong." She shrugged.

His lips parted to speak, then clamped shut again. Torchlight lit his face as he looked away down the hall. His brows furrowed. It was clear his mind worked to figure this out. She'd been pronounced barren. He'd told her he was as well. Maybe he'd finally understand her anger, her outbursts, and her confusion.

His brows lifted and realization bloomed on his face.

"That's why you refused to see me." His lips pressed in a thin line.

Breen nodded.

He paused again. "We're getting out of here together. Tonight."

She shot to her feet. Her limbs wavered, but she stayed aloft. Her fingers wrapped around the cool metal bars, brushing his warm fingers.

"You mean it?" He nodded. Tears spilled down her cheeks, hot and filled with relief. She leaned her forehead against his fingers. "Thank you."

"It'll be all right, Breen." His fingers wrapped hers, as much as they could through the bars.

Emotion burned her throat and stopped her from speaking. The intense relief, and the uncertainty for tomorrow welled in her chest, bubbling into her throat. But they were going to get away. She was going to be free. And her baby was going to live.

Her heart clenched.

Her baby was going to *live*.

FOURTEEN

rakkone's plan was simple. During the cell shift change, she'd pretend to be sick—which wasn't far from the truth. Nausea rolled through her stomach and rose inside her throat. She clamped her lips shut. She'd pretend to be ill and Drakkone would take her to the infirmary on his way out at the end of his shift.

He promised her they'd get away. He promised her they'd be safe. The hardest part would be getting her out of the Academy. Then they could flee Seaburn.

Then she would be free.

Her heart raced, stirred by anticipation.

"It's getting late, isn't it?" Drakkone's deep voice signalled her to initiate phase one of their plan.

Breen moaned, gripping her stomach and doubling over on the floor. The two guards shuffled somewhere outside, but not toward her.

She groaned louder, edging her voice with as much pain as she could. Boots shuffled nearby.

Drakkone peeked through the bars. "I think this one is sick."

"Probably just from hunger," another soldier said. His armor rustled.

Breen groaned again.

"It's the end of my shift. I'll take her to the infirmary on my way out."

Breen smiled.

"Whatever." The other guard shuffled away.

Her breath fled her lungs in a relieved sigh.

The click of her door's lock slid free. The wooden slats creaked as the door opened. She still had a part to play in case anyone saw her. Drakkone wrapped his hand around her arm and towed her to her feet. He did so as gently as possible, unable to hide his smile as she glanced up at him.

Holding her stomach with one hand, and hanging her head, she stepped from her small prison, Drakkone leading the way.

He called a goodbye to his comrade before they shuffled up the hall, Drakkone half supporting her until they reached the stairwell. Her body relaxed and she stood tall.

"We're not clear yet," he said.

"It's still good to be out of there." She flexed her fingers.

Drakkone nodded his agreement and led the way up to the main floor of the Academy. The rest of his plan banked a lot on luck. They needed to get to the infirmary where he'd stashed some clothes and supplies, without being stopped or noticed by any patrolling soldiers.

This late at night, they shouldn't raise much suspicion, or encounter anyone on their path. Not until the actual escape began at least.

Smooth stone walls rose on either side of them. Tapestries hung from the walls, and stone arches led to the main corridor. They passed by carefully, glancing between joining halls and the path ahead.

The door of the infirmary appeared not long after. Drakkone peeked inside first, before slipping within. He gave the all clear and motioned her after him. Breen followed.

Only moonlight lit the room. The doctor was long gone for the night.

Drakkone pulled a rucksack from beneath one of the cots. They couldn't bring much with them, not if they wanted it to appear like any normal day. Their plan banked on that. He handed her a small bag of her own.

She peered inside the leather. Fresh clothes, a leather soldier uniform and boots. She smiled. Finally, she'd be able to get out of these foul smelling rags.

Breen stepped into the moonlight next to the washing basin, stripping the worn leathers from her flesh and quickly washing some of the dirt from her skin.

Drakkone's gasp made her freeze. She glanced over her shoulder.

He stared at her with a half open mouth.

A grin spread across her face before she could help it. "You've seen me nude before." She chuckled.

His lips clamped shut fighting a grin as he spun away.

Breen rolled her eyes and replaced her clothes with the fresh ones, slipping on her boots. Her leather vest was tight to her stomach, unlike the outfit had been in the past. She tightened her belts below her bump and joined Drakkone.

He handed her a sheath.

She grabbed it and tied it to her belt. A weapon. This is what she needed. Now she'd be able to defend herself against any foe that may present itself.

She was getting out of here tonight, or she was going down fighting. She'd not be taken back to the dungeons again.

Once Drakkone attached the small sack to the belts wrapping his hips, he motioned for her to follow. It was time. The next part of the plan could get them killed. But it'd be worth it if, no, *when*, it worked.

Drakkone led the way through the hall lined with arches. They passed through one and into the main corridor, where they fled through the front entrance. The stone pillars outside cast long shadows on the front of the Academy.

Her stomach turned. She would *not* miss this place. Not one bit.

Two guards stood at the front gates. Drakkone and Breen headed for the side door.

Only one guard would remain at the back gate. If need be, they'd take him down. Drakkone was certain the guards at the Palace entrance wouldn't know them. The Emperor kept his own personal guard, ones who lived inside the Palace and would be unfamiliar with Breen's constantly swinging military career and Drakkone's fairly insignificant one.

"Just act natural, and let me do the talking." Drakkone shot her a look.

"You're the boss." She shrugged, though the anxiety was eating away at her stomach.

Breen wanted her freedom more than she wanted to exercise her dominance in this messed up situation.

They trudged across the sand. It crunched beneath her boots. She couldn't help but glance at the surrounding walls. Soldiers did their usual rounds. None were close enough to see who they were. If they could get past the soldier on the other side of the door, Drakkone had said it would be smooth sailing from there.

Whatever that meant.

They paused before the door. Drakkone wrapped his knuckles on the thick wood. So this is why it had been strange she'd come barging through the door. She was supposed to knock.

The door creaked open, revealing a yawning palace guard in gold armor.

"Yes?"

"We'd like to slip through to use the… uh… facilities." Drakkone's brows waggled suggestively.

Breen shot him a wide-eyed glance. What on earth was he doing? They'd never discussed this part. Her lips thinned, but she didn't say anything. She had promised to trust him, and she was determined to do so.

"The facilities, huh?" A smirk replaced the bored stare of the soldier.

"We won't be long."

"Have fun." He winked and stepped out of the doorway.

Drakkone returned his grin and led the way through, taking Breen's hand and pulling her through the archway.

Once they'd fled out of earshot and stepped through the topiary garden, she squeezed Drakkone's warm fingers, pulling him to a stop.

"The *facilities?*" she hissed.

Drakkone chuckled, keeping his normal timber low. "Soldiers often need a break from the Academy grounds and come over to the palace gardens and hot springs for a dalliance."

Her jaw dropped. "What?"

His grin only grew. "It was the only way to get by without much suspicion."

She shook her head. "Unbelievable."

Drakkone squeezed her fingers and released her hand. He nodded in the direction of the main gate, out of sight of the door they'd just passed through. "We should get going. I hope you've learned your soldier routine well."

She nodded. She'd spent enough time among Seaburn's military to mimic them. "Let's go."

He led the way through thick foliage, tall palm trees, and flowerbeds until their boots hit the main path—smooth cobblestone lined with large rocks.

The main path ended at the Palace's main entrance on one side, and the gates to the tall sandstone walls on the other. Drakkone led them toward the latter.

Cold sweat beaded on her forehead and dripped down her temple. If they didn't get this right, if they didn't get through these doors, they'd be in for one hell of a fight.

One for their lives.

Drakkone put his shoulders back and straightened, picking his feet up a bit as he marched toward the gate. Breen stayed at his side, straightening her spine and mimicking his gait.

Smooth stone tapped beneath the thick soles of their leather boots. She had hoped the shadows would disguise them against the leering gazes of the men guarding the main entrance, but as they crested the dip of the hill, torches lined the main gate. The warm light of flames bathed the two guards, clad in thick metal armour from head to toe. They wielded large rounded shields with Seaburn's crest engraved upon them, and a spear in their opposite hand.

They stood stiff, tall and at attention. They watched their approach through narrowed eyes.

Damn. Maybe it wouldn't be so easy after all.

When at last they reached the gates, Drakkone halted and nodded to the military men. Breen stopped several paces behind him, allowing him to take the lead as requested.

"State your business," the man to the left of the gate said.

"Patrol." Drakkone left it at that.

Breen resisted glancing at Drakkone, and the guards. Instead she stared straight ahead, like the city patrolmen did as they exited the Academy for their daily routes.

"Late patrol doesn't leave through these gates."

Cool air licked her arms, pulling goose bumps to her flesh. Breen bit the inside of her cheek in an attempt to rein in her emotions and keep her expression clear of anything incriminating.

They were supposed to be here. This was normal.

"There was an issue with the gates. Sand crud stuck in the hinges again." Drakkone's tone shifted from formal to cordial. Again, Breen resisted glancing at her partner.

The second man scoffed and lowered his shield slightly. "We have the same problem every few weeks. What a pain."

"A pain is putting it mildly." Drakkone groaned dramatically.

The second man chuckled and motioned up to the men atop the wall. One nodded and together they heaved upon the mechanism holding the doors in place.

The door creaked as they shifted open.

"Don't be late." The man winked.

"We won't." Drakkone nodded and exchanged an amused smile with the man before continuing through the parted gates.

They passed through, shadows descending upon their shoulders from the stone overhang. Her fists clenched at her sides until they passed, and torchlight warmed her back.

Drakkone was much better at playing the unsuspecting escapee than she had expected. He led the way down the main road until they disappeared west down an adjoining path.

Once they were out of sight of the palace guards, Breen breathed a great sigh of relief. Her shoulders sagged and a laugh bubbled from her chest.

"You did it," she said.

Drakkone smiled stiffly. "I told you I'd get you out of there."

He had. And he did. But at great cost to himself she was sure. When they finally realized she was gone, they'd know it had been him. There wouldn't be a doubt about it. He'd never be able to return to Seaburn, to his home, to the family he spoke so rarely of.

Her stomach rolled. He'd never talked much about his family, other than they were a long line of military men and women. How much would he miss Seaburn? Would he resent her for taking him from his home? She hadn't realized until now how much she asked of him. Whatever family he had, he'd just left behind. His life, his job, his Emperor—he'd left it all behind for her and their child.

Her cheeks warmed. Never before had someone sacrificed so much for her.

"Are you all right, Breen?" His brows furrowed, and concern lit his gaze.

Breen nodded. Her eyes were leaking. She wiped tears from her cheeks with the back of her hand and cleared her throat. "Yes. I'm fine."

After a long moment of assessing her face, he nodded and stared ahead.

"We still have a bit of a journey ahead of us," he said. "Seaburn is no small place. It'll take a few hours on foot to reach the outskirts."

"As long as we're long gone by morning."

"We will be." Drakkone took her hand, squeezing her fingers before releasing them. She couldn't help the smile pulling at her lips.

She'd made the right choice after all.

* * *

HER FEET, back, and thighs ached by the time the tall homes of Seaburn ended. Shorter clay and wood homes occupied the edge of town, untamed tall grass in their front yards. Large unoccupied lots sat between each, the distance slowly increasing between each one.

The sky had begun to lighten. Pre-dawn pale blue crested the horizon. She imagined the dawn would be beautiful from the Academy roof, where the entire city fell away to ocean stretching for miles.

Breen sighed and wrung her hands together. Nerves soured her stomach. She'd grown tired on the long journey, but refused to stop until they'd put some distance between them and the Academy—no matter how many times Drakkone thought they should stop for rest.

"The stables should be just a few more yards." Drakkone glanced at her from the corner of his eye. Worry wrinkled his forehead.

She only nodded between ragged breaths. Haze clouded her mind. Her feet stung with blisters in boots a size too small. The heel dug in every step or two, scraping her skin raw. She'd need to clean them up soon, but couldn't bear to stop.

Not yet.

Drakkone sighed and glanced forward again.

Foul manure drifted on the breeze. She wrinkled her nose. The stables were near indeed. It had been some time since she'd lived close to animals. Though she missed the freedom of embracing the wild beasts and riding across the open sand, she *didn't* miss the smell.

"There it is." Drakkone pointed between two small homes with hay for roofs. Between the lots, across the unpacked dirt, large stables sat atop the open sand. Four horses grazed lazily at their bales of hay, kicking their feet in the dirt and shaking their long hair to rid them of flies.

Breen smiled, the sight of such beautiful beasts somehow reassuring her she would be okay.

"I only have enough money saved for one. But it should be able to get us a fair distance by noon." Drakkone steered from the uneven cobblestone path riddled with dirt and grass growing between the stones.

She followed. Tall stalks brushed her fingers until they emerged on a packed dirt path.

Though she hadn't been able to see a home beyond the barn, once they rounded the wooden stables, a small, but cozy home sat a dozen feet from it, candlelight already lit in the open windows.

"They're up early," Breen remarked.

"Most traders are." Drakkone stopped by the barn doors, which stood ajar.

Inside the hay strewn wood floor was lit by torchlight. Bales stood stacked against the one wall she could see, while stalls lined the rest. Only two stalls were occupied by horses, while the other six remained empty. Racking hay from the bales was a tall man with gray hair, and black skin. He wiped sweat from his forehead and paused, stabbing the large pitchfork into the floor.

"Excuse me, sir." Drakkone stepped inside.

The man jumped and stepped back toward the pens.

Once he got a look at Drakkone, he took a breath and dipped his beige hat in greeting. "Morning." His tone was raspy, as if unused.

"I'm looking to buy a horse."

"Really?" The man glanced back at the stalls. "Not used to getting that kind of request here. Usually I cart folks between towns."

Her heart leapt. That could work just as well. If he could take them now, they'd be long gone before Seaburn soldiers caught up to them. Then again, she couldn't be sure how fast this cart driver would ride. It could be evening by the time they reached another village.

"Really." Drakkone nodded. "Your fastest, preferably. We have a long journey."

The man's gaze slid from Drakkone, to Breen, as if realizing for the first time he wasn't alone. He twisted his thick grey moustache and leaned his pitchfork against the barn wall before stepping outside. "What's your offer?"

Breen knew nothing about their currency, how much Drakkone had of it, or what a fast horse would be worth. In her tribe, they simply had to tame their own wild horse if they wanted one. Otherwise they'd be stuck on foot or by cart if someone chose to bring them along on their travels.

"Thirty gold searken." Drakkone withdrew a burgundy coin purse from the satchel at his hip. He displayed the gold coins through the mouth of the open pouch.

The man's eyes flew wide. "You've never bought a horse before have you, boy?"

Drakkone paused, his eyes widening slightly. "No."

The old man laughed and grinned. "You're lucky I'm an honest man. My fastest stallion will get you to Drunfal before sunset. Fifteen gold will do. I'll throw in some canteens for your travel."

Mischief flashed in the man's dark gaze. He had to know they were on the run, yet he gave them a bargain and would send them away with more supplies. Her heart swelled. She had yet to experience kindness outside of Drakkone in this city.

"Thank you," she murmured.

The man simply nodded. "Only a fair trade."

She smiled.

Drakkone stepped back as the man shuffled from the barn and around to the pen beside the stables. Long wooden logs created a fence, twine holding the pieces together. He unlocked the gate and whistled.

Each of the four horses stopped their grazing and pricked their ears.

"Dullahan, come here boy." The man motioned, and a tall black stallion trotted from between two white snouted mares. His tail flicked as he halted before his master, dipping his head in greeting. "This is Dullahan. He's a good boy, and should fair you well."

The man laced a cord around the horse's neck and led him back to the barn, where Drakkone aided him in saddling the stallion before he fetched two canteens and filled them from a well next to the stables. He hooked them to the back of the leather saddle before leading the horse back into the yard.

He passed the reins to Breen before stepping back. Drakkone produced fifteen coins, placing them in the man's gloved hands before returning his coin purse to his satchel. Once he was set, he bent to help Breen into the saddle.

She rolled her eyes and motioned him aside. Breen gripped the leather and stirrups, swinging herself up into the seat in a single graceful movement. She'd ridden horses all of her life, and even tamed a few wild ones. An already tame one wasn't going to give her trouble.

The man chuckled as Drakkone swung up behind her, slipping his feet into the stirrups while she sat in front of them, the saddle digging into her lower abdomen. She held her belly and glanced down at the bump in her shirt.

"I wish you both the best of luck."

Breen glanced at the man and smiled. "Thank you, truly."

He nodded and waved them off, returning to his barn.

Drakkone took the reins and wiggled into what she hoped was a more comfortable position than her own. Once they were ready, she laced her fingers through the long black hair of the horse, and patted his thick neck with her free hand.

"Let's go," Drakkone said.

Breen nodded and glanced back at him, smiling over her shoulder.

He smiled too, though there was a grimness to his gaze. He was leaving all he'd ever known behind. For her.

Breen placed her hand on his, which lay on her upper thigh, reins in hand.

He met her gaze. "Ready?" Uncertainty clouded his dark eyes.

"Yes."

Drakkone snapped the reins, and Dullahan trotted forward, his hooves crunching on the packed earth.

As they rode out onto the main road leading straight out of Seaburn, the sun crested the horizon, casting long shadows along the ground, and brilliant orange and pink atop distant mountains.

They'd done it. Drakkone had done it. She was free. At last.

FIFTEEN

$\mathcal{H}$er thighs ached and her stomach rolled with nausea the further they rode. Sand dunes spread out for miles over the barren wasteland. Crops of gnarled bushes and dying trees spotted the land every few miles.

No matter how much it hurt to keep going, they couldn't stop. Even as the sun rose high in the sky and they stopped to rest, her heart raced. She glanced into every shadow, for fear Seaburn soldiers would leap out at her.

By morning they were on the move again, having given rest to their steed and her weary limbs. Weeks passed through open desert, village ruins, and small outcropping towns. They passed Sarton, a small village outside Seaburn borders, and then they embraced the desert once again, flying as far west as fast as they could.

As the sun lowered on the horizon, the jungle rose to the south, a dark mass across the sand.

Drakkone steered Dullahan towards it. Breen shifted to glance back at him. Though the jungle would provide much needed shelter from the heat, the predators prowling the forest floor would provide a new danger on their long journey.

"Are you sure the jungle is best?" Breen arched a brow. Her back ached from the constant riding. Her thighs had gone numb and a headache welled behind her eyes.

Drakkone nodded. "It'll be easier to hide inside."

"What about the jungle cats?" Again, Breen shifted. It was impossible to get comfortable atop horseback.

"If we light a fire, they'll stay away." Drakkone met her gaze as his fingers brushed her elbow.

She wasn't so sure. Though she'd only been in the jungle during the day, she'd heard tales of night crawlers in the trees. Her stomach twisted. A groan escaped her lips.

"Are you all right?" His brows furrowed.

Breen nodded stiffly. She wasn't about to lay her burdens on him.

"Sore?" He raised a brow. She froze. How did he know? She didn't know many men familiar with pregnancy. "Is it your back?" His warm fingers brushed her bare spine where her shirt rode up.

"Maybe." She flushed as he handed her the reins and gripped her hips, rubbing his thumbs up her lower back. Breen gasped, unable to hold back her relief.

His thumbs kneaded her skin, just outside of her spine, sending pleasant waves through her aching back. He moved from her lower back to her shoulder blades, his hands slipping up her shirt.

"How are you so good at this?" she moaned.

Drakkone smiled as she arched against him. "My mother was pregnant with my younger sister when I was ten. She didn't complain, but my father rubbed her back and feet constantly."

Breen quirked a brow. He'd hardly ever mentioned his family before. She hadn't known he had a sister. "What a good man."

He chuckled. "Yes, he is."

"Are you much like him?"

His thumbs worked the knots from her back, continuing until she leaned back against him. His hot breath brushed her ear. "We're both military men who love our country and despise our Emperor." He paused. "He liked his job, but was never so good at following the rules."

"Not like you at all," she teased.

Drakkone's chest shook with his laugh. "Maybe we are alike after all."

"You said he *liked* his job. Has he retired?"

"Yes, he was injured in battle, broke his leg. He never fully recovered."

"That must have been hard on your family." Her heart clenched. It must have been difficult to get by after his father left the military. How did they support themselves?

Drakkone shrugged. "It was, but at the time I advanced to Third Rank and was receiving enough pay to feed the family most weeks."

"So you took on the burden of your entire family?" Breen laid her hand on his thigh. She couldn't imagine what that was like. She'd always had her family and her tribe to support her.

He hesitated. "I suppose."

A thought occurred to her. Her brows cinched as she turned in her seat to face him. "Is that why you were so hesitant to free me? You had your whole family depending on you?" If they still depended on him, she'd taken him away from them. How would they survive without him?

Drakkone stiffened. His hands stopped kneading her back. She was right. He'd left his entire family to save her and their child. Tears burned the back of her eyes.

"They'll be all right, Bree. My sister will join First Rank in a few years, and my father will sell crops. He's been working on his field since his retirement." He smiled in an attempt to reassure her.

She shook her head. "You should have told me." Her heart swelled with something she'd never experienced before. Heat spread through her face, to her chest and limbs. Was this love, or simple appreciation?

"I should have."

Breen leaned back, turning her head as much as possible. She pressed her lips to his. Drakkone smiled as he kissed her back. He wrapped an arm around her waist before kissing her forehead and embracing her.

Thank you.

She didn't say it, but she had a feeling he knew.

As the sun dipped below the horizon, leaving a pale blue glow over the desert, they arrived at the jungle.

Vines hung from tall, thick trees. The forest sprouted from the sand as if by magic, something she never quite understood.

Dullahan slowed at the forests edge, his hooves crunching against thick ferns and twigs. Drakkone swung from the horse's back, stretching his limbs before returning to help her down.

Breen had already swung to the ground. Though her back continued to ache, she was grateful to be off the horse. Her legs shook beneath her, threatening to give way. The feeling in her thighs had not yet returned.

"How far in will we go?" Breen stretched as much as she could with the weight growing in her belly.

"Not far." Drakkone took the reins and led the way inside the thick brush.

He parted the wide leaves until they arrived at a small clearing. Though vines covered most of the ground, tall grass rose at the center. At least the foliage would be much more comfortable to sleep on than the shifting sand.

"This should do fine for the night." Drakkone glanced up as if asking her approval.

She agreed.

While Drakkone tied Dullahan to a nearby tree and went about gathering firewood, Breen yanked tall grass from the center of the clearing until she had created a large enough circle to house a small fire. Once she was finished, she collected stones, creating a ring around the bare soil.

By the time flames sparked over the pile of wood Drakkone had gathered, night had fallen. Perfect timing.

Heat radiated from the small fire, casting warm light over the surrounding foliage. Shadows flickered across wide leaves and thick vines, creating monsters in the darkness licking at the edges of their camp.

Drakkone laid out two bedrolls. As he had the night before, he kept them apart from each other, making sure she knew he expected nothing of her.

Breen smiled. It still seemed impossible that Seaburn had produced such a fine man. As Drakkone sat back on one, he produced two canteens and some dried meat from his rucksack.

"Tomorrow I'll see what I can hunt." His brows furrowed.

They hadn't much rations. Enough to get from Sarton to the next village if they were lucky. Catching wild game would improve their odds tenfold.

"We'll catch something." Breen glanced between her bedroll and his.

"We?" He raised a brow.

"Yes, *we*." Breen narrowed her eyes as she sat beside him.

Drakkone said nothing of it, but a smile lit his face nonetheless. "Are you sure you should hunt in your… condition?"

Breen rolled her eyes. "Tribe women have done much more than hunt during their pregnancies."

"Like what?" Drakkone passed her a strip of meat and a canteen.

She accepted both, taking a deep gulp of water before answering. "We fight until the day the baby is born. We wrestle, hunt, forage, tame horses, teach lessons." She paused. "And even mate." Her cheeks warmed. Breen avoided his gaze as she tore off a slice of meat. She could no longer remember what type they'd purchased. Though the salt was overpowering, at least it was food.

"Is that so?" His voice grew teasing.

"Yes." Breen cleared her throat as she devoured the rest of her meal. She swallowed another great gulp of water before sighing. Not long ago she'd been forced to starve. She'd never take food for granted again, no matter how hard and chewy.

Drakkone ate in silence, trying unsuccessfully to tame his smile.

Breen crossed her legs beneath her and leaned towards the fire, splaying her fingers over it.

Something inside her belly shifted.

Breen jumped. What on earth was that?

"What is it?" Drakkone placed his canteen and meat aside.

Again, something shifted. She laid her hands on her belly, her brows furrowed. Again, a smaller shift this time. It pressed against her fingers. Was this her child?"

"Bree…" Drakkone scooted closer, his hands hesitating midair as if he didn't know where to check for injury.

"The baby." Her heart raced. "I think it's moving."

His eyes widened as he glanced down at her protruding stomach. Again, he hesitated. "May I…?"

Breen glanced up. She smiled. "Of course."

Drakkone laid his hands on her stomach, his fingers splayed across her shirt. His hands were warmer than the fire, sending a shiver up her spine. The night had chilled far more than she realized.

The baby shifted.

Drakkone gasped, his fingers nearly flying from her belly. Instead, he moved them around slowly, as if seeking another miracle. "Our child."

Her eyes burned and her heart swelled. She had no idea what this feeling was, but it moved through her until she leaned against him, resting her head in the crook of his shoulder. "Our child." She rested her hand beside his. Their fingers entwined as the baby kicked again.

"Our miracle." Drakkone kissed her forehead. Her heart fluttered.

Breen closed her eyes, letting his warmth wrap her in its embrace.

* * *

THE SUN PEEKED through the trees the next morning, brushing her cheeks in warm light. Breen shifted. Her whole body ached from their journey, but at least her head had cleared.

"Good morning."

Breen peered over her shoulder. Drakkone's arm wrapped her waist. He smiled, his head propped up in his hand.

She flushed. "Have you been awake long?"

"Not long."

A branch cracked nearby. Something shifted in the trees. Her heart raced as she leapt to her feet alongside Drakkone. The calm of morning was shattered as they ripped their swords from their sheaths.

Another branch snapped only a few feet away.

Could it be Seaburn soldiers? Had they been found already?

Cold fear laced every bone in her body. She couldn't go back.

Drakkone stepped through their small camp and into the trees. Thick antlers peeked through the dense foliage. The large head of an elk whipped in their direction. Its nostrils flared as it leapt away over a fallen log.

Her racing heart slowed. "An elk! It's just an elk!" She took a deep breath.

Her nerves were shot. Whatever peace she'd had with Drakkone the previous night was far off.

Drakkone's shoulders relaxed. "At least we've found dinner."

"Dinner?"

Drakkone turned, a wide grin on his face.

The hunt. "Right." Breen lowered her blade. With her blood pumping through her veins, adrenaline sent her mind racing. "Now is as good a time as any, I suppose."

Breen joined Drakkone as they made their way through the trees.

"Are you sure you should be hunting? I wouldn't want to startle you and be sliced in half." Drakkone flashed a sly smile.

Her eyes widened as she froze. "Excuse me?"

"When that branch snapped you nearly leapt from your skin."

He was teasing her at a time like this? Breen narrowed her eyes. "I did not."

"Are you sure?" He continued through the foliage.

Thick vines brushed her shoulders as she gathered her wits enough to follow. "Yes."

"Could have fooled me."

"How do you expect to catch anything while you prattle on?"

Drakkone chuckled. "That's fair."

He stepped over a fallen tree ripe with moss. Dew amassed along every leaf, sprinkling her shoulders and hair in drops of water as she brushed passed.

As they emerged in the next clearing, a wide oasis lay between the trees. Thick grass ringed its borders, as did several elk.

"There are so many," she whispered.

Drakkone paused at the edge of the clearing. "There are."

Breen stepped into the open space, her sword up and ready. Drakkone grabbed her arm. "What are you doing?"

"I'm going to catch one." Her brows furrowed. Obviously that was what she was doing.

"With your sword?" Drakkone's grin returned. He flashed his teeth.

"Yes." Her cheeks heated.

"I'd like to see that."

Breen bristled. "Well, you're about to!"

She spun from Drakkone and approached slowly through the brush. The elk had their backs turned. If she could get close enough, she might be able to injure one to keep it from running. Though she'd always been much better at taming horses, than catching game, she'd never done it without a spear. Maybe Drakkone had a point.

A branch snapped beneath her boot. Damn.

The elk rounded, their ears flicking up and their eyes wide. They raced for the trees. Breen spit a curse as she leapt after them, slicing at the hind legs of the closest.

Her blade sailed inches away from its flesh. *Damn.*

Breen gritted her teeth as her sword pulled her off balance. Her weight slid from under her and her heart leapt into her throat.

Drakkone grabbed her arm and yanked her into his arms.

Her heart hammered against her ribs as she looked up into his face. His sly smile teased along with the amused glint in his eyes.

"My weight is off because of... because of the pregnancy," she stammered her excuse.

"Of course."

"It's your fault." Her cheeks flushed with indignation. "You're the one who put this baby in me."

He chuckled. "You're right."

Breen froze. She was? "Of course I am."

Drakkone bent, pressing his lips against hers. He stole the breath from her lungs with even the smallest of kisses. "You're the most beautiful creature I've ever seen. Pregnant or not."

AFTER THEIR LARGE meal in the jungle, nothing could compare. They hadn't the means to salt the meat, or else their rations might have been enough. The days turned to weeks, and weeks into a month. Even as the distance grew, pricks of anxiety still rose on her skin every time a caravan passed on the road or a pack of soldiers slowed on the sand.

But with their soldier uniforms still tight on their shoulders, they'd appear to be one of them, even if their style of riding was a bit peculiar.

After over a month on the road, their meager rations bought in Sarton finally came to an end, just in time for another town to rise on the horizon.

Darkness lay heavy on the desert. Their horse slowed from a trot, its hooves clopping against the worn dirt road.

"Kelna," Drakkone said.

Though Breen wasn't familiar with Seaburn geography, Drakkone thankfully was. He'd plotted a course deep into the wasteland to keep them free of Seaburn soldiers. Despite his careful planning, Seaburn's presence could be felt in every town. Soldiers marched the roads, eyes darting to every passerby as if seeking another for imprisonment.

Her heart ached. Though fewer tribesmen were forced into duty this far from Seaburn, a few still leered as they passed.

Breen kept her eyes low. She couldn't believe her tribesmen capable of such hate, such servitude. She wrinkled her nose. Her thin cloak snapped against her thighs in the breeze. She kept her hood drawn over her face, just in case.

Drakkone urged their stallion into the village. Squat sandstone homes sat meters apart, pens for cattle, sheep and chickens beside most.

Kelna spread over the dirt and sand for miles, the largest town they'd seen since their departure. Though most of the roofs were made of straw, and the homes hardly decadent, a thriving market sat at the center of town, wooden carts and stalls lining the streets to trade for wheat, rice, produce and meat.

Her mouth watered as they eased passed a butcher's cart. His large knife *thunked* against the wooden boards of his stall as he sliced a fat chunk of red meat in half. Never before had she salivated at the sight of raw meat. But after a month of dried meat and rice, she could hardly bear to remain seated on their horse while real food passed her by.

"We'll get something to eat at the tavern."

Breen glanced back at Drakkone, who smiled down at her. He must have caught her gaze lingering. She flushed and smiled, thankful to have Drakkone on her side.

Breaking through the small crowd, Drakkone eased the stallion to a halt outside a wooden tavern, the only two-storey building in town. A small sign hung from the front, *Kelna Inn and Tavern*, a simple a name as any.

"We should stay here for the night and rest up," Drakkone continued. He slid from Dullahan's back and landed with a thump.

"Do we have the coin for that?" Breen took Drakkone's outstretched hands and slid the few feet to the ground. Her knees shook and her thighs continued to ache. She'd be grateful for a nice bed and supper, but they had few coins when they left Sarton, and she didn't want Drakkone to spend the remainder on luxuries they couldn't afford.

"We do." He released her hands and tied their horse's reins to a long wooden bar outside the tavern. Two mares kicked the ground beside them. The tavern must be a frequent stop for travellers.

"All right."

Drakkone led the way inside, past a worn, dark oak door, and inside the dim building. Straw covered the stone floors, and the pungent scent of ale laced the air, turning her stomach.

Breen wrinkled her nose, and followed Drakkone to the wooden bar beside a staircase leading to the second floor.

A few patrons twisted in their wooden booths to eye the newcomers, but Breen kept her hood drawn tight and her gaze set ahead.

While Drakkone garbled his Seaburn language to the bartender, Breen inspected the establishment for exits in case they needed to make a quick escape. Another door stood off the back of the long room, and several windows lined the wall of occupied booths. Evening light filtered in, the growing darkness dimming the open space.

Lanterns sat on every table, though only one group of patrons thought to light theirs.

"We have our room." Drakkone startled her from her reverie.

"Good." She nodded, catching her breath.

"They serve dinner for a few more hours. Once we're settled, I'll return for some." Drakkone motioned to the stairs at their back.

Her stomach rumbled. She could not wait for food. *Fresh* food. The baby kept her hungry at all times, and today would be no different. But at least there would be something good, something new to add to her diet.

Breen mounted the stairs to a landing before turning upward to the second floor. A window at the end of a long corridor filtered in enough light for her to see by.

"Room five," Drakkone said.

One. Two. Three. Four. *Five.*

At the far right-hand side of the hall, a bronze *5* was nailed to the wood.

Drakkone slid in to unlock the door before pushing it open.

Used to sleeping in a dorm full of other trainees, or a large tent owned by her parents, Breen had never shared a room with a man before, unless she counted the one-night dalliance in Drakkone's Seaburn chambers. Though they'd slept beside each other most of the time on their journey, her sleeps were restless and she often chose to sleep alone. One of them had to stay alert when morning came.

She stepped inside.

Each wall was wooden, as were the furnishings. A large bed occupied the far wall beside a shuttered window. Thick furs lay atop it, flat feather pillows at the head.

Her aching legs shook, threatening to give way.

Before taking anything else in, she collapsed in bed, soft wolf pelts tickling her bare arms and cheeks. Drakkone chuckled as she wrapped her arms around the grey fur and cuddled the softness. The baby shifted inside her, but then stilled, as if sensing it was time to rest.

"I never thought I'd see a bed again." She sighed. Her eyelids grew heavy, and her tense muscles relaxed.

"I'm glad you like it."

Breen peeked over her shoulder. Drakkone inspected the rest of the room. A small closet with an extra blanket, a dresser with nothing inside, a small table and chair against the far wall. Each piece of furniture could fall apart at any moment. But this bed was worth it. This fur was worth it.

She closed her eyes and smiled.

Her stomach rumbled.

"Hungry?"

Breen narrowed her eyes at Drakkone, who grinned. "Maybe."

He simply chuckled and nodded. "I'll get dinner."

She squeezed the furs and rolled onto her other side. "Thank you," she whispered. Her heart clenched with unspoken words as the door shut softly. She wasn't just grateful for the food, or his generosity. She was grateful for *him*.

* * *

THE DOOR SLAMMED against the wall, and Breen's eyes shot open. She spun to her back, tearing her sword from its sheath at the bedside.

Drakkone entered with wild eyes. He closed the door behind him.

She took a deep breath, her heart slowing as she lowered her blade.

"Gods, you scared me." Breen sat up, wiping sleep from her eyes. She wasn't sure when she'd drifted off, or how long she'd been out, but the fear widening Drakkone's eyes sent her heart plummeting towards her gut. "What is it?"

Drakkone sat on the bed beside her and handed her two folded pieces of parchment. "We're wanted."

Her brows cinched together until she unfolded the pages. A crudely drawn image of her marked the page, but she didn't understand the lettering above her face. The numbers on the bottom on the other hand, spoke volumes.

One thousand.

She flipped to the second. Drakkone's image stared back at her, the same number below. She looked up at him, her brows raised. "What is this?"

"We're wanted by the Emperor." He motioned to the lettering above their images. "Our bounty is set at one thousand gold coins."

"How could this have reached so far already?" Her heart raced. "We've only just arrived."

Drakkone shook his head. "We didn't ride directly here. We stuck to the jungle's edge instead of the wasteland. Riders could have gotten to every town in Seaburn's Empire by now."

Her fists clenched around the pages. Why did the Emperor, this terrible man, keep trying to ruin her life? Why did he and his men insist on seeking her out even after her escape?

"I should have seen it coming." Drakkone sighed. "They've done this in the past, but never for so much coin."

"But where will we be safe now?" Her hands flew to her stomach, which protruded over her belt. "Where will our baby be safe?" She could hardly discern her own whispered voice over the pounding in her ears.

This couldn't be happening. Not now. They'd come so far. They'd escaped. She had been *free*. Yet, Seaburn continued to threaten not only her, but their unborn child.

Heat built in her chest so fast it knocked the breath from her lungs. She would *not* let them harm her baby. She would not let her child grow up in such a place, such a *life*. "We need to keep running."

Drakkone nodded. "We will."

Breen squeezed her eyes shut. Where would they be safe? Her eyes flashed open.

Home.

Her home. The only one she'd ever known. "The Savage Lands."

Drakkone looked up from studying his hands, his brows pulled together. Hope lit his dark eyes. "You're sure?"

She nodded quickly, sparks of anticipation dancing across her skin. "Yes. We can go to my tribe. They'll protect us."

He took her hand, his warm fingers squeezing hers. "Then that's where we'll go."

Breen pushed forward, wrapping her arms around his neck. She buried her face against his hair, now growing long and thick from lack of regular trimming. "Thank you."

Drakkone wrapped his arms around her and squeezed tightly; his fingers hot against her bare lower back. Her shirt only seemed to ride higher by the day. "I told you, I'd do anything for you."

She only nodded, tears burning the back of her eyes.

Finally. She was going home. Finally, she'd see her family again.

* * *

THEY RODE OUT THAT NIGHT, Dullahan kicking up sand as they flew from Kelna and back into the open wasteland. Drakkone got their money back, and spent it on the supplies they needed to reach the Southern Delica Tribe.

The journey would be long, and hard, but with her belly growing larger every day, they had to get away from Seaburn fast, or their baby would be caught between the warring worlds.

Months passed in the Wasteland. Small towns and lonely homes became far and few between, until days passed between them. Eventually the jungle rose on their left, giving them cover at night and water for the day. A large oasis, much bigger than the one they'd previously found, occupied the western most half of the jungle.

They rested as much as they could, her constant need to pee and aching muscles becoming overbearing. Even as the jungle thinned, her breathing grew laboured, the baby pressing against her bladder and lungs.

When they finally reached the Delic River, the thunder of its waves could be heard for miles. Home was so close. Just across the river. But getting across the wavering surface posed a problem. Even if she weren't pregnant, swimming the rapids would be suicide. The calmer portions were not to be trusted either. Alligators lurked in the depths closest to the jungle, reed clusters and the sudden flight of birds the only sign of danger.

So they continued east for the sea, where the river narrowed and grew shallow enough for Dullahan to cross.

Drakkone leapt from the horse's back, taking the reins and urging the stallion out into the water. The black stallion flared its nostrils and pulled back on the leather straps, but Drakkone was determined, pulling the beast out into the ankle-deep water.

"It's all right," he cooed gently, patting the horse's neck and pulling him deeper until the water rose to Drakkone's knees. Finally, Dullahan marched forward, kicking up water as he splashed quickly through the river.

Drakkone laughed as he struggled to keep up, losing the reins as Dullahan rushed to the other side.

Breen leaned forward and snatched the fallen reins. She held on tightly, the reins digging into her palms. She tried not to grin too widely as Dullahan stepped onto the far bank. Drakkone scrambled up to join them, soaking wet below the waist.

"Did you enjoy your swim?" She smiled, unable to hold back her wicked grin.

"Very funny." Drakkone brushed sand from his boots. "You won't be laughing when I get back up there with you."

Her grin dropped into a pout. "You'll get me all wet."

"You'll deserve it for mocking me!"

Breen narrowed her eyes, and it was Drakkone's turn to grin.

SIXTEEN

Sand crunched beneath Dullahan's hooves as they followed the river west to the Southern Delica Tribe. Breen's heart raced with each step bringing her closer to a home she never thought she'd see again.

Drakkone sat at her back, a warm and sturdy presence against her mounting excitement. Her fingers danced in Dullahan's long course hair. She wanted to be there now. She wanted to see her mother, her father, her tribesmen, her students—everyone.

The sand sloped up a small hill until they emerged at the top. At the crest of the next hill, mere yards away, white tents stood out on the sand, glittering in the harsh sunlight.

Home.

Breen grinned and swiped the reins from Drakkone's hands, snapping them in one quick motion.

Dullahan whinnied and took off down the slope before climbing the next. Drakkone chuckled, his voice barely audible over the wind whipping in her ears. Sand blew in a flurry at their back, while the white tents of her tribe grew larger and larger.

Several heads peeked from their tents, familiar tawny skin and dark eyes curious and wary.

They crested the hill, Dullahan snorting as she slowed his gate with a swift tug.

Tribesmen flooded from their tents, warriors wielding swords, young ones with curious big eyes, and elders peering outside with concern. This wasn't the joy, and freedom she remembered. No children flew between tents or shouted their laughter. No warriors wrestled and grunted in the sand at the center of the village.

Her heart fell, stamping out her excitement.

This was fear.

This was concern for being taken again by Seaburn's army. Her heart clenched as she guided Dullahan through the tents toward her father's at the center of camp.

Whispers sprung up all around them, and their swords slowly lowered.

"Be careful." Drakkone's breath was hot on her ear.

Breen glanced over her shoulder. Worry cinched his brows and flattened his thick lips. This wasn't the first time he'd voiced his concerns, but her people would accept him given time. She nodded.

"Breen!" a high voice carried on the wind.

Her heart leapt. "Mother!"

Kianne pushed through the gathering tribesmen, who slowly parted around her. Her hood fell back as she breached the open space surrounding their horse.

Breen slid from her steed's back before Drakkone could leap down to help her. She stumbled, thrown off by the weight of her belly. Kianne embraced her before she could fall, her warm arms encircling her shoulders and pulling her close.

"My daughter, you've returned to us!" Wet tears hit Breen's cheeks as Kianne pressed her lips to her forehead. "I can't believe you're alive." She squeezed tighter.

"Mother." Breen clung to Kianne's thick robes.

During the months she'd been forced to stay in Seaburn's Academy, she'd almost forgotten what home was like. The hearty smell of wild boar drifted through camp. The murmur of tribesmen and the warm embrace of the sun and sand on her skin. This was home. *Her* home.

Tears burned the back of her eyes, but she would not let them fall in front of her tribe. Drakkone hit the ground with a thump. Kianne startled, her whole body jerking. She glanced over Breen's shoulder, her fingers tightening on Breen's arms.

"Who is this?" Kianne's voice edged with reproach.

Drakkone was clearly not of the tribes. With the dark complexion of Seaburn's people, those her family had grown to despise, it would be difficult for them to accept he was not the bad person they thought.

Not all of her tribesmen lowered their blades. Some even pointed them right at the father of her child.

"Drakkone." Breen stepped from her mother's embrace and took his hand, pulling him away from the vicious snarls and barred teeth of the clan warriors. He squeezed her fingers. "He saved my life."

Kianne's narrowed eyes relaxed, and her smile returned. She sighed deeply. Relieved. "You saved my Breen?"

Drakkone nodded, his gaze sullen.

A small grin tugged at Breen's lips. He'd done so much more than that.

"Then you are welcome in the Southern Delica Tribe." Kianne held out her hand. Drakkone took her forearm, as Kianne took his. They both squeezed before releasing one another.

Kianne turned to the rest of the clansmen. "This man is *welcome* in our tribe. He has saved my daughter, and brought her back to us. You will treat him as one of our own." A growl of command seeped into her voice.

It had been many years since Breen heard such an edge to her mother's tone. Normally, her voice was light, and free like the wild horses of the savannah. Breen had nearly forgotten her mother was the wife of the Chief, and as such, a strong warrior in her own right.

Mumbles surrounded them, but slowly the crowding tribesmen

nodded their approval and slipped off to return to their duties. Even with Kianne's seal of approval, wary glances flickered their way.

"Much has changed, hasn't it?" Breen glanced back at her mother.

"Yes, much has, my daughter." Kianne's lips pressed into a thin line. "As it clearly has with you, as well." She raised her eyebrows at Breen's obviously large belly. "You're pregnant." A smile pulled at her lips and tears stung her eyes. "I never thought I'd see the day."

Breen smiled. "I told you, it'd never be Lukerin."

Kianne nodded. "That you did. You must be at least six months along." Her brows cinched. "Is it, Drakkone's?" Her gaze flicked to the tall man.

"Yes." Breen couldn't help but laugh. "And you're right, it must be at least six." Truth be told, she'd been unable to keep count after so long on the road.

"The gods bless you, my daughter." Kianne wiped tears from her eyes. "Come. Your father will want to see you."

Breen nodded. Her heart set once again to racing. She was home. Truly home. And her family was still alive, still together. Sparks of hope bubbled inside her chest. It had been so long since she'd been this excited, or happy. The last moment such joy filled her heart had been in the jungle as her baby kicked for the first time.

Drakkone squeezed her fingers and released her hand.

They followed Kianne through the twisting paths between tents, until they arrived at the Chief's. The large tent stretched out at least twenty feet in either direction, with a large fire pit in the open space before it. A large hog lay cooking on a metal poker strung over low flames.

Her stomach growled, much as it had been for a long time now.

The flap to the tent snapped open, and a tall, broad man with long dark hair braided away from his face emerged. Her father. A smiled pulled at her lips.

But Chief Ruin didn't see her. His gaze landed on Drakkone, and his eyes widened. He ripped his dual blades from their sheaths on either hip before anyone could react and leap forward to explain.

Drakkone went rigid, while her father lunged across the sand.

Even in middle age, his movements were precise like a wild cat. A snarl tore from his throat as he lunged between Kianne and Drakkone.

"Ruin!" Kianne reached for her husband's arm.

The Chief had already leapt.

Breen's eyes widened. She tore her curved blade from its leather sheath and jumped between the men. Her sword clanged loudly against her father's, drawn high, inches from her head.

"Father!" she snapped.

His eyes widened. Confusion furrowed his brow and flashed through his gaze. "Breen?" She could barely make out her name over the pounding in her ears.

"You will not harm this man." She gritted her teeth and narrowed her eyes at her father, who continued to remain stiff, and poised for battle.

"You're alive." His swords hit the sand with a thump. Her father's arms wrapped around her shoulders and squeezed her tight.

Her breath flew from her lungs as he pressed her against his chest. His shoulders shook and his grip tightened further.

"Father!" she gasped. "You're crushing me!"

Ruin stiffened and squeezed one last time before stepping back. He held her shoulders in his large hands, his eyes glazed. "My daughter, you've returned to us."

"Of course." She smiled. Her breath caught in her throat, nearly cutting off her words. Her heart clenched as she clamped down on the rising tears.

"I never thought I'd see you again. My blood. My life." He embraced her again.

The back of her eyes burned, and she stared at the bright blue sky to hold back the thick drops of water forming against her lashes. "Neither did I."

He released her, stepping back, his gaze flicking from her, to Drakkone. Again, he stiffened. "And you've brought... company." He plucked his swords from the ground. Red leather strapped the hilts;

the long ends dangling against his thighs, as he stood straight. He didn't return them to their sheaths.

"Yes." Breen turned to Drakkone. His brows remained furrowed, his hand on the hilt of his blade. She reached for his wrist, motioning him forward to join them. "This is Drakkone."

"And you've brought this... Seaburn man into our midst?" His voice hissed out between his teeth.

"He saved my life, Father."

The Chief's eyes returned to hers, wide and uncertain.

Never before had the daughter of the Chief needed saving.

"I've welcomed him as one of our own, husband." Kianne placed a hand gently on Ruin's back. "He brought our Breen back to us."

Ruin's lips pressed into a thin line. He regarded Drakkone for a long moment, sizing him up, much like men do. "You saved my daughter from that wretched place?"

Drakkone nodded, his brows relaxing, though he didn't remove his hand from the hilt of his blade.

Her father returned his swords to their sheaths in one swift movement. He breathed a heavy sigh. "Then you are welcome among our tribe. Thank you for returning my daughter."

Drakkone bowed his head. She had to imagine he wasn't sure what to say, or how to say it. She hoped he didn't miss his family as much as she had. Her heart clenched.

"Come, join us." Ruin extended a hand to his tent.

The Chief led the way, Kianne flashing a smile at Breen and Drakkone as she followed. Breen joined them, Drakkone bringing up the rear. Cool shade embraced her shoulders, soothing them from the heat she'd endured for too long.

Her father's tent remained exactly as she remembered it. At the center front, a small pit held embers where flames once rose. An opening in the ceiling allowed smoke to escape, though no smoke was present at the moment. Surrounding the pit, several small wooden benches occupied the packed earth. Tapestries and thick furs adorned the walls. Weapons hung from racks, and were mounted to the wooden walls carving her room, and her parents, from the large space.

Chief Ruin and her mother sat beside each other beside the pit. The acrid smell of ashes climbed up her nostrils as Breen held her back, lowering herself to sit. The baby rolled inside her, pushing the breath from her lungs. By the time she reached the bench, she had to take deep breaths. She ran her hands over her protruding belly, grateful to sit somewhere that wasn't a horse's back or sand to crawl inside her clothing.

Drakkone hesitated, ready to offer his aid, but she didn't need it. Once she was settled, he joined them, keeping a respectful few inches between them.

"You're pregnant," her father gasped.

Kianne squeezed her father's hand, her eyes glazing again as she leaned against her husband. "She is."

"What a blessing in these times." Ruin grinned. "The gods favor you, my daughter."

Breen smiled, though her lips twisted ruefully. She wasn't sure she agreed. Though her child was surely a blessing, that was true, the gods hadn't favored her in a long time. Even though things had turned out all right in their flight so far, she'd been through too much to agree the gods gifted her with anything but this child.

"Surely they favor all of us, as you've finally returned to us." Kianne leaned her head against her husband's arm before she released his hand. "Finally, I will be a grandmother. You will surely have the most beautiful of babies in all the Lands."

Drakkone nudged her arm and smiled down at her. Breen flushed and shrugged her shoulders. Kianne was right. Her son or daughter would be the most beautiful of babies, the most loved and the most desired in the Savage Lands. She held her belly with her fingers. Warmth radiated from inside as her child nudged her hands.

Now that she was finally home, her child would be safe. Her child would be loved, and cared for. Her child would be free.

Though only weeks ago, it seemed that all had been lost, she had finally returned to the place she missed most. And in just a couple months, her baby would be born, and her family complete. She'd dreamt for years of having a child, for her, for her family and for her tribe. But never had she imagined that child would be born like this.

To a savage mother, and a Seaburn father.

* * *

THE SUN WARMED her cheeks as she ducked outside her family's tent the next morning. Though nausea had stirred her from sleep, the soreness of her backside and limbs began to fade, replaced with earnest delight to be among her fellow tribesmen.

Drakkone remained asleep in her old quarters. Though her parents had a small spat over where Drakkone should stay, Breen insisted he stay with her until they pitched their own tent.

"Good morning." An elderly tribeswoman smiled and nodded as she passed, a large basin of water in hand.

"Morning." Breen couldn't help the grin breaking across her face.

Frying eggs and the savoury scent of sausages drifted between tents, sending her stomach back into rumbles. Breen followed the smell, her nostrils flaring to catch more of the delicious scent.

She craved fresh meat like she'd never craved anything else. Her mouth watered as she rounded the white tents. Outside her mother's Lesson Hut, a woman kneeled in the sand, braids drawn into a bun atop her head. She smiled as she pushed thick sausages across a thick black pan over a fire pit. Flames flicked at the base of the metal, causing the frying white of the eggs to bubble and sizzle with the heat.

"That smells incredible." Breen inhaled deeply.

The woman glanced up, hazel eyes dancing with amusement. "Breen. It's good to see you."

"Mum!" a high voice pierced the stillness of morning. From the tent at the woman's back came rushing a small girl with wild eyes and thick braids. She froze on the sand, her eyes flying wide. "Breen!"

Breen cocked an eyebrow. "Aura?"

She hardly recognized the girl. Though it had been nearly a year since they'd last seen one another, she'd shot up several inches and grown into her lanky limbs.

Aura flew across the sand and flung herself into Breen's arms. Her warmth enveloped Breen's shoulders, and her tiny fingers dug into her shoulder blades.

"Mum said you were back, but I didn't believe her." Aura squeezed tighter.

A laugh bubbled from her chest. Breen embraced her favorite student, lifting her from the ground and spinning her in a circle. Aura giggled as her spin ceased, and Breen set her back on the sand.

"She was right." Breen ruffled her hair.

Aura scowled and quickly flattened the stray hairs atop her head. "Class hasn't been the same without you."

"I imagine not. Who's been teaching you?"

"Kianne." Aura heaved a sigh. "She prefers teaching over demonstration."

Breen laughed. "I remember."

"Now that you're back, will you teach us?" Hope lit her wide eyes.

"Of course."

"Will we start today?" she gasped.

Aura's mother rose to her feet and laid her hands on her daughter's shoulders. "Now, now, Aura. Breen might need a few weeks before she returns to training you." The woman nodded at Breen's belly, cloaked in a thin brown top with wide sleeves. None of her old clothes fit any longer. She'd had to borrow the shirt from her mother.

Aura's eyes flew wide as she took in Breen's large belly. "There's a baby in there?"

Her mother laughed. "Yes."

"Can I touch it?" Aura poked a finger toward her stomach.

Breen laughed. Aura had always been curious, but in her absence she'd also become bold. "Go ahead."

Aura slowly stretched out her splayed hands, gently laying them on Breen's belly. Her baby shifted inside, surprising a gasp from both of them.

"It moved!" Aura looked up at her with eyes like round coins.

"Babies do that." Breen rubbed her fingers across her abdomen, tiny little bumps lurching inside her, pressing against her fingers.

"Bree?" Drakkone's deep voice carried over the sand.

She twisted her neck to glance over her shoulder. He appeared between two tents close together, brows furrowed and eyes filled with concern. He'd needed the sleep much more than she, so she'd left him in bed. Clearly, she should have left word of where she'd gone.

"I'm here," she said.

Drakkone's eyes met hers, honest relief filling their widened depths. Though he didn't say a word of it, it was obvious she'd frightened him. Though she hadn't meant to scare him, the fact that he had been concerned for her warmed her heart.

Aura's mother reached for her child, her lips pulling back to bare her teeth.

"Who is *that?*" she hissed.

Breen glanced between the woman and Drakkone, who froze a few feet away.

"This is Drakkone." Breen held up her hands. "He won't hurt you, or Aura, I promise. He's not like them."

The woman glanced between them both, slowly releasing Aura's arm. "You're sure?"

"Positive." Breen smiled.

She quickly nodded and stepped back up to the breakfast she'd been cooking. Her stiffened shoulders didn't relax, and she glanced beneath thick lashes. "Why don't you come eat?"

"Oh yes, join us!" Aura bounced up and down, oblivious to the tension between the adults. "Will you be back to teaching this afternoon? It's been *moons* since I had a good lesson!"

"Aura. Be polite," her mother warned.

Aura huffed a sigh and collapsed onto a flat rock protruding from the sand. "Yes, Mum."

"So you've been enjoying your fighting lessons since my... departure?" Breen inclined a brow.

Aura beamed. "Yes! I can wield a real sword now—" She quickly glanced at her mother. "Though Mum doesn't let me practice outside class."

Breen grinned. "That's probably for the best."

Once they were all seated on the benches surrounding the pit, Aura's mother handed out smooth wooden plates of eggs and sausages.

Breen's mouth watered and her stomach growled. She wasted no time in devouring her breakfast, savouring each mouthful like it was her last.

Drakkone smiled as she ate, not bothering to hold back his amusement. He knew she'd hated the dried chicken and even after a full pig roast dinner the night before, she still remained famished.

"So *will* you be teaching?" Aura scooted closer as she finished her meal, big eyes staring up at her, begging for a lesson on fighting.

Breen smiled. "I don't see why not."

"Are you sure you should be teaching her how to fight...?" He didn't say it, but she knew the end of his sentence. *In your condition.* It wasn't the first time he'd asked her that.

Aura's mother scoffed loudly. "You clearly haven't seen many pregnant tribeswomen. We fight until the baby is on its way out our doors!"

Drakkone's eyes widened, and Breen burst into laughter. That's exactly what she'd told him once.

"Mum!" Aura gasped.

"It's the truth." The woman grinned. "I fought with you in my belly until the day you were born!"

Aura remained aghast, staring wide-eyed at her mother.

"Yes, I will teach your lessons." Breen grinned. Excitement burned through her chest, lighting sparks over her limbs. It had been some time since she wielded a sword to teach instead of fight.

Her heart ached. She hadn't realized how much she'd missed her students until now.

"Yes!" Aura leapt to her feet. "Can we start now?"

Breen chuckled and stood as well, holding her belly as she rose. Her balance shifted, and Drakkone held her elbow to steady her. She gave him a grateful look. "Gather the others. We'll meet when the sun is at its highest."

Aura grinned and took off through the tents, sand kicking up in her wake.

Breen shook her head and smiled, watching her go.

Aura's mother bid her farewell and brought their plates inside her tent, disappearing back into the shade.

Once she was gone, Breen turned back to Drakkone. His rough fingers brushed her elbow, beckoning her to face him.

His brows furrowed low over concerned eyes.

"What's wrong?" Breen trailed her fingers along his arm.

Drakkone shook his head. "All my life, I was told we were helping the tribes by taking them from a life of miserable suffering in the Wastelands, and giving them a purpose in the Seaburn armies."

Her jaw hardened, and she dropped her hand.

"They lied to us, didn't they? No one here seems miserable, only afraid—" He paused, the words caught on his tongue. He didn't need to say it.

They were only afraid of *him*.

"Seaburn takes us from our homes and throws us into their world without a second thought for who we are or what we want." Her voice was hard, unyielding.

"I see that now." Drakkone sighed, squeezing his eyes shut. His thumb and index finger pressed against the bridge of his nose. "I should have seen it. I should have learned for myself before joining them. At the very least, seen it in how they treated you when you first arrived, in the fire in your eyes and spirit. I shouldn't have let this go on for so long."

"But you did."

"And I'll never forgive myself for it." His hand fell to his side. His gaze affixed to the sand, his fists clenched. "I'll stop them, Bree. I'll stop Seaburn no matter the cost." His eyes rose, meeting hers, steel in their dark brown depths.

Her heart fluttered.

Did he truly mean it? Stopping Seaburn and the Emperor meant betraying everything he'd ever known. His home. His family. It meant betraying his way of life.

He took her hands, squeezing them between both of his. "I promise you, I won't let this continue."

Warmth spread through her chest, and burned the back of her eyes. She kissed his fingers. "We'll fight them together."

Drakkone nodded and enveloped her in his arms, blocking out the rest of the world with his embrace. Breen melted into him, laying her cheek against his chest.

They would fight Seaburn. Not just for her, or her tribe, but for their child. They'd fight Seaburn, and they'd win.

SEVENTEEN

$\mathcal{B}$reen settled on the burlap floor of the Lesson Hut, crossing her legs beneath her. The shade was a welcome reprieve from the sun, even with Drakkone's warm presence mere inches away.

"Good afternoon, students." Breen smiled at the dozen children spread out before her. Aura sat in the front row, eyes wide and eager for knowledge.

For days she'd resumed their lessons, teaching them to fight with swords and shields; how to dodge, lunge and parry. But today she would teach them something different. Some were nearly thirteen, the age when the Wrestling Ritual became part of their lives.

She'd always enjoyed wrestling with her brethren. Lukerin's absence had left an empty spot in her heart, even though she didn't love him romantically, she missed the man she considered her brother. At thirteen, every child became a warrior apprentice, and would join in wrestling matches to bond with their brothers and sisters.

"Do you know what the Wrestling Ritual is for?" Breen asked her students. Aura's hand shot up faster than all the others, pulling a toothy grin to Breen's face. "Aura."

"To bond with the other tribesmen!" Her fingers nearly vibrated against her leather tunic.

"That's right." Breen nodded. "When you become a warrior apprentice, you are only a short year from being a full fledge warrior of the Delica Tribe. You will protect your people, serve your Chief as you must, and above all, you will become an adult in our tribe family."

Drakkone shifted at her side, his hand resting on her bare lower back. Her open-backed tunic helped with her constantly growing belly. His fingers sent shivers up her spine as he drew circles on her skin.

"Wrestling helps you bond with your brothers and sisters. It creates a familiarity with your new kin, while helping prepare you for battle. Several of you will start the Wrestling Ritual soon, correct?"

Two of the older boys, and one girl, nodded. They were the tallest, sitting at the back of the class, spines straight, eyes attentive, and ready to join the rest of their clansmen.

She smiled. "Do you remember the rules?"

They all nodded.

"Tell me."

One of the boys straightened further, his head and shoulders peeking over the crowd of younger children like a sand fox sticking its head from its den.

"Wrestling isn't for hurting, or injuring another clansman," he said.

The girl perked up next. "No weapons can be wielded during a match."

"And?" Breen faced the last of the trio.

His eyes widened slightly, and he gulped before straightening. "When your brother is down, he must remain there for five seconds or tap out in order to win."

"Right." Breen placed her hands on her knees. "I'm glad you've all been paying close attention."

Drakkone's fingers froze on her back. Breen continued questioning her students, ignoring her disappointment at his abrupt stop.

"Now, in what circumstances does the crowd determine a victor?" It didn't happen often, but it was important to know.

Each of their brows furrowed, seemingly perplexed.

"None of you know?" Her gaze roamed each of them.

Drakkone grew rigid. She glanced over her shoulder. He stared at the entrance of the tent, his head cocked, ear facing the outside. What was wrong?

"When it isn't clear who's won." Aura beamed up at Breen.

"Right." She smiled at the small girl before glancing back at Drakkone.

"Horses," Drakkone said. His eyes met hers, edged with fear.

Her heart sank into her gut. Her stomach flipped. "You don't mean…"

"Seaburn."

The word crashed around her, sending a torrent of hot and cold swirling through her belly. Fear. Rage. Uncertainty.

She needed to protect her baby. She needed to protect her students. Her tribe. Everyone. Breen's fingers wrapped around the hilt of her sword, sheathed, and resting on the burlap beside her. She had to protect them. She *would* protect them.

"Children, I need you to stay here." Breen stood with some effort. Drakkone followed.

Curious and concerned gazes met hers. "Why?" Aura squeaked.

"You remember last time you saw me before I left?" Her voice quaked. Her fingers shook. The students nodded. Fear crept into their gazes. "I need you to stay here." Her gaze flicked up to meet the three soon-to-be warriors at the back of the class. "Protect them, and keep them *here.*"

They leapt to their feet like she'd thrown fire at their toes. They understood immediately. "Arm yourselves. They're coming."

Breen swept to the flap of the tent, Drakkone on her heels.

"You should stay with them." He grabbed her elbow, stopping her mere inches from the exit.

"I will not leave my people to fight against those savages alone." She tore her arm away and stepped out onto the sand.

Hooves beat the earth, a distant rumble like storm clouds. They approached from the east. Tribesmen ran between the tents in a flurry of motion, some barrelling toward the noise, others away.

"Bree, I'm serious."

"I am too." She drew her sword from its sheath with a soft *shing*. The sharp blade glinted in the afternoon sunlight, reflecting harsh light onto her dark shirt.

Breen glanced between the coming noise and her family's tent not far away. She knew the direction she should go. She should face the coming terror head on, as she had before. But something stole her courage and ate at the heat coursing through her veins: fear.

Fear for her life. Fear for Drakkone's. Fear for their child's.

Her heart raced, and her palms grew slick with sweat.

When had she become so weak? When had she begun to question leaping into battle? She shook her head and gripped her blade tighter.

The hilt laced with red cloth absorbed the sweat from her fingers and kept her grip from slipping. She took a deep breath and turned toward the fight.

Breen jogged across the sand, her boots sinking in more than she was used to, slowing her pace.

The roar of horses grew louder, edged with the battle cries of her tribesmen. Breen ran, her breath heavy in her throat. She dodged between tents until she was met with open sand.

Down in the valley between their camp and the sand dunes twenty feet away, her brethren fought Seaburn soldiers clad in leather armour. Their blades clashed loudly, echoing over the desert.

Breen gritted her teeth, ready to lunge down the hill.

Rough fingers closed on her elbow.

"Breen, you can't." Drakkone twisted her to face him. "You'll get hurt."

"I can fight," she hissed. She yanked her arm back, but Drakkone held strong, his fingers digging into her skin.

"You're *six months* pregnant." He met her gaze, his brows raised.

"You can't win this fight. You'll injure yourself or the baby. We need to *run*."

Her heart sank. "I can't run away from my family."

"You must."

Breen glanced between the battle below, and the camp at their back. Two riders broke from the fight and climbed the hill.

Her gut clenched and bubbled with fear. She'd never been afraid of a fight before. She loved the thrill of battle, and she'd die for her tribe. But she had more than herself to think about now. She had Drakkone, and this baby.

But her tribe was her family too. And she couldn't leave them behind.

Breen wrenched her arm from his grasp.

Drakkone spun, unleashing his sword from its sheath. The two Seaburn soldiers rode toward them.

They didn't have a choice now. They had to fight.

Long curved blades sliced at Drakkone as he dove in front of her. The clang of blades echoed in her ears, before they *shinged* apart.

"Go!" Drakkone bellowed.

Both of the riders flew past, yanking on their reins to turn their horses back around.

Her feet remained rooted to the sand. She couldn't go without Drakkone. She wouldn't leave him. Breen faced the coming soldiers.

"*Breen!*" Drakkone hissed an exasperated sigh.

Hooves beat toward them, too far apart for Drakkone to block both.

Two brown mares lunged forward.

Breen ducked to the right side of the one bearing down on her. Her sword clashed against his before she slashed the leather strap of his saddle, sending him to ground.

The man thumped to the earth, air exploding from his lungs. His eyes widened, stunned. While Drakkone took care of the other, Breen jumped in, her sword flying for his throat.

But her weight slowed her, giving him time to recover and roll from her path. Her lips pulled back and a growl rumbled in her throat. She could do this. She had to.

The soldier spun to his feet; sand dusting every piece of him as he reached for his blade.

Breen swung, catching his raised sword. She pushed the blade back, forcing him to stumble. She spun to deliver her killing blow. Only her belly offset her spin, and she tumbled sideways instead.

Sand flew up at her too fast. She crashed into it, thin grains coating her skin and tongue.

She coughed sand from her mouth, turning to jump back to her feet.

The soldier raised his blade, ready to bring it down upon her.

Her breath caught in her throat and her eyes widened.

The blade stabbed down like a hawk diving for its prey.

This was it. This was how it ended.

Her life. Her baby. They were both dead.

The man stopped. A curved blade pierced his chest. Drakkone stood at his back, breathing heavily as he thrust his sword deeper.

Blood spurted from between the soldier's lips. His eyes rolled back.

Drakkone pushed the man from his blade, letting his body fall limp in the dirt.

Her racing heart slowed, and she met Drakkone's gaze.

"Are you all right?" He stooped, his hands flying across her skin, searching for injury.

"I'm fine." Breen pushed him back, climbing to her feet with some effort. Her offset weight hadn't bothered her much before. Why did it have to affect her now when she needed it most?

Several horses rode past them, the blades of Seaburn soldiers cutting through tents as they went. Hot anger flared inside her chest. She gritted her teeth. She needed to help her people. Yet, she was useless like this.

"I need to get you out of here." Drakkone took her arm, pulling her from the blood pooling in the sand.

"What about my tribe? My parents?" Her heels dug in, stopping them both between two vacant tents.

Drakkone paused, searching the camp. "We'll find your parents. Then we need to go."

Heat continued to build inside her, but she nodded. He didn't understand why she needed to stay, but she needed to find her parents at the very least and make sure they were all right. Though her parents had once been great warriors in their own right, old age was settling on them, especially her mother, who frequently complained of back pain.

Drakkone led the way, winding through the tents. He skirted the soldiers and the screams ripping through their home. Tears stung the back of her eyes.

It was all happening again. Her home. Her tribe. They were being ripped apart. And for what? For their bounty? Or was this just another raid for soldiers? They had most of their warriors already. What more did they want?

"Stay away from them!" Her mother's high voice rose on the sand.

Breen stopped in her tracks.

The Lesson Hut.

Of course. Her mother would want to protect the children. The young warriors wouldn't be enough in her eyes.

Breen stepped off Drakkone's path and raced as fast as her feet and big belly would allow, between white tents sprayed with flecks of dirt and blood.

"Breen!" Drakkone snapped. His boots crunched in the sand as he followed.

Her mother stood just outside the doorway of the Lesson Hut, twin blades in hand, and a fierce snarl on her lips.

"Stay back!" she growled. Two soldiers boxed her in, smirks on their faces and swords flashing in the sunlight.

They spoke garbled words, few of which Breen understood while her heart pounded in her ears.

She still had twenty feet between them. She needed to hurry. She cursed her weight. She cursed the slowness of her feet. Her mother *needed* her.

Both soldiers flashed forward. Her mother raised her swords. They clashed against both of the soldiers. Kianne spun, forcing them back. One stumbled, while the other remained balanced. The man leapt forward, thrusting his blade out.

While Kianne dived in to finish the first, the second brought his blade up.

It pierced her mother's gut, thrusting into her abdomen and through to the other side. Blood spilled down the blade and onto the sand.

Kianne's eyes widened and her fingers shook around her blades.

"Mother!" Breen screamed, tears blurring her eyes.

Kianne turned slightly, her gaze meeting Breen's for a moment. Her lips parted, but no words escaped them. Slowly her eyelids closed and she slid to her knees before collapsing in the sand.

"No!" Breen closed the space between her and the soldiers. She cut through the one sent to ground, her blade spilling his crimson blood across the earth.

The second spun in time for her to block.

He growled at her, pushing her blade back.

Drakkone dove in front of her, slicing his twin blades clear across the man's throat. The soldier fell back, dropping his sword and clutching his neck. Red seeped between his fingers as he collapsed.

Drakkone spun toward her.

Breen only stared at her mother's still form lying in the sand. Blood pooled around her, sand soaking it up. Her whole body froze. Her mind cleared.

No. This couldn't be happening. Her mother. She was the wife of the Chief, one of the best fighters in the Tribe. Or she had been once.

Her lips parted to speak, to scream, to cry—something. But nothing came.

Her chest hollowed, weightless and empty.

"Bree." Drakkone stepped in front of her, blocking the view of her mother. "Breen, look at me."

She shivered. Her whole body gave way. Drakkone caught her in his warm embrace, keeping her standing. "We have to go." His fingers tightened at her back.

Breen shook her head. She couldn't go. Her mother was dead. It wasn't fair. It wasn't right. She couldn't leave her father, or the children in the tent.

Drakkone lifted her from the ground, one arm braced beneath her back, the other beneath her legs. Even with her weight, he flew across the sand.

Her mother's body drew further and further away, until white tents blocked Kianne from view.

Her hammering heart slowed and nausea rolled inside her.

Her mother was dead. This couldn't be happening; couldn't be real.

Drakkone shook beneath her with each step until they reached the wooden stables at the far end of camp, hastily thrown together with thick boards. He pulled their steed from its stall. Dullahan chuffed and kicked the ground, happy to be of service.

He must have been out earlier that day, as he was already saddled, ready for their escape.

Drakkone sat her in the rough leather saddle before swinging up behind her. He took the reins and kicked his heels into Dullahan's sides.

The stallion flew from the pen and out onto open sand.

Breen remained still. Cold. Lost. She couldn't think. Couldn't feel. Couldn't see anything but the red scorching the sand.

Seaburn had come again. And they'd left the Savage Lands drenched in the blood of her people. Her fists clenched against her thighs, which ached with the familiar movements of Dullahan's gate.

The Emperor had sent his men once again into her home, to rob her people, and steal her happiness. And there had been nothing she could do to stop them. She cursed her inability to fight, her clumsy movements and off-set balance. She should have been able to stop them. She should have been able to save her mother.

Breen squeezed her eyes shut. No matter the cost, she would see to it Seaburn never interfered with her home again. Heat burned through, embers burning up her throat.

This was the Emperor's fault. The greedy, self-serving, glutinous man. He would pay. She'd kill everyone he'd ever loved for this. She'd kill them all. For her family, her *mother*.

Fire burned to life, flickers of flames scorching her skin.

She'd kill them all.

EIGHTEEN

*D*ullahan rode across the sand dunes of the open wasteland, slowly banking toward the river, back the way they'd come several days prior.

Breen's heart ached with every step. The further away they travelled, the darker it became. Evening turned to night. Her mother was dead. Maybe her father too. Who knew how many more soldiers Seaburn would take. The apprentices? Her students? They were so young. They didn't deserve this. None of them did.

A crop of dead, gnarled trees sprouted along the river bend, slowing Dullahan's quick pace. While empty despair continued to fill her chest with cold, her eyes burned and her jaw worked. Heat slowly overtook the chill, burning up her throat and behind her eyes.

Her fingers closed on the leather reins. She snapped them taut, pulling them right from Drakkone's fingers.

Dullahan whinnied, caught off guard by the sudden tug. He stopped beside a tall grey tree with twisting branches leaning over the river.

"Breen, what are you doing?"

She slipped from their steed's back and onto the cooling sand. What was she doing? She didn't know. She couldn't take this hurt. This fear. This despair.

It'd eat her alive if she let it.

"Bree?" Drakkone sighed and slipped to the ground next, tying the reins to a low hanging branch before following her to the water's edge.

The slow current drifted by, fish flicking their tails above the surface as they dove below. She wished she could join them, sink into the black depths of the river, never to return. Maybe there she'd be able to fight. There she'd be weightless. There she'd be free. No one could touch her there, taint her or take her back.

Breen slowly shook her head, wrapping her arms around herself. Her cold fingertips dug into her biceps.

"Bree, you can talk to me." Drakkone rested his hand on her shoulder.

She shrugged it off.

"I'm tired." Her voice barely carried over the gentle breeze.

"We'll rest once we're further away."

A humorless laugh bubbled from her chest. "I'm tired of everything. I don't need your protection. I've always been fine on my own."

"It's okay to need help." His boots crunched in the sand as he shifted.

"Not for me. Not for my people. I can fight for myself."

Her chest burned with feelings he didn't understand. She'd never needed a man's protection. Never needed their help before Seaburn and this pregnancy. She should never have trusted him.

She didn't trust him.

She couldn't. Even after all they'd been through, she didn't know where this was going. She couldn't see it. Couldn't dream of a proper end.

"I just want you to stay safe." His fingers brushed her waist.

Breen spun, pushing back. "I was safe before *you*. Before Seaburn. I was safe before your people took me away." Her eyes burned with tears. "I was happy, and I could protect *everyone*. I can't have this baby in this world, Drakkone. She won't be safe. She'll never be safe. I can't protect her."

His brows cinched together, and he reached forward. She slapped his hand away. She didn't want his affection. She didn't want his trust. And she certainly didn't want his pity.

"She'll die in this world, and it'll all be because of me. Because I can't protect her." Hot tears seared her cheeks.

"You don't have to do this alone." Drakkone reached for her again. Even as she stepped away, he caught her hand. His warm fingers closed around hers, tugging her closer. "I won't let you do this alone, Bree."

Breen slowly shook her head, unable to stop the tears or the waves of terror and despair rolling through her. Her breath hitched in her throat, caught in a sob. Drakkone pulled her against his warm chest, wrapping his arms around her and holding her close.

She sank into him, unable to do anything else, craving the comfort found in his arms. Her baby would never be safe in this world. Not anymore. She hated her inability to protect her own. Her mother had already fallen due to her weakness. Would her child be next?

Wrapping her fingers around Drakkone's leather shirt, she clung to him. If she couldn't protect this baby, someone had to. Someone had to be their baby's guardian. Someone had to be her protector.

"We'll protect our child together," Drakkone said, as if echoing her thoughts.

Breen could only nod. She didn't trust her voice. Her whole body shook and quivered.

"You can trust me." He squeezed her shoulders and she buried her face against him.

Could she trust him? He'd given up so much for her. His entire life, his family, his home and his country. If she couldn't trust him, than who could she trust? She shivered.

Breen nodded against him. She didn't dare step away. He was the only thing holding her aloft.

"This baby will be born, and loved and cared for. We'll protect it from anything that comes at us. Your strength will return once this pregnancy is over."

Again, she nodded. He was right. He had to be. If he wasn't, she might never be able to protect anyone again.

* * *

THE JOURNEY back to the Wastelands in the North took longer than she remembered. With nothing to look forward to, and no home to go back to, Drakkone led them around the jungle and back to Kelna. Even with their wanted posters hanging in shop windows, they had nowhere else to go.

The other Tribes wouldn't accept Drakkone, not like hers had. She couldn't let him be put in such danger. So they would travel Seaburn's outlying towns until the baby was born, or soldiers caught them.

They had no other choice.

Her eyelids remained permanently heavy from lack of sleep. Her bulging belly only seemed to grow by the day, her baby's kicks becoming more frequent. Though it stirred her heart to know that her baby was alive and well, ready for the freedom of the outside world, it also brought cold fear to her bones every time she thought of it.

With less than a few weeks to go before her due date, Breen couldn't imagine what they'd do with a baby on the road. How would they survive and keep the baby safe while fleeing from town to town? It'd never be able to survive the Wastelands. But did they have another choice?

She wrapped her arms around her belly as they rode into town.

Drakkone led them past the outlying homes, and through the bazar until they reached the Kelna Inn and Tavern.

Though darkness lay upon their shoulders, stars twinkled overhead. She hoped no one recognized them. Breen pulled her cloak tight to her shoulders, keeping her hood slipped up.

They hadn't seen any wanted posters on the ride into town, but she was sure they'd see some at daybreak.

Goose bumps washed her skin as Drakkone hitched Dullahan

outside the Inn's stables. Once he helped her to the ground, they made sure their steed had food and water before wandering inside.

"Stay close to me," Drakkone whispered. The door creaked as it swung open.

Drakkone stepped inside first, leading the way. Breen did as he said, staying close, and keeping an eye out for trouble.

Rowdy laughter broke out through the bar, several men stomping their feet and slamming their mugs of ale on the wooden tables.

Drakkone went straight for the bar, slipping coins from the small purse at his belt. He spoke his garbled tongue, and handed the coins to the barkeep, who nodded and tossed a key at him.

As his shoulders relaxed, and he turned back to Breen, another round of laughter broke out. Her fingers inched toward the blade hidden beneath her cloak. She didn't trust these people, or this place. But they had no choice. Her eyes were so heavy; her entire body ready to give way. It had been days since she had a decent night's sleep. After sleeping in her old bed, lying in sand night after night felt like a cruel punishment on top of everything else she'd suffered. Her mother's death replayed over and over in her dreams.

Drakkone led the way upstairs, where the same long hall stretched out before them. At the end of the hall, the same bronze number 5 remained nailed to the door.

"The same room?" Breen raised a brow.

He shrugged and slipped the key in the hole, twisting it with a click. The door swung inward. "It seems so."

Before they settled for the night, Drakkone inspected their quarters quickly for a second exit. Outside the shuttered window, the first floor bar's roof lay only a few feet below. They'd be able to leap from the window with ease and climb to the ground from the first floor.

Sure that they would either be killed in their sleep or sleep like the dead, Breen collapsed inside the bed furs, hardly taking a moment to unstrap her sword before she fell into sleep.

* * *

DRAKKONE INSISTED they remain in Kelna to rest for a few days.

After Breen passed out cold the night before, Drakkone had disappeared some time in the night, removing all of their bounty posters from town. There had been a scarce few left, but with the posters gone, they should be safe for a few more days.

In truth, she didn't mind remaining. Her back, legs and feet ached with every moment of wakefulness. She hated the idea of sitting atop Dullahan's back for another week in search of the next town they *might* be safe within.

Warm morning light filtered between the crack in the shutters, illuminating a long strip up her belly and over her chest. Breen sat propped against the wall, a thick pillow at her back, and her belly in her hands.

She ran her fingers over the cotton, tracing light patterns over her stomach. How had she grown so large in what seemed like such a short amount of time? Though she'd seen pregnant bellies much larger in her village, she still couldn't believe the nearly seven inches of flesh protruding from her once toned abdomen.

Drakkone slept at her side, having fallen asleep after he returned from a long night's work. His once short hair stuck up in all directions, mussed from sleep. His eyes darted back and forth beneath his lids, perhaps fighting some demon in his dreams.

Sighing, Breen tilted her head back against the wall.

Alone in this small room, she couldn't picture the life where she remained on the run for months on end. She couldn't picture the soldiers chasing them, or the despair leeching into her every pore. Instead, with her soon-to-be baby in her hands, and its father at her side, she saw a different life. One she never imagined, not even before she was taken to Seaburn.

Breen was going to be a mother. Given a month, this belly would be a baby, and this man would be a father. Warmth blossomed in her chest, warming the bare patches of cold skin along her collar.

What would her baby be like? Would she be strong like Drakkone? Determined and stubborn like Breen? Would she be a warrior? A leader?

She couldn't wait to find out.

Carts creaked outside her window as they passed for the bazar down the road. Chatter drifted through the shutters, children's laughter on the street, families shopping for supplies.

Her stomach rumbled, breaking the quiet of the room. She flushed, though Drakkone wasn't awake to hear the embarrassing gurgle.

Inching off the bed, Breen peered through the crack in the wooden shutters. Bright blue sky shone overhead, giving light to the dozens of pedestrians roaming the streets below.

Her stomach rumbled again.

Breen narrowed her eyes at her belly. "Hungry, are you?"

Shaking her head, she pulled on her boots, washed her face from the water basin atop the dresser, and pulled on her cloak before plucking Drakkone's coin purse from the bedside table.

Though she should wait for him to awaken, the baby would not appreciate her patience. Neither would her rumbling stomach.

Breen left the room, closing the door quietly behind her. It creaked, but didn't send Drakkone flying to his feet, so she assumed he must be deep asleep. She padded down the hall to the stairs, avoiding the gaze of the barkeep as she slipped outside.

A warm breeze ruffled her thick braids, slipping loose strands of hair across her cheeks. She brushed them back, following the flow of cloaked townspeople. Though their cloaks were certainly more colorful than her own, she appreciated the thin fabric's protection, especially as it hid her large bump beneath its folds.

The bazar began a street down from the Inn. Stretched on either side of the lane, carts and wooden stands occupied every inch of the street's edge, selling fruit, meat, grain, beads, weapons, and other assorted items. Families and individuals alike strode between them waving to the vendors and chatting with others while small children ducked between their legs, playing with sticks or wooden swords.

Breen continued down the long main street of carts that seemed to go on forever. Her mouth watered and her stomach rumbled. Her fingers itched at her waist. With only a few coins remaining, and no food back at the inn, she had to use their funds wisely. Though she loathed it, dry meat and rice should be the cheapest, with fruit and fresh meat being the most expensive.

Rolling the leather purse between her fingers, she stood between two carts, one full of apples, and the other with dried meats hanging in strips from the stand's roof.

It had been months since she'd tasted fresh fruit. The sweetness of red apples called to her. They had to be rare in Kelna. She hadn't seen an orchard nearby. Maybe from north of Seaburn's main city, where forest grew next to the sea. From the third floor Academy windows in Drakkone's room, she'd seen the dark green haze on the horizon. Maybe that's where they could go. To the forest. If there were apples, she might not mind.

Breen shook her head. She'd been gone long enough, and should be getting back before Drakkone woke and grew worried.

She stepped toward the cart of dried meat as a rough hand closed on her elbow. Her brows furrowed and she turned. Drakkone? A tall man with ivory skin and pale blue-grey eyes stared from under a black-hooded cloak.

She yanked her elbow back. He didn't release her.

"Excuse me," she hissed between her teeth. "Let me go."

The man stared through her with vacant grey eyes. He said nothing.

"Release me!" Breen pulled her arm from his grasp this time, stepping away.

"You're coming with me," he said. Though his accent was thick, he spoke her language. She'd never seen a man like him before. No man of skin pale like his wandered the Wastelands, let alone Seaburn. Not that she'd seen anyway.

"I'm not going anywhere." Her fingers closed around the hilt of her blade.

The man said nothing, simply gazed through her, no recognition in his eyes. Had he even heard her? What was the meaning of this?

Breen circled to return the way she'd come, back to the inn. The man blocked her path. "Move," she snapped.

She stepped around him. He stepped into her path. "You're coming with me."

"No, I'm not." Breen leapt back as he reached for her once again. Her heart pounded against her ribs. She tore her sword from its sheath, her cloak whipping over her shoulders as she pointed her blade at his chest.

The surrounding chatter dulled.

The man reached inside his cloak, withdrawing a long straight sword—another thing unseen in her lands. Who was this man? And what did he want with *her*?

"You're coming with me," he repeated in the same monotone voice.

"Make me." Breen narrowed her eyes.

The man stepped forward.

Breen lunged, snapping her blade at his gut. His sword clashed against hers, knocking hers back. She growled and thrust again.

Again, he parried her blade.

Whispers flooded the street. Families gathered their children, holding them back away from the fight.

The man danced around her, strangely graceful for his large form. He slapped her blade away with each blow, but never made a move to strike her.

Her breath hissed between her gritted teeth. Her muscles ached with each turn of her blade. She couldn't keep this up, not in her condition. But she couldn't let this man take her either. Wherever he was from, whatever he wanted, she couldn't let him near her baby.

Breen spun, using her momentum to slap his blade outward. While he was knocked back, arms splayed, she drove the tip of her sword at his gut.

It *thunked* into his abdomen, pushing through flesh, muscle and bone until it emerged on the other side of him. Warm blood trickled down her hands from the hilt of her blade.

Vacant eyes met hers, staring right through her.

Whatever light remained within them dulled, and he slid from her blade, collapsing to the sand at her feet.

"Breen!" Drakkone's deep voice carried across the bazar.

She turned to Drakkone, who raced toward her, sword withdrawn. "Drakkone." Breen lowered her blade. His eyes widened, scanning her blood drenched weapon and the body at her feet.

"What happened?" He stopped by her side, pulling her away from the blood slowly sweeping the sand. "Who is that?"

Breen shook her head. "I don't know."

Drakkone wrapped his arm around her shoulder and squeezed. "Are you all right?" His hot breath whispered against her ear.

"I'm fine."

He stepped back, doing a quick assessment of his own. His eyes scanned her body until they reached her hips. He froze. "You're bleeding."

Her brows cinched together. Over her bump, she couldn't see any blood. She couldn't feel any cuts, scrapes or other injuries.

Her heart clenched. "The baby."

Drakkone's eyes flew wide. "We need to get you back to the inn."

Breen nodded slowly, her heart racing. She'd overexerted herself. She'd gone too far. She'd endangered her *child*.

Drakkone wrapped his arms around her back and beneath her knees, hoisting her into his arms. She wrapped her arms around his neck, burying her face in his shoulders. Cramps filled her lower abdomen, sending striking pain like lighting through her stomach.

She let go of Drakkone's neck and wrapped her arms around her belly. She would not let this child be hurt. She would *not* let her baby die.

"Hurry," she whispered.

Drakkone squeezed to let her know he'd heard.

NINETEEN

Drakkone raced up the stairs of the inn to the second floor. His boots beat loudly against the wood, echoing down into the dining room below. Once they stopped bouncing up the steps, he ran the length of the hall. The door to their room cracked off the wall as Drakkone kicked it open.

The bronze number five *dinged* several times as it fell from the door and bounced across the wooden floorboards.

Pressure built in her gut, pushing harder and harder against her insides. Pain came in waves, flooding her with agony for several long moments before subsiding.

Her fingers wrapped around the leather of Drakkone's shirt, the fabric rough and ripping beneath her long fingernails. Another wave hit, faster than waves eating the sand from a beach.

"Drakkone." Her head lolled back as he set her gently on thick furs. "Something's wrong. Something's wrong with the baby."

Drakkone simply nodded, his eyes wide, and brows cinched. "I'll get a doctor."

"Don't leave me." Her heart lurched and she reached out. He took her hand, his fingers wrapping hers as he kneeled at her bedside.

He met her eyes. "I'll be *right back*. You're going to be all right. The baby is going to be all right. I promise."

Tears burned her cheeks. "You can't promise me that."

"I can." His jaw set. "And I do."

He squeezed her fingers one last time before releasing her and dashing from the room. As his heavy footfalls faded, another burst of agony tore through her. She snapped her teeth shut, her fingers curling around her belly.

As the pain subsided, she took a deep, steadying breath.

Breen had never once thought she'd be in this mess. She never could have imagined having a baby with a Seaburn soldier. What had she been thinking, going to his bed? Had she been mad? Had he seduced her? She shook her head. Drakkone wasn't capable of such things. He was too kind. Too honest. But he'd left her here alone. He'd left her to these thoughts, and this agony.

Another wave had her toes curling and a cry flying from her lips between her clenched teeth. She needed a healer now. It was too early for this baby. Much too early. She had several weeks left of this pregnancy, and here she was bleeding at a wayward inn, in the middle of the Wastelands.

She wanted her mother. She wanted her family. She wanted Drakkone here to tell her everything would be all right.

Pain pierced her stomach, sending her writhing across the blankets beneath her. She needed a hand to hold. She needed a doctor to tell her what to do. She needed *someone*. She'd take the damned barkeep at this point.

Another wave had black creeping across her vision. Breen squeezed her eyes shut. She couldn't hold back the cries anymore. Each burst of pain came closer together, ripping through her insides.

She hardly heard the footfalls over her cries of pain.

Drakkone appeared at her side, gripping her fingers, kneeling beside the bed.

"Breen." He squeezed. "Bree, I'm back. I brought a doctor."

Her lashes fluttered, but she could barely keep her eyes open any longer. Breen squeezed his hand, sweat clamming her palm. "You're here."

"Of course I'm here."

"How late is she in the pregnancy?" The gruff voice of a man broke through her pain.

At the end of the bed, a short man with black skin and hazel eyes pulled cloths from a bag, followed by a small pair of scissors.

Her entire body tensed. "What are those for?"

The man glanced up, meeting her gaze. "I'll need to get the pants off of you somehow."

A laugh bubbled from her chest. She shook her head. The last time someone talked the pants off of her, she'd gotten pregnant. It was a fitting end to have the opposite occur.

Breen nodded, and turned her gaze back to Drakkone. She didn't care what the doctor did, as long as he helped get this baby out of her safely.

Drakkone smiled, though his eyes remained wide and sweat beaded on his forehead. He was worried. More worried than she'd ever seen him. Drakkone kissed her forehead and smoothed her hair.

"It'll be all right," he said.

She parted her lips to speak, but a cry broke through instead. Agony filled every inch of her being, stealing her breath and every last wit she'd so desperately tried to hold on to.

"Your contractions are getting closer together," the doctor mumbled. She wasn't sure if he spoke to her, Drakkone, or himself. "You're having this baby."

"It's too early," she gasped.

"She's only a little over eight months along." Drakkone squeezed her fingers.

"Far enough. The baby wants out, and it's coming whether we like it or not."

A cold breeze brushed her skin. She wasn't sure when, but at some point the doctor had cut her pants from her body.

She should feel embarrassed, flushed, something. But all she could think was she wanted this baby the hell out of her.

"The baby is already crowning."

More pain surged through her. At this point it was hard to tell from where.

"I need you to push, Breen."

Breen nodded, if only slightly. She squeezed her eyes shut, her fingers around Drakkone's, and pushed with all of her might.

"You're doing great," Drakkone whispered. His fingers brushed loose strands of hair from her face.

Her breaths came quickly, puffing in and out in loud gasps.

"Again," the doctor snapped.

Breen did as he said.

"Again!"

Pain exploded through her. She screamed, like she'd never heard a person scream before. Her eyes burned. Her lungs burned. Everything hurt.

Then relief.

Her breathing slowed, the pain and pressure dulled.

A high pitch cry broke the stillness left by her scream. Tears flowed down her cheeks and pooled against her throat.

"A baby girl." The doctor smiled as the crying continued.

Drakkone's gaze whipped between her, and the bundle the doctor was holding. She could hardly see her baby, her daughter, over her remaining bump.

Her limbs shook as she struggled to sit up.

The doctor's smile dropped. "Careful now. Careful."

Drakkone helped her into a half sitting, half lying position, propped on pillows and blankets alike.

The crying continued to fill the quiet, though it grew quieter, less desperate.

The doctor stood, turning from her line of sight. Using a wash cloth and clean water from a basin, he cleaned the blood and other matter from their daughter before he wrapped her in a thin blanket.

Then he turned, and she could finally see her.

Their baby. Their daughter.

The doctor set the pink bundle in her arms, stepping back as she cradled the baby in her arms. Warmth emanated from her, filling her heart to capacity, so that she may never love someone as much as this tiny girl again.

Her lips parted wordlessly. Her daughter's cries slowly ceased. Tiny little pink fingers stretched by her delicate, round face, brushing her flat nose and rosy cheeks.

"Nina," Breen whispered. She held her daughter closer, wrapping her arms around her and cradling her against her chest. Tears continued to spill down her cheeks, filling her mouth with salt as she smiled.

"Nina. A beautiful name." Drakkone sat beside her, wrapping one arm around her back while his hand lay atop hers on their daughter's blanket.

"Have you ever seen something so perfect? So wonderful?" Breen brushed the tips of her fingers along Nina's cheek.

Her eyes slowly blinked open, as blue as the aqua sea surrounding Seaburn, with rings of dark blue, like the bottom of the ocean, surrounding the outer rim, and her pupil.

Warmth blossomed inside her chest, filling every inch of her with heat.

"Never," Drakkone agreed.

Breen grinned. She couldn't help it. She'd never beamed at anyone, or anything like this before in her life. This was their baby. Their daughter. Nina was theirs. Somehow they'd created this tiny little creature together. And somehow they were going to raise her.

A splinter of cold fear cut through the heat warming her body. Her fingers tightened around her child. As long as she lived, she would never let someone harm this baby. Nina would be safe with her, and Drakkone. She'd be safe, and loved.

Forever.

Breen leaned down, placing a kiss on Nina's forehead. Her soft, warm skin soothed any fear, any doubt, and any pain from her mind. She smiled, the cold fleeing and her warmth returning.

Breen would love this baby forever.

PART TWO

NINA

TWENTY

Breen ran, her boots slamming against the cobblestone at her feet. Her breath fled her lungs in deep huffs. Her heart pounded to the rhythm of her steps.

"Mumma." Nina clung to her torso, her thin arms wrapped around Breen's neck, and her legs wrapping Breen's toned waist.

"I know, Nina."

Breen risked a glance down at her daughter. Blue eyes shone up at her, and blonde curls bounced around her face. How she and Drakkone had created such a beautiful little girl, she'd never truly understand. But Nina's widened eyes, filled with terror, sent her heart racing and her legs pumping faster.

No one was taking her little girl away from her. She'd spent three years regaining her strength for this, and she would not let her down.

Loud footsteps pursued them down the hill. Tall, gnarled trees lined the path on either side. Their trunks stood close together. Too thick for her to slip through and onto the open sand. The dunes would just slow her down anyway.

The town at the base of the hill might be her only hope. If she could steal a horse, or a carriage, she could flee faster than any man on foot.

She bit her lip. If only she could reach Halivaara in time.

Her feet slipped from under her. The cobblestone came up fast.

Damn.

Breen wrapped her arms tightly around Nina. Squeezing her eyes firmly shut, she twisted as fast as she could. Pain exploded through her left shoulder as she collided with the street.

A gasp escaped her lips, joining with Nina's high-pitched cry.

Her heart clenched. No. No. No. This couldn't be happening. Not now. Where was Drakkone when she needed him?

Breen rolled across the ground, Nina safely in her arms. She dug her heels between cobblestone bricks, and leapt to her feet as fast as she could. Her shoulder throbbed. Not pulled from its socket. Nothing broken. Good enough.

But it was too late.

Pale-faced men in black cloaks dove across the lane, vacant eyes locked onto Nina. Their pursuers were nearly upon them.

Breen ripped her sword from its sheath, balancing Nina on her left hip, while wielding her blade in her right hand. This is what she'd trained for. This is what she'd spent the last two years preparing for. This fight. The day someone came for her. The day someone threatened Nina.

A snarl on her lips, Breen faced the five men slowing their gait. They encircled her, strange straight swords drawn and pointed at her baby.

"What do you want?" She gritted her teeth, and narrowed her eyes at the men.

No one said a word.

Nina whimpered in her grip, burying her face against Breen's aching shoulder. Breen squeezed her waist to reassure her. Everything would be all right. She'd fight until her last breath to keep them away from Nina. As long as she stood long enough for help to arrive, they'd be fine.

"You're coming with us," one man said. Grey vacant eyes. Sunken cheekbones, and stringy black hair along his forehead.

"Never." Breen pointed the tip of her blade at the man's chest.

Pebbles clacked over the cobblestone as two shifted on either side of her.

Breen spun low, avoiding the two blades of the men leaping toward her. Their swords clanged together as Breen rolled from their reach. She leapt back to her feet in time to meet the blade of the man who'd been at her back.

He stabbed for her hip. She brought her blade up, the side of the metal *shinging* against his foreign blade as she parried his attack.

With his chest open, she stabbed him through the abdomen. The hilt of her blade *thunked* against his leather armour. Blood poured from between his lips.

She withdrew, letting his body collapse lifeless on the road.

Breen spun for the remaining four. While the first man waited patiently at the back, her twin attackers, with nearly identical faces, frames and movements, leapt.

Nina squeezed her neck tighter, her whimper hardly audible over the crashing of Breen's blade against those of her attackers.

She growled, her heart ramming faster in her chest. The hot flames of fury licked at her throat and stifled her breathing.

How dare they attack her? How dare they attempt to take her only daughter? She'd see them all dead before this was over. She'd see their blood turn the sand red, and their lightless eyes stare unseeing at the blue sky.

She couldn't forgive this. She wouldn't.

Breen pushed the blade of the first astray. Before she could lunge in for a final blow, the second twin leapt in the way, his sword clanging against hers, inches from either of their faces.

"She's coming with us." He pushed back.

Gritting her teeth, she pushed harder. "You will not touch her."

Her breath hissed between her bared teeth. Breen stepped back, letting the man's own strength betray him, sending him face-first onto the street.

The other brother returned, slapping her blade aside before diving in for a stab of his own.

Her heart skipped, and she twisted. Pain sliced through her right bicep, leaving a long line welling with blood.

She bit down on a gasp, and spun away from further damage. While he continued forward with his stab, Breen brought up her blade, piercing his abdomen and spilling his blood across his brother's back.

He fell in a heap, pinning his sibling to the ground.

Breen turned on the final two as shouts rose from the village.

She glanced over her shoulder, unable to help it. What if more attackers were on their way? What if it was another riot?

With most of Seaburn's citizens growing restless with the Emperor's gluttony, riots had risen throughout the city and even in the surrounding towns. This wouldn't be the first time she'd been caught in one.

Boots thumped quickly across the cobblestone. Breen turned, her blade ready. The first man to speak slapped her blade aside and dove at her, not stabbing for her body, but instead reaching for Nina.

Her eyes widened as she spun to protect her daughter from the man's touch.

He collided with her like the wind of a hurricane ripping a tree from the earth. She sailed across the bodies of the men she'd killed and hit the ground hard. Pain rocked up her arms. She'd have many new bruises tomorrow.

The man wrapped his arms around her waist, pinning her to the ground. Her sword flew from her grasp—as did Nina.

"Nina!" she cried.

Her beautiful blonde baby slid across the cobblestone, her exposed knees scraping along the cobblestone road. Blood blossomed in the cuts, and tears welled in her wide blue-eyes.

Fury lit Breen's veins, driving embers to full-blown flames that flickered through every inch of her body.

Breen slammed her elbow into the face of her attacker. He gasped, his hold loosening enough for her to shimmy forward. Once free of his grasp, she thrust her heel into his nose. Blood spurted from his face, seeping down his mouth and chin.

Leaping to her feet, Breen plucked her blade from the ground as the last black-cloaked man jumped in, his hands wrapping around Nina's arms and yanking her to her feet.

Nina cried out, tears streaking her tawny cheeks. Breen spun, glancing between her bloodied attacker, rising to his feet, and the other one, who dared to put his hands on her child.

"Let her go!" she snapped.

The man simply stared with the same vacant expression.

"I'll kill you for this." Breen leapt at the man clutching her daughter.

He jumped back, holding her aloft, Nina's small body blocking the man's vital points. Breen pulled back, frustration burning her skin and stealing her breath.

"Give her *back*!"

The man behind her lunged, his boots scraping the earth. Breen spun in time for her blade to clash against his. He pushed her down with all of his strength. Her muscles ached and her heart raced.

He pressed his blade harder, until one of her legs gave way, driving her to one knee.

"Mumma!" Nina screeched.

The man paused. This was her chance.

Breen rolled from the path of his blade and leapt to her feet as his sword hit the cobblestone. He stumbled and she slashed through his neck with every ounce of her strength.

He fell to the ground in a pool of blood.

Another cry filled the silence, that of a man. She spun in time to see Drakkone's blade pierce the abdomen of the man clutching Nina.

Her daughter fell to the ground and scurried away from the falling body. Wide-eyed and crying, she sat inches from the dead man.

"Nina." Breen sheathed her sword, ran over to her daughter and scooped her into her arms.

Cold relief stilled her heart and sent the heat of her rage racing to the recesses of her mind. Thank the gods she was all right. But again, she'd required the assistance of Drakkone. Time and time again he'd saved them on the road. Nina could have been taken if he hadn't shown up.

Her inability to protect her only child sent her eyes burning. She buried her face in Nina's silky curls and held her tight to her chest.

"Are you all right?" Drakkone breathed heavily. He sheathed his curved blade and gently laid his fingers on her arm.

Breen gasped, the sting of her cut sending hot pain through her entire arm. "Yes." She turned from his hand. "I'm fine. It's only a scratch."

Hooves beat the western road, coming toward them. Her heart leapt.

Nina leaned back, her tears gone, and worry creasing her brow. "Mumma, you're hurt."

She shook her head. "I'm fine, Nina. We need to go, *now*."

Drakkone nodded, breathing a sigh of relief as he ushered them both away from the bodies littering the road.

Someone grunted from behind them as he pushed to his knees. Breen narrowed her eyes. The one twin she hadn't killed.

A snarl rose to her lips.

"There isn't time." Drakkone took her elbow and yanked her toward the village.

Smoke filled the sky and shouts arose from within the small town.

"We can't take Nina there." Breen dug in her heels.

"We can escape in the riot." Drakkone paused, glancing over his shoulder. "There are always more of these cloaked men. We must go."

Breen glanced between the bodies littering the road, and Halivaara at the base of the hill, a mere forty feet or so away. She bit the inside of her cheek. "All right."

Nina clutched her shirt and nuzzled into the crook of her shoulder. The ache reminded her she'd taken a bad fall. She'd need to ice it tonight or risk having a worse injury in the morning.

Drakkone led the way down to the village, which burned with smoke. Cries filled the afternoon, while the approaching beat of hooves sent her heart racing. They needed to escape. But how?

Drakkone had entered Halivaara for supplies, but they had no horse, not any longer. They needed food more than they needed fast travel. They made due on foot, taking turns carrying Nina when she grew tired.

Her heart clenched. It had been weeks since she'd wished for the return of Dullahan. Maybe if they'd kept the stallion, they wouldn't be in this mess.

Sandstone homes with straw roofs rose from the dunes, bushes, and gnarled trees surrounding them. She'd hardly seen any trees in weeks, especially in the wasteland. But being so close to Seaburn's main city, where rivers occasionally flowed and the sea remained not too far away, some greenery lent the landscape substance.

Cries and shouts rose from the town square several blocks in. Drakkone led them as far around it as possible, but with the distant pounding of hooves drawing near, they needed a way out—and fast.

Whether the approaching men be Seaburn soldiers coming to save the day from the rebellion, or more mysterious cloaked men seeking her daughter, they needed to flee. And they needed to do it now.

Smoke filled the air, and flames rained down from the straw rooftops, aided by the wind. Her lungs burned, and a cough exploded from her chest.

"Cover your face." Breen raised the front of Nina's dress to cover her mouth. Unfortunately, Breen's leather armor wasn't so pliable.

"For the rebellion!"

Shouts filled the air, and boots trampled the nearby earth. Between two homes, the town center came into view, a large two-storey building, one of the few in town, rose high above the other homes. The crest of Seaburn, made of bronze, and nailed to two thick-wooden doors, burned with surrounding flames.

A crowd stood outside, fists in the air, weapons in hand.

"We need to get out of here. The riot is getting out of hand." Drakkone's pace quickened.

Breen lengthened her stride to match his. "How?" Her heart beat wildly against her rib cage. He was right, but she had yet to see any horses. Aside from the crowd at the center of town, there didn't seem to be any civilians around.

Drakkone remained quiet, leading the way out of the cloud of smoke and into a bazar. Most of the stands remained vacant, while a few carts spilled fruit across the street—abandoned.

If they had more time she'd pluck the fruit from the ground. Her stomach ached. When was the last time she'd eaten? A day ago? Two?

"Excuse me!" Drakkone called.

Breen twisted to peer around him. At the far end of the bazar, an old man with a carriage loaded crates of wheat and eggs into the back.

His eyes widened as he glanced over his shoulder.

"Stay back!" The man trembled as he withdrew a short dagger. He stepped back, knocking over several bags of rice piled by the wheels.

"We aren't going to hurt you," Drakkone returned in Seaburn's tongue.

Over their time on the run, he'd taught her much of his language. Finally, she understood the garbled words and strange nuances of their bizarre language.

"I said, stay back!"

Drakkone froze, as did she. Nina peeked from Breen's shoulder, blinking curious eyes at the old man.

"Are you headed out of town?" Drakkone raised his hands in a sign of surrender. They didn't want to hurt the man. They simply needed help.

"Yes."

"Is there any way you could spare a ride for three strangers?"

The man's dark gaze flickered from Drakkone to Breen and Nina, resting for a few moments on the sheaths at their waists. He hesitated, his mouth remaining open. "I-I can't..." He shook his head and lowered his blade.

Shouts rose closer, and the thundering hooves finally crested the hill. A wave of Seaburn soldiers rode over the cobblestone at the far edge of town. At least thirty men and women raced toward them, ready to injure and arrest anyone in sight.

Sweat beaded on her forehead, and her eyes widened. They needed to go. *Now.* Breen glanced between Drakkone and the man's cart.

"Please." She stepped in front of Drakkone, clutching Nina tight.

The man froze, his blade rising higher.

"We just need a way out of town," Breen explained, fumbling with Seaburn's language. She might understand it, but speaking it was another matter.

"I can't—" He paused. His eyes locked on Nina, who stared back, eyes glittering in the afternoon sun.

The terrified expression of the farmer, or whatever he was, turned soft. The creases of his forehead smoothed and his cinched brows relaxed.

Breen glanced down at her daughter. Though Nina didn't move, her eyes shone bright, nearly glowing in the sun. What was happening? Since Nina had been only a few months old, something beautiful and captivating had always drawn people to her. They'd received more help than they ever had before—from food and lodging, to protection from Seaburn soldiers on patrol.

But that help only ever came after their eyes lay on Nina. Could it be they simply wanted to help a young family? Or something more? Nina was certainly a special girl, smart for her age, and always learning. But was there something else pushing these people to lend their aid?

Her gut twisted and soured. What caused Nina's bizarre affect on strangers?

"All right..." The man shook his head, as if breaking from a daze. "All right, hurry. Get in." He sheathed his dagger and motioned them into the back of the cart.

His horse snorted and shook its mane, tapping the ground impatiently.

"Thank you." Drakkone smiled and approached. He heaved the bags of rice from the street and set them in the back of the cart before taking Nina from Breen's arms and setting her in the back as well. Once Nina was inside, his fingers locked around Breen's hips, and he helped her into the back over a short wooden plank nearly four feet off the ground. It'd be hard to get into the cart on her own, though his help only reminded her of her inability to protect their child when the moment had come.

Breen bit the inside of her cheek as she slid to the hay-strewn floor. Drakkone heaved himself into the back as Nina crawled onto her lap.

The man scurried around the raised bars on either side of the cart. The wood shook beneath them as he clambered onto the small bench at front of the carriage.

"All set back there?" he called back.

"Yes." Drakkone nodded, though the driver would never see him over the dozens of crates piled on top of one another.

With a snap of the reins, the cart lurched forward, away from the shouts of the rebellion, the cries of coming battle, and the last cloaked man who was certain to follow.

TWENTY-ONE

The carriage slowed to a stop at the edge of a large plantation north of Halivaara, far enough from any town that Breen could finally relax. A large two-storey wooden home occupied the end of the driveway, a lone gnarled tree at the center of the short road breaking the path in two.

Diagonal from the large house, a wooden barn stood tall, nearly the same size as the main home. A short wooden fence stretched out in either direction to indicate their land, while several pens inside held cows, horses and a few pigs. Beyond the buildings, large fields of wheat spread out to the horizon. The setting sun cast eerie shadows across the tall stalks.

"We're here." The man in the driver's seat glanced over his shoulder, an uncertain smile on his lips.

Drakkone leapt from the back of the cart first, stretching his muscles before reaching in to help Nina down to the dirt driveway. Nina clung to his neck as her father held her, overcome with exhaustion.

Without waiting for Drakkone's aid, Breen leapt out, glad to have solid ground beneath her. She stretched her aching limbs, relief sweeping her spine as she cracked her back. With the sun dipping over the horizon, it had been hours since they'd left Halivaara. Sitting still wasn't her strong suit, and after being stuck in the back of a cart for half a day, she was bursting with energy and ready for movement.

The tall, brown-skinned man circled the cart and extended his hand to Drakkone, who returned the gesture, shaking his hand in greeting.

"Thank you," he said. "We appreciate the help."

The man smiled. "Not at all. Excuse my earlier rudeness. The riots had me on edge."

"Understandable."

"My name is Jer."

"Drakkone." He nodded. "And this is Breen and our daughter Nina."

"Nina." Jer grinned; his eyes alight as Nina blinked open her heavy-lidded eyes. "What a beautiful name."

"Thank you." Drakkone adjusted his grip on Nina, letting her rest comfortably if she chose to sleep. It wouldn't be the first time she slept while they walked.

"Where are you headed?"

Breen glanced across the yard. Warm candlelight spilled from every bottom window of the house, while the upper rooms remained dark. Little curious eyes peeked from between thin curtains, but the child ducked back inside the moment she was caught.

"North." Drakkone shrugged. Non-committal. It couldn't hurt to be vague, just in case soldiers showed up at Jer's doorstep one day, asking where they'd gone.

"Ah. Bredon, I'm guessing?"

"Yes."

"A lovely town. Much cooler at the base of the mountains. Great for a vacation from this never-ending heat." He chuckled.

"Exactly." Drakkone smiled.

"It's a little late for travel now. You three should stay for the night.

My wife will have dinner ready any time, I'm sure. We have plenty of extra rooms for you."

Breen blinked at the man in surprise. Though he'd shown kindness at driving them from Halivaara and having them stay the night, feeding them was a new kindness in itself. Even Nina's affects weren't typically this generous.

"We wouldn't want to interrupt your evening any further—"

Jer scoffed. "Think nothing of it. I insist."

Drakkone glanced at Breen. His dark eyes met hers for a long moment, eyebrows raised. Breen shrugged. Nina was too tired for further travel tonight, and none of them had eaten since this morning.

The thought of a hot meal sent her mouth watering and her stomach growling. Though she wasn't sure if they could trust Jer, she did trust their ability to fight their way out of most situations. She only hoped it didn't come to that.

"All right," Drakkone agreed. "Thank you. Your generosity is unparalleled."

"It's nothing." Jer waved them off before leading the way to the house.

"Daddy!" The front door whipped open, slamming off the inside wall. A small girl, not many years older than Nina, ran across the sand, her dark curls bouncing as she leapt into her father's arms.

"Hila." Jer chuckled and embraced her. From the tone of their skin, to the slightly protruding ridge of their noses, it was clear this had to be his daughter.

"Daddy, you're home so late!"

He set her back on the ground, taking her hand as he led her back to the house. "Yes, I'm sorry about that." Hila glanced over her shoulder as Jer led her into the warm light spilling from the front door.

"Who are they?"

Jer glanced back, an amused smile on his lips. "New friends."

"Friends?" Hila beamed.

"Yes."

Nearly vibrating with excitement, Hila smiled back and forth between Drakkone, Breen, Nina, and her father.

Jer's heavy boots thudded against the wood floor as he stepped over the threshold several inches above the rough dirt path outside. "Come in."

Drakkone stepped in first, gaze darting around the foyer, searching for traps and enemies, she assumed. Breen joined them next. Lantern light filled the home, warming her skin as she passed by the thin glass. A small flame flickered inside, stirred by their movement.

"Jer! Is that you?" The high-pitched voice of a woman called from deeper inside the home. "You're late!"

"Apologies, my love."

A tall woman, a few inches short of her husband, appeared in the doorway. Her eyes widened as they met Breen's. "You brought guests." Her voice rose an octave. It was clear Jer didn't bring home many unexpected guests.

"Yes. This is Drakkone, Breen and the little one is Nina."

"Nina," the woman echoed. Her eyes met Nina's, which had opened with all the shouting. The woman smiled, warmth blossoming in her dark eyes. "What a beautiful little girl! Please come in."

Jer closed the door behind them, while his wife ushered them out of the foyer and into a wood-panelled dining room with red tapestries woven with gold hanging from the far wall.

Two more children sat at the table, one merely a few years younger than Breen, and the other no more than twelve. Each of them bore the same resemblance to their parents.

"Who is this?" The elder girl stood, her eyes widened as they landed upon Nina's dazzling gaze.

"Emha, Gelda, this is Drakkone, Breen, and their daughter, Nina." The woman swept inside, embracing her eldest daughter's shoulders as the girl stood from her meal.

The savory scent of stew wafted from half-empty bowls, filling her nostrils and stirring the hunger gnawing at her belly. Breen couldn't resist licking her lips, her stomach rumbling loudly.

"My apologies, you all must be starved! Please have a seat!" Jer's wife smiled and waved them all to the long wooden dining table with eight chairs surrounding it.

"Thank you." Drakkone smiled, shimmying through the tight space between the chairs and the window against the left-hand wall. "You're too kind."

"It's nothing." She turned to the kitchen through a curved archway.

Breen slowly sat beside Drakkone. Though her muscles urged her to stand, move, and get exercise, her stomach would not have it—not until she ate.

Nina sat in Drakkone's lap, her shoulders and head just cresting the lip of the table. Her eyes wide with curiosity, she glanced around the unfamiliar dining room, at the girls sitting across from them, Jer taking a seat at the head of the table, and his wife returning with wooden bowls. Steam rose from the contents, and Breen's mouth watered.

"Here you are," she said. "I'm Sula, by the way."

Jer flushed at the head of the table. "Apologies. Introductions are not my strong suit."

Sula gave him a teasing smile before slipping back into the kitchen for more bowls.

Emha leaned over to them. "Father is *always* forgetting his manners."

Breen smiled, and Drakkone chuckled.

While Breen took a deep breath, ushering the scented steam through her nostrils, Jer's daughters stared at Nina, wide-eyed and all smiles.

Drakkone remained stiff at her side, clearly uncomfortable with the attention their daughter was getting and unsure of this bizarre situation. She couldn't blame him. They didn't typically stay with strangers, and seeing how these strangers reacted to Nina, Breen and Drakkone could no longer ignore or explain away this bizarre affect Nina had on people.

From her blonde hair, and blue eyes, which neither of them

possessed, to her interest in reading over playing with other children, it was clear Nina wasn't a normal child.

"Eat, eat!" Sula flicked her fingers at them as she returned, two bowls balanced on one arm. She set them before her husband, and Hila, who'd climbed up into her father's lap, very similar to how Nina sat.

Once they were all seated with food in front of them, Sula returned to the opposite end of the table, taking her own seat before a slightly less steamy bowl of stew.

Breen's hunger could be ignored no longer. Licking her lips, she plucked the wooden spoon from the bowl and tried a sip. Heat scorched her tongue. Salt. Meat. Vegetables. Savory broth. Her shoulders relaxed as she devoured her first bite—ignoring the sting of her tongue.

"It's delicious," Drakkone said, before taking his second mouthful.

"It truly is," Breen mumbled around her next bite.

"Why thank you." Sula beamed.

Once the stew had cooled, Drakkone shared his bowl with Nina, who hardly ate anything. With her drooping eyes, Breen couldn't blame her. After all the day's excitement, she deserved a good night's sleep.

"So, where are you headed?" Sula asked.

"Bredon," Jer answered for them.

Breen was grateful they'd already told him their little lie. It gave her more time to devour her stew. It had been some time since her hunger was satiated.

"Ah, yes. A beautiful town. Very cool below the mountains."

Jer chuckled. "The very same thing I told them."

Sula flushed. "Well, it's common knowledge, dear."

"True."

"Will you be staying with us long?"

"Not long," Drakkone said. "Just for the night, if that's all right."

"Oh yes, yes! Please stay as long as you'd like! We don't get many guests so far out of town." Though Sula spoke to Drakkone, she was hard pressed to remove her gaze from Nina.

Discomfort stirred in Breen's belly. She shifted, swallowing her stew around the lump forming in her throat.

"You're very kind." Drakkone nodded.

After a few minutes of eating, they finished up, and Sula and her daughters quickly scurried between the table and the kitchen, rounding up dishes.

Now that she was well fed, energy surged through her limbs, lighting her veins with sparks. Breen shifted in her seat, glancing between Drakkone, Nina, and the others.

"You're fidgeting." Drakkone leaned in close to her ear.

"We've hardly moved since this morning." She shot him a sideways glance.

Drakkone sighed.

For years they'd trained every night after Nina went to bed. It was getting to be that time, and her muscles ached to be used. Even with the bit of blood and dirt coating her skin from her small battle in Halivaara, she'd rather fight than wash up and relax.

"Fine, but we should get Nina to bed first." Drakkone quirked a brow.

Breen sighed. "All right."

"I think Nina is ready for bed." Drakkone cleared his throat.

"Of course! Emha, would you show them to the guest room?" Sula glanced at her daughter, who hovered by the kitchen door.

Emha nodded, short brown curls bouncing around her heart-shaped face. "Of course, Mama."

"Thank you, Dear."

They all stood, Drakkone carrying Nina with her head on his shoulder as they shimmied out from behind the table, and up the stairs in the main entry. Emha carried a lantern up the narrow passage into a wider hallway of the same wood. Many doors occupied the walls on either side. They did have a fairly large family, and quite a big house. They must make good money off farming if they had a few extra rooms.

"Here you are." Emha paused at the end of the hall, holding the lantern aloft as she swung the door inward and motioned them inside.

"Thank you," Drakkone said.

Breen stepped inside, Drakkone following, with Emha at their heels. Her bare feet thudded against the wood before being muffled by a thick rug. She lit two lanterns and several candles.

Warm light filled the small space. Thin sheets and a single thick pelt lay across a wide bed in the corner, while a washbasin sat atop an old dresser, worn wood cracking with age.

"Do you need anything?" the girl asked.

"This is perfect, thank you." Ever the gentlemen, Drakkone smiled, and Emha blushed before nodding and rushing from the room.

The door clicked closed behind her. While Breen paced the room, inspecting the yard beyond the window, Drakkone placed Nina in bed, pulling the sheet and pelt over her shoulders before sitting at her side.

"You should take a few minutes to relax." Drakkone leaned back against the wall at the head of the bed.

Breen glanced over her shoulder. Though her muscles still itched, ready for action, she shouldn't force Drakkone right into practice so soon after eating. "Fine."

She joined Nina and Drakkone in bed, sliding up the other end closest to the wall. With Nina sound asleep between them, she leaned against the wall in the same way Drakkone was.

"Jer took us all the way from Halivaara, and even still he lends us aid."

Breen sighed and pulled her legs up to her chest. She knew exactly where he was going with this. It wouldn't be the first time someone had went above and beyond to help them, but only after their eyes met Nina's. Everything changed after that.

"He seems like a good man." Breen shrugged.

"Yes. But you know it's more than that."

She met his gaze. His brows furrowed over dark eyes. "I know."

"What are we going to do?"

"Nothing." There was nothing they could do. Whatever Nina's ability, or affect on those around them, she was their daughter, and Breen would be damned if she'd let anything happen to her.

Drakkone sighed. "It's as if she uses her ability to protect us sometimes."

Breen glanced at him. She'd noticed as much too.

"She understands so much more than she should," Drakkone continued. "When my little sister was her age, all she did was run around playing. She hated naps and despised sitting quietly at dinner." He smiled at the memory.

Breen's heart clenched. It had been a long time since he spoke of his family. After her mother was killed, she had a feeling he stopped speaking of them on purpose, for fear it would make her relive it all over again. He wasn't wrong.

"She's special," Breen said.

Drakkone shook his head. "It's something more."

She quirked a brow. "Like what?"

He paused, staring at the wall at the far side of the room. "I'm not sure."

"We'll figure it out." Breen turned onto her side and reached across Nina's sleeping form. She took his hand and squeezed.

Drakkone smiled. "We will."

* * *

DIRT CRUNCHED beneath their boots as they stepped across the lane, small pebbles kicking up beneath their heels. Every night after Nina went to bed, Drakkone and Breen would train. While Drakkone had spent her pregnancy and the last three years growing stronger, she'd spent her time regaining the strength she had.

She was determined to reach his level and beat him in their sparring matches.

Her fingers itched by the hilt of her blade, eager to begin. They stood across from one another, a few yards from the main house.

Drakkone drew his sword from his sheath and stepped back into his usual defensive stance. Breen pulled hers from her hip, pointing her blade in his direction.

Her heart raced as she waited for his signal. She would improve, and she would protect their daughter.

Drakkone held up his blade. "Begin."

Breen lunged forward, driving her blade against his. They clanged together, Drakkone swiping hers back. She leapt away before he could drive his blade at her gut. After three years training together, she knew his tactics well.

He shifted forward to stab her shoulder. She spun from reach, flashing her sword for his neck.

Drakkone ducked, slamming his shoulder into her chest.

Wind exploded from her lungs as she fell backward. She hardly caught herself, shifting into a crouch.

He'd won. Again.

"You're fast, but you aren't guarding your chest enough," he chided. Drakkone stepped back, waiting for her a few feet away, in the same stance as before.

Breen took a few deep breaths before she straightened. She stood opposite to him in her ready stance.

"Again," she said.

Drakkone nodded stiffly. He knew how seriously she took these practices, and disapproved of her overzealous attitude.

"Begin."

Again, Breen leapt. Instead of throwing her blade at his, she dove to the side, slicing for his hip. Drakkone jumped back as she leapt up, driving her blade at his gut. His sword slammed against hers, sending it sailing across the yard.

"Damn," she hissed.

"Wrap the cloth around your wrist so you don't lose your blade."

"*I know*," she snapped.

Breen retrieved her blade from the ground and returned to her ready stance. Drakkone inspected her face, her furrowed brows and irritated frown. He sighed before nodding. "Begin."

This time Breen didn't move. Let him make the first move.

Drakkone smiled. He already knew what she was doing.

A light breeze tickled the hairs on her neck. She remained poised, taking even breaths through her nose to keep calm.

After several long moments, Drakkone lunged. He sliced for her gut. She jumped back. He drove the tip of his sword at her shoulder. She slammed her blade against his, opening up his chest.

Finally.

Breen drove her sword for his heart.

He ducked. As her blade sailed over his head, he grabbed her elbow, twisting her arm painfully. She released her blade as he swept her feet from beneath her.

Her breath whooshed from her lungs as she fell.

Drakkone wrapped an arm around her waist, keeping her several feet from the ground, stopping her fall. His warm chest pressed against hers, radiating heat even through her leather top.

Breen blinked at him with wide eyes, her heart pounding in her ears, far louder than it had in battle. His hot breath brushed her cheeks. She flushed. They hadn't been this close in awhile.

"Breen..." he began, but didn't finish his sentence.

Drakkone leaned down, pressing his lips against hers. Her heart leapt as heat rushed through her chest. Breen kissed him back, wrapping her arms around his neck, her fingers twining in his hair. Drakkone pulled her back up, his hand on her neck and arm around her waist, holding her tightly to his body.

The door to the house creaked open.

They leapt apart, faces flushed red and eyes wide.

"Apologies." Sula smiled sheepishly from the doorway. "I just wanted to ask if you'd like one of the girls to watch Nina while you practice."

Breen shook her head and cleared her throat. Embarrassment at being caught flew through her limbs. "No, that's fine. We're done." She paused. "Our practice I mean!"

Sula's knowing smile didn't leave her face as she nodded and stepped back inside, shutting the door quietly behind her.

"Bree." Drakkone's fingers brushed her elbow.

Breen stepped away. "I should go check on Nina." They hadn't been intimate in nearly a year. Her heart raced and her mind flew in all direction. She didn't know what to say or do, so instead she fled.

TWENTY-TWO

Drakkone slept soundly, his heavy breathing filling the silence of their small room. One lantern remained lit, casting shadows across the wall.

Breen lay on her back, her heart pounding and her fingers tapping against her stomach. Even after practice with Drakkone, where she'd underperformed yet again, she couldn't rid the anxiety bubbling in her chest. Their kiss flashed across her mind. Heat filled her.

She shook her head. She couldn't think about that now. She needed to move. To act. To do *something*.

She sighed. Thinking about it wasn't helping. But what could she do?

Her gaze flickered from the ceiling, to the door, to the window.

Maybe fresh air would clear her mind. Or perhaps a few laps around the property. Breen bit the inside of her cheek. If Drakkone woke and she wasn't there, he'd worry. Even worse, what if Nina woke to her mother missing?

Squeezing her eyes tightly shut, Breen bit back a frustrated growl.

She couldn't remain still any longer.

Shimmying from beneath the fur draped over her lap, Breen slipped from the bed and onto the floor. By the light of the lantern she found her boots, leather top and pants. She slipped them on before strapping her sword to her hip. Just in case.

Breen paused for one last look at her sleeping daughter. Nina lay curled up against Drakkone's side. Her soft blonde curls lay across her cheek and shoulders, while her fingers wrapped around the fur blanket. She sighed and shut the thick wooden door behind her with a click.

Shadows drenched the hall in black. Boards creaked beneath her feet. Breen stepped as lightly as she could, but nothing could prevent the creaking of the hall. She descended the stairs to the foyer, where a single lantern remained lit next to the door, hung on a metal hook.

She peeked outside. Cool night air brushed her cheeks. The moon shone down upon the yard, casting cold blue light over the gnarled tree at the center of the drive. Its branches swayed in the breeze.

Breen stepped onto the driveway and stretched. She'd have just enough light to see by. Enough to run by. Breen took deep breaths, letting cold air wash her lungs.

A stab of recognition halted her steps.

Cold this dense hadn't entered her lungs in a long time. Not since she'd been drowned repeatedly. She shivered. Goose bumps crawled across her skin. She couldn't think about this now. She couldn't think about it ever again. It was behind her. All the way back in Seaburn city, where she prayed it'd remain.

So instead of thinking, she ran.

Dirt crunched beneath her boots as she loped across the long drive. Wind brushed her thick braids over her shoulders. Her sword tapped against her leg with every bound, a welcome reminder.

She hardly made it across the driveway when a crack cut through the quiet.

Breen spun toward the barn and froze.

What was that? The entire house had been asleep, her family included. Who was in the barn?

Warm lantern light seeped from between a crack in the barn

doors. Murmuring voices drifted on the light breeze. Not just *someone* in the barn, but perhaps many.

Breen glanced back at the house. Only a single lantern lit the front entry window. If the house was quiet, who could be inside?

She gulped the lump forming in her throat. She had to know.

Breen crept forward.

Whether Jer's family had somehow slipped out of the house without her notice, or Seaburn soldiers staged an attack—she had to be ready.

The thick wooden doors to the barn muffled the sound, but the thin space permitting light between them might allow her to listen to the conversation within. She crossed the yard, lightening her steps until she reached the door. Breen crouched and narrowed her eyes as she peered between the slats.

"We need to formulate an attack," a man said. Tall, with black skin and haunted eyes. His fists shook at his sides.

"Don't be so rash." Jer rolled his eyes as he paced the barn floor. Hay kicked up beneath his boots, and horses chuffed in their stalls, unhappy at the late night disturbance.

"If we want to stage a coup, we have to be smart about this." Another man, short, and blue-eyed with tawny skin. She'd only ever seen this shade of blue eyes on another tribesman once before. Moigrin's sister. Could this man be related to them? He was certainly old enough to be their father. But why would a tribesman from the North be so close to Seaburn?

"But an attack could hurt their resources—"

Jer cut him off. "An attack is *not* the way to go. Not yet."

The man snapped his teeth shut, and narrowed his eyes, not pleased at being overruled.

What was going on here? What attack could they be planning? One against the clans? Or Seaburn? Had an official rebellion finally risen?

Breen shifted, glancing left and right at the dim barn, trying to see who else might be inside. Though several other shadows occupied the space, they turned from the door, their faces hidden. She sighed, her brow cinched as she shifted on her heels.

The sheath of her sword scraped pebbles, sending several knocking against the thick wooden door.

She froze.

Damn.

All eyes turned to the door.

Breen quickly stood, stepping away from the barn. Her heart leapt. She couldn't make it back to the house without being seen. She could try hiding in the fields, or around the barn. Maybe they'd think it was simply the wind?

She bit the inside of her cheek. Footsteps thumped against the inside.

Too late.

Breen threw the doors wide in time to meet the first man who'd spoken. His dark eyes met hers, a splinter of fear registering in their depths.

"Breen." Jer flew across the floor, shooting panicked glances at the other men and women present. "What are you doing here?"

"What's going on?" Breen narrowed her eyes.

Jer glanced at the man beside him. "A meeting."

"I can see that. What is it for? Why have it in the middle of the night?"

Jer sighed and shook his head. "Come inside, and we'll explain."

Breen did no such thing. The second she stepped inside they might try to overpower her and attack. She remained in the doorway.

Once Jer seemed to realize she wouldn't be going anywhere without an explanation, his rigid brow softened and his shoulders relaxed. "This is a meeting of the rebellion, Breen."

The rebellion?

Her eyes widened. So she'd been right.

"Jer!" the other man growled. "What are you doing? You're risking us all!"

Jer levelled him a look. "If we can't let tribesmen in on our plans for the Empire, someone we're readily trying to aid, then why should we bother?"

The man's lips snapped shut.

Riots thrown in the name of the rebellion had been cropping up for years. Though they'd started in Seaburn City, they'd started showing up everywhere, which was evident from the riot they'd ran through in Halivaara.

"*You're* the rebellion?" Breen quirked a brow.

Jer smiled. "Yes."

She glanced around the barn. Two other men stood with two women. Two more tribesmen, and two more Seaburn-born, one a man, one a woman. So the rebellion was being thrown on both sides. The tribes were getting involved.

Her heart clenched.

She had been waiting for this day. The day when Seaburn no longer had a hold on her people—the day when they could fight back.

"Part of it at least." A woman standing further back motioned them back in.

Breen only hesitated a moment before following, Jer and his comrade leading the way. When they all stood in a circle, only then did the rebels seem to relax.

"We plan to overthrow the Emperor and put into place a democracy of equal rights." The tribeswoman met her gaze. "We've let Seaburn take our children for far too long."

Heat flamed through her chest. She knew all too well.

"We want a better life for this kingdom. Too many are starving or dying in the streets." The man next to Jer grew rigid, his jaw hardening. So these Seaburn men and women did believe in this. They believed the tribes deserved better.

Finally.

"Where are our manners?" Jer shook his head. Sula was right; he did forget introductions quite often. "I'm sure you've guessed most of this. But we should introduce ourselves. You already know me." He paused and motioned to the tall black-skinned man. "This is Vasily."

"Vas," the man corrected.

"Yes, he goes by Vas." Jer smiled. "This is Arowyn." He nodded at the tribeswoman. "And these are Sundas, Elgen and Hana."

"We're calling ourselves the Seaburn Council," Vas said.

"Yes," Jer agreed. "Until the time where elected officials can be put into place. We'd have both men and woman of Seaburn and the tribes involved."

"And how do you plan on overthrowing the Emperor?" Breen raised a brow. "He has thousands of soldiers. Most of which are loyal to him. They have no choice but to be."

Jer's brows rose, and his eyes held pity. Breen bristled.

"You wear Seaburn military garb." Jer glanced at the leather's wrapping her body. "You were taken, weren't you?"

Her jaw hardened. She nodded.

"Then you know not all Seaburn soldiers are loyal to the Empire."

He was right.

She hadn't been the only soldier smart enough to fool the dungeon guards into believing she was broken. Moigrin had chosen to remain, for a purpose much like this.

"We have contacts among the soldiers' ranks," Vas explained. "They'll help us get inside and stage a coup."

"And you're sure you can trust them?" Her stomach soured, overcome with nerves. She couldn't help it. Every word they spoke could be her family's salvation—or ultimately their ruin.

"We're sure."

Pebbles crunched outside. Each of the council members froze.

Breen spun for the door, her hand on the hilt of her sword.

Drakkone appeared at the edge of the lantern light. He held Nina in his arms. Her blue eyes scoured the inside of the barn, wide and alert.

"Nina. Drakkone." Breen stepped toward them, but paused.

Drakkone's dark eyes clouded, staring ahead unseeing.

"Mumma." Nina beamed.

Drakkone stepped inside, as if driven by some unknown force. He didn't look at her, or the other men and women present. He simply stared, sightless.

"Drakkone." Her eyebrows tightened. "What's wrong?"

He said nothing.

She glanced at Nina. "Nina, what's going on?"

Nina smiled, tilting her head. "I wanted to see what was going on, Mumma."

Breen glanced between her daughter, and the Seaburn Council. Each of their eyes had grown wide, filled with wonder and adoration. Their gazes locked on Nina, smiles pulling at the corners of their lips.

"Nina, what's wrong with your father?" Breen joined them in the entry, as did the council members. They cooed and bathed Nina in compliments.

Her daughter simply giggled, beaming at the men and women— clearly satisfied with their attention.

Breen pressed her fingers to Drakkone's cheeks, and turned his face down to look at her. His dark gaze was slicked with grey. His lips remained slightly parted, as if he remained asleep.

Her heart plummeted and she backed for the door. Cold slithered through her chest. Her heartbeat sped.

It was as she had feared for so long now. Nina's powers went beyond drawing kindness out of strangers. She could control their minds.

Dirt crunched beneath her boots as she backed onto the driveway.

What was her daughter? What gave her this power?

She shook her head. Whatever it may be, it wasn't normal.

And neither was Nina.

"Nina, whatever you're doing, I need you to stop." Breen met Nina's gaze.

Her brows furrowed. "What do you mean, Mumma?"

"Let your father go."

Nina twisted her lip between her teeth.

"*Nina.*" Though cold washed her limbs, she had to get Drakkone back.

Nina sighed. Drakkone set her on the ground. The moment she left his arms, Drakkone thumped against the barn floor.

Breen gasped and rushed forward. She kneeled at his side. It had been as she thought, Drakkone had never awoken.

* * *

BREEN PACED the village bazar of Halivaara. Even after the riot the previous day, the streets still bustled with people, who seemed no longer concerned over the rebels haunting their town.

Drakkone crunched behind her, rushing to catch up.

"Breen."

She didn't slow.

"Bree!"

Drakkone's warm fingers wrapped her elbow. He didn't stop her, only pulled her back gently, slowing her pace. "What's wrong?"

She glanced at him. Her stomach turned. Unease filled her.

"You still have no memory of last night?"

Drakkone shook his head. "None. If Jer hadn't confirmed it, I might have thought you were dreaming."

Breen scoffed. "I'd know if I had been dreaming."

He smiled.

"I think we should leave. Whatever is going on, it isn't safe for her. It isn't normal." Her voice cracked around her dry throat.

His expression grew slack with surprise. "Leave? Why would we do that?"

"Because it isn't safe."

"What about the Seaburn Council? The rebellion?"

When Drakkone had woken that morning she told him all about what she'd learned. His eyes had lit with his smile. This is what he had wanted since the day he met her family and realized the tribes were fine on their own.

She shrugged. "They can do whatever it is they're planning without us."

Drakkone's jaw hardened. "Bree. You can't be serious."

"Of course I'm serious. We should leave tomorrow. Get Nina far away from all the chaos. Maybe Bredon isn't such a bad idea."

He shook his head. "But we could help them create a better Seaburn for everyone. Not just Seaburn citizens, but for your tribes."

Her heart clenched.

As much as it warmed her heart and stirred her affection for the man, to think he wanted to fight for the tribes, they didn't need his help. They needed Seaburn to leave them alone. She couldn't go along with any of the Council's plans. She had to think of Nina. She was the priority.

"It isn't our problem anymore. We need to get away before we're found." She looked ahead, unable to stand the look of disbelief on Drakkone's face. Her heart pounded in her ears and her mind swirled. Cold fear slicked her throat.

Following the Council's plan could mean putting her family in danger. Though she'd never run from a fight before, she had to flee this one. Her head ached. She could hardly think with her mind spinning.

"Bree," he pled.

She shook her head. She wasn't changing her mind.

They continued in silence. Seaburn men and women strode by with wicker baskets, and children at their sides. Instead of fighting with wooden swords or dancing across the streets, the children remained close at their parent's sides, their dark eyes darting across the street.

Smoke no longer clouded the air, but the acrid scent of ash remained. Most of the damage had been toward the center of the village, so the bazar had moved several streets over, where the fire hadn't reached.

Somewhere along the row, Jer sold wheat and wicker toys for children—a hobby of his wife's. They were to meet him before sunset. He'd return them to his farm for one more night. They had to gather supplies for the coming journey.

While Drakkone paced in silence at her side, Breen eyed several carts of fruit and vegetables. Brilliant greens, vivid reds and mouthwatering blues. She licked her lips, but continued on. They couldn't afford such frivolities.

Tall wooden stands holding weapons slowed her pace. The glint of steel flashed sunlight into her eyes. Several shields hung from the front of the stand, while swords sat atop the counter.

The metal shined, new and well cared for. She stepped toward them.

The shields were cleaned so thoroughly they reflected the surrounding bazar. Breen's own tawny cheeks and dark braids appeared in one. Drakkone stood at her side, strangely malformed on the sleek surface.

A shadow moved at their backs.

Breen froze.

A man in a dark cloak hovered across the street, in an alley between two stands. Several people passed by the surface, obscuring him. She straightened and glanced at Drakkone. His gaze lingered on a cart across the street, freshly cut red meat and a butcher behind the stand.

"Drakkone," she hissed under her breath.

The people in the shield passed. The cloaked man remained. Watching. Waiting. She swallowed.

"Drakkone." She spoke slightly louder, but didn't dare move.

His dark eyes met hers.

"They're here." She nodded in the direction of the alley across the way.

His jaw hardened. He held her eyes for a long moment before relaxing his shoulders and stretching. He glanced over his shoulder as he did.

When his arms dropped back to his sides, he met her gaze, eyes wide. He'd seen the man. Or men. However many there were this time.

"We need to go. Now."

Though Jer wouldn't be expecting to leave for another few hours, they couldn't wait. They'd steal his horses if they had to.

Drakkone nodded abruptly and steered back the way they'd come, toward Jer's cart at the end of the long street.

"Stay calm." Drakkone squeezed her elbow.

Breen nodded. Her heart thumped against her ribs. She swallowed, thankful they'd left Nina with Jer's family. At least she'd be safe while they were gone.

"We should try to lose them." Breen wrapped her arm around his; as if it were any other day and they were simply a couple walking the market. His skin warmed hers.

It had been some time since she'd touched him for anything other than training. Until their kiss at least. Her cheeks warmed at the memory. She missed the passion that had kindled their relationship and given them their daughter. Maybe one day they could stop running and marry.

She shook her head. There was no time to think about that now.

"Agreed."

Drakkone pressed against her side, steering her down a joining street. Breen didn't dare look over her shoulder. She didn't dare try to find the shadows at their backs. Any unusual movements would have them found. The faster they were found out, the sooner they'd need to flee. If the men in cloaks realized who they'd come with, not only would they endanger Nina, but Jer's entire family.

Breen bit her tongue to hold back her panic. Pain flooded her mouth. It cleared her mind. They could do this. They could get away.

They turned onto another street.

Her heart thumped faster.

She glanced into a home's window. The glass reflected the street, and two shadows at their backs.

Damn.

Her grip tightened around Drakkone's. He met her eyes and squeezed back briefly. His immediate understanding blossomed warmth through the cold drawing goose bumps to her flesh. They'd been partners for some time now. Even if they hadn't been as romantically involved as they once had, this man knew her better than anyone.

Drakkone had them winding down street after street, through alleys, between gnarled trees in someone's yard, and back into the bazar.

Surely the men couldn't still be following.

She had to know. She had to risk it.

Breen glanced over her shoulder.

No one but Halivaara citizens remained in sight.

She exhaled a long, relieved breath. "They're gone."

Drakkone's rigid shoulders relaxed. "Thank the gods."

They continued through the bazar until they reached Jer's cart. He'd already sold several of the dolls he'd brought with him, along with half his supply of wheat.

"We need to go," Drakkone said.

"Already?" Jer raised his brows beneath a straw hat.

"The men we told you about this morning—the ones following us. They're here."

His eyes widened and he nodded quickly. "Let's not waste any time."

TWENTY-THREE

*S*moke rose in the distance, dark grey clouds rising into the setting sun. Breen's heart hammered in her chest as she stared wide-eyed at the horizon.

The smoke came from Jer's house.

"Faster. We need to go faster!" Breen gripped Drakkone's arm.

The three of them hardly fit on the front bench. Wedged between the two large men, Breen wanted nothing more than to lunge into action, to whip the reins and send the horses speeding up the sandy path.

Jer nodded. Sweat dripped down his temples as he whipped the reins.

The two mares whinnied and took off. The earth rumbled by below, bouncing them up and down in their seat.

Only a few minutes left until they arrived. The peak of the barn crested the sandy hills. The high branches of the gnarled tree rose next. Almost. They were almost there.

Breen bit the inside of her cheek. Her heart raced in time with the hooves of the mares. They shouldn't have left Nina behind. They should have brought her with them. It had been foolish of them to trust in Jer's family. Foolish of them to trust anyone's protection but their own.

What if Nina had already been taken? Or worse, what if she were hurt? Or killed?

No. She couldn't think that. It wasn't possible. It couldn't be.

Fear gripped her heart in a vice. Her breath fled her lungs.

Dense black smoke rose from flames licking the roof of the barn. Cries came from within.

Nina's cries.

The back of her eyes burned, and she half stood in her seat, ready to leap out.

The cart lurched closer and closer until they skidded left onto their road and then right into the driveway. Jer yanked up on the reins and Breen leapt with Drakkone to the pebbled path before they'd come to a full stop.

"Nina!" Her throat burned with her scream.

Breen raced across the driveway, heat scorching her skin as she drew close to the gaping barn doors.

"Nina! Where are you?" Drakkone cried. His chest heaved with each breath, and his gaze darted through the smoke clouding the barn.

"I'm going in." Breen leapt through the dense, acrid air.

"Bree, wait!"

She was already gone.

Her throat burned with every inhale. Breen covered her mouth. Fire lapped at the hay along the far side of the barn. Horses whinnied and cried, stomping the ground inside their pens.

Her heart tightened.

She spared a quick moment to throw open the gates of the closest two. Their chests slammed against the bars, forcing it open the moment she threw the latches. The horses ran from the smoke and out the door, their hooves trampling the wood, the sound echoing in the hollow barn.

"Nina!" she called.

Her heart rammed in her chest.

"Mumma!" Nina screamed. Her voice rose high. Sobs permeated the crackling of the flames.

Between the creak of wood, swords clashed.

Breen ripped her blade from its sheath, ignoring the smoke, ignoring the fire. Her daughter was in trouble.

She emerged at the back of the barn, smoke clearing just enough for her to see the battle waging in the center of the floor.

Two cloaked men lay dead, blood pooling around their limp bodies. Another man stood against four others, his eyes sightless, and his jaw slack. His sword collided with those of the other cloaked men.

What was going on? They were fighting each other now?

Nina cowered in the corner against a hay bail. Her shoulders shook with her sobs and her red face was streaked with tears.

"Nina!"

Breen dashed around the skirmish and knelt beside her daughter, scooping her up into her arms.

"Mumma!" Nina burrowed her face into the crook of her neck.

"Shh my girl. I'm here now."

Nina nodded half-heartedly.

The cloaked man continued to fight, through every cut, every stab, every hit. Her brows cinched. Why would he do this? Why would he risk his life to protect her daughter?

She froze and glanced down.

Nina.

She was controlling him. She was using him to fight for her.

Breen swallowed the lump in her throat and stood, leaving Nina on the floor as she stepped between her daughter and the enemy.

"Mumma." Nina whimpered.

"Hush," she soothed. "Mumma will protect you."

Nina nodded slowly and embraced herself as Breen pointed her blade at the five men before her.

One stabbed his blade through the gut of Nina's protector. That was it for him. He fell to the ground, blood gushing from between his lips.

The other four advanced.

Breen's lips pulled back in a snarl.

"She's coming with us," one of them said, his voice flat and monotone.

"*Never.*"

Breen leapt, her sword clanging against that of one man. He didn't growl or snap like a man in battle typically did. He simply stared through her with vacant eyes, much like those of men and women Nina affected.

Her brows pulled together.

Could someone like Nina be controlling these people? If so, who? And how could she find them?

A roar broke through the crackling of flames, and Drakkone leapt through the smoke, driving his blade through one of the cloaked-men's backs.

Wordless surprise spread on the man's face before he collapsed.

Breen pushed back on the blade of her attacker until she pushed him off balance. The man stumbled, but recovered before she could plunge her sword through his gut.

He twisted from her path, his blade whipping out to catch her shoulder. Pain flared through her skin, but didn't drive deep enough to hit muscle.

She leapt back, slapping her blade against his. He pushed on, pressing his advantage.

Breen let him, allowing him to push her back with all of his might.

She stepped to the side. He toppled forward.

Sticking out her foot, she tripped him. He crashed to the ground in a tangle of cloth and limbs. Breen drove her blade through his spine before he could twist away.

He fell limp.

Breen spun as motion flashed in her peripheral. She leapt back on instinct. A long sword flashed in front of her eyes, fraying the ends of her braids.

Her heart rose into her throat.

Too close.

Instead of lunging for her again, the man went for Nina.

Wrong choice.

Breen leapt in, thrusting her blade at his spine. He spun out of reach.

Damn.

Her lungs burned and her eyes stung as she squinted through the smoke. She needed to end this, and end it quickly—before she passed out.

The man leapt, and she dove to the side, bouncing back quickly to her feet. She brought her sword up in time for his to clang against hers. She gritted her teeth as he pressed down. Breen narrowed her eyes at him.

He pushed harder.

Her leg gave way and she fell to one knee. She couldn't push him back, and from this position, she'd be a fool to try and roll away again. She'd be dead in moments, a blade through her back.

Breen growled, fury lighting her veins. She couldn't let Nina down. She couldn't let herself down. She had to kill this man. Or they'd take her daughter. They'd take her to the gods only knew where. She couldn't allow that. She wouldn't.

She wrapped her left hand around her blade. Her palm stung as she pressed back. Her sharp sword sliced into her palm. She had no other choice. She had to push him back.

Breen rose to her feet, her muscles straining under his weight. He might not be a huge man, but he could overpower her if she didn't use all of her strength.

Her blade continued to cut deep into her hand. She gritted her teeth. Just a few more seconds and she'd kill him. Heat flared through her chest.

How dare these people come into this home and try to take her daughter? How dare they attempt to harm those she loves?

She'd make them pay.

Breen thrust with all of her might. The man stumbled back. A brief look of surprise passed over his smooth features. She smashed her boot into his hand. His sword flew.

With a battle cry, Breen leapt. She thrust him back, her blade sinking into his abdomen. His back collided with a wooden beam and her blade sunk into the wood on the other side.

He stared at her with wide eyes.

Her breath fled her lungs. Tears welled in her eyes from the smoke.

But she'd done it.

Breen pulled her blade free and stepped from reach.

Drakkone scooped Nina into his arms. The remaining men were already dead. Blood bubbled on the hot wood.

A crack above sent her heart racing.

"We need to go!" She shot a desperate glance at Drakkone.

He nodded, and ran for the exit.

Breen was quick on his heels, her muscles pumped, her breath coming in quick gasps as she dove back through the dense smoke.

Her lungs burned and she coughed violently. Her whole body shook. Then clear air embraced her and cooled her throat.

They raced away from the burning structure, back to Jer's house.

Drakkone flung the door in and leapt inside. "Jer!"

Breen joined him, slamming the door behind her before she stooped to catch her breath. Cool air slipped down her raw throat. She desperately craved water to soothe the burning, but it'd have to wait. Coughs racked her chest.

"Jer!" Drakkone called again.

They stepped out of the foyer, and into the dining room.

Drakkone froze, and she nearly slammed into his back.

Copper tinged the air.

Her skin went cold. No. Not them.

Breen peered around Drakkone. Two bodies sat in their usual seats. Emha and Gelda. Their wild dark hair spilled over the table. Blood slowly dripped down Gelda's long fingers, creating a small pool by her chair.

Her heart skipped. Her breath fled.

Sula lay in the archway between the dining room and the kitchen, face first in a pool of red. Jer sat near her head, back against the cupboards, Hila cradled in his arms. Tears streaked his face. His blood shot eyes refused to leave his wife's body.

"Jer," Drakkone whispered. He held Nina tighter, keeping her facing Breen instead of the horror before them.

"My girls." Jer shook his head slowly. "My girls."

Tears stung the back of her eyes. All words fled her. For what could she say when this man had lost everything—every*one* he loved?

The door to the home thudded off the wall.

Breen spun, flashing her sword out.

She froze mid swing, the point of her blade a mere inch from Vas's throat. Her racing heart stilled. "Vas."

"Breen." The man's eyes widened as he stared down at her curved sword.

"Apologies." Breen lowered her blade.

"It's all right." Vas swallowed before he cleared his throat. "What's happened? Why is the barn on fire?"

"They came." Breen couldn't help the widening of her eyes. "They killed them all. They nearly took Nina."

"*What?*"

Breen shook her head and stepped aside to reveal Jer's family.

Vas gasped, his eyes flying wide. "No."

Again, tears burned her eyes. This time they fell.

"Jer." Vas rushed forward, rounding the bodies before kneeling at his friend's side. He reached out, gripping Jer's shoulder. "Jer."

The man only shook his head and gripped his daughter tighter. His mouth quivered as he tried to form words. But nothing came.

"Jer, my friend." His voice cracked. "I'm so sorry. So, so, sorry."

Drakkone stepped out of the dining room and back into the foyer, taking care to block Nina's view of Jer's family. Her lids were heavy anyway, fluttering half-closed in her attempt to stay awake.

Whatever she'd done to protect herself—whatever she'd done to that man—it had taken a lot out of her.

Breen joined Drakkone, letting Jer and Vas have their privacy.

Flames of anger licked her throat, chasing her tears away. It wasn't fair. None of this was fair. This poor family had taken them in, only to be slaughtered for gods only knew what purpose.

Where was the justice in this? What was the point?

"Are you all right?" Drakkone's fingers brushed her elbow.

She shook her head, unable to meet his gaze. "This is why we should have left. This is why we must *leave*." She dropped her voice to a whisper. "Those people are dead because of *us*."

Blood dripped to the floor from her clenched fist. Pain shot up her arm to her elbow. She was injured. Right. But compared to the tragedy in the other room, it didn't matter.

Drakkone wrapped his free arm around her shoulders. Though fear and frustration burned in her stomach, she embraced him. The warm bodies of her daughter and Drakkone pressed against her chest.

She squeezed her eyes shut.

They should have left that morning like they'd intended. But Jer had convinced them to stay another day and gather supplies before their long journey to Bredon. One they'd never planned on in the first place.

Breen wrapped her fingers around the back of Drakkone's leather shirt as she buried her face against his chest. He stroked her hair, his fingers soft and gentler than she'd ever expect from such a large man.

She wanted to blame him, or Jer—or someone for this. But there was no one to blame but the men lying dead in the barn.

Someone cleared their throat in the arch of the door.

Breen stepped back quickly, swiping tears from her cheeks. It wasn't the time to feel this pain. It was time to run.

"We should go before Seaburn soldiers descend upon us." Vas shifted uncomfortably, his hands bunching his long cloak as if he were unsure what to do with them.

Drakkone nodded. "We'll leave."

"Come with us." Vas met Drakkone's gaze before flicking to Breen.

"We can't," she blurted.

"The rebellion could use people like you two." Vas smiled half-heartedly. "We can protect you too. You and Nina."

Hot anger flared into her throat. How dare he use protection for their daughter to manipulate them into agreement? Breen narrowed her eyes.

"What is your plan?" Drakkone sighed. She'd never heard him so exasperated.

"To assassinate the Emperor. We have a small group inside the Academy. They're going to help us get inside and stage a coup. Once we have the Palace, we'll be able to instate new laws, new rules. We'll be able to protect you and the tribes."

Breen worked her jaw. It all sounded too good to be true. Yet, with every word Drakkone's eyes grew wider—filling with hope.

"You know the rebellion is the right thing for this Kingdom. It's the right thing for *everyone*." Vas met her gaze, brows raised.

"You want us to put ourselves and our daughter back in harms way." Breen hardly kept the growl from her words. Whether she wanted Seaburn pushed into a better future or not, she couldn't risk Nina.

"As I said, you'll all be protected. There's no reason to fear. We have a safe haven outside Seaburn's capital. We'll be close for when we make our move. We have dozens of warriors protecting the compound. You won't find any place safer in all of Seaburn." Vas glanced between them both.

While Drakkone slowly nodded, her stomach turned. She didn't like this. Not one bit. They didn't know this man. They hardly even knew Jer and his family. Yet this man invited them—strangers—to join a rebellion years in the making. How could *he* put his trust in them?

Breen slowly shook her head.

"We should help them, Mumma."

She glanced at Nina, who blinked heavy lids in her direction.

"We should help them make Seaburn better." Nina nuzzled her father's arm. "If it'll make Daddy happy."

Drakkone smiled down at her.

Breen sighed. This wasn't right. This wasn't safe. But with fire eating the barn and only the horses Vas must have brought with him to escape, what choice did she really have? They had to run before Seaburn, or worse, arrived.

"All right."

"Excellent." Vas smiled and nodded. "I'll get Jer and we'll be on our way."

TWENTY-FOUR

The cart lurched across the cobblestone path, sending her tumbling left and right. Breen growled, biting her tongue as she righted herself in the back of the trolley—only to be thrown once again.

"By the gods. When will this trip end?"

Drakkone chuckled. She leaned against his shoulder, unable to do anything else with the constantly bouncing cart. She shouldn't have let them convince her to sit in the back. Though riding up front couldn't be much better.

"We're almost there." He smiled.

"How can you be sure?" She narrowed her eyes.

Drakkone tilted his chin up, motioning to the road ahead.

Seaburn's capitol rose from the sand, the cliff at its back a harsh contrast to the blue sky. The palace stood tall, nearly blocking out the sun. Bright rays pushed past the smooth sandstone, leaving white spots across her vision.

Breen rubbed her eyes and looked away. She hadn't been this close to Seaburn in over three years. The last time she'd seen the golden domes and thick pillars, she'd been riding in the opposite direction—

away from Seaburn's madness. She'd never looked back. Never regretted her decision to flee.

But instead of fleeing for the Wasteland like she so desperately wished, they rode toward enemy territory—the last place she thought she'd ever willingly go again.

"Can't say I miss it." Breen leaned her head against Drakkone's shoulder. His shoulder warmed her ear. Nina slept in his lap, cradled in his arms. How she slept through all the bumping, Breen couldn't be sure.

Drakkone smiled, though the warmth didn't reach his eyes. He wasn't from her world. Though he'd seen all the horrible things Seaburn had done to her and other tribesmen. This place was still his home. His family lived there. He once lived there. He'd grown up in the streets of Seaburn and until a few years ago, he'd never thought of his home as evil or wicked, like she'd been raised to believe. She had to remember that while evil things had been done there to her and many others, not all in Seaburn were evil. The man whom she leaned on, the man she loved, was proof of that.

"Do you miss it?" She avoided his gaze, instead watching the sleeping Nina.

Drakkone shifted slightly. His eyes bore into her scalp, but she refused to look in his eyes. Whatever he told her, she wanted that to be the truth. She didn't want to read something else in his eyes.

"We're here!" Vas called back.

Breen straightened up to peer out the side of the cart.

In the shadow of the Seaburn Palace, a wide lake spread across the sand, several extravagant homes surrounding it, including a large compound with a black iron gate.

Maybe they would be safe with the rebellion. Maybe this would be a good place to protect Nina from harm. With the high walls, it wouldn't be easily penetrated. Yet, Seaburn soldiers weren't the only thing she had to worry about anymore. Could these walls keep out the foreign, cloaked assassins? She hoped so.

The cart continued up the main road until they reached an inter-section, where Vas turned onto a slightly smoother path headed north, toward the compound. The high stone walls towered above as they drew near, casting shadows on her face.

They didn't stop until their horses stood directly before the iron gates.

"State your business," a man atop the wall shouted, half-hidden by a guardrail. "And your names."

"Vasily," the council member called back, an irritated edge to his voice. "You know very well who I am, Gerin. Let us in."

The man froze. "Sorry, sir."

Moments later, the gate lurched upward, slowly retracting into the wall above. As soon as it settled into the arch of the gate, Vas snapped the reins and led the horses in.

Inside the compound, the main home rose two stories tall—sand stone walls, with a beautiful flat porch and palm trees on either side. Stables sat near the gates, and a second building made of wood sat in the corner, half the size of the main house. Possibly servant's quarters.

Breen stilled. Only one entrance meant only one exit. Though there might be a hidden escape route somewhere, she could only see one. Her heart leapt into her chest. What if they'd walked right into a plot by the Emperor?

The cart halted by the stables and Vas jumped out. Jer slowly slid to the ground after him, his whole body sagging with the weight of his family's demise.

Her heart pounded faster.

"All right. We're here." Vas circled the cart and waited patiently while the three of them dismounted.

Half a dozen guards stood atop the walls while another dozen or two roamed the yard, carrying bales of hay, or practicing with swords. They spared a few glances, but none approached.

Her heart slowed. Maybe they weren't in any danger. After all, no one had leapt at them yet or come running with chains and cuffs.

"This is an old summer home, isn't it?" Drakkone stared at the beautiful home at the sunniest corner of the large compound.

"It is." Vas nodded. "It belonged to my family."

"It's beautiful."

"Thank you." Vas smiled and motioned to the house. "You'll be safe here. We have everything you could possibly need, and of course trained men to protect you." Vas took the lead, his boots crunching in the dirt as he made his way to the extravagant home.

"I used to go to the lake outside every summer when I was a boy." Drakkone grinned. His eyes shone with pleasant memories.

"It's a popular spot," Vas agreed.

"Can we go to the lake, Daddy?" Though Nina continued to curl up in Drakkone's arms, her eyes were wide open and alert.

"I don't know if that'd be wise, Nina." Drakkone's smile drooped.

"I'm sure we can arrange an escort if the little one wants to swim." Vas paused before the few steps leading to the wide porch.

"She doesn't know how to swim yet," Breen said.

"I could always teach you." Drakkone smiled at his daughter, and Nina beamed up at her father.

"Can we please?" Her small fingers wrapped into tiny fists.

Drakkone chuckled. "As long as it's okay with your mother."

He shot her a glance. Breen narrowed her eyes. This was already an unfamiliar place, and yet he wanted to leave the safety of it for a lake surely occupied by enemy soldiers. Madness. All of it.

"We could wait until sundown if it'll ease your concerns, Breen," Vas said. "The soldiers disappear around then."

Breen worked her jaw back and forth. She still didn't like it. But Nina continued to give her big eyes, begging for the chance at adventure.

"Fine." Breen sighed.

Nina grinned and squealed while Breen shifted from foot to foot, unsure of what to say or where to go in this new world of theirs.

* * *

THE SUN DIPPED in the sky, bathing the earth in warm light. Pink and orange filled the horizon. They'd have more good weather tomorrow, typical of Seaburn.

Nina screeched as she splashed through the lake's once still surface. Drakkone held her hands while she kicked, laughing in her attempt to keep above water. They both smiled. They were both so happy here. It had been a long time since they'd felt safe for more than a few hours. They'd been on the move for years and they were tired of it, as was Breen.

Despite this fatigue, she couldn't still her pulse pounding in her ears or the writhing anxiety twisting in her gut. They'd been running for so long it seemed impossible to stop. At any moment Seaburn soldiers could descend upon them. Any moment the men in black cloaks could return to try and take her daughter.

Breen brushed her fingers against the worn leather of her sheath. It lay in the sand at her side, ready in case of danger. Breen shook her head, a frustrated sigh hissing between her teeth.

"You don't look very relaxed."

Breen jumped, nearly twisting to her feet.

"Apologies. I didn't mean to startle you." Vas smiled, a few feet from where she sat in the sand.

She took a deep breath and her heartbeat slowed. "It's all right."

"May I join you?"

She shrugged. Vas sat in the sand a few feet from her, keeping a respectful distance as he watched her family in the lake. Before they'd been escorted to the lake, Vas had told them to relax, take the night off and tomorrow they'd return to fighting. Tomorrow they'd plan a war. Tomorrow they'd worry. But today they deserved rest.

But was rest simply the calm before the storm? Was this quiet evening, this delightful smile on her family's faces—were they the last good thing she'd see before the fight started up again?

"I found information on the men in the barn."

Breen whipped toward the man. "What?"

Vas met her widened gaze. "This isn't the first time they've been spotted near Seaburn." He paused. "Have they been following you for long?"

Breen nodded. "Years now."

"They don't come from this land." She'd guessed as much from their pale skin and strange weapons. "They come from across the sea, from the kingdom of Warshard. They're quite different than us." Vas smiled faintly. His dark eyes blazed with curiosity. He clearly wanted to know much more about this new land. "We've had visitors from these lands over the years, but none have caused trouble quite like this."

"Why do they want Nina?" Her voice was small, even to her.

"I'm afraid I don't know."

Her shoulders slumped. She knew it was too good to be true.

"What do you know?" she asked.

"There are six kingdoms. Though similar to the Empire, each kingdom has a royal bloodline resulting in a monarchy."

Breen tilted her head. "And how is that different than Seaburn?"

Vas smiled. "It isn't really. But apparently they work much better together with a system to share their supplies. Their armies are all volunteers and most of the kingdoms get along from my understanding."

Breen quirked a brow. "Is such a thing possible between *six* kingdoms?"

Seaburn and the Savage Lands had a hard enough time getting a long. Having six nations working together seemed impossible.

He shrugged. "I'm not sure. It's simply what I've been told."

"I still don't understand what these people want with Nina."

"I don't either. But knowing where they're from is a start."

Breen nodded. He had a point.

"I'm glad you and your family decided to stay."

She couldn't help but snort. They hadn't really been given much of a choice. Come with them for protection and to help the rebellion, or be lost to the desert and all the dangers it held. Between the dangers posed by simple survival, the Emperor and his armies, and that of these strange foreigners, having a place to protect them seemed like the only choice—especially when Drakkone and Nina wanted it.

"Nina is an incredible little girl." He shifted in the sand, crossing his hands in his lap. She had a feeling he didn't spend much time sitting on the ground. His finely stitched robes certainly conveyed upper class.

"She is." Breen bit the inside of her cheek.

"She might be able to help in this rebellion."

Breen started. "She has nothing to do with this rebellion. What do you want from her?" She knew there had to be an alternative reason for their invitation.

Vas smiled. "May I tell you a little story about a boy much like Nina?"

Breen worked her jaw. "Why not?"

"My family wasn't always wealthy. I grew up in a tiny village west of Larwik." The name sounded familiar, most likely somewhere Drakkone had mentioned they could go. "Growing up, there was a boy only a year older than I. Somehow, and to this day I don't understand how he did it, but he could control the minds of others."

Her breath caught in her throat.

"He was eventually killed in a raid, but my point is, he helped our village more than anything. He swayed marauders to leave us alone, got information from strangers so we knew they could be trusted. He even brokered a deal with Larwik to deliver water to our village at a more than fair trade." Vas smiled at the sky, lost in memories. "Our village would have disappeared without him. We all would have died."

"And you think Nina is like this boy?" Her voice cracked around her tight throat. If this was true, maybe there were more people out there like her daughter.

"Maybe, maybe not. Either way, it could be Nina's destiny to help Seaburn too. One day she could do great things, just like that boy did." Vas lowered his gaze to meet hers. His dark eyes were solemn, his mouth set in a thin line. He'd cared about this boy, and continued to mourn his loss. That hadn't been an easy story to tell.

"Maybe," Breen agreed. Maybe her daughter was meant for great things. Maybe she would save them all from the Emperor's wrath.

Breen looked at her giggling daughter, paddling away in the lake alongside Drakkone. She smiled and sighed wistfully. Whatever they did, as long as Nina was safe, Nina could save anyone she wanted.

TWENTY-FIVE

urved arches adorned the ceiling of the two-story dining hall. Pillars lined the room, with several halls leading to the rest of the house. Morning light spilled through the upper windows, warming her cheeks and dusting the room in a soft glow.

Breen leaned against her hand, propping her chin in her palm wrapped in linen. She stifled a yawn. She hadn't gotten a good sleep the night before. Too many thoughts swirled through her mind, threatening to keep her from sleep for the rest of her days.

Was what they were doing safe? Should they stay? Leave? Where would they go? Each question kept her up until the horizon brightened. When she'd finally fallen asleep to the heavy breathing of Drakkone, and light snoring of Nina, crows outside their window cawed her awake.

The world seemed bent on keeping her out of bed.

But as much as the soft furs called to her, she couldn't stay. Instead, she joined her family and the rest of the compound for breakfast.

"This is amazing," Drakkone mumbled around a mouthful of eggs.

Breen smiled. She twirled the tip of her fork against the plate. For the first time in a long time, she wasn't hungry. Her gut remained empty, hollow, like a cold void sitting at her core. They were close to

Seaburn. *So* close. And still in danger. No matter what Vas said, she didn't know these people, and she couldn't trust them.

Nina might be meant to do great things, but she would do them when she was older. When she could *fight*.

"Good morning." Vas passed through the dual pillars marking the main entrance to the dining hall. He waved briefly at the others, seated randomly around three long banquet style tables.

"Good morning." Drakkone nodded in greeting.

"The Council will meet shortly and we'd love for you to join us." Vas smiled. He held his hands together in his long sleeves, his skin barely peeking out.

Breen glanced at Drakkone. He met her gaze. She shrugged and nodded; she couldn't see any harm in it.

"All right. Where should we meet you?" Drakkone asked.

"I can take you there now." Vas motioned back to the door.

Drakkone had already devoured his breakfast, and Nina had done the same, clearing her plate of eggs and bacon in minutes. Breen on the other hand still had most of her food present.

"Apologies, I thought you'd be done with breakfast by now."

Breen shrugged. "I'm done." She stood, leaving no room for questions.

Vas smiled and nodded before leading the way out of the dining hall.

Breen held Nina's hand as they followed. Her tiny warm fingers wrapped around Breen's, and her gaze darted around the unfamiliar building. Nina had been ready to explore since she awoke. Sitting through a meeting might not be the best use of her energy. If they could get her to sit still at all.

Colorful tapestries of the jungle hung from each wall, depicting a different scene or animal. Nina's eyes widened as they passed a particularly fearsome jungle cat. Its lips pulled back, stretching around long teeth. Yellow eyes glared at some foreign attacker.

"What is *that*?" Nina yanked on her hand and motioned to the animal.

"A tiger." Breen smiled as warmth blossomed in her chest. There was so much Nina had yet to see—so much for her to learn. If only she could join her mother in the Lesson Hut one day.

Her heart ached. Nina would never meet her mother, maybe not even her father if he hadn't survived the attack.

"Here we are." Vas halted before two thick wooden doors with iron clasps and handles. "We should be the last to arrive."

Vas flung the doors open and stepped inside.

A long room, not quite as large as the dining hall, spread out before them, held in by thick walls adorned in paintings, and an arched roof. Tall arched windows cut from stone gave them a view of the compound wall. The walls must not have always been around.

"Good morning!"

At the center of the room, a long wooden table waited, with over a dozen high-backed chairs pushed in. Only half were occupied.

"Good morning." Vas gave a small half-bow before he closed the doors behind them and took an empty seat next to Jer, who slouched against the table, staring at his hands. "I believe you've met some of the Council before."

Breen nodded. She recognized them all from the barn, though their names evaded her.

"Drakkone, you weren't... yourself, that night." Vas motioned to each of the Council members. "These are the rest of the Seaburn Council members. Arowyn." The tribeswoman. "Elgen." A Seaburn-born man, clearly a soldier in his early years. "Hana." A Seaburn woman. "And Sundas." A tribesman.

Each bore a red circle on the arms of their tunics—the sign of the rebellion.

"It's nice to meet you all." Drakkone took a seat across the table from Vas. Breen sat beside him, hoisting Nina up onto her lap so she could see above the table.

"We'd like to make a proposition," Vas continued. "We need your help."

"*Our* help?" Breen quirked an eyebrow.

"Well." Vas paused for a long moment, glancing at each of the other council members. Dread swelled in her stomach, turning her insides.

The story about the boy like Nina came to mind, and she knew what Vas would ask of them. "We need Nina's help. Her abilities. We want her to help us infiltrate the palace."

Breen's mouth fell open.

This was exactly what she'd been afraid of.

Vas rushed to continue, "Using her powers of persuasion, we could get access to the chambers of the Emperor easily. With the help of our contacts inside the Academy and the Palace guard, we'll be able to take out the Emperor and take hold of the Palace in one fell swoop."

Her stomach soured. She wrapped her arms around Nina, cold rushing through her limbs and numbing her fingers.

"No."

Everyone in the room turned their gaze on Breen.

"Breen—"

"*No.* I will not let you put my daughter in danger." Breen held onto Nina tightly, who shifted uncomfortably in her rigid grip.

"Bree…" Drakkone reached for her hand. She pulled away.

Would he truly side with them when the safety of their daughter was at stake?

"Please take a few moments to think this over," Hana urged. Her dark eyes met Breen's. "We know what we're asking of you is a lot, but we wouldn't be asking if we weren't sure we could protect Nina."

"I said, no. I will not allow you to bully me into accepting this. I will not allow you to bring Nina into that place, and I will not allow you to make me think this is even a remotely good idea." Her lips pulled back, and she bared her teeth.

Arowyn, the tribeswoman, met her gaze, her brows cinched together—sympathetic. "Breen, I know what we're asking, but—"

"Mumma, why can't we help them?" Nina tilted her head back, her eyes meeting Breen's. Bright blue swirled in their depths. Mesmerizing.

"Because, it isn't safe." She froze, but she didn't mean to. Her grip loosened, allowing Nina to turn and face her.

"But you can keep me safe, Mumma."

Breen shook her head, her neck stiff, and her head heavy. "No."

"You and Daddy can. I want to help them, Mumma. I want to help you."

"Nina, do you know what could happen?" Drakkone's brows furrowed.

"I know about the men in the hoods. Bad things happen when they appear. They die and you and Mumma get hurt." Nina glanced between them with wide eyes. "I want to help so we can live in a real home."

Breen's heart clenched painfully. Nina had grown quickly, her intelligence increasing far past that of a three-year-old. Breen had always known she was different. She'd always known she was special. Nina understood far more than she let on. She'd only been with the rebels a day, and she knew she wanted to help them. She knew she could.

"We... can't." The words fell off Breen's tongue like sap. Slow.

Her mind raced, yet her body wouldn't behave. She wanted to take Nina's hands, look in her eyes and make her understand. But the swirling, endless depths of blue weren't just those of her daughter — they were those of her power. Nina was doing something to her, whether she meant to or not.

"Nina." Drakkone laid his hand on her shoulder, but she hardly felt it. Everything went hot, then cold. Numbness spread through her body. "What are you doing?"

Nina didn't remove her gaze from Breen's. She didn't blink. Didn't move. "Mumma, we *need* to help them."

She couldn't shake her head. Couldn't force the word *no* from her lips. Her jaw locked and her fingers twitched in her lap.

Nina was controlling her.

This is what it felt like to be controlled by her daughter. She had no say. There was nothing she could do. She was stuck. Wooden. Frozen in time.

"Yes." She didn't say the word. But it was her voice that spoke.

Nina smiled, her rosy cheeks puckering with dimples.

Breen slumped back. She gasped as if rising from water after holding her breath for too long. Like she'd been doused by buckets of ice water in the Seaburn dungeons. Her fists clenched but her skin went cold. She could move. She could breathe. She could control herself. Her fingers wrapped around the arms of her chair, her nails scratching the wood.

Her body shook as Nina turned to sit back in her lap, facing the others, as if nothing had happened.

"Bree." Drakkone wrapped his fingers around hers. "Are you all right?"

Breen didn't have the strength or energy to shake her head.

"Then it's settled." The rough voice of Elgen broke the silence. "We'll have Nina's help in this."

Drakkone's jaw hardened as he met the man's gaze. "We will be there with Nina the entire time. She will *not* leave our side. If it becomes too much for her, we're out, and you're on your own."

Vas nodded stiffly. "We agree to your terms."

BREEN STUMBLED through the double doors of the meeting room and into the hall. She gasped in a breath, trying to still her shivering as she held herself up against the doorframe.

"Bree." Drakkone's boots followed.

She flung herself from the door and further into the hall. Her legs shook beneath her, and her lips quivered.

"Bree!"

She shook her head, fleeing down the hall, away from the council and away from Nina.

"*Bree!*"

She kept going.

Never before had she been afraid of her own daughter. Never before could she have imagined Nina would use her powers on her own mother. Yet she had. And she *hated* it. The cold. The heaviness. The sudden weight and stiffness of her own limbs. She couldn't control herself. She couldn't do *anything*. If this is what it felt like to have her mind controlled, she couldn't wish it upon anyone else. It was a violation. A breech in trust.

Rough fingers wrapped around her elbow and spun her around.

Her legs buckled beneath her, dumping her into Drakkone's arms. He embraced her, holding her tight to his chest, keeping her aloft.

"Bree." His warm breath brushed the strands of hair from her face. "I'm sorry."

She shook her head. Her eyes stung. "You all just sat there. You let her do that to me." She could hardly hear her own voice. Never before had she felt so small. So weak. Only she had felt like that once. In the bowels of the Academy.

"I'm sorry." His arms tightened.

"Tell me you felt it too. Tell me you didn't just sit there and let our daughter control me." Her fingers closed into fists.

Drakkone sighed. "I'm sorry."

So he had. He let her. He allowed Nina to betray her. To use her. What kind of man did that? What kind of man allowed his lover, or whatever they were to each other, to suffer in such a way?

"No." She got her feet under her. "No, you're not."

"Bree."

"Leave me be." Breen pushed away from him.

His eyes widened, and his brows tightened. Hurt passed through his gaze.

Breen shook her head and left.

TAKING OFF ON HORSEBACK, Breen rode out of the compound, her heart racing with the wind rushing through her hair. She snapped the reins, and her mare took off, kicking up sand.

She needed to think to clear her head. She couldn't stay in the compound and have herself further influenced by Nina's mind control. Whether she was using it for what she thought was the good of others, or not, it wasn't right. It wasn't normal, and it wasn't fair.

Breen shook her head.

Cold air assaulted her bare arms, bringing goose bumps to the surface. She bit down on her lip and dug her heels into the mare.

Their gallop turned into a sprint. Though the sun was rising higher, she couldn't feel its heat. She couldn't feel its rays.

What would her mother do if she were here? What would her father say?

She scoffed.

Her father would lunge into battle at the first chance he got—but he'd never let her fight before her time. Bringing Nina into a war zone would be out of the question—even if it gave them the advantage.

But her mother would stop. Her mother would think. She'd mull it over until she was completely sure they were doing the right thing. She'd weigh the pros and cons. The good of the many versus the good of the few.

She'd do it. Her mother would take Nina to Seaburn if it meant saving all the tribesmen. She'd give up her own daughter to save them all. She'd always been a proud woman—but not like her father. She could be reasoned with. She was the smartest woman Breen had ever known.

But which of her parents should she emulate?

Which knew the correct path? Which would get her daughter out alive, *and* help her people at the same time? There were risks with both. And could she truly pull Nina away if Nina wanted to stay?

Her mind control proved she couldn't.

Breen had no say in this. She was trapped. Locked into a game she didn't agree to play.

Her eyes stung with the wind, sending tears streaking over her cheeks.

Maybe Drakkone was right. Maybe they should help the rebellion. But at the cost of their daughter? She gritted her teeth.

Never.

That left only one option. Breen had to protect her. She'd go with the raiding party, or whatever they were calling it. She'd keep Nina close, and guarded. She'd insist on as many other soldiers as they could possibly send. And at the first sign of trouble, she'd get Nina out. She'd knock out her own daughter if it meant saving her life.

Breen bit back a sigh. She hated the position they'd driven her into. But this was the position she had been born for. This is the one she'd been bred to deal with. She'd been trained to fight since an early age. She could best almost anyone in her tribe. She could do this. She'd kill anyone she had to for Nina.

She yanked up on the reins, slowing the gait of her horse.

By the time she turned around, the sun blazed high in the sky, ready to dip in the east. Gnarled trees rose out of the desert. She had to be halfway to Sarton. Maybe closer.

Breen urged her mare back towards Seaburn. Her heart slowed. She could do this. She had no other choice.

With the wind whipping in her hair, she hardly thought through the rest of the ride. Instead, she embraced the calm. The quiet.

When the lake finally crested the horizon, the sun had begun to dip behind the palace atop the cliff. Long shadows blocked out the sunlight, leaving dark claws to rack the desert.

Breen slowed by the lake's edge. No children played in the water today. The cold breeze kept them away. Trotting past the large expanse of water, Breen approached the compound on the far side— the home deepest in shadow.

A rumble like thunder broke across the stillness of evening.

Her heart leapt.

What was that?

Shouts rose from the compound.

Nina.

Breen snapped the reins and dug in her heels. Her mare whinnied, rearing before she took off running. "Come on!" she snapped, sitting high in her saddle as she rode for the rebels' headquarters.

TWENTY-SIX

reen burst through the gates of the compound, her heart pounding in her ears, and eyes wild. Swords clanged in every direction as Seaburn soldiers and men in black cloaks fought the rebels.

"Nina!" she cried, pushing through to the main house, which swarmed with soldiers on the steps.

Her horse leapt up the stairs as Breen ripped her sword from its sheath. She sliced her blade across the necks, shoulders and backs of the men she passed, leaving a trail of blood in her wake.

"Nina!" she called again, her voice rising high above the chaos.

Rebels leapt in to fend off the attackers while Breen slid from the mare's back, and dove into the main house.

Shouts, cries, and the roars of battle filled the home, echoing off the sandstone walls. Her legs pumped with newfound energy, steady beneath her as she raced through the halls.

She shouldn't have gone—shouldn't have left. She should have stayed to protect her daughter. She should have stayed with Drakkone. She should have accepted his apology and dealt with it like a warrior would.

Breen shook her head. Her self-pity could wait.

Her family could not.

Swords clashed in the main dining hall, filing the empty space with the rumble of battle.

She skidded to a halt between the two pillars leading down to the main floor. She searched the crowd for the blonde hair of Nina, the tall frame of Drakkone.

Nothing.

"Damn." Breen leapt back into motion, her heart racing with her steps.

Why had the black-cloaks suddenly teamed up with the Seaburn soldiers? She shook her head. She didn't believe in coincidences. She couldn't believe this was some accident. Whatever this was, it had been planned—and planned well.

"Nina!" Her voice echoed off the high walls of the hallway.

She couldn't live with herself if something happened to Nina or Drakkone. She couldn't go on without her family. She'd tried so hard for so long to keep them together. She wouldn't give up now.

Swords clanged before a loud thump sent a soldier flying from the meeting room. His back cracked against the wall opposite the doors.

Drakkone leapt out after him, thrusting his blade through the chest of the soldier.

Her breath exploded from her lungs in a relieved sigh. "Drakkone!"

He turned, yanking his blade from the body of the man. "Breen. Where have you been?" His brows pulled up, not in anger, but in concern.

"I had to think." She shook her head. Now wasn't the time for this.

Drakkone nodded. He understood.

"Where is Nina?"

He motioned her back inside the meeting room. "She's safe."

Inside the large room, the council members waited. Those of Seaburn descent cowered at the back of the room, all but Elgen. Though he had to be reaching his sixties, he stood tall, his sword drawn. The tribesmen waited by the end of the table, their swords up until they realized who stepped inside.

"Everyone's safe." Drakkone shut the door behind them. The bar to lock the door lay in splinters across the smooth floor.

They couldn't stay here.

"Nina," Breen said.

The blonde hair of her daughter peeked around Elgen's leg. Her blue eyes met Breen's. Her heart tightened. The last time she'd stared into her daughter's eyes, she'd taken control over her body.

"Mumma!" Nina leapt from her perceived safety and raced across the room. Her eyes welled with tears, glittering in the low light of lanterns.

Her heart leapt. She bent to one knee as Nina threw herself into Breen's arms. She embraced her daughter, squeezing her tightly, her heart pounding. She couldn't stay mad at this girl. She couldn't be upset with Nina. She was so young, and though she understood much, she couldn't be held accountable for powers she had yet to truly grasp. There'd be time to teach Nina when and where to use her powers. Now was not the time.

"Nina, you're all right." Silk curls slipped between her fingers.

"I'm sorry, Mumma." Nina nuzzled against her neck, her fingers clutching her tunic.

Breen smiled. "I know."

A crash in the hall had her leaping to her feet. Breen held Nina tightly, and swung toward the door.

The clamor of battle continued—heavy footfalls, grunts and the clang of swords. They couldn't stay here. Not now. Whatever was going on—whoever had staged this attack—none of it mattered. Getting Nina to safety had to be the priority.

"We need to go." Breen met Drakkone's gaze.

He nodded. "Elgen, how far is the drop from those windows?"

The elderly man stepped from his protective stance to the large windows cut from stone. His shoulders filled the width of the center window. Though the home was built on a platform, she couldn't imagine much lay between the windows and the ground below.

"Eight feet. Maybe nine," Elgen reported. "No signs of the enemy."

"Then we head out that way."

Breen quirked a brow. "Are you certain? How will we escape the compound?"

Drakkone met her gaze. "The gates were open upon your arrival?"

"Yes."

"Then we sneak to the stables, and flee on horseback."

Breen nodded slowly. Though she hated to run from a fight, there was much more at stake than her warrior pride. "All right."

"There's still twenty feet of open space between the house and the stables." Arowyn joined them, concern creasing her brow.

"If the battle is still waging; they'll be distracted."

"It's our best bet." Sundas lay a hand on Arowyn's shoulder. They exchanged a long look before she gave a swift nod.

"Let's go."

"I'll protect the door until you have everyone out." Sundas stepped passed them and held his sword aloft, waiting by the double doors.

Arowyn's jaw hardened. "Then so will I."

Sundas sighed but offered a small smile. "What else could I have expected?"

Arowyn smiled back as she joined the man, their battle stances familiar. It had been a long time since she'd seen the warrior stance of the tribes.

Elgen leaned outside the middle of the trio of windows, glancing left and right. "We're clear." He stepped back. "I should go first, just in case trouble comes."

"Agreed." Drakkone stalked the length of the room to join the council members.

Climbing atop the ledge, Elgen sat and shimmied out as far as he could. Drakkone stepped up beside him and offered his hand. Elgen accepted, holding onto Drakkone as he slipped from the sill. Drakkone's bicep bulged under the weight of the man. He leaned out, slowly lowering Elgen until his boots came within a foot of the ground. Elgen let go and landed with a soft thump.

"Who's next?" Drakkone turned his gaze on the rest of the council.

One by one, Drakkone helped lower Vasily, Jer, Hana and then

Nina to the ground below. When they'd all safely stepped aside, Drakkone turned to Breen. "You're next."

Breen raised a brow. "You think I can't handle myself up here?" she teased.

Drakkone smiled. "You know that isn't true."

Breen flashed a toothy grin. "Then you go and I'll lower you."

Drakkone laughed, shook his head and winked. "Maybe I will."

Breen just grinned and stepped onto the ledge. She trusted him. He wouldn't be far behind her. Breen sat and gripped Drakkone's warm hand. His fingers squeezed hers before she'd even slid forward to drop. He met her gaze, his dark eyes warm. She squeezed his fingers. They would get out of this. They would save their daughter. Together. And then they would learn to live life like other families, again, together.

She slid from the ledge. Drakkone kept her aloft, lowering her until she reached the ground. He gave her fingers one last squeeze before releasing her and turning inward. He should be next. He should join them.

Yet he didn't appear on the ledge.

Her heart hammered as Nina clung to her pant leg.

"Where's Daddy?"

Breen glanced down at Nina's watering eyes. "He's coming."

Nina nodded, while Breen watched the arched window.

He didn't reappear.

A crash from within sent her heart racing. "Drakkone!" She stepped for the window, but she'd never be able to climb back up. "Drakkone!"

Arowyn appeared in the arch. She leapt, and the council members scattered to let her land. She landed on her feet.

"What's happening in there?" Breen snapped.

"Soldiers busted inside." The woman stood. "Sundas forced me out the window."

Her heart pounded in her ears. Damn him. Damn Drakkone and his need to protect others he hardly knew. He should have come after her. He should be down here. What if he was injured? What if he needed help?

Sundas leapt from the window. He rolled as he landed, not quite as graceful as Arowyn had been. A long cut marred his shoulder. Blood dripped down his bicep.

"Sundas!" Arowyn reached for him.

"I'm fine." He stood.

That was it. That was all of them. All but Drakkone.

Breen faced the window. No one appeared in the arches.

"We should head for the stables," Elgen barked. He faced the length of the narrow alley, ready to head along the wall to the corner. Once they rounded the corner they'd be able to slip along the wall until the house ended and open space began.

"Not without Drakkone," Breen snapped.

"We need to get everyone to safety." Elgen growled.

Breen faced him, her lips pulling back in a snarl. "We *wait* for Drakkone."

Elgen parted his lips to speak, but Nina stepped in front of her mother. "We wait for Daddy." She narrowed her big eyes at the man.

He froze, his eyes flying wide as he met Nina's.

Breen glanced between them. At least Nina's abilities came in handy.

Another crash from inside had her turning back to the arches, in time for a black-cloaked man to sail outside and into the compound wall. A loud snap filled the empty space. He slid lifeless to the ground.

Heavy boots hit the ground behind her.

"Why isn't everyone moving?"

Breen turned to find Drakkone at her back. She sighed with relief. "Never do that again."

He raised a brow and grinned that grin that always made her heart thump a little harder. "Worried for me?"

Breen narrowed her eyes, making him laugh. *Always.*

"Daddy!" Nina embraced her father. He plucked her from the earth in one swift movement, hoisting her into his arms.

"We should go." Arowyn shifted uncomfortably.

"Yes," Drakkone agreed.

Elgen snapped from his spell and glowered at Nina. He only paused a moment before he spun in the direction of their escape and stomped off.

The rest of the council crowded after him, leaving Breen to bring up the rear. She held her sword at the ready, glancing over her shoulder every few steps. The cries of battle still waged—though with all the sandstone between them, the sounds were muffled. Distant. She could almost believe they were far away.

The group turned the corner at the edge of the compound. In seconds they reached the edge of the house, and their last layer of protection. Elgen stopped, kneeling by the edge of the stairs as he peered into the open yard.

"There's suitable distraction. We should go two at a time." Elgen glanced back at the group.

They all nodded.

Elgen and Vas crouched at the edge of the home for one last moment before leaping out. They ran as fast as their legs could take them, kicking up dirt in their wake. When at last they reached the wooden stables across the yard, Arowyn led Hana. Both women disappeared inside the shadows of the stables.

Breen glanced out. Ten feet from the far end of the stables, soldiers fought. The rebellion was losing.

Breen glanced at Drakkone. "You're next."

He scoffed. "You should take Nina and go."

"Not after the stunt you just pulled." Breen glared. *"You're next."*

He met her gaze for a long moment. No hint of a smile remained on his face. She wasn't giving on this. "Fine."

Drakkone crouched for a moment longer before he leapt from behind the house. Only her, Jer and Sundas remained. Sundas kneeled beside her, watching the battle with hunger in his eyes, while Jer watched with wide, fearful, round eyes. Sundas wanted to fight as much as she. Breen understood, but neither of them had time to join. The council needed saving. If this rebellion was to win, they needed protection.

Her family disappeared inside the barn.

"We should go," Sundas said. He didn't peel his gaze from the battle.

"We should," she agreed. Breen stood as one of the rebels went down across the yard. His body hit the dirt in a puddle of blood. Her heart clenched.

They were leaving these men here to die.

Yet, none tried to escape. None fled for the gates. Instead, they stood their ground and fought. For the Council. For the rebellion. For Seaburn the way it should be, the way it could be someday.

Her heart swelled. She was so proud of them. Proud to be one of them. She'd be forever grateful for their sacrifice.

Sundas leapt from cover, pulling Jer with him and sprinted across the yard. Breen followed, her heart racing with her quickened breaths. She couldn't help glancing towards the far end of the yard. Body after body marred the sand and dirt. Rebels. Soldiers. Foreigners.

What was this fight for? What was the point?

The doors to the stables burst open, and she followed Sundas inside the dimness.

Horses chuffed and tapped their hooves against the ground.

Hay crunched beneath her boots, and the musty sent of wet wood filled the space. Elgen, Vas, Hana and Arowyn had already mounted their steeds and waited at the far edge of the stables, in front of the wide double doors.

"Everyone's here." Drakkone nudged her elbow, startling her.

"Good." Breen shifted further inside.

Sundas swung up onto his horse, as did Drakkone. Nina sat in front of him, eyes wide with concern. A saddled horse remained beside Drakkone, ready for her to ride. The gray and white dappled mare snuffed the air and dipped her head, awaiting her rider.

Breen fit her boot into the stirrup and swung up. She gripped the leather reins, ready to take off.

"Is everyone ready?" Elgen called back.

They all nodded. Anticipation sent her heart racing—awaiting the run to the gate and their flight across the desert. She hoped the rebellion had more than one safe house. More than one army.

"Let's stay tight in formation." Elgen straightened. "We race for the gate. Once we're beyond and a safe distance from the compound, we'll make a plan."

"Let's just go already." Jer sighed, the same defeated huff she'd come to expect from the man recently.

Elgen gave Jer a long look before he nodded.

They burst from the stable doors, flying fast over the sand. Breen urged her mare forward with her heels, snapping her reins.

Their small party rumbled outside and through the compound. Soldiers froze in battle or dove from their path. Elgen led them straight and true, through the open gates and out onto the sand.

Breen spared a glance back at the compound. Blood pooled in the sand. The rebels had given so much to help better Seaburn. Yet, all she could think of was fleeing their foul country. Was it possible to instil this council and a new regime?

If the rebellion won, and truly made changes to the kingdom, Seaburn might some day be a beautiful place.

Heat licked her heart and burned her throat. She'd never believed in this rebellion until now. They were willing to give up so much for the proper treatment of citizens and tribesmen alike.

She steeled herself.

The Emperor would die for the deaths of many, the abuse of her fellow tribesmen, and for so much more.

AFTER THEIR FLIGHT from the rebel compound, Elgen led them south, just outside of Sarton. Upon their arrival, Breen agreed to their plan to kill the Emperor. This time not under duress. It was time to end the tyranny of the glutinous Emperor. It was time to end the suffering of her people, all her people.

Though she'd first agreed under Nina's spell, the rest of the council relaxed at her uncoerced agreement. Nina had never beamed so brightly, and Drakkone had never gazed at her quite like he did.

Love swelled in the dark depths of his eyes. Finally, she'd come around to what the rest of these men and women had expected of, and hoped for her.

The real battle would begin tomorrow. Tomorrow, they'd kill the Emperor.

TWENTY-SEVEN

t first light, Breen rode with her family, Vas, Arowyn, Sundas and Elgen from Sarton, to Seaburn city. Hana and Jer, the final members of the council, stayed behind. With no formal training, they'd only get in the way.

Though the rebellion didn't have a second army to speak of, they still gathered nearly a hundred supporters through the night. Vas had further assured them more soldiers for the cause waited within the walls of Seaburn. He'd sent word to the movement inside, and they'd be waiting.

Rebel soldiers surrounded the small group as they made their way through the streets. Pale light fell on their shoulders in the cool morning air. The sun had yet to rise, keeping the earth cold and their anticipation heavy. This early in the morning, they shouldn't encounter many patrols—if any. That didn't stop Breen's heart from racing, or her gaze from darting toward every shadow.

The majority of their newfound army would join them from the opposite edge of town. From the Academy. They'd meet at the palace, where their inside informant would leave the main gates open when the sun crested the horizon.

For now, they were left in the dull morning light, the world cast in cold blue.

A shiver worked its way up her spine.

So much could go wrong. So much was at stake. But if somehow they succeeded and things went right, a new Seaburn would be born from the ashes of the Empire.

Breen sighed, her warm breath fogging the cool morning air. Nina squeezed her fingers. Her daughter walked at her side, awake and alert—ready for anything. She couldn't help but smile. Though Nina was barely three years old, she was wise beyond her years. Breen couldn't wait to see her grow up—see the woman she became.

Nina glanced up, curiosity in her big eyes.

Breen smiled and squeezed Nina's fingers. Nina beamed and looked forward.

Through the shadows of morning, they crept through the streets of Seaburn, cloaked and silent like night. Arowyn led them, often scouting ahead a street or two to be sure they weren't about to run into any patrols.

Her dark braids disappeared around the bend in the road, between tall sandstone homes. They continued ahead, Drakkone and Nina on either side of her.

Around the bend, the street narrowed. Arowyn was nowhere to be seen.

Surely she couldn't have cleared the entire street so quickly. Did she duck into an alley? Hide among the gnarled bushes in the small yards?

Movement in her peripheral had her spin for the right side of the group. Two Seaburn soldiers emerged from the shadowed alley, their leather armor all too familiar.

Her heart skipped.

She spun again, to their left. Two more soldiers. One clutched a knife to Arowyn's throat. The woman snarled and struggled, even with blood leaking down her neck.

Out of the next two alleys ahead half a dozen men emerged.

Damn.

She froze.

A man with tawny skin over a wide set jaw met her gaze with cold brown eyes. Her heart skipped before plummeting into her stomach.

It had been a long time since she'd seen Lukerin. He hadn't aged a day.

"At the ready, men!" Elgen snapped.

The *shing* of swords leaving their sheaths filled the air, but Breen couldn't move. She couldn't breathe. Her breath stuck in her throat, heavy like honey. At Lukerin's side she scarcely recognized two more of her fellow tribesmen. So they'd given up.

They'd been broken.

Breen swallowed the forming lump in her throat. Her fingers shook at her sides.

"Mumma?" Nina looked up at her with cinched brows and wide, worried blue eyes. "What's wrong?"

Breen slowly shook her head. She'd never thought Lukerin would give up. He'd stayed in the dungeons for months. Yet, here he was— eyes vacant. No flash of recognition lit their dark depths. He didn't know her. Didn't recognize her.

She couldn't fight them. She couldn't fight her kin.

They needed to be saved. They needed to be released from the tyranny of the Emperor. And they were about to do just that. They only had to hold on a little while longer.

"Halt," Lukerin said, voice low, and empty. "In the name of the Emperor, sheath your weapons and give yourselves up for punishment."

"For what, boy?" Elgen huffed.

"You have two escaped fugitives in your midst." Lukerin looked right through her. Though he knew of her and her escape, he didn't *know* her. Not like he once did.

"Lukerin," Breen whispered. "We're going to save you."

Her heart swelled, clenching in her chest. He'd once been her closest friend. The only man to best her in battle before Drakkone. Even if it had only been once.

"Submit." The same hollow voice rang across the cobblestone street.

Breen shook her head. "Never."

The soldiers lurched forward, swords drawn. Their blades clanged against those of the rebels. Breen ripped her own sword from its sheath. Her fingers trembled. She didn't want to do this. She didn't want to fight them. But she couldn't let them take her, or Drakkone. She couldn't leave Nina without a mother, without a father.

Elgen and Sundas took the first two soldiers, but four more pushed through the center. Drakkone leapt in front of her, his sword crashing against Lukerin's. Breen pulled Nina back, stepping in front of her. She gave her hand one last squeeze before releasing it.

"I'll protect you." Breen met Nina's gaze. She nodded.

Two soldiers came in from either side.

A growl ripped from her throat as she swung for the first. The man leaned back, the tip of her blade inches from his exposed throat. The second dove in. She stepped back and elbowed his chest as he passed. Too much forward momentum. He should be smarter than that.

Air exploded from the man's lungs as he crashed to the street. The first lunged over his comrade, whipping his blade at her chest.

Her sword clanged loudly against his, reverberating all the way up her arm. He put too much strength behind his attack. She'd be able to trick him off balance, if only she could keep him far from Nina.

Breen pushed back and swung. Their blades collided again and again. As he fought for the offensive, so did she. Her chest burned with anger, and her heart pounded in her ears. These broken men would never separate her from her daughter. She couldn't let them. No matter how much it hurt to fight against her kin.

The clashing of blades sent sparks flying as he dragged the edge of his sword along hers. She gritted her teeth, her muscles clenching and straining beneath his weight.

She stepped back, and he pressed his advantage.

Her breath hissed from her lungs before she inhaled sharply. She'd been in this same situation hundreds of times. Even the strong could be outfoxed.

Breen stepped aside abruptly, letting the man's forward momentum take over. He flew forward, eyes going wide as the ground came up at him. Breen twisted to sink her blade into his back.

"Mumma!" Nina screamed.

She stopped.

The man hit the ground as she spun. A man reached for her daughter, but froze in motion. Another soldier stood ready to shove a sword through her back. But again, he remained a statue.

"Nina." Breen slipped between the frozen men.

Every Seaburn soldier remained still, gaze empty.

"Did you do this?" Breen pulled Nina away from the man reaching for her. Breen kneeled. Nina nodded. Her lips twitched into a smile. "Smart girl."

Nina's furrowed brow relaxed, and she beamed up at her mother.

Breen turned to the others. "Knock them out."

Drakkone, Elgen and Sundas met her gaze. They each exchanged a look before nodding in agreement. Maybe they needn't fight their way to the palace after all.

Taking the hilt of their swords, the men smashed the metal into each of the enemy's skulls. Arowyn returned to their midst before dragging the soldiers into the alley. Once they were finished, Drakkone hoisted Nina up into his arms. Her eyelids sagged with exhaustion.

They'd barely begun their rebellion and Nina might fall asleep at any moment. Her stomach rolled with anxious nausea. Much of their plan depended on Nina. If they couldn't take the palace—and hold it— they'd be done for, and the rebellion would die with them.

Nina blinked slowly and met Breen's gaze. "I'm okay, Mumma."

Breen's lips pressed into a thin line. She said nothing, and simply nodded. Hopefully Nina's powers would be accessible by the time they reached their next roadblock.

Arowyn returned to the lead, her stride lengthening, and her fists clenched—most likely furious at having been caught. Sundas joined her at the head of the group, scouting with her each time she disappeared around a bend.

The palace towered ahead. The high sandstone walls crested even the tallest of Seaburn's noble homes. The pillars of the castle rose higher even than the walls.

Her heart raced much faster than her feet. She should save her worries, crush her anxiety into a tiny box inside her mind and lock it away, but she couldn't. Not yet. Her fear kept her going. Kept her fighting. She'd be a better protector if she had things to lose.

They rounded the final street and came level with the palace walls. Two enormous wooden doors stood ajar. The gates. They were open.

Her heart skipped.

Whoever was on the inside had done it. They'd gotten them inside the palace walls. Now they only needed to get passed the castle guards and find the Emperor. With their army on its way, and Nina's abilities, she couldn't imagine they wouldn't find him. She sighed with relief, glad she put her trust in the rebellion after all.

Two soldiers waited inside the gates. One, a tall woman with her hands on her hips, and a sly smile. The other, a man she didn't recognize.

"Breen." The woman grinned, stepping forward.

"Moigrin," Breen gasped. She hadn't seen the warrior in years. A new scar ran diagonal along her cheek. Another ran through her right eyebrow. Her hair was no longer braided. Instead it remained straight and short, framing her face and tickling her narrow chin.

"You're alive." The group stopped and parted, allowing Moigrin to step inside and embracing Breen.

"So are you." Gold armour lay on Moigrin's shoulders. So she'd risen high in the ranks, all the way to palace guard, or perhaps an army general.

"I've tried my best." Moigrin shrugged and stepped back. Her grin didn't leave her face. "I'm surprised you joined the rebellion. When you left I thought you'd never want to come back."

"It took some convincing." Breen shot a look at Drakkone and Nina.

Moigrin eyes widened. "Is she yours?"

"Yes. Her name is Nina."

"She's the one who can control the minds of men?"

Breen nodded.

"Incredible." Moigrin let her hands fall limp at her sides.

"She truly is." Breen smiled.

"We should get inside, Moigrin." Elgen stepped forward. Moigrin's smile dropped and she nodded.

"Yes, we'll take the servants entrance." Moigrin gave Breen one last long look before turning and leading the way up the palace steps.

Breen glanced around the open yard. No guards were stationed on the walls of either the palace or the Academy, whose walls she could just see down the slope. No soldiers stood at the front of the palace, and none wandered the yard.

Moigrin truly had connections if she'd removed so many from their path. Were there that many rebels inside the palace walls? Or had Moigrin used other means to dispose of them?

The sandstone palace walls shaded them from the coming sun as Moigrin led them around the side of the enormous building, to a door etched from stone. She motioned for them all to halt before she rapped on the door—once, then two quick taps, then a third softer tap. A code.

The door flew open.

"Finally." A woman sighed loudly, narrowing her eyes at Moigrin. Her white apron was smeared with soot, and her cheeks marred with flour. "The staff will be up soon. Hurry." She stepped aside.

"Apologies, Agnes." Moigrin grinned and pecked the woman on the cheek before stepping inside.

Breen raised a brow. She hadn't known Moigrin was interested in women. Then again, she'd never asked, nor had she the occasion to find out.

Agnes blushed and shook her head before stamping back inside.

Moigrin motioned the party in. Dim lantern light lit the large stone kitchen. Baked goods filled the air with sweetness, and somewhere coffee beans brewed. A delicacy she was sure only the Emperor could afford.

Moigrin led them around the marble counters, silver pots and dark oak furnishings, and into the hall. "It isn't far from here. But be careful, and be *quiet*. Not every palace guard is as rebellious as I." She flashed a mischievous smile over her shoulder.

Breen nodded.

They followed quietly down the white marble floored hall, and up a narrow stairwell to the second, then third floor. When they emerged from the cramped space, torches lit the hall, sitting in bronze casters. Plush red carpet lined the marble floor, and paintings and tapestries hung from every wall.

Soft murmurs drifted down the hall.

Breen crept ahead to join Moigrin, leaving Sundas and Arowyn to bring up the rear, and Drakkone and Nina in the middle. She wanted to assure their protection, and any guard they encountered would meet the sharp end of her blade.

Soft light spilled between a crack in two large golden doors with ivory handles near the end of the hall.

Her brows furrowed. That had to be the heaviest door in the world.

Moigrin paused, and motioned for silence. The group froze several feet from the door. Breen joined her old friend on either side of the golden slabs.

The tribeswoman peeked through the crack. A strip of light lit her face, turning her brown eye, gold. What was she seeing? Who was inside? Her heart raced.

Breen shifted, and Moigrin stepped back, a puzzled look on her face.

Unable to tame her curiosity, Breen pressed her face to the cold metal of the door.

Inside was a room more luxurious than she'd ever seen. Thick furs of jungle cats, desert coyotes, and other patterns she'd never imagined, lay strewn across a wide king-size bed in the interior chamber. In the sitting room, several sofas and chairs sat around a square leather table.

A fireplace sat imbedded in the far wall, flames licking the air.

Two figures stood before it. One, a tall but plump man with his gut hanging over his brown trousers, and thick golden rings on his fingers. The other, well built, with wide shoulders, long white hair and an irritated scowl on his face.

"You can't expect me to let this slide," the Emperor snarled. "You assured my rule of this kingdom for the rest of my days."

The other man sighed. "You've lost hold of your own country, Ragus."

"*Emperor* Ragus."

He smirked. "You know not to take that tone with me."

The Emperor froze, his mouth hanging open. After a moment he gulped and straightened. "Apologies, Solipher. It's the stress. I've forgotten my manners."

Solipher nodded slowly, quirking a brow.

Though the Emperor stood before this strangely beautiful man, with pale skin and startlingly blue eyes, Ragus appeared the inferior man, while Solipher might be the most regal person she'd ever seen.

"Apology accepted." Solipher turned, pacing to the fireplace. He laid a hand on the mantle, his absurdly long nails clicking against the marble. "You've called upon me for which grievance this time?"

"Just... what I've told you." Ragus paused. "The rebels are getting out of hand. Even your own men weren't able to capture the girl."

Solipher slid him a narrow look. His eyes turned to blue fire. "They aren't *my men*. Your entire kingdom would cower at my feet if I unleashed *my men*."

"Gods, yes. You're right," the Emperor stammered.

"What's going on?" Moigrin whispered, her breath hot on Breen's shoulder.

Breen pulled her gaze from the Emperor's chambers, her brow furrowed. "I have no idea. Who is that inside?"

Moigrin shook her head. "I don't know."

They stepped back from the door and joined the others.

"What do we do?" Breen asked.

"Should we risk going in now?" Moigrin worked her jaw. If it truly was so strange for the Emperor to have this visitor, it might be best if they held off until the man left.

"We haven't the time to wait," Elgen snapped, his beard shaking beneath his frown.

Breen exchanged a glance with Moigrin, but the others seemed to agree now was best—before more soldiers came—before they were found out.

She sighed and stepped back to the door, taking one last look.

The Emperor had taken a seat, sighing dramatically as Solipher placed a hand on his hip. "You still owe me that favor, Ragus, and yes you have yet to deliver."

"I know. I know. But they've evaded my soldiers for years. Who's to say where they are now?" The Emperor stared at the floor, his brow creased. He played with the rings on his chubby fingers.

"That's your job to find out." Solipher hissed out each word—the threat was clear. Whoever the Emperor was to deliver, he'd suffer greatly if he failed to meet their arrangement.

A loud thump broke the quiet of the hall.

Breen snapped back from the door to find Elgen staring wide-eyed at a picture frame knocked from its place. It leaned against the wall and the floor.

Her heart skipped.

Had they heard?

She turned back to the crack in the door.

Solipher faced the doors, his eyes narrowed, something dark curling around his fist. His nostrils flared. "Your security has grown lax, Emperor." He stepped into the center of the room. "But you've finally done something right. You've brought me my gift."

He extended his hand toward the door. Black smoke spilled from his palm to the floor, curling in upon itself before leaping forward.

Breen jumped back. The doors flew open, the harsh breeze whipping her cheeks.

Dark soldiers, constructed of the gods only knew what, leapt from the now empty room, swords drawn.

She ripped her sword from its sheath. What were those things?

And what was Solipher?

TWENTY-EIGHT

lack soldiers rolled from the shadows by the dozens, forcing Breen and Moigrin back down the hall.

"What are those things?" Elgen balked.

A shadow man leapt forward, slicing his straight blade toward her head. Breen ducked and stabbed her sword up through its gut.

It disappeared in a cloud of smoke. Two more stepped into its place.

"Run!" Arowyn's high-pitched shout rang through the hall.

Breen spun with Moigrin, and ran back toward the servant's steps. Cold fear gripped her heart and pushed her breath from her lungs.

This couldn't be possible. Magic like this didn't exist.

Sundas leapt into the stairwell first, and the rest followed. Moigrin pushed her ahead, and spun to face the shadows.

"Moigrin!" Breen froze on the first step.

"Go!" Moigrin shouted before she spun back to face the shadows. Sword drawn, she dove into the fray. Darkness enveloped her.

Breen fled.

Her boots beat the stairs as she spun round and round, down to the ground floor. Her heart hammered and her hands shook. Would Moigrin make it out alive? Was she dead already? What were those shadows? And how could the rebels fight and win against something that couldn't die?

Breen hit the first floor moments behind the others. She glanced over her shoulder, only to find shadows pouring from the passage, creeping across the ceiling and walls.

"GO!" Breen raced after the others.

They reached the door to the kitchens, only darkness had already crept over it, and no one wanted to trod into the black.

"The main doors!" Sundas cried.

They couldn't stop now for fear of being overtaken.

Sweat beaded on her forehead as they passed tapestry after tapestry, images of the ages, the beasts of Seaburn, soldiers, men and women she didn't recognize. At the end of the arched hall opened a three-storey entryway, with twin staircases rising on either side to the second floor landing, before continuing up to the third.

Two arched doors of gold sat at the far end, thick handles ready to pull free so they could throw themselves outside.

"There!" Elgen called.

He led the charge to the exit, Drakkone and Arowyn on his heels. Sundas wasn't far behind, and neither was she.

Her heart pounded in her ears. She couldn't hear the shadows—if they made any noise at all. She desperately wanted to turn and see how close they were.

She didn't for fear they licked at her heels.

The long room spread out further than she'd originally thought. Large pots and vases held flowers and ferns, while a wide fountain lay at the center.

Half dashed around the pond on one side, while the other ran around the left.

Shadows flew across the ceiling, encircling them in black. The tendrils wisped forward, ready to envelop the doors.

"No!" she gasped. This couldn't be happening. Not now. They were so close.

Only a few feet from the doors, the shadows descended, blacking out the gold.

The group skidded to a halt on the thick carpet. This was it. They were done. There was nowhere else to go.

Shadows descended upon the staircases, the high vaulted ceilings, the walls, and the passages into the large room. Blackness encroached, ready to snuff out the fires burning in large bronze pots. Once their light was gone, only the shadows would remain. Only the blackness. Only their deaths.

She'd failed. Failed to protect her family. Failed to protect Nina.

Her heart rose into her throat. Her stomach twisted. This wasn't fair. This wasn't right. They deserved freedom. They deserved *life*.

"This isn't over yet," Drakkone snapped.

She turned towards him. His gaze met hers, burning like flames. Determined. Ready to fight until his last breath.

Her fingers clenched around the hilt of her sword.

He was right. They couldn't give up. Not now. Not ever. Even if she went down fighting, at least she'd go down in glory. At least she'd fought for something worth dying for.

Breen swallowed the lump in her throat and nodded.

She faced the coming shadows. Soldiers leapt from the darkness, their straight swords trained on the rebels.

Breen held her sword aloft, her breaths quickening with each step they took. This was it. This was her final battle.

The shadow soldiers opened their wide mouths in a roar, though no sound escaped. They leapt.

Breen swung her blade at the darkness. She cut through their chests, guts, arms, and legs until they disappeared into dust.

The battle cries of her comrades filled the hollow space as they joined her in this fight. The clang of blades filled the room. They swung harder than ever before, ducking the shadow swords, cutting through their armored bodies, and destroying every one that leapt from the growing blackness.

Sweat poured down her forehead, stinging her eyes. Her heart hammered in time with her swing. She stabbed one through the gut, pushing it back with her foot before it fell into wisps. Another took its place. She cut off its head. Another parried her blade and drove her back. She spun from its reach.

She would not go down. She would fight.

A blade sliced her arm, as sharp as any sword she'd seen. Her breath hissed out. She sliced off the hand of the shadow. Its sword fell before turning to smoke. She drove the tip of her blade through its neck. Again, the shadow dissipated.

But there was always another. Always one more to take its place. There was no end. There was only futility.

They couldn't kill all of them. Not when they couldn't find its source.

Her eyes stung and her limbs tired.

Another slice brought a shot of adrenaline through her veins. Another had her gritting her teeth. Blood dripped down her arms. Pain exploded through her skin. Not yet.

She couldn't go.

Not yet.

Breen sunk her blade through the spine of another shadow. The gut of a second. A third pushed her off her feet, sending her sailing across the floor.

Her breath exploded from her lungs.

Her limbs were so weak. She hadn't trained hard enough. She wasn't good enough to protect them. To protect Nina.

Drakkone leapt in front of her, blocking the coming shadow.

Breen sat up, catching her breath. "Drakkone." They'd never get to return to her tribe. They'd never get to bring Nina back. She'd never spend another night with him. Never kiss him again.

He glanced over his shoulder, eyes wild from battle. And he smiled. He grinned down at her, as if this were the most fun he'd ever had.

Her heart skipped.

A black sword ran through his gut.

Her heart stopped.

Blood splattered her cheeks. Her eyes widened. His eyes widened. He turned on his assailant, cutting off its head before falling to his knees. The dark blade disappeared. But the damage was done.

"Daddy!" Nina screamed.

"No." Tears stung her eyes as she reached for Drakkone.

"Take Nina, and run." His rough voice hardly carried.

"I can't leave you." Her breath fled her as she gripped his shoulder. She met his gaze. His brows furrowed.

Nina collapsed by his side, tears spilling over her cheeks. "Daddy!"

Breen took his hands, wrapping her fingers around his.

"Go." His brows rose. His fist tightened around the hilt of his sword. He climbed to his feet. Breen and Nina came with him. "*Go.*"

Breen glanced between them both—her heart torn in two.

There was no decision. Nothing left to choose.

Breen scooped Nina off the ground, cradling her against her hip and embracing her with one arm.

"I love you." Breen met his eyes, unable to stop the tears from streaking her cheeks.

Drakkone smiled. "I love you." He turned back to the battle.

Breen forced her gaze from his back as he lunged for the shadow soldiers continuing to cut through their comrades.

She leapt for the door, Nina screeching in her ear. "We can't leave Daddy!"

Breen sliced her blade through the shadows protecting the door. They dissipated across her blade, but only for a moment.

"We have to," she whispered. She sliced again, and again. "We have to, Nina."

Nina shook her head and buried her face against Breen's shoulder. Her tears slicked her skin. Breen squeezed her tight.

She could get through these shadows as long as Drakkone held off the soldiers. She could get through them and get out. They could run. They could make it. Nina would live. She had to. There was no world for her without Nina. She had to end this.

Breen sliced harder and faster, her breath rushing from her lungs with each swing. The faster she cut, the more time she had. The golden door appeared below the blackness.

The handle.

There it was. Their salvation.

Breen let out a battle cry as she sliced through the shadows one last time. The last tendril disappeared from the handle. "Hold on!" She grabbed it with both hands and pulled as hard as she could.

The door creaked loudly, the sound echoing in the large hall. Nina clung to her neck as Breen towed the door open.

One foot.

Two.

She slipped through.

Her shoulder hit the sandstone outside, as she rolled onto the sand. The door shut behind them with a bang.

Breen took a few deep, steadying breaths, clinging to Nina. "Are you all right?"

She slowly loosened her grip and tore her gaze from the two doors sealing Drakkone inside the palace. Nina looked up at her with wide, bloodshot eyes. Her lip trembled as she nodded.

"Good." Breen stood, brushing sand from them both and drawing her sword. She might need it yet.

"Mumma. What about Daddy?" Nina whimpered.

Breen shook her head. "I had to save you. I'm sorry, Nina."

Her eyes welled with tears, and she nodded slowly.

Breen squeezed her eyes shut for a moment. Her heart broke. She tightened her grip on Nina, embracing her daughter before she adjusted her grip. They couldn't stay. They had to go now, before soldiers came after them, before the city woke up. Before whatever those shadows were decided to follow.

She didn't know where they'd go. But they had to leave.

Now.

Breen wiped her eyes, flicking away her tears before she started down the palace steps.

A whoosh from above sent her leaping back.

Her heart rose into her throat as she skidded across the sand, falling back onto the path.

Solipher stood in her place; eyes alight with something akin to madness, and a wide smirk on his angular face. "How good of you to come."

Breen narrowed her eyes. "What do you want?"

She rose to her feet, keeping Nina close and angled away from the man. She pointed her sword in his direction, glad to have a weapon between them.

"The girl." He nodded toward Nina, whose eyes widened with fear.

A growl ripped from her throat. "You won't touch my daughter."

His smile spread. "How feisty."

Breen stepped back. Under his black robes and around his gold trimmed belt, he held no weapon she could see. No sword, no dagger —not even a shield. He was defenseless against her.

"Step aside," she snapped. "You have nothing to defend yourself, and I won't fight an unarmed man."

"Who's to say I'm unarmed?" Solipher chuckled, his voice deep, yet edged with ice. His menacing gaze moved from Nina, to her. He splayed his fingers at his side. In the palm of his hand, shadows swirled, just as they had before.

Her breath caught in a gasp. What *was* this?

From the darkness, a long straight sword emerged, two points sticking from the black hilt. It widened slightly at the end, curving to point outward. Not the same as her scimitar, but not quite the straight sword of the foreigners.

Who was this man? And what did he want with Nina?

"I won't let you take her," Breen hissed. She stood her ground.

"And how are you going to stop me?" Genuine curiosity lit his blue eyes, ringed with white around the iris, white just like his hair.

Breen glanced between Nina, and Solipher. She slowly lowered Nina to her feet and ushered Nina behind her.

He wanted a fight. That much was clear. His fingers twitched up and down on his hilt, anticipating whatever came next. She couldn't let him get through her. She couldn't let him take Nina.

Taking a deep breath, she gathered whatever strength she had left.

"If you insist." He grinned and flipped his blade around his hand. It swung in a wide arc before settling in his grip. He stepped back into an offensive stance unlike she'd ever seen. His feet parted, sword up, level with his head, pointing down slightly. His other hand danced against the air in front of him.

"Stay back, Nina." Breen didn't risk a glance over her shoulder.

"Yes, Mumma." Her small footsteps retreated a few paces.

Breen was surprised she could still stand at all. She'd been exhausted since they reached the palace, even more so when the shadows arrived. Could they somehow have drained her power? Or had Nina been trying to control the darkness and save them all this whole time?

"Ladies first." Solipher bowed slightly.

Breen narrowed her eyes. "If you insist."

Leaping forward, Breen drove her sword for his unarmed hand. He stepped aside, impossibly fast. She dug her heels in and drove her elbow back.

He sucked in a breath as her elbow smashed against his gut.

Something hard collided with her back, and she flew through the air, dropping into the sand several feet away. Air exploded from her lungs. She struggled to catch her breath.

What in the name of the gods had that been?

She struggled to sit up, coughing loudly.

Solipher spun his blade in his hand once more. "Apologies. That wasn't fair." He grinned. So he had done it, yet he hadn't used his sword or his free hand. Was it the same darkness? "You caught me by surprise."

Breen stood, dusting sand from her clothes. She circled, again putting herself between Nina and Solipher.

"I'll try to behave this time."

Breen gritted her teeth.

Solipher dove across the sand in one graceful motion, closing ten feet of space in the blink of an eye. She stepped back in time to avoid his sword, which sailed over her shoulder.

Breen parried his blade, tossing it aside before driving hers in.

Again he stepped aside, impossibly fast.

She spun again, flashing her sword out. He dodged, dancing artfully around her strikes.

Breen growled and leapt in with a quick slice at his chest, then his abdomen. He slapped her blade away with a twitch of his wrist.

How could he fight like this? It was inhuman. Impossible. Unbelievable.

She dove closer, her cuts fewer in between.

Solipher leapt back. But she pressed forward. She had to land a blow. Had to stun him somehow. The smile didn't leave his face as he leapt back again and again. Her blade narrowly missed his gut, his limbs, and his chest.

She drove her blade in, heart hammering in her ears. Again he stepped aside. Mid-lunge, Breen swiped outward with all of her strength.

His eyes flew wide as the very tip of her blade cut a thin line across his cheek.

Breen grinned. Finally. Something. Though the scrape didn't bleed, a clear line still broke the perfectness of his ivory skin. So he could be hurt.

If he could he hurt, he could be killed.

Solipher's eyes narrowed. He leapt in a flurry of strikes.

Breen gasped and brought her blade up to protect herself. His blade clanged against hers time and time again, the pressure knocking her back further and further, forcing her to step away.

She couldn't get a hit in, couldn't return thrusts. The only thing she could do was block and hope for a moment to parry.

His blade slammed against hers, forcing hers aside. But his swing was slightly too wide. It took a second longer for him to bring it back in.

This was her chance.

Breen thrust her blade into his gut with every ounce of her strength. Her whole body shook with the effort. Her hands grew slick with sweat.

The tip of her blade pierced through to the other side, spreading copper through the air.

Solipher exhaled a hiss, his pupils narrowing as he met her gaze. He slammed the back of his hand into her cheek, sending her swirling through the air and bouncing across the sand.

"Impudent girl." He hissed.

Breen rolled to a stop, breathing heavily, the fire of adrenaline in her veins. She'd gotten him. Sand fell from her hair as she leaned up. Her arms shook under her weight.

She was weak, getting more exhausted by the minute. But she'd done it. Maybe this would weaken him enough for her to get away with Nina.

She peered through her thick braids, which clung to her face. She couldn't stop the smile from rising to her lips.

Solipher's face twisted while his nose wrinkled and his lips drew back in a snarl. His brows descended over his eyes like two dark shadows. He held his wound, crimson seeping from between his fingers.

The scent of copper and ash filled the air. Her nostrils flared.

Breen stood, her knees shaking. She plucked her blade from the sand. "It's over."

Solipher straightened, flipping his long hair from his face. His sneer relaxed into a smirk. The corners of his lips twitched. "You stupid, stupid little girl. You really think your puny weapons can kill *me*?"

Breen narrowed her eyes. Whatever he was, he could bleed. And if he could bleed, she could kill him. Puny weapon or not.

Solipher let his bloody hand fall to his side. Drops of red hit the sand and sizzled. Breen quirked a brow as he stepped across the sand, his hand out and ready at his side.

Breen straightened. He wasn't done yet? Her whole body ached with weakness. She needed to rest. But he had hardly broken a sweat.

Had his injury been an accident? He seemed overconfident enough, so much so he'd let her get a hit without meaning to.

Solipher broke into a run, sailing across the sand, his feet hardly touching the ground. Breen dove to the side, rolling over her head and back to her feet, leaping forward and racing back to the palace steps a few feet away. He turned and followed, a growl on his lips and rage burning in his eyes.

Nina watched with large eyes. She sat on the steps; her body nearly limp with exhaustion. So she was trying to control this man. But clearly she was unable.

Wet fingers closed around her wrist and yanked her off her feet. Breen gasped, her flesh burning beneath his touch. He threw her down the steps. Her shoulders slammed into the stone. Her breath fled her lungs. He leapt after her. His blade drove down at her chest. She rolled from his path. But he'd anticipated this and slashed sideways.

The tip of his blade scored her cheek. Her blood sprayed the sand.

"Mumma!" Nina shrieked.

Breen twisted aside, onto her knees, ready to leap to her feet.

Pain exploded in her abdomen—hot and searing.

Her heart stopped. Her breath stopped. She froze. Solipher's black blade sunk through her ribs.

His smirk returned. He thrust deeper.

She gasped. Pain exploded through her torso, hot claws scraping across her insides.

"Stupid girl," he purred. Solipher stepped back, ripping his sword free. Her blood dripped from the dark blade and splattered the sand. Her heart pounded in her ears. Her eyes stung.

She'd failed. She'd failed her daughter.

TWENTY-NINE

Solipher stepped away, his blade disappearing.

Breen fought for breath, fought to hold on to rationality. Her mind fled in all directions. Her family. Her failures. Her life. Her daughter.

She got one foot under her.

A crack from the front gates restarted her heart. Battle cries filled the yard. Breen stood, while Solipher watched the rebellion pour in like ants through the palace gates.

Her fingers clenched around her blade. She stepped closer, each step filled with wrenching agony. She had to do this. For Drakkone. For Nina. For her.

She steeled herself and thrust.

Her blade pierced his ribs, in nearly the same spot in which he stabbed her.

His roar drowned out the rebels as he turned fiery blue eyes on her. He ripped the blade from his gut, tearing it out of her hands. His blood sizzled against the sand, spraying across the earth. He stumbled across the steps and into the sand.

"Leave my daughter alone."

Breen breathed hard, her gut clenching around the pain of each breath.

Solipher glared. "This isn't over."

In a wisp of smoke, he disappeared.

Breen stared for a long moment at the place he'd once occupied. He was gone. With whatever magic he'd used, he'd just disappeared.

Her legs gave out and she collapsed to her knees.

"Mumma!" Nina raced across the sand, tears streaking her face. She threw herself against Breen, her arms clutching her neck.

Breen gasped, pain flooding her abdomen. "Nina." She winced.

"Mumma, I couldn't stop him. I couldn't." Her sobs shook her small body.

A smile pricked at her lips. So she'd been right. Nina had been trying to control Solipher. "It's all right." Breen wrapped her arms around Nina, and buried her face in her hair. "It's all right now."

Rebels roared by, rumbling across the sand. Their cries filled the air until they reached the palace.

Breen sighed and slowly stood. "We've got to go." Her legs shook beneath her. *Walk*, she commanded them. They had to get away, in case the rebellion went awry. She wouldn't have them caught up in all of this.

Nina nodded and clung to Breen's neck.

Balancing Nina on one hip, she slipped her blade back into its sheath. She hoped they could get out in one piece. She hoped they didn't run into any more patrols. She wasn't sure she could fend off one more person, or engage in one more battle.

Breen stepped forward slowly, her body shaking beneath her. Blood continued to pour from her abdomen, soaking her shirt. Once they were outside the palace walls she'd find something to stop the bleeding. But Nina had to be the priority. She was always the priority.

She kissed Nina's hair. Each step brought fresh agony coursing through her limbs. But she kept going. She couldn't stop. Not when they were so close to freedom.

The arch of the gates grew closer until she could see the detail of the golden doors—the intricate patterns etched into their surface.

Twin tigers fought along jungle leaves, their claws extended and tails whipping behind them.

Her knees gave way, and she tumbled into the sand. Nina rolled from her hands. She coughed up sand, thin grains clinging to her hair and face.

Damn legs.

How dare they betray her now?

Breen groaned as she shifted onto her side, then her back.

Blue sky shone overhead, fluffy clouds dazzlingly white against the intense blue. It had to be mid-morning. How long had they been engaged in battle?

Hours at least.

"Mumma?" Nina knelt at her side, shaking her arm.

"Yes, Nina?" Fog lay on her mind, heavy like winter furs.

"You said we need to go."

Right.

She had said that. Breen got her arms beneath her, and had nearly sat up when they gave way too. She slid back down into the sand, her eyelids heavy. "Just give Mumma a few minutes to rest."

Nina glanced from the blood soaking her abdomen, to the cut across her cheek. "You're bleeding, Mumma."

"I know."

"You need help."

"I know."

Nina's fingers clenched against the sleeve of her tunic. "Mumma, get up."

Breen sighed. "Just a minute, Nina."

"Mumma, get up."

Something stirred in her mind. Something sharp and uninvited. It pulled at her limbs, straining them to move.

"Stop, Nina." Breen inhaled sharply.

"But—"

"Just a minute." Her voice sounded far away, unlike her own.

"Breen!" a deep voice carried over the sand. Boots beat the ground, approaching fast.

Her heart leapt, stirring her unresponsive limbs. They needed to go. They needed to flee. She needed to get Nina to safety.

"Breen," Drakkone gasped. His knees hit the ground hard as he collapsed by her side. Blood marred his shirt and his arms. Linen wrapped his abdomen. He reached for her anyway. "Bree, what happened?" He pulled her shoulders up so she lay in his lap. He cradled her there, blocking the sun from her eyes.

"Drakkone." She blinked slowly.

He'd been left behind. Left for dead.

But he was alive. How was he alive?

Her brows furrowed.

"Bree, you'll be all right. We'll find a doctor." His voice rose higher. Panicked.

Mumbles came from all around, voices vaguely familiar.

"She's going to be fine!" he snapped, twisting to look at someone she couldn't see. "She'll be fine." He looked back down at her. Worry filled his eyes.

Nina inched closer, holding onto her hand. "Mumma, where are you going?" Tears welled in her eyes.

Breen glanced from Drakkone, to Nina's beautiful face. She smiled. "I'm not going anywhere." Nina squeezed her hand.

"But I can feel it." Nina's eyes widened. "You're far away."

"I'm right here."

Tears slipped down Nina's face, dropping onto her bare arm.

"Nina, can you keep her here?" Drakkone squeezed her shoulders.

Nina looked up. "How?"

He shook his head. "I don't know, just try."

Nina nodded and clenched her hand harder.

This little girl. This *beautiful* little girl. She was alive. She was safe. She'd finally done her duty to protect her. After years of trying to return to who she once was—the *warrior* she once was—she'd finally done it.

She saved her daughter. She saved Nina. She protected her when she most needed it. Her heart warmed and the fuzziness encroaching upon her mind blossomed with heat. Her eyelids drooped.

"Breen, wait." Drakkone shook her. "Wait. We'll get you a doctor."

"She's going, Daddy," Nina cried. "She's going."

Drakkone dug his fingers into her arms. She hardly felt it. "No. Don't."

Breen smiled. She'd done her job. She'd done the one thing she always wanted to do.

Protect those she loved.

"Bree."

The blue sky disappeared. Drakkone's worried gaze disappeared. Nina's dazzling eyes, like the endless sea, disappeared.

I love you.

EPILOGUE

rakkone wrapped his arms around Nina. Her warmth pressed against his chest. Seaburn city fell away to the sea, stretching to the horizon, which glowed with pinks and orange.

Breen had loved the sunset. She'd loved the colors. She'd loved the sea.

She'd loved to fight. She'd loved to protect. She'd loved their daughter.

And yet, she was gone.

His heart tightened in a vice, stealing his breath and stinging his eyes. Drakkone held Nina tighter at the top of the hill. Hot sand lay beneath him, and his sword at his side.

The Emperor had been deposed. Once the rebellion breached the walls, they easily overtook the palace and killed him. Somewhere in there he'd seen a doctor, gotten stitched up before riding out of the city with Nina and the council members. They separated at the base of the hill, where the council continued to Sarton and he continued up the opposite hill—much smaller than the one the city sat upon, but large nonetheless.

He'd always sat upon this hill as a boy. He'd dreamed of the future, of a better Seaburn. He was finally getting his dream. But at the cost of someone he loved.

His chest tightened.

He'd give it all back to have her. To have Breen alive and safe.

Nina stirred, glancing up from her nap. She yawned, her lids heavy as she blinked up at him. "Daddy?"

Drakkone took a deep breath, reining back in as much as he could. He had to be strong for Nina. Breen wasn't around to be strong for them both anymore.

"Yes?"

Nina shifted into a sitting position. "Mumma isn't coming back."

Drakkone froze. He wasn't sure how much Nina understood. She was so young, and though bright, and wise beyond her years, she was still just a child. "No, she's not."

Nina leaned her head against his chest, watching the sunset out over the sea. "Was Mumma happy?" Her small voice broke. She reached up to wipe her eyes.

Was Breen truly happy?

She'd lived a good life up until Seaburn came and took her. After that she'd endured hell for a long time. Even after their escape it had been nothing but running. Nothing but constant turmoil and a need for freedom.

But she had been free. And they'd been together.

Was that enough for her like it was enough for him?

He'd never get to ask her. Never get to see if they could be happy together. Never get to see if they'd be married, or return to her tribe.

Had Breen been happy?

She had been once, he was sure of it. All she'd wanted was to protect Nina, to keep her safe. In the end, she'd done just that. Did that make her happy? Did that make her life worth living?

Drakkone sighed.

More than anything, he wished he could ask her.

"I think she was happy, Daddy." Nina looked up at him.

His brows furrowed as he met her gaze. "You think so?"

Nina smiled slightly. Though he didn't know the extent of her powers, maybe she did know. She could sense Breen's passing—could feel her slip away. But had she been able to do these things all along? Was she some sort of empath, able to feel the emotions of others?

"Yes." Nina nuzzled closer.

He squeezed her tighter and his gaze returned to the horizon. The sun dipped low, the golden mass giving way to night.

Maybe Breen had been happy. In the end she'd truly protected their daughter—truly saved her.

That had been all she'd ever wanted.

THE END

ASHEN

CHRONICLES OF WARSHARD
BOOK THREE

KATHERINE BOGLE

PREVIEW

ONE

Cold slithered across the bare nape of her neck. Adni shivered. A breeze inside the Cinder Mountains? Shadows fled from the flames of Renley's torch. Fire licked the oil-slick rag wrapped around the long branch.

But Renley's light wasn't the only illumination.

Cool blue, like the sky, grazed the jagged cavern walls. Wet glistened on its surface, and thunder roared inside the tunnel system. Somewhere ahead, rapids pounded the rocks.

Finally, she thought, *Father's treasure hunt is almost over.*

"Can you hear it?" Her father glanced over his shoulder. His gray beard strained over his face, stretched in a manic grin, its length only a reminder of how long it had been since they'd left home. Three? Four days?

"Rapids?" Renley's voice seized with excitement. He didn't see their father for what he was—a greedy madman.

Adni sighed, her breath fogging the cool autumn air. Only the bliss of a hot spring could ease the cold from her bones. After all, it had been months since they'd travelled to one.

Her fingers wrapped around the leather-strapped hilt at her waist - Adni's eighteenth birthday present. For years, she'd longed for a sword like the knights of Salander. She'd escape from this wretched place and convince someone—anyone—to train her. Once she had the skills, she could join the Salander army, or even the King's palace guard. She shook her head. After the Insane had been brought to justice ten years ago, there wasn't much need for armies anymore.

"Yes! We've nearly arrived, my boy!" Her father lengthened his stride; flying past the pulley system on the opposite wall, the one delivering fresh rainwater to the nearby village. His fingers tightened around the map he clutched. The dozen gold and silver rings on his fingers winked in the torchlight.

Renley grinned over his shoulder at her. Adni quirked an eyebrow and grimaced. Renley humored their father far too much.

His grin dropped. The flames of his torch turned his green eyes into emerald fire. He turned back to the coming tunnel, a frown curving his wide mouth. Renley was only fifteen, three years younger than Adni. He didn't understand the hundreds of trips that still waited him when treasure hunting stopped being fun.

"I knew today would end well when I heard songbirds this morning!" Her father rounded a bend in the rock.

They emerged in a large cavern, slick with mist from the pounding of a waterfall. At least it drowned out her father's insane mumblings.

Her father, Bran, paused by the edge of an underground lake. The brilliant blue-green water twisted into violent waves as it fled down a tunnel near the entrance of the cavern. A jagged hole in the ceiling, just above the tip of the waterfall, blazed with sunlight.

Adni's heart fluttered.

When was the last time she'd seen the sky? A week? A month? She couldn't remember. Though several skylights could be found through the mountains, they hadn't encountered any on their last few trips. She wasn't lucky enough to have one near their home either.

Her father pumped a fist in the air. She imagined his hoot of impending victory. She bit her lip to keep from rolling her eyes. *"It wasn't ladylike,"* her mother always said. Her fingertips brushed the red jewel of the amulet hung around her neck. The precious stone rested on her chest, nestled just below her collarbone. Her mother had given it to her so many years ago she could hardly remember its meaning any longer. Her siblings didn't have one, but her mother insisted she never take it off.

She shook her head. Maybe father was right about one thing. Her mother had always been eccentric, even in her youth.

While her brother and father raced for the stairs carved into the curved cavern wall leading to the cliff from which the waterfall bubbled, Adni pulled her sword from its sheath.

If her father insisted on forcing her along every one of his journeys, she'd at least take the time to practice her swordsmanship on the open ledge.

The heavy metal pulled her left and right as she twisted it, awkward in her unpracticed hands. It was far different than the wooden sword she'd fashioned years ago from driftwood. Its edges weren't as jagged, though they were certainly dull.

She narrowed her eyes at the uncooperative blade. She wouldn't let her lack of strength stop her.

Adni spun, swinging her blade out. The weight tore her off balance. Her stomach flew into her throat, and her eyes widened as her boot caught on a rock.

Her elbows slammed against the rough stone floor.

"Ow." She winced.

"Adni, what in blue skies are you doing down there?" Renley called over the thunder of the waterfall. He stood at the top of the steps, his eyebrows twisted with worry instead of amusement.

She glanced up, her cheeks burning. Damn. She had hoped they were too busy to see.

"Nothing!" Adni shook her head, her shoulder-length black hair flicking her cheeks. She stood quickly, dusting her thick trousers. Damp clung to her knees.

Renley waved her up the steps.

Adni nodded, but she was in no rush. While Renley disappeared back over the cliff side, Adni sucked in a deep breath. Cold hair filled her lungs. She needed to get used to the weight of her blade. Swinging her sword left and right, Adni steadied herself on the edge of the lake. How else was she going to join the Salander guards and be free of this mountain?

Her heart ached for the thick pine forests and open plains of the six kingdoms where her fondest childhood memories dwelt. It had been far too long since she'd lived in Warshard.

Adni wandered closer to the steps, bending her knees as she parried a non-existing enemy. The blade cut through the air, the metal glinting in the sunlight. She smiled. Her fingers tightened around the hilt. She could do this. She could learn. The native clansmen knew how to fight. Though they usually stuck to their bows and arrows, they were unbelievably fast with a dagger. Someone would teach her. And then she would go. She'd return to the home the Insane Queen ripped away from her ten years ago.

"Adni!" her father bellowed.

She winced. Cold seeped through the warmth blossoming in her chest. She bit back a snarl and sheathed her blade. Damn him, and his treasure hunts. Damn him and his constant need for her presence. Damn him, and everything he made her do.

Adni trudged up the slick stone steps, ready to share her irritation loudly with her father. He'd probably found his treasure and was ready to head home. Only he needed to gloat first of course. He *always* needed to gloat. Heat boiled through her limbs and tightened her fists.

She reached the top of the steps and froze.

The cliff side was flat and wide. The river leading to the waterfall disappeared into a narrow mouth at the far side of the cliff. Only blackness waited inside.

Where was the treasure?

Her stomach turned. If her father didn't find the treasure, she'd wish for his gloating, for his rage was second to none.

"Where is it?" her father screamed. His shouts echoed in the hollow cavern, carrying his words back to her over and over until they rung in her ears.

She gritted her teeth. *Damn.*

"I'm sure it's here somewhere," Renley said. His brows turned up as he glanced between them, frantically searching for what to do.

How could she tell him there was nothing to be done? If father's map lied, and there was no treasure to be found, the best they could do was flee before their father lashed out. Her cheek ached at the memory of his hand on her flesh from the last time he'd been disappointed.

Adni stepped up beside her brother. Her fingers brushed the fur wrapping the wrists of his jacket—similar to her own. His gaze met hers, and his lips pressed into a thin line.

Maybe he was old enough to remember their father's rage.

"The map is *very* clear!" Bran twisted to face them, his eyes wide and wild with lust for riches. His teeth gnashed together as he ripped the twine from the parchment. He splayed it between his hands. "It should be *here!*"

Light filtered behind the map, showing her every detail her father saw. The twisting tunnels, large caverns, waterways, and clues. She couldn't quite recall where he'd gotten the map, but the waterfall gushing beside a large X was unmistakable. They were at the right spot, with no treasure in sight.

"Maybe we took a wrong turn," Renley began hesitantly.

"There was no wrong turn!" he hissed. His face twisted in a snarl, fist clenched in front of him. His gaze flickered to Renley before falling back on his map.

Adni narrowed her eyes as she stepped in front of Renley. Her heart clenched with a need to protect her kin. Their father's gaze didn't rise from the page. He spun in every direction, looking at the map in every possible light.

"Head back to the camp," Adni whispered over her shoulder.

Renley's eyebrows rose as he met her concerned gaze. "What? I can't leave father now."

"Trust me."

Renley shifted from foot to foot, humming and hawing. "Fine." He spun for the steps and descended slowly, as if a thousand boulders lay on his shoulders.

She smiled. Ever the drama queen.

While her father's shuffling and muttering continued, Adni watched her brother go. Someone had to stay with their father and be sure he didn't hurt himself again. She moved to the edge of the waterfall, pushing her bare fingers into her pockets. Water sprayed a mist at the base of the falls, fogging the edge of the clear water.

Sunlight glazed the surface, a startlingly beautiful mix of greens. She revelled in the sun warming her cheeks, and turned her face to the skylight.

"Where is it?" her father's shout broke her reverie.

Her full lips twisted into a frown. She opened her clear blue eyes. Her mother always said her eyes might as well be the winter sky.

She looked back down into the lake below, ignoring her father's fury. Though it appeared still, the twisting current at the far end meant it was anything but. The underwater channel would be a dangerous one. She was sure many had lost their lives thinking it was simply a pretty pool to swim in.

"What is that?"

Adni glanced at her father. He leaned close to the edge, peering over her shoulder. His eyes widened as he leered into the clear depths.

She followed his gaze. Just in front of the waterfall's spray, something gold glistened at the bottom of the lake. She raised an eyebrow.

Could it be the treasure?

"You found it, my girl." His mouth stretched into a grin so wide his upper gums showed—pink and red, blotchy with color, just like his yellow, rotting teeth. "My good little Adanza."

Her nostrils flared. No one used her full name, not unless her father was drunk on the thrill of the hunt.

His fingers clamped down on her shoulders, digging into her skin even through the thick fur trim of her hood. He squeezed, pinching her skin.

She winced, and tried to step away. He held too tightly.

"You've always been my special little girl." His dark gaze shifted from the pool to her face. With his smile so wide, and his face this close, his wrinkles were far more apparent. "You'll survive it."

Her eyebrows furrowed. *Survive it?*

His fingers left her shoulders before his palms slammed into her back. Her breath fled her lungs and her eyes widened. The dark cliff side fell away. Her feet met air. The green-blue water flew up at her, gold glinting just below the surface.

Her heart rose into her throat where a scream ripped free. She hardly heard her father's cackle above the roaring in her ears.

Her whole body froze as pain and cold slapped her like the hand of winter itself.

ABOUT THE AUTHOR

Katherine Bogle's debut young adult novel, Haven, came second in the World's Best Story contest 2015. She currently resides in Saint John, New Brunswick with her partner in crime, and plethora of cats.

Follow Katherine for all the latest updates:
katherinebogle.com
TheHavenSeries@outlook.com

facebook.com/AuthorKatherineBogle

twitter.com/KattyB3

instagram.com/katherinebogle

goodreads.com/katherinebogle

The world is made of monsters.

Adni might be one of them.

After the Evil Queen Kadia razed Warshard, leaving thousands homeless or dead, many of Salander's people fled to the Cinder Mountains seeking refuge.

Adni, the daughter of a treasure hunter, has always despised her father's bizarre occupation and loathes every family trip in search of riches. Always desperate for more, her father shoves her off a waterfall to retrieve treasure at the bottom of a lake. Instead, Adni is swept up in a violent underwater current, only to be rescued by Julian, a mysterious woman with a flirtatious smile.

Desperate to flee the oppression of her family and the mountains, Adni escapes with Julian to Salander in search of her real father – who might just be a worse monster than the man she left behind.

Join Haven and her siblings on four unique adventures in a time when war ravaged the six kingdoms...

HAVEN has always hated royal gatherings, and jumps at the chance to sneak away for a race through town on horseback. But when the young princess is injured, her ancestry is brought into question.

Much is expected of the heir to the Rythern throne, but when **LUCIAN** is forced to leave the warfront by his father, his reluctant agreement comes at a price.

The battle for Helms Keep has disastrous consequences for **MARCEL**. Soon he finds himself fighting both enemy forces and his own memories.

ASTRID is sent to the family summer home in the Cinder Mountains for her own safety. Only she doesn't expect the knee-high snow and frigid temperatures. With only her guards to protect her, Astrid must dig deeper than she ever thought herself capable of in order to survive.